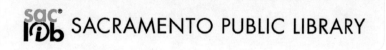

Also by Ian McEwan

# Lessons

Alfred A. Knopf

*New York*  2022

# LESSONS

◄◄ ►►

# IAN MCEWAN

THIS IS A BORZOI BOOK PUBLISHED BY ALFRED A. KNOPF

Copyright © 2022 by Ian McEwan

All rights reserved. Published in the United States by Alfred A. Knopf,
a division of Penguin Random House LLC, New York. Simultaneously published
in hardcover in Great Britain by Jonathan Cape,
an imprint of Vintage, a division of Penguin Random House Ltd.,
London, in 2022.

www.aaknopf.com

Knopf, Borzoi Books, and the colophon are registered trademarks
of Penguin Random House LLC.

Ian McEwan is an unlimited company no 7473219 registered
in England and Wales.

Page 435 constitutes an extension of this copyright page.

Library of Congress Cataloging-in-Publication Data
Names: McEwan, Ian, author.
Title: Lessons / Ian McEwan.
Description: First United States edition. | New York : Alfred A. Knopf, 2022. |
"This is a Borzoi book"—Title page verso.
Identifiers: LCCN 2022013935 (print) | LCCN 2022013936 (ebook) |
ISBN 9780593535202 (hardcover) | ISBN 9780593535219 (ebook)
Subjects: LCGFT: Novels.
Classification: LCC PR6063.C4 L47 2022 (print) | LCC PR6063.C4 (ebook) |
DDC 823/.914—dc23/eng/20220323
LC record available at https://lccn.loc.gov/2022013935
LC ebook record available at https://lccn.loc.gov/2022013936

Jacket illustration by Tina Berning/Synergy
Jacket design by John Gall,
based on a design © Suzanne Dean

Manufactured in the United States of America
First United States Edition

To my sister, Margy Hopkins,
and my brothers,
Jim Wort and David Sharp

First we feel. Then we fall.

—James Joyce, *Finnegans Wake*

# Part One

# I

This was insomniac memory, not a dream. It was the piano lesson again—an orange-tiled floor, one high window, a new upright in a bare room close to the sickbay. He was eleven years old, attempting what others might know as Bach's first prelude from Book One of *The Well-tempered Clavier*, simplified version, but he knew nothing of that. He didn't wonder whether it was famous or obscure. It had no when or where. He could not conceive that someone had once troubled to write it. The music was simply here, a school thing, or dark, like a pine forest in winter, exclusive to him, his private labyrinth of cold sorrow. It would never let him leave.

The teacher sat close by him on the long stool. Round-faced, erect, perfumed, strict. Her beauty lay concealed behind her manner. She never scowled or smiled. Some boys said she was mad, but he doubted that.

He made a mistake in the same place, the one he always made, and she leaned closer to show him. Her arm was firm and warm against his shoulder, her hands, her painted nails, were right above his lap. He felt a terrible tingling draining his attention.

"Listen. It's an easy rippling sound."

But as she played, he heard no easy rippling. Her perfume overwhelmed his senses and deafened him. It was a rounded cloying scent, like a hard object, a smooth river stone, pushing in on his thoughts. Three years later he learned it was rosewater.

"Try again." She said it on a rising tone of warning. She was musical, he was not. He knew that her mind was elsewhere and that he bored her with his insignificance—another inky boy in a boarding school. His fingers were pressing down on the tuneless keys. He could see the bad place on the page before he reached it, it was happening before it happened, the mistake was coming towards him, arms outstretched like a mother, ready to scoop him up, always the same mistake coming to collect him without the promise of a kiss. And so it happened. His thumb had its own life.

Together, they listened to the bad notes fade into the hissing silence.

"Sorry," he whispered to himself.

Her displeasure came as a quick exhalation through her nostrils, a reverse sniff he had heard before. Her fingers found his inside leg, just at the hem of his grey shorts, and pinched him hard. That night there would be a tiny blue bruise. Her touch was cool as her hand moved up under his shorts to where the elastic of his pants met his skin. He scrambled off the stool and stood, flushed.

"Sit down. You'll start again!"

Her sternness wiped away what had just happened. It was gone and he already doubted his memory of it. He hesitated before yet another of those blinding encounters with the ways of adults. They never told you what they knew. They concealed from you the boundaries of your ignorance. What happened, whatever it was, must be his fault and disobedience was against his nature. So he sat, lifted his head to the sullen column of treble clefs where they hung on the page and he set off again, even more unsteadily than before. There could be no rippling, not in this forest. Too soon he was nearing that same bad place. Disaster was certain and knowing that confirmed it as his idiot thumb went down when it should have stayed still. He stopped. The lingering discord sounded like his name spoken out loud. She took his chin between knuckle and thumb and turned his face towards hers. Even her breath was scented. Without shifting her eyes from his, she reached for the twelve-inch ruler from the piano lid. He was not going to let her smack him but as he slid from the stool he didn't see what was coming. She caught him on his knee, with the edge, not the flat, and it stung. He moved a step back.

"You'll do as you're told and sit down."

His leg was burning but he wouldn't put his hand to it, not yet.

He took a last look at her, at her beauty, her tight high-necked pearl-buttoned blouse, at the fanned diagonal creases in the fabric formed by her breasts below her correct and steady gaze.

He ran from her down a colonnade of months until he was thirteen and it was late at night. For months she had featured in his pre-sleep daydreams. But this time it was different, the sensation was savage, the cold sinking in his stomach was what he guessed people called ecstasy. Everything was new, good or bad, and it was all his. Nothing had ever felt so thrilling as passing the point of no return. Too late, no going back, who cared? Astonished, he came into his hand for the first time. When he had recovered he sat up in the dark, got out of bed, went into the dormitory lavatories, "the bogs," to examine the pale globule in his palm, a child's palm.

Here his memories faded into dreaming. He went closer, closer, through the glistening universe to a view from a mountain summit above a distant ocean like the one fatty Cortés saw in a poem the whole class wrote out twenty-five times for a detention. A sea of writhing creatures, smaller than tadpoles, millions on millions, packed to the curved horizon. Closer still until he found and followed a certain individual swimming through the crowd on its journey, jostling with siblings down smooth pink tunnels, overtaking the rest as they fell away exhausted. At last he arrived alone before a disc, magnificent like a sun, turning slowly clockwise, calm and full of knowledge, waiting indifferently. If it wasn't him it would be someone else. As he entered through thick blood-red curtains there came from a distance a howl then a sunburst of a crying baby's face.

He was a grown man, a poet, he liked to think, with a hangover and a five-day stubble, rising from the shallows of recent sleep, now stumbling from bedroom to the wailing baby's room, lifting it from its cot and holding it close.

Then he was downstairs with the child asleep against his chest beneath a blanket. A rocking chair, and by it on a low table a book he had bought about world troubles which he knew he would never read. He had troubles of his own. He faced French windows and he was looking down a narrow London garden through a misty wet dawn to a sole bare apple tree. To its left was an upturned green wheelbarrow, not moved since some forgotten day in summer. Nearer was a round metal table he always intended to paint. A cold late spring concealed the tree's death and there would be no leaves on it this year. In a hot three-week drought that had begun in July he could have saved it, despite the hosepipe ban. But he had been too busy to haul full buckets the garden's length.

His eyes were closing and he was tilting backwards, remembering once more, not sleeping. Here was the prelude as it should be played. It had been a long time since he was here, eleven again, walking with thirty others towards an old Nissen hut. They were too young to know how miserable they were, too cold to talk. Collective reluctance moved them in time like a corps de ballet as they went down a steep grass slope in silence to line up outside in the mist and wait obediently for the class to begin.

Inside, dead centre, was a coke-burning stove and once they were warm they became riotous. It was possible here, not elsewhere, because the Latin teacher, a short and kindly Scot, could not control the class. On the blackboard, in the master's hand: *Exspectata dies aderat*. Below it, the clumsy writing of a boy: *The long-awaited day had arrived*. In this same hut, so they had been taught, men in more serious times once prepared for war at sea, learning the mathematics of laying mines. That was their prep. While here, now, a large boy, a famous bully, swaggered to the front to bend, leering, and offer his satirical backside to be ineffectually beaten with a plimsoll by the gentle Scot. There were cheers for the bully, for no one else would dare so much.

As the din and chaos mounted and something white was chucked across the desks, he remembered, it was Monday and the long-awaited and dreaded day had arrived—again. On his wrist was the thick watch his father gave him. *Don't lose it*. In thirty-two minutes it would be piano lesson. He tried not to think of the teacher because he had not practised. Too dark and scary in the forest to arrive at the place where his thumb went blindly down. If he thought of his mother he'd go weak. She was far away and couldn't help him so he pushed her aside too. No one could stop Monday coming round. Last week's bruise was fading, and what was it, to remember the piano teacher's scent? It was not the same as smelling it. More like a colourless picture, or a place, or a feeling for a place or something in between. Beyond dread was another element, excitement, he must also push away.

To Roland Baines, the sleep-deprived man in the rocking chair, the waking city was no more than a remote rushing sound, swelling with the passing minutes. Rushing hour. Expelled from their dreams, their beds, people were moving through the streets like the wind. Here, he had nothing to do but be a bed for his son. Against his chest he felt the baby's heartbeat, just under twice the rate of his own. Their pulses fell in and out of phase, but one day they would be always out. They would never be this close. He would know him less well, then even less. Others would know Lawrence better than he did, where he was, what he was doing and saying, growing closer to this friend, then this lover. Crying sometimes, alone. From his father, occasional visits, a sincere hug, catch up on work, family, some politics, then goodbye. Until then, he knew everything about him, where he was in every minute, in every place. He was the baby's bed and his god. The long letting go could be the essence of parenthood and from here was impossible to conceive.

Many years had passed since he let go of the eleven-year-old boy with the secret oval mark on his inner thigh. That evening he had examined it after lights out, lowering his pyjamas in the bogs, bending to look closer. Here was the impression of her finger and thumb, her signature, a written record of the moment that made it true. A photograph of sorts. It didn't hurt when he ran his own finger around the borders where pale skin shaded greenish into blue. He pushed down hard, right in the centre where it was almost black. It didn't hurt.

→►

In the weeks that followed his wife's vanishing, the visits from the police and the sealing of the house, he often tried to account for the haunting on that night he was suddenly alone. Fatigue and stress had pushed him back on origins, on first principles, the endless past. It would have been worse if he had known what lay ahead—many visits to a careworn office, much waiting with a hundred others on plastic benches bolted to the floor for his number to be called, multiple interviews pleading his case while Lawrence H. Baines squirmed and babbled on his lap. Finally he won some state aid, a single-parent's stipend, a widower's mite, though she wasn't dead. When Lawrence was one year old, there would be a nursery place for him while his father took up a chair—in a call centre or similar. Professor of Helpful Listening. Completely reasonable. Would he let others toil to support him while he languished all afternoon over his sestinas? There was no contradiction. It was an arrangement, a contract he accepted—and hated.

What happened long ago in a small room by the sickbay had been as calamitous as his present fix but he kept going, now as then, outwardly almost OK. What could destroy him was from the inside, the feeling of being in the wrong. If he had been a misguided child to feel that then, why indulge the guilty feeling now? Blame her, not himself. He came to know her postcards and her note by heart. By convention, such notes were left on the kitchen table. She had left hers on his pillow, like a hotel's bitter chocolate. *Don't try to find me. I'm OK. It's not your fault. I love you but this is for good. I've been living the wrong life. Please try to forgive me.* On the bed, on her side, were her house keys.

What kind of love was this? Was giving birth the wrong life? It was usually after a serious drink that he fixed on and loathed the final sentence she had failed to complete. *Please try to forgive me,* she should have said, *as I have forgiven myself.* The self-pity of the absconder against the bitter clarity of the left-behind, the abscondee. It hardened with each finger of Scotch. Another invisible finger that beckoned. He hated her progressively and every thought was a repeat, a variation on the theme of her self-loving desertion. After an hour of forensic reflection, he knew the tipping point was not far ahead, the pivot in the evening's mental work. Almost there, pour another. His thoughts were slowing and then they abruptly stopped for no reason at all, like the train in the poem that their class had to learn by heart on pain of punishment. A hot day at a Gloucestershire halt and stillness into which someone coughs. Then it would come to him again, the lucid notion as clear and keen as birdsong close by. He was drunk at last and liberated into loving her again and wanting her back. Her remote seraphic beauty, the frailty of her small-boned hands, and her voice barely inflected from a German childhood, a little husky, as though from a bout of shouting. But she had never shouted. She loved him, so the blame must be his and it was sweet of her to tell him in her note that it was not. He didn't know which defective part of himself to indict, so it must be all of him.

Woozily contrite, in a sad-sweet cloud, he would make ruminative progress up the stairs, check on the baby, fall asleep, sometimes fully clothed, across the bed, to wake in the arid small hours, exhausted and alert, furious and thirsty, totting up in the dark his virtues and how he was wronged. He earned nearly as much as she did, had put in his half-share with Lawrence, including nights, was faithful, loving, never tried it on as the poet-genius living by special rules. So he had been a fool, a sap, and that was why she had left, for a real man perhaps. No, no, he was good, he was good and he hated her. This is for *good*. He had run full circle—again. The closest he could come to sleep now was to lie on his back, eyes closed, listening out for Lawrence, otherwise lost to memories, desires, inventions, even passable lines he had no will to write down, for an hour, and another, then a third, into the dawn. Soon he would replay once more the visit from the police, the suspicion that lay on him, the poisonous cloud he had sealed the house against and whether the job needed doing again. This worthless process had brought him back one night to the piano lesson. The echoey room he had stumbled into and where he was forced to watch.

Through Latin and French he had learned about tenses. They had always been there, past, present, future, and he hadn't noticed how language divided up time. Now he knew. His piano teacher was using the present continuous to condition the near future. "You're sitting straight, your chin is up. You're holding your elbows at right angles. Fingers are ready, slightly bent, and you're letting your wrists stay soft. You are looking directly at the page."

He also knew what right angles were. Tenses, angles, how to spell continuous. These were elements of the real world his father had sent him 2,000 miles away from his mother to learn. There were matters of adult concern, millions of them, that one by one would be his. When he arrived from the Latin lesson, breathless and on time, the piano teacher interrogated him about his week of practice. He lied to her. Then she sat close again. She wrapped her perfume around him. The mark she had made on his leg last week had faded and his memory of what happened was uncertain. But if she tried to hurt him again he would run from the room without pausing. It was a kind of strength, a murmur of excitement in his chest, to pretend to her that he had practised for three hours during the week. The truth was zero, not even three minutes. He had never deceived a woman before. He had lied to his father, whom he feared, to get out of trouble, but he had always told his mother the truth.

The teacher softly cleared her throat, which indicated that she believed him. Or perhaps it didn't.

She whispered, "Good. Off you go."

The large thin book of easy pieces for beginners was open at the centre. For the first time he noticed the three staples in the crease that held the book together. These did not have to be played—the stupid thought almost made him smile. The stern upright loop of the treble clef, the bass clef coiled like the foetus of a rabbit in his biology book, the black notes, the clear white ones you held for longer, this grubby dog-eared double page that was his own special punishment. None of it now looked familiar or even unfriendly.

When he started, his first note was twice the volume of the second. He moved warily to the third note and the fourth and gathered speed. It was caution, and then it felt like stealth. Not practising had set him free. He obeyed the notes, left hand with right and ignored the pencilled fingerings. He had nothing to remember but to press the keys in the correct order. The bad place was suddenly on him but his left thumb forgot to go down and then it was too late, he was already clear, on the other side, moving smoothly across the level ground above the forest where the light and space were cleaner, and for a stretch he thought he could discern the hint of a melody suspended like a joke above his steady march of sounds.

Following instructions, two, perhaps three, every second needed all his concentration. He forgot himself, and even forgot her. Time and place dissolved. The piano vanished along with existence itself. It was as if he were waking from a night's sleep when he found himself at the end, playing with two hands an easy open chord. But he didn't take his hands away as the breve on the page told him he should. The chord resounded and diminished in the bare little room.

He didn't let go when he felt her hand on his head, even when she pressed down hard to rotate his face in her direction. Nothing in her expression told him what would happen next.

She said quietly, "You . . ."

That was when he lifted his hands from the keys.

"You little . . ."

In a complicated movement, she lowered and inclined her head, so that her face approached his in a swooping arc that ended in a kiss, her lips full on his, a soft prolonged kiss. He neither resisted nor engaged. It happened and he let it happen and felt nothing while it lasted. Only in retrospect, when he lived and relived and animated the moment in solitude, did he get the measure of its importance. While it lasted, her lips were on his and he numbly waited for the moment to pass. Then there was a sudden distraction and it ended. A flash of a passing shadow or movement had fallen across the high window. She pulled away and turned to look, as he did. They had both seen or sensed it at the same time, on the edge of vision. Was it a face, a disapproving face and shoulder? But the small square window showed them only ragged cloud and scraps of pale winter blue. He knew that from the outside the window was too high for even the tallest adult to reach. It was a bird, probably a pigeon from the dovecote in the old stable block. But teacher and pupil had separated guiltily and though he understood little, he knew that they were now united by a secret. The empty window had rudely invoked the world of people outside. He also understood how impolite it would have been to raise a hand to his mouth to relieve the prickling sensation of drying moisture.

She turned back to him and in a steady calming voice that suggested she had no concern for the prying world, looked deep into his eyes as she spoke, this time in a kindly voice in the future tense, which she used to make the present seem reasonable. And now it was. But he had never heard her say so much.

"Roland, in two weeks there's a half-day holiday. It falls on a Friday. I want you to listen carefully. You'll come on your bike to my village. Erwarton. Coming from Holbrook, it's after the pub, on the right, with a green door. You're going to come in time for lunch. Do you understand?"

He nodded, understanding nothing. That he should cycle across the peninsula by narrow lanes and farm tracks to her village for lunch when he could eat at school baffled him. Everything did. At the same time, despite his confusion, or because of it, he longed to be alone to feel and think about the kiss.

"I'll send you a card to remind you. From now on you'll have your lessons with Mr. Clare. Not me. I'll tell him you're making excellent progress. So, young man, we are going to do major and minor scales with two sharps."

→→

Easier to ask where than why. Where did she go? Four hours passed before he reported Alissa's note and disappearance to the police. His friends thought that even two hours was too long. Phone them now! He resisted, he held out. It was not only that he preferred to think she could return at any minute. He did not want a stranger reading her note or her absence officially confirmed. To his surprise someone came round the day after his call. He was a local police constable and seemed hard-pressed. He took a few details, glanced at Alissa's note and said that he would report back. Nothing happened for a week and in that time her four postcards arrived. The specialist came unannounced in the early morning in a tiny patrol car which he parked illegally outside the house. It had been raining heavily but he was oblivious to the trail his shoes left across the hallway floor. Detective Inspector Douglas Browne, the flesh of whose cheeks hung in swags, had the friendly aspect of a large brown-eyed dog. He sat hunched at the kitchen table across from Roland. By the detective's immense hands, their knuckles matted with dark hair, were his own notebook, the postcards and the pillow note. A thick overcoat, which he did not remove, added to his bulk and enhanced the canine effect. Around both men was a litter of dirty plates and cups, junk mail, bills, a near-empty feeding bottle and the smeared leftovers of Lawrence's breakfast and his bib.

These were what one of Roland's male friends called the slime years. Lawrence was in his high chair, unusually silent, gazing in awe at this hulk of a man and his outsized shoulders. At no point during the meeting did Browne acknowledge the baby's existence. Roland felt faintly offended on his son's behalf. Irrelevant. The officer's soft brown eyes were on the father alone and Roland was obliged to answer routine questions. The marriage was not in difficulty—he said this louder than he intended. No money had been removed from the joint account. It was still the holidays, so the school where she worked wouldn't know she had left. She had taken a small black suitcase. Her coat was green. Here were some photographs, her date of birth, her parents' names and address in Germany. She might have worn a beret.

The detective was interested in the most recent card, from Munich. Roland didn't think she knew anyone there. Berlin yes, and Hanover and Hamburg. She was a woman of the Lutheran north. When Browne raised an eyebrow, Roland told him that Munich was in the south. Perhaps it was the name of Luther he should have explained. But the detective looked down at his notebook and asked another question. No, Roland said, she had never done anything like this before. No, he didn't have a copy of her passport details. No, she had not seemed depressed lately. Her parents lived near Nienburg, a small town, also in north Germany. When he had phoned them about another matter, it became clear she hadn't been there. He had told them nothing. Her mother, afflicted by chronic resentments, would have erupted at this news of her only child. Desertion. How dare she! Mother and daughter habitually squabbled. But his parents-in-law and his own parents would have to be told. Alissa's first three postcards, from Dover, Paris then Strasbourg, had come in four days. The fourth, the Munich card, came two days later. Since then, nothing.

Detective Inspector Browne studied the postcards again. Each one the same. *All fine. Don't worry. Kiss Larry for me. xx Alissa.* The invariance seemed deranged or hostile, as did the loveless sign-off. A plea for help or a form of insult. Same blue felt-tipped pen, no dates, illegible postmarks, Dover apart, the same bland city view of bridges over the Seine, the Rhine, the Isar. Mighty rivers. She was drifting eastwards, ever further from home. The night before, on the edge of sleep, Roland summoned her as Millais's drowned Ophelia, bobbing on the Isar's smooth clean waters past Pupplinger Au with its naked bathers sprawled on the grassy shores like beached seals; on her back, head first, floating downstream, unseen and silent through Munich, past the English Garden to the Danube confluence, then unremarked through Vienna, Budapest and Belgrade, through ten nations and their savage histories, along the borders of the Roman Empire, to the white skies and boundless delta marshes of the Black Sea, where he and she once made love in the lee of an old mill in Letea and saw near Isaccea a flock of rowdy pelicans. Only two years ago. Purple herons, glossy ibis, a greylag goose. Until then he had never cared about birds. That evening before sleep, he had drifted away with her to a locus of wild happiness, a source. Lately, it was an effort of concentration to remain long in the present. The past was often a conduit from memory to restless fantasising. He put it down to tiredness, hangover, confusion.

Douglas Browne was saying consolingly as he bent to his notebook, "When my wife had had enough, she chucked me out."

Roland started to speak but Lawrence cut in with a squawk. A demand to be included. Roland stood to unstrap him from his chair and settled him on his lap. A new angle, face to face, on the giant stranger silenced the baby again. He gazed fiercely, open-mouthed and dribbling. No one could know what passed through the mind of a seven-month-old. A shaded emptiness, a grey winter sky against which impressions—sounds, sights, touch—burst like fireworks in arcs and cones of primary colour, instantly forgotten, instantly replaced and forgotten again. Or a deep pool into which everything fell and disappeared but remained, irretrievably present, dark shapes in deep water exercising their gravitational pull even eighty years later, on deathbeds, in last confessions, in final cries for lost love.

After Alissa left he had watched his son for signs of sorrow or damage and found them at every turn. A baby must miss its mother, but how if not in memory? Sometimes Lawrence was silent for too long. Shocked, numbed, scar tissue forming within hours in the lower regions of the unconscious, if such a place or process existed? Last night he had screamed too hard. Enraged by what he couldn't have, even as he forgot what it was. Not the breast. He was bottle-fed from the start at his mother's insistence. Part of her plan, Roland thought in bad moments.

The detective inspector finished with his notebook. "You understand that if we find Alissa, we can't tell you where she is without her permission."

"You can tell me if she's alive."

He nodded and thought for a moment. "Generally, when a missing wife's dead it's the husband that's killed her."

"Then let's hope she's alive."

Browne straightened and rocked back just a little in his chair, miming surprise. For the first time he smiled. He seemed friendly. "It often goes like this. So. He does her in, disposes of the body, down in the New Forest say, lonely spot, shallow grave, reports her missing, then what?"

"What?"

"Then it starts. Suddenly he realises, she was adorable. They loved each other. He misses her and he begins to believe his own story. She's done a runner. Or a psychopath has done her in. He's tearful, depressed, then he's furious. He's not a murderer, he's not lying, not as he sees it now. She's gone and he really *feels* it. And to the rest of us it looks real. It looks honest. Hard to crack, those ones."

Lawrence's head lolled against his father's chest, and he began to doze. Roland didn't want the detective to leave just yet. When he did it would be time to clean up the kitchen. Sort out the bedrooms, the laundry, the dirty trail in the hall. Make a list for the shops. All he wanted was to sleep.

He said, "I'm still at the missing her stage."

"Early days, sir."

At that, both men began to laugh quietly. As if it was fun and they were old friends. Roland was well disposed towards the collapsed face, its soft hangdog look of infinite wear and tear. He respected the detective's impulse to sudden confidences.

After a silence Roland said, "Why did she throw you out?"

"Worked too hard, drank too much, late every night. Ignored her, ignored the kids, three lovely boys, had a lady on the side which someone told her about."

"Well shot of you then."

"That's what I thought. I was about to become one of those blokes with two households. You hear about them. The old doesn't know about the new, the new is jealous of the old and you're running between them with a white-hot poker up your arse."

"Now you're with the new."

Browne sighed loudly through his nostrils as he looked away and scratched his neck. The self-made hell was an interesting construct. Nobody escaped making one, at least one, in a lifetime. Some lives were nothing but. It was a tautology that self-inflicted misery was an extension of character. But Roland often thought about it. You built a torture machine and climbed inside. Perfect fit, with a range of pain on offer: from certain jobs, or a taste for drink, drugs, from crime coupled with a knack of getting caught. Austere religion was another choice. An entire political system could opt for self-imposed distress— he had once spent some time in East Berlin. Marriage, a machine for two, presented king-sized possibilities, all variants of the *folie à deux*. Everyone knew some examples and Roland's was a crafty construction. His good friend, Daphne, had laid it out for him one evening, long before Alissa left, when he confessed to months of feeling low. "You did brilliantly at the evening classes, Roland. All those subjects! But everything else you tried, you wanted to be the best in the world. Piano, tennis, journalism, now poetry. And these are only the ones I happen to know about. As soon as you discover you're not the best, you throw it in and hate yourself. Same with relationships. You want too much and move on. Or she can't stand the pursuit of perfection and chucks you out."

Into the detective's silence Roland rephrased his question. "So, new lady or old, what is it you really want?"

Soundlessly, Lawrence was crapping in his sleep. The odour wasn't so bad. One of the discoveries of middle life—how soon you came to tolerate the shit of the one you loved. A general rule.

Browne gave the question serious thought. His gaze moved distractedly around the room. He saw chaotic bookshelves, magazine piles, a broken kite on top of a cupboard. Now, with elbows on the table and head lowered, he stared down into the grain of the pine while he massaged the back of his neck with both hands. Finally, he straightened.

"What I really want is a sample of your handwriting. Anything. A shopping list will do."

Roland let a wavelet of nausea rise and fall. "You think I wrote these messages?"

A mistake, after a heavy night, to have skipped breakfast. No slice of buttery toast and honey to set against hypoglycaemia. Too busy dealing with Lawrence. Then tremulous hands made the coffee come out triple strength.

"A note to the milkman would be fine."

From the pocket of his coat Browne brought out a boxy leather object on a strap. With grunts and a sigh of exasperation, he freed a camera from its worn case, a task which involved turning a silver screw too small for his fat fingers. It was an old Leica, 35 millimetre, silver and black with dents in its body. He kept his eyes on Roland and made a purse-lipped smile as he unclipped the lens cap.

He stood. With pedantic attention he arranged the four cards and the note in a row. When all had been snapped, both sides, and the camera was back in his pocket, he said, "Marvellous, this new fast film. Go anywhere. Interested?"

"I used to be keen." Then Roland added, accusingly, "As a kid."

Browne took from the other pocket of his coat a sheaf of plastic. One by one, he picked up the postcards by a corner, and slid them into four transparent envelopes, which he sealed with a pinch. Into the fifth he put the pillow note. *It's not your fault*. He sat down and made a neat pile, squaring it off with his big hands.

"If you don't mind, I'll take these along with me."

Roland's heart was beating so hard that he was beginning to feel refreshed. "I do mind."

"Fingerprints. Very important. You'll get them back."

"They say things get lost in police stations."

Browne smiled. "Let's take a tour of the house. So, we need your handwriting, item of her clothing, something with just her prints on it and uh, what was it? A sample of *her* writing."

"You already have it."

"Something historic."

Roland stood with Lawrence in his arms. "Perhaps it was a mistake getting you involved in a personal matter."

The detective was already leading the way towards the stairs. "Perhaps it was."

When they reached the narrow landing Roland said, "I need to sort the baby out first."

"I'll wait here."

But five minutes later, when he came back with Lawrence on his hip, he found Browne in his bedroom, their bedroom, diminishing it rudely with his bulk as he stood by the window near the small desk Roland worked at. As before, the baby stared in astonishment. A notebook and three typed-up copies of recent poems were scattered around the typewriter, an Olivetti portable. In the underlit north-facing bedroom the detective was holding a page tipped towards the light.

"Excuse me. That's private. You're being bloody intrusive."

"The title is good." He read it tonelessly. " 'Glamis hath murdered sleep.' Glamis. Lovely girl's name. Welsh." He put the page down and came towards Roland and Lawrence along the narrow space between the end of the bed and the wall.

"Not my words and Scottish actually."

"So you're not sleeping well?"

Roland let this go. The bedroom furniture had been painted by Alissa in pale green with blue stencilling in an oak leaf and acorn pattern. He opened a drawer for Browne. Her jumpers were smoothly folded in three rows. The various scents she used made a muted blend, a rich history. The moment they first met overlaid with the time they last spoke. It was too much for him, her perfumes and sudden presence and he stepped back, as though from a strong light.

Browne bent down with effort and took the nearest. Black cashmere. He turned aside to ease it into one of his plastic bags.

"And my handwriting?"

"Got it." Browne straightened and tapped the camera bulge in his coat pocket. "Your notebook was open."

"Without my permission."

"Was that her side?" He was looking towards the head of the bed.

Roland was too angry to answer. On her bedside table was a red hair clip with clenched plastic teeth perched on a paperback book, which Browne picked up by its edges. Nabokov's *Pnin*. Delicately, he lifted the cover and peeked.

"Her notes?"

"Yes."

"Have you read it?"

Roland nodded.

"This copy?"

"No."

"Good. We could call in forensics but at this stage it's hardly worth the bother."

Roland was getting himself under control and tried to sound conversational. "I thought we were at the beginning of the end for fingerprints. The future is genes."

"Fashionable rubbish. Won't see it in my lifetime. Or yours."

"Really?"

"Or anyone's." The detective made a move towards the landing. "What you've got to understand is this. A gene isn't a thing. It's an idea. An idea about information. A fingerprint is a thing, a trace."

The two men and the baby descended the stairs. At the bottom Browne turned. The transparent bag containing Alissa's jumper was under his arm. "We don't turn up at a crime scene looking for abstract ideas. We're looking for traces of real things."

They were interrupted again by Lawrence. Flinging out an arm he gave a full-throated shout that began on an explosive consonant, a *b* or *p,* and he pointed meaninglessly at the wall with a wet finger. The sound was practice, Roland generally assumed, for a lifetime of talking. The tongue had to get in shape for everything it was ever going to say.

Browne was walking down the hall. Roland, following behind, said with a laugh, "I hope you're not implying that this is a crime scene."

The detective opened the front door, stepped out and turned. Behind him, parked up on the kerb at a tilt, was his tiny car, a Morris

Minor in baby blue. The low morning sun highlighted the sad droop-
ing creases of his face. His lecturing moments were not persuasive.

"I had a sergeant who used to say that where there's people there's
a crime scene."

"Sounds like complete nonsense."

But Browne had already turned away and seemed not to hear.
Father and son watched him go down the short weedy path to the broken garden gate that had never closed. When he reached the pavement
he spent a half-minute, slightly stooped, rummaging in his pockets for
his keys. At last he had them and opened his door. Then, in one movement and with an agile twist of his bulk, he folded himself backwards
into the car and slammed the door behind him.

➤➤

So Roland's day, a cool day in the spring of 1986, could begin and
it weighed on him. The chores, the pointlessness with a new element,
the untidy unwashed feeling of being a suspect. If that was what he
was. Almost like guilt. A deed, wife-murder, clung to him like the
breakfast that had dried to a crust on Lawrence's face. Poor thing.
Together they were watching as the detective waited to pull into the
traffic. By the front gate was a spindly sapling tied to a bamboo stick.
It was a robinia tree. The garden-centre assistant told him it would
flourish in traffic fumes. To Roland, from this threshold everything
looked randomly imposed as though he had been lowered from a forgotten place into these circumstances, into a life vacated by someone
else, nothing chosen by himself. The house he never wanted to buy
and couldn't afford. The child in his arms he never expected or needed
to love. The random traffic moving too slowly past the gate that was
now his and that he would never repair. The frail robinia he would
never have thought to buy, the optimism in the planting he could no
longer feel. He knew from experience, the only way out of a disassociated state was to carry out a simple task. He would go to the kitchen
and clean up his son's face and do it tenderly.

But as he kicked the front door shut he had another idea. Now,
with only one thought in mind, he went up the stairs with Lawrence

to his bedroom to his desk to examine his open notebook. He could not remember his last entry. Nine poems published in literary journals within fifteen months—his notebook was the emblem of his seriousness. Compact, with faint grey lines, dark blue hard covers and a green spine. He wouldn't allow it to become a diary tracking the minutiae of the baby's development or the fluctuations of his own moods or forced musings on public events. Too commonplace. His material was the higher stuff. To follow the obscure trail of an exquisite idea that could lead to a lucky narrowing, to a fiery point, a sudden focus of pure light to illuminate a first line that would hold the secret key to the lines that must follow. It had happened before, but wanting it, longing for it to happen again, guaranteed nothing. The necessary illusion was that the best poem ever written was within his reach. Being clear-headed didn't help. Nothing helped. He was obliged to sit and wait. Sometimes he gave way and filled a journal page with weak reflections of his own or passages from other writers. The last thing he wanted. He copied out a paragraph by Montaigne on happiness. He wasn't interested in happiness. Before that, part of a letter by Elizabeth Bishop. It helped to appear busy but he could not fool himself. Seamus Heaney once said that a writer's duty was to turn up at the desk. Whenever the baby slept in the day Roland turned up and waited and often, head on desk, slept too.

The notebook was open as Browne had left it, to the right of the typewriter. He wouldn't have needed to move it to take his pictures. The light from the sash window was cool and even. The lines were at the top of the verso page: his teenage years transformed, the course of his life diverted. Memory, damage, time. Surely a poem. When he picked up the notebook the baby lunged for it. Roland moved it out of reach, provoking a squeal of protest. Behind the typewriter, gathering dust, was a fives ball. He had never played but had squeezed it daily to strengthen an injured wrist. They went into the bathroom to clean the baby's face and wash the ball. Something for Lawrence to get his gums into. It worked. They lay together on the bed on their backs, side by side. The tiny boy, just over a third of his father's length, sucked and chewed. The passage was not as Roland remembered, for he was reading it through a policeman's eyes. It had not improved.

When I brought it to an end she didn't fight me. She knew
what she'd done. When murder hung over all the world. She
lay buried, but on a sleepless night she springs up out of the
dark. Sits close on the piano stool. Perfume, blouse, red nails.
Vivid as ever, as though dirt of the grave in her hair. Ah, those
scales! Horrible ghost. She won't go away. Just the wrong
time, when I need calm. She must remain dead.

He read it twice. It was perverse to blame both women, but he did:
Miss Miriam Cornell, the piano teacher who meddled in his affairs by
novel means over distances of time and place; Alissa Baines, née Eberhardt, beloved wife, who held him in a headlock from wherever she
was. Until she asserted her existence he would not be free of Douglas
Browne. To the extent that he was responsible for shaping the cast
of the policeman's mind, Roland also blamed himself. On the second
reading he thought his handwriting was obviously distinct from that
on the postcards and note. It wasn't all bad. But it was bad.

He rolled onto his side to look at his son. Here was a discovery
he had been too slow to make—in the sum of things Lawrence was
more comfort than chore. The fives ball had lost its charm and rolled
from his two-handed grasp. It lay against a blanket, shiny with saliva.
He was gazing upwards. The blue-grey eyes were a blaze of attention. Medieval artists showed vision as light beaming outwards from
the mind. Roland followed the beam towards speckled ceiling tiles
that were supposed to retard fires, and a ragged hole from which once
hung the previous owner's bedroom chandelier. A hopeful gesture in
a low room ten feet by twelve. Then he saw it, right above them now,
a long-legged spider making its way upside down towards a corner of
the room. So much purpose in so small a head. Now it paused, rocking
in place on legs as fine as hairs, swaying as though to a hidden melody. Did the authority exist who could explain what it was doing? No
predators around to baffle, no other spiders to seduce or intimidate,
nothing to impede it. But still it waited, dancing on the spot. By the
time the spider went on its way, Lawrence's attention had shifted. He
turned his outsized head and saw his father, and his limbs went into
spasms of leg straightening and bending and arm flailing. This was

dedicated work. But he was communicative, even questioning. His eyes were locked on Roland's as he kicked out again, then he waited with an expectant half-smile. *How was that?* He wanted to be admired for his feats. For a seven-month-old to show off he would need some idea of minds like his own and of what it might be like to be impressed, of how desirable, pleasurable it could be to earn the esteem of others. Not possible? But here it was. Too complicated to follow through.

Roland closed his eyes and gave himself up to a slow spinning sensation. Oh to sleep now, if the baby would sleep too, if they could sleep together here on the bed, even for five minutes. But his father's closed eyes suggested to Lawrence a universe shrinking into frozen darkness, leaving him the last remaining being, chilled and rejected on a vacated shore. He inhaled deeply and howled, a piteous piercing wail of abandonment and despair. For speechless helpless humans, much power lay in a violent switch of extreme emotions. A crude mode of tyranny. Real-world tyrants were often compared to infants. Were Lawrence's joys and sorrow separated by the finest gauze? Not even that. They were wrapped up tight together. By the time Roland had roused himself and was at the top of the stairs with the baby in his arms, contentment was restored. Lawrence clung to the lobe of his father's ear. As they went down he probed its whorl with clumsy stabs.

It was not yet 10 a.m. The day would be long. It was already long. In the hall the watery trail of shoe-dirt across the low-grade Edwardian tiles led him back to Browne himself. Yes, yes, it was bad. But here was the place to start. Eliminate. One-handedly he fetched a mop, filled a bucket and cleared up the mess, spreading it widely. This was how most messes were cleared up, smoothed thin to invisibility. Tiredness turned everything to metaphor. His domestic routines made him resent and resist the demands and lures of the worldly life beyond. Two weeks back there was an exception. International affairs invaded his past. US warplanes in a raid on Tripoli, Libya, destroyed his old primary school but failed to kill Colonel Gaddafi. Now, to read a report of a speech by Reagan or Thatcher or her ministers made Roland feel excluded and guilty for not paying attention. But it was time to keep his head down and stay faithful to the tasks he set himself. There was value in thinking less. Manage the fatigue and care for the essentials:

the baby, the house, the shopping. He hadn't seen a newspaper in four days. The kitchen radio, which was on low all day, sometimes used a quiet voice of virile urgency to woo him back. He tried to ignore it as he walked by with his bucket and mop. *This is for you,* it murmured. *Riots in seventeen prisons. When you were about in the world you used to care for precisely this kind of thing . . . An explosion . . . developments came to light when Swedish authorities reported radioactive . . .* He hurried past. Keep moving, don't nod off, don't close your eyes.

After the hall he started on the kitchen while Lawrence sat in his chair eating and playing with a peeled banana. The sink-and-table clean-up was roughly achieved. He carried Lawrence upstairs. In the two bedrooms the order he imposed was cosmetic but the slide towards chaos was stayed. The world seemed minimally more reasonable. Here, after all, at the top of the stairs was a pile for the washing machine. Alissa was no better at this stuff than he was. In fact—but no, today he was not thinking of her.

Later, Lawrence sucked dry a bottle of milk and slept and Roland went next door to his bedroom. Rather than sleep he had in mind some changes to his poem about sleeplessness. "Glamis." In an understated way—it had to be understated because he didn't know enough—it was about the Troubles. In '84 he had spent some days in Belfast and Derry with a London Irish friend, Simon, newly rich from a chain of fitness gyms, and idealistic. Simon's idea was to start a few tennis schools for kids across the sectarian divide. Roland was to be the head coach. They were looking for locations and local support. They were innocents, fools. They were followed, or thought they were. In a Knockloughrim pub a fellow in a wheelchair—kneecapped, they decided—advised them to "be careful." Simon's anglicised Ulster accent provoked indifference everywhere. No one was much interested in children's tennis. They were held for six boring hours at a roadblock by British soldiers who didn't believe their story. During that week Roland barely slept. It rained, it was cold, the food was atrocious, the hotel sheets were damp, everyone chain-smoked and looked ghastly. He moved about in a bad dream, constantly reminding himself that his state of fear was not paranoia. But it was. No one touched them, or even threatened to.

He worried that his poem owed too much to Heaney's "Punishment." How the figure of a woman long preserved in a bog evoked her Irish "betraying sisters," victims tarred for consorting with the enemy while the poet watched on, both outraged and complicit in his understanding. What could an outsider, an Englishman with one week's faint engagement, have to say about the Troubles? His fresh idea was just that—to shift the poem towards his ignorance and insomnia. Tell how lost and fearful he had been. Now there was a new problem. The typed draft before him had been in Browne's hands. Roland read the title and heard in his thoughts the detective's flat voice and was repelled by "Glamis hath murdered sleep." Weak, portentous, riding free on Shakespeare's back. After twenty minutes he put the poem aside to contemplate his latest idea. He opened the notebook. The piano. Love, memory, harm. But the detective had been there too. In his presence privacy had been violated. An innocent pact between thought and page, idea and hand, had been ruptured. Or polluted. An intruder, a hostile presence had made him dismissive of his own phrasing. He was forced to read himself through another's eyes and struggle against a likely misreading. Self-consciousness was the death of a notebook.

He pushed it away and stood, remembered his immediate circumstances and their weight. They were enough to make him sit again. Think carefully. It was only a week ago that she left. Enough weakness! Precious when he should be robust. Some poetic authority had said that writing a good poem was a physical exercise. He was thirty-seven, he had strength, stamina and what was written remained his own. The poet would not be deterred by the policeman. Elbows on desk, chin propped in hands, he lectured himself in these terms until Lawrence woke and began to scream. The day's work was done.

In the early afternoon, as he was dressing the baby for a shopping trip, the sound of birds squabbling in the roof gutter at the rear of the house prompted a thought. Downstairs, with Lawrence under his arm, he checked in the desk diary he kept by the phone in the hall on top of a pile of directories. He hadn't noticed that it was already May. Since it was Saturday then it was the 3rd. All morning the small dusty house had been warming. He opened a window on the ground floor.

Let the burglars come while he was at the shops. They would find nothing to steal. He leaned out. A butterfly, a peacock, was sunning itself on the brickwork. The sky he had ignored for days was cloudless, the air smelled richly of next door's mowing. Lawrence would not need his coat.

Roland was not quite carefree as he left the house with the baby in the pushchair. But his constricted life seemed less important. There were other lives, bigger concerns. As he went along he attempted a breezy indifference; if you've lost a wife, then do without or find another or expect her back—there was nothing much in between. The heart of wisdom was not to care too much. He and Lawrence would get by. Tomorrow they would go for dinner with good friends a ten-minute walk away. The baby would fall asleep on the sofa protected by a line of cushions. Daphne was his old friend and confidante. She and Peter were excellent cooks. They had three children, one of them Lawrence's age. Other friends would be there. They would be curious about fresh developments. Douglas Browne's visit, his style of questioning, the shallow grave in the New Forest, the outrageous intrusions, the little camera in his pocket, what his sergeant had said—yes, these Roland would reshape into a comedy of manners. Browne would become Dogberry. He smiled to himself as he walked towards the shops and imagined the hilarity among his friends. They would admire his resilience. To some women a man caring alone for a baby was an attractive even heroic figure. To the men he would seem a dupe. But he was a little proud of himself, of the laundry churning in the washing machine even now, of the clean hallway floor, of the contented well-fed child. He would buy some flowers from a zinc bucket he had passed two days before. A double bunch of red tulips for the kitchen table. The shop was just ahead, more newsagent than florist, and while he was in there he would buy a newspaper. He was ready to embrace the wider turbulent world. Lawrence permitting he might read it in the park.

It was not possible to buy a paper without seeing its headline. "Radiation cloud reaches Britain." He had already heard in the murmur of his kitchen radio fragments of the explosion story. While he waited by the till for the flowers to be wrapped he wondered how it was possible to know something, if only in vaguest terms, and at the same time deny it, refuse it, steer round it, then experience the luxury of shock at the moment of revelation.

He reversed the pushchair out of the shop and continued towards his errands. The normality on the street had a sinister slow-motion look. He had thought he could burrow down but the world had come to find him. Not him. Lawrence. An industrial bird of prey, a pitiless eagle, in the service of the machinery of fate, come to snatch the child from the nest. The idiot parent, virtuous with the morning dishes in the sink, with a change of cot sheets, some tulips for the kitchen, had been looking the other way. Worse, was determined to look the other way. He thought he was immune because he always had been. He imagined it was his love that protected his child. But when a public emergency erupts it becomes an indifferent leveller. Children welcome. Roland had no special privileges. He was in there with the rest and would have to listen out for public announcements, the quarter-credible assurances of leaders who, by convention, talked down to the citizenry. What was good for a politician's idea of the masses might not be good for any individual, especially for him. But he was the mass. He would be treated like the idiot he always was.

He stopped by a letter box. Its quaint red and royal insignia, George V, were already a memento of another time, of risible faith in continuity by way of posted messages. Roland stowed the flowers in a bag that hung from the pushchair handle and unfolded the paper to read the headline again. It was of the deadpan science-fiction kind, bland and apocalyptic. Of course. The cloud always knew where it was heading. To get here from Soviet Ukraine it would have crossed other countries that mattered less. This was a local affair. It appalled him how much of the story he already knew. A nuclear power station meltdown, explosion and fire in a faraway place called Chernobyl. An old aspect of normality, prison riots, still simmered further down the page. Below the newspaper Roland had a partial view of Lawrence's fuzzy almost bald head swivelling as he tracked each passer-by. The headline was not as alarming as the line above it in smaller print.

"Health officials insist there is no risk to public." Exactly. The dam will hold. The disease will not spread. The president is not seriously ill. From democracies to dictatorships, calm above all.

His cynicism was good protection. It prompted him to take measures that would let him feel that he was not a faceless member of the mass. His child would survive. He was a knowledgeable man and knew what to do. The nearest pharmacy was less than a hundred yards away. At the prescription counter he queued for ten minutes. Lawrence was restless, squirming, arching his back against the buggy's safety straps. As only the well-informed knew, potassium iodide protected the vulnerable thyroid against radiation. Children were at special risk. The pharmacist, a friendly lady, smiled and shrugged stoically as she might at a day of heavy rain. All sold out. As of last night.

"Everyone is going crazy for it, love."

Two other pharmacies in the area told him the same, though in less friendly terms. One old fellow in a white coat was irritable: had he not seen the sign on the door? Further along the street Roland bought six one-and-a-half-litre bottles of water and a strong bag to carry them in. Reservoirs would be irradiated, tap water must be avoided. At a hardware shop he collected up packs of plastic dust sheets and rolls of sticky tape.

In the park, while Lawrence gripped in his fist a crushed portion of his second banana of the day and fell asleep, Roland scanned the pages and formed a mosaic of impressions. The invisible cloud was sixty miles away. British students arriving at Heathrow from Minsk were radiated to fifty times normal levels. Minsk was 200 miles from the accident. The Polish government was advising against drinking milk or eating dairy products. The radiation leak was first detected by the Swedes 700 miles away. Soviet authorities had passed on no advice about contaminated food or drink to their own people. It could never happen here. But it had already. A leak at Windscale had been kept secret. The Third Secretary at the Russian embassy in Stockholm had been dispatched to ask Swedish authorities how to deal with a graphite fire. The Swedes didn't know and referred the Russians to the British. Nothing else was publicly known. France and Germany had said there can be no harm to the public. But don't drink the milk.

In the centrefold a detailed cutaway drawing of the power station showed how it happened. He was impressed that a newspaper could know so much so soon. Elsewhere were warnings that experts had given long ago about this design of reactor. Bottom of the page, an overview of British power stations of roughly similar design. An editorial advised that it was time to shift to wind power. A columnist asked what happened to Gorbachev's policy of openness. It was always a fraud. Someone wrote in the letters page that wherever there was nuclear power, East or West, there were official lies.

Across the broad asphalt path that cut through the park, on a bench like his, a woman was reading a more popular paper. Roland had a view of the headline. "Meltdown!" The entire story, the accumulated details, were beginning to nauseate him. Like eating too much cake. Radiation sickness. Two women, each pushing an old-fashioned well-sprung pram, walked past. He heard one of them use the word "emergency." There was a general light-headed sensation that came from there being only one subject. The country stood together, united in anxiety. The sane impulse was to run. If he had the money he would rent a place somewhere safe. But where? Or buy a plane ticket to the States, to Pittsburgh where he had friends or to Kerala where he and Lawrence could live cheaply. How might that look to Detective Inspector Browne? What he needed, Roland thought, was a conversation with Daphne.

The weather report on the back page of his own paper predicted a north-easterly breeze. More of the cloud was on its way. His first duty was to hump the bag of bottled water home and start to seal the windows. He must continue to keep the world out. It was a twenty-minute walk. As Roland took the front door key from his pocket Lawrence woke. For no reason, in the way of all babies, he started to bawl. The trick was to pick him up as soon as possible. It was hot and clumsy work, unfastening the straps, lifting the screaming red-faced child, getting the pushchair, the water, the flowers, the dust sheets into the house. He was in, and saw it lying on the floor, writing side up, another card from Alissa, her fifth. More words this time. But he left it where it was and carried Lawrence and the shopping towards the kitchen.

# 2

He and his parents arrived in London from North Africa in the late summer of 1959. There was said to be a heatwave—a mere 89 degrees Fahrenheit and "sweltering," a new word to Roland. He was disdainful, a proud native of a place where the light of mid-morning was a blinding white, where the heat struck your face as it bounced off the ground and the cicadas fell silent. He could have told his relatives. Instead, he told himself. Here, the streets near his half-sister Susan's rooms in Richmond were orderly, with a look of permanence. Colossal paving stones and kerbs too heavy to lift or steal. Smooth black roads empty of dung and sand. No dogs, camels, donkeys, no shouting, no car horns pressed for half a minute on end, no handcarts piled high with melons, or dates still clinging to their palm branches or blocks of ice melting under sackcloth. No smell of food in the street, no hiss and clatter, no stench of burnt oil and rubber from the workshops under awnings where they pressed old tyres into new. No calls to prayer by muezzins from their high minarets. Here the surface of the clean road was slightly curved as though mostly buried out of sight was a fat black tube. To allow the rain to run off, his father explained, which made sense. Roland noted the heavy iron drains in the unlittered cobbled gutters. So much work to make a few yards of ordinary street, and no one noticed. When he tried to explain his black-tube idea to his mother, Rosalind, she didn't understand. The Tube was a railway, she said. The underground part didn't reach as far as Richmond. Along the visible portion of his black tube the traffic processed evenly, with no sense of striving. No one was trying to get ahead of everyone else.

In mid-afternoon of their first full day back "home" he went with his father, Captain Robert Baines, to the English shops. The light was golden treacly thick. The dominant colours were rich reds and greens—the famous buses and the startling postboxes over which rose tall horse chestnuts and plane trees and, lower down, hedges, lawns, verges, pavement crack weeds. Red and green, his mother said, should never be seen. These clashing colours were associated with anxiety, with a tensing in his shoulders that made him lean forward as they walked. The day after next he and his parents would travel seventy miles from London to inspect his new school. The term would not begin for several days. The other boys would not be there. He was glad, for the thought of them made his stomach contract. The word "boys," boys en masse, conferred on them an authority, a thuggish power. When his father referred to them as "lads" they became taller in his thoughts, stringier, irresponsibly strong. In a town six miles from his school—*his* school—he and his parents would visit an outfitter to buy his uniform. That prospect too tightened his stomach. The school colours were yellow and blue. The list included a boilersuit, gumboots, two different kinds of tie, two different kinds of jacket. He had not told his parents that he didn't know what to do with such clothes. He did not want to let anyone down. Who could tell him what a boilersuit was for, what gumboots were, what a blazer was, what "Harris tweed with leather patches" meant and when the right time was to put them on and take them off?

He had never worn a jacket. In Tripoli in winter, sometimes he wore a jumper knitted by his mother with a twisting cable pattern down the front. Two days before they caught the twin-propellor plane that brought them to London via Malta and Rome, his father had shown him how to knot a tie. In the sitting room he had proved to his parents several times over he could do it. It was not easy. Roland doubted that when he stood with other boys, tall *lads*, hundreds of them in a line, in front of gigantic mirrors like the ones he had seen in a picture of the Palace of Versailles, he would remember how to fix his tie. He would be alone, mocked and in trouble.

They were walking to buy his father's cigarettes and to escape the two small rooms Susan lived in with her husband and baby daughter. Already his mother had packed away the camp beds and was vacuuming the dustless carpets. The little girl, with two molars coming through would not stop crying. It was only correct that "the men" should be out of the way. They walked side by side for fifteen minutes. It was where their street met the main road that the enormous horse chestnuts rose, forming an avenue towards the first of the shops. He was well used to high eucalyptus with their dusty dry rustling leaves and flaking barks, trees that seemed to live on the edge of death from thirst. He loved the high palms leaning into deep blue skies. But London's trees were rich and grand like the Queen, as permanent as the postboxes. Here was a deeper anxiety. The lads, the boilersuit and the rest were as nothing. The individual leaves of the horse chestnuts, like the line of the Mediterranean horizon, like the writing on the blackboard in his Tripoli primary school, held a secret, one that he could barely tell himself. His vision was blurring. A year ago, he could see more clearly by screwing up his eyes. That no longer worked. There was something wrong with him and he could not bear to think about it, about where it was leading. Blindness. It was a sickness and a failure. He could not tell his parents because he dreaded their disappointment in him. Everyone could see clearly, and he could not. This was his shameful secret. He would take his condition away with him to boarding school and deal with it alone.

Every horse chestnut was a cliff of undifferentiated green. As they approached the first its leaves began to appear, each one an exuberant friendly five-eared spread. Stopping to look closely might have given his secret away. Examining leaves was not the sort of thing his father approved of.

When they reached a newsagent, the Captain bought, unasked, along with his cigarettes, a chocolate bar for his son. Years of being an infantryman in barracks in Fort George, Scotland before the war, low-paid and always hungry, had made Roland's father appreciative of the treats he could bestow on his son. He was also stern, dangerous to disobey. It was a powerful mix. Roland feared and loved him. So did Roland's mother.

Roland was still at an age when a mix of chocolate, toffee, sugary biscuit and crushed peanuts could dominate his senses and obliterate his surroundings. When he came to, they were entering another shop. Beer for the men, sherry for the women, lemonade for himself. Later that afternoon on television there would be football miraculously beamed from Ibrox Park, Glasgow. And tomorrow a variety show from the London Palladium. There was no television in Libya, not even talk of its absence. The wireless programmes from London broadcast to the forces families abroad faded and swelled among the hiss and whine of cosmic mayhem. For Roland and his parents television was not a novelty. It was a wonder. To watch it was to celebrate. There must be drinks.

Now father and son retraced their steps from the off-licence with their heavy loads in stout paper bags. When the avenue was still five minutes ahead, with the newsagent just behind, they heard a loud bang like the sharp crack of a rifle, like the .303 Roland had heard many times at the firing range out at Kilometre Eleven. What Roland saw as he turned remained with him for the rest of his life. At its end it would feature in the dying forms and whispers of his retreating consciousness. A man in white helmet, black jacket and blue trousers was flying in a low arc. Because he went head first it looked like a choice, a feat of daring and defiance. He landed on all fours and collapsed face down on the road as he slid along the asphalt with a rasping noise. On impact his helmet tumbled away from him. By a conservative estimate he travelled thirty feet, perhaps forty. Behind him was a small car with smashed-in front and shattered windscreen. The man had flown over its roof. The upended wreckage of a motorbike lay twisted in the gutter. In the car was a woman screaming.

The traffic stopped and stillness settled across the city. Roland ran across the road after his father. As a young soldier in the Highland Light Infantry, twenty-three-year-old Corporal Baines had been on the beach near Dunkirk and had seen much death and men split apart by bombs, still alive. He knew not to move the motorcyclist off the road. He put an ear to the man's mouth to check his breathing and felt for his pulse in the blood-spiked hair at his temples. Roland watched closely. The Captain turned the man onto his side and parted his legs for stability. He took off his own jacket, folded it and tucked it under the man's head. They went over to the car. By now, there was a crowd. Captain Baines was not alone—all the men, except the youngest, had been in the war and knew what to do, Roland thought. The car's front doors were open and three men were leaning in. There was general agreement that the woman should not be moved. She was young, with blonde curly hair and a satin blouse with colourful polka dots streaked with her blood. There was a gash across the width of her forehead. She was no longer screaming but repeating, over and over, "I can't see. I can't see." A man's muffled voice came from within the car. "Don't worry, pet. It's the blood run into your eyes." But still she kept on calling out. Roland turned away in a daze.

Next thing two ambulances were there. The woman, silent now, was sitting on the kerb with a blanket across her shoulders. An ambulanceman was turning a dressing around her head wound. The unconscious motorcyclist was on a stretcher by the ambulance. Its interior was creamy white, lit with yellow lamps. There were red blankets, two single beds and space in between, like a child's bedroom. His father and two other men went forward to help with the stretcher but they were not needed. There was a murmur of sympathy in the crowd as the woman began to cry as she too was helped onto a stretcher. The blanket was tucked round her and they carried her into the other ambulance. All the while, Roland now saw, the blue lights on both had been flashing. Flashing heroically.

These several minutes were frightening. In his eleven years he had known nothing like them. They had a disjointed dreamlike quality. In memory they would blur, slip out of sequence. Perhaps they had run first to the car, then to the man on the ground because no one else was attending to him. There was a gap, like a sleep, during which the ambulances had arrived. Their sirens must have sounded and yet he didn't hear them. A police car was there but he had not seen it arrive. Perhaps it was a woman in the crowd who had fainted and who was sitting on the kerb with the blanket. Perhaps the woman in the car remained in place as an ambulanceman staunched her bleeding. The yellow illumination inside the ambulance may have been reflected sunlight. Mcmory was not easily examined for greater detail like a horse chestnut leaf. The man shooting through the air—that was incontestable. So was the way he landed and surged forwards face down with the white helmet rolling away onto the grass verge. But what stayed with Roland and changed him was what happened when the rear doors were slammed shut and the ambulances pulled out into the stilled traffic. He began to cry. He moved away so that his father wouldn't see. Roland was sorry for the man and the woman but that wasn't it. His tears were for joy, for a sudden warmth of understanding that did not yet have these terms of definition: how loving and good people were, how kind the world was that had ambulances in it that came quickly out of nowhere whenever there was sorrow and pain. Always there, an entire system, just below the surface of everyday life, watchfully waiting, ready with all its knowledge and skill to come and help, embedded within a greater network of kindness he had yet to discover. It seemed to him then, as the ambulances receded with their distant sirens sounding, that everything worked, and was decent and caring and just. He hadn't grasped that he was about to leave home forever, that for the next seven years, three-quarters of his life would be at school and that at home he would always be a visitor. And that after school came adulthood. But he sensed he was at the beginning of a new life and now he understood that the world was sympathetic and fair. It would embrace and contain him kindly, justly and nothing bad, really bad, could happen to him or to anyone, or not for long.

The crowd was dispersing, everyone was returning to the everyday. Now Roland noticed three policemen standing by their patrol car. Captain Baines's arm was covered in dried blood the colour of rust from fingertips to elbow. He rolled down his sleeves as he and Roland went to retrieve his folded jacket from the gutter. There was blood on its grey silk lining. They carried their bags back across the road and stopped while he put the jacket on. He explained that he had to conceal the blood from the police. He did not want to be called to court as a witness. He and Roland's mother had their plane to catch home next week. This reminder that he would not be travelling with them brought Roland's moment of enlightenment to an end. In its place came all the old anxieties. They walked to his sister's flat in silence. Later they were joined by her husband, Keith, a bandsman, a trombone player in the army. While the baby slept at last, they drank beer, sherry or lemonade and watched football on TV with the curtains drawn.

Two days later Roland and his parents took the train from Liverpool Street to Ipswich. Outside the comatose Victorian station they waited for a number 202 bus, as instructed in a letter from the headmaster's secretary. It came after forty-five minutes, an empty double-decker in exotic maroon and cream. They sat upstairs so the Captain could smoke. Roland had a seat by a window open for the heat. They went down a long straight main road past cramped terraced houses in dark red brick. By a boatyard they turned onto a narrow road that ran along a foreshore. Suddenly the wide River Orwell was in view, at full tide looking clean and blue. He was turned away from his parents so he scrunched up his eyes, hoping to see more clearly. On the far side, upriver, was a power station. The lonely road snaked through a marshland of muddy pools whose scent of salt and sweet decay rose through the late summer warmth and filled the bus. On the far bank of the river now were woods and meadows. He saw a barge with high masts and sails the colour of the blood on the Captain's sleeve. Roland pointed out the boat to his mother but she turned too late to see it. This was a novel landscape and he was enchanted. For several minutes he forgot the purpose of their journey as the bus climbed a hill past an ancient tower and the river was lost from view.

The bus conductor came up the stairs to tell them in the local accent that sounded like a song that theirs was the next stop. They stepped out into the cool deep shade of a vast spreading tree. It grew from the far side of the road by a wooden bench. Not a horse chestnut but it recalled Roland to his secret and the pleasures of the bus ride were forgotten. His father took the secretary's letter from his jacket to consult her directions. They went through open cast-iron gates by a lodge and followed the drive. No one spoke. Roland took his mother's hand. She gave his a squeeze. He thought she looked anxious and tried to think of something interesting and tender to say. But all he could think of and could not mention was what lay ahead, out of sight behind the trees. The separation to come. It was his duty to protect her from it for a few moments longer. They passed a Norman church and, in a dip of the drive, a small pink-washed building from which came the sound and smell of pigs. As the drive rose there came into view, 300 yards away across a wide expanse of green, a grand building of grey stone, with columns and curving wings and high chimneys. Berners Hall was a fine example, Roland would one day read, of English Palladian architecture. Set well apart, half hidden among tall oaks, was a stable block with a water tower.

They stopped to look. The Captain gestured towards the Hall and said, unnecessarily, "There it is."

They knew what he meant. Or Rosalind Baines knew precisely and her son understood only in vague terms.

→→

Few people in Britain knew of Libya. Fewer knew of the British army contingent there, a remnant of the vast sweeping desert campaigns of the Second World War. In international politics Libya was a backwater. For six years the Baines family made a life in an obscure crevice of history. A good life as far as Roland was concerned. There was a beach known as Piccolo Capri where the families met in the afternoons after school and work. Officers at one end, Other Ranks further along. Captain Baines's best friends were men like himself who had fought in the war and risen through the ranks. The Sandhurst officers and their families belonged in another world. All Roland and Rosalind's friends were the children and wives of the Captain's friends. These were their points of reference: this beach, Roland's primary school housed within Azizia barracks on the south side of the city—the target the Americans would one day destroy; the YMCA where Rosalind worked in the heart of Tripoli: the tank and light armoured workshop at Gurji camp where the Captain worked; the Naafi where they did their shopping. Unlike most families they also bought vegetables and meat in the Tripoli souk. Rosalind pined for home, knitted constantly for babies she would never meet as babies, wrapped birthday presents most weeks, wrote letters daily to relatives that usually ended, "Must rush now to catch the post."

There were no secondary schools and when Roland turned eleven he would have to be sent to England. Captain Baines thought his son was too girlishly close to his mother. He helped her out with the housework, slept in her bed when the Captain was away on manoeuvres, still held her hand, even at the age of nine. Her choice, if she'd had one, would have been to return home to England to a normal life and a local day school for her son. The army was reducing its numbers and offering early retirement on good terms. But his father, as well as being generous and stern, kind and domineering, was wary of change long before he had lined up his arguments against it. He had other motives for getting Roland out of the way. Two decades later, one evening over beers, Major (retired) Baines told his son that children always got in the way of a marriage. Finding a state boarding school in England for Roland was good for everyone "all round."

Rosalind Baines, neé Morley, army wife, child of her times, did not chafe or rage against her powerlessness or sulk about it. She and Robert had left school at fourteen. He became a butcher's boy in Glasgow, she was a chambermaid in a middle-class house near Farnham. A clean and ordered home remained her passion. Robert and Rosalind wanted for Roland the education they had been denied. This was the story she told herself. That he might have attended a day school and stayed with her was an idea she must have dutifully banished. She was a small nervous woman, a worrier, very pretty, everyone agreed. Easily intimidated, fearful of Robert when he drank, which was every day. She was at her best, her most relaxed, in a long heart-to-heart with a close friend. Then she told stories and laughed easily, a light and liquid sound that Captain Baines himself rarely heard.

Roland was one of her close friends. In the holidays, when they did the housework together, she told stories of her childhood in the village of Ash, near the garrison town of Aldershot. She and her brothers and sisters used to brush their teeth with twigs. Her employer gave her her first toothbrush. Like so many of her generation she lost all her teeth in her early twenties. In newspaper cartoons people in bed were often shown with their false teeth in a glass of water on the bedside table. She was the oldest of five and spent much of her childhood minding her sisters and brothers. She was closest to her sister Joy who still lived near Ash. Where was their mother when Rosalind was minding the children? Her reply was always the same, a child's view unrevised in adulthood: your granny would take the bus to Aldershot and spend the day window-shopping. Rosalind's mother fiercely disapproved of make-up. In her teens, on rare nights out, Rosalind would meet her friend Sybil and together they would hide in a special place, a culvert under the road on the edge of the village, to apply their lipstick and powder. She told Roland that at the age of twenty, already married to her first husband, Jack, expecting her first child, Henry, she believed he would come out of her bottom. The midwife put her right. Roland laughed along with his mother. He did not know where babies came from and knew it was not right to ask.

The war came to Rosalind in a startling moment. She was an assistant to an old lorry driver named Pop. They were delivering supplies near Aldershot. A bomb hit the road and the blast knocked their lorry into a ditch. Neither of them was hurt. She continued with Pop after the war. By then Jack Tate had been killed on active service and she was the mother of two children. Henry was living with his granny on his father's side. Susan was in a London institution for the daughters of dead servicemen. During the war there was plenty of work for women. In 1945, making regular runs to an army depot outside Aldershot, she became aware of the handsome sergeant in the guardhouse. He had a Scottish accent, an erect posture, a trim moustache. After many encounters he asked her to a dance. She was frightened of him and refused several times before she gave in. They were married in January two years later. The year after that Roland was born.

She always spoke of her first husband in a low voice. Roland came to understand without being told that this man was not to be mentioned in front of his father. His name had a heroic sound to it: Jack Tate. He had died of stomach wounds received in Holland four months after the D-Day landings. Before the war he had been a wanderer. Whenever he was away Rosalind and her two children lived "on the parish," which meant they were extremely poor. Sometimes the village policeman would bring Jack Tate back. Where had he been? Rosalind's answer to Roland's question was always the same— he slept under hedges.

Roland's half-brother and sister, Henry and Susan, were distant, romantic figures, adults making their own way in England, with jobs, marriages and babies. In his spare time Henry played the guitar and sang in a band. Susan had been part of the household until Roland was six. He thought she was beautiful and he loved her. But they were the children of Jack Tate and there was something forbidden about them that rendered them indistinct. Why were they sent away in 1941 to live with a strict and unloving granny, Jack's mother, in the years before their father's death? Henry stayed there right through his teens until his National Service. Susan was sent later to the harsh place in London, founded in the nineteenth century to train girls to be chambermaids. She became ill with an abscess in her throat and was eventually brought home.

Why hadn't Susan and Henry grown up with their mother? He didn't pose these questions, even in his thoughts. They were constituent parts of the cloud that lay over family relations. That cloud was an accepted feature of life. During the half of his childhood that was Libya he was never encouraged to write to his brother and sister. They never wrote to him. He overheard that Susan's marriage to Keith the bandsman was in trouble—in itself, a hazy enough concept. She was to fly out to Tripoli to stay for a while. The day before they went to RAF Idris to collect her Rosalind took Roland aside and spoke sternly. She said everything twice, as if he had done something wrong. He was never, *ever* to tell anyone that he and his sister had different fathers. If anyone asked he was to say that his father was Susan's father. Was that understood? He nodded, understanding nothing. This serious adult matter belonged in the familiar cloud. Not speaking about it seemed proper and reasonable.

At the beginning, when Roland and his mother arrived for the first time in Tripoli to join the Captain, they lived in a two-bedroom, third-floor flat with a tiny balcony. The king's palace was close by. The heat and alien culture of central Tripoli and daily trips to the beach were exciting. But there was something wrong in the family and soon there was something wrong with seven-year-old Roland. Nightmares, with much screaming, attempts to jump from his bedroom window while sleepwalking. Sometimes his parents left him alone in the early evening in the flat. He would sit in an armchair with his knees drawn up, listening in terror to every sound, waiting for their return.

Then he found himself in a nearby apartment, spending afternoons with a friendly lady—she was part Italian—and her daughter, June, a girl his age who became his best friend. June's mother was a thera-pist and must have been the one to suggest a practical solution. The Baineses moved to a white single-storey villa on a farm on the west-ern edge of Tripoli. Here, peanuts, pomegranates, olives and vines grew. If he leaped from his bedroom window he would fall no more than two feet. The gift of a puppy, Jumbo, might also have been the therapist's idea. June and her mother returned to Italy and for a while Roland was desolate. The farm revived him. A mile away, where the olive groves ended and scrub desert began was Gurji military camp where the Captain worked. Roland sometimes walked there alone to a school friend's house along a narrow sandy track flanked by high cactus hedges.

In another part of the family cloud was his mother's sadness. He took it for granted. It lay hidden in her subdued tone, her nervousness, the way she paused in a task and looked away, drawn into a daydream or a memory. It was in her sudden outbursts of irritation with him. She always made up with kind words. Her sadness bound them closer. Every three or four months, for a couple of weeks at a time, Captain Baines would be in the desert with his unit on manoeuvres. The plan was to be ready for the day when the Egyptians, backed by the Rus-sians, attacked Libya from the east. The Centurion tanks that the Captain's workshop serviced needed to practise their defensive moves. Roland, who knew something of these warlike preparations, got into his mother's bed at night not only to receive comfort but to give it, just by being there. He was protective of her even as he needed her.

But he needed his father too. Caution and a military sense of order became a disabling obsession in Captain Baines's old age. But in his forties he had a taste for adventure. When travelling Arab musicians came by the house, he went out onto the sand with them and took hold of their *zukra*—bagpipes—and played along with the group. His army colleagues would not have put their mouths where an Arab's mouth had been. The excursions alone in the car with his nine-year-old son may have been part of his programme to instil masculine virtues and skills. They drove to a troops' training ground where Roland learned to climb a rope and swing hand over hand along netting. At the Kilo-metre Eleven rifle range, he lay beside his father and looked down the sight of a .303—number four mark one, he was taught to say—at distant targets in a sandbank. Roland pulled the trigger and the Captain took the recoil in his shoulder. The noise, the danger, the deadliness were exhilarating. He arranged for Roland to go with a sergeant and drive a tank round the training ground of steep sand dunes. He taught his son Morse code and brought home two key sets and a hundred yards of wire. He drove him to the grand parade ground at Azizia so he could roller skate across great distances. Captain Baines took a manly view of swimming. He taught his son how to dive and hold his breath under water for half a minute and how to swim the crawl—the rightly named breaststroke was for girls. At the beach they developed together a game they called "the record." The Captain stood chest-deep in the sea counting slowly while Roland stood unsupported on shoulders slippery from Brylcreem. Before it came to an end, not long before they took the plane to London, the record stood at thirty-two.

When Roland mentioned that he would like to find a scorpion, he and the Captain set off into the scrub desert west of Tripoli. On such journeys, his father would say, "Three-eighths?" and Roland would shout out, "Point three seven five!" Or the Captain would say, "Twenty miles?" and Roland would make the mental calculation—divide by five, multiply by eight—and give the answer in kilometres. His father was priming him for the eleven-plus exam with the sort of questions he thought were bound to come up. None of them did.

"Capital of West Germany?"

"Bonn!"

"Name of the prime minister?"

"Mr. Macmillan!"

They pulled over by the side of the empty road that led to Tunisia. For ten minutes they walked into the immense stony desert of small cacti and brush. It did not surprise Roland that under the first stone his father turned was a large yellow scorpion. Its tail and sting were raised. It had been waiting for them. The Captain recklessly pushed it into a jam jar with his thumb. For a week Roland fed it stag beetles but the scorpion cowered. Rosalind said she could not sleep with it in the house. Robert took it into the workshop and brought it back floating in formaldehyde, sealed in a jar. For years, Roland imagined the scorpion's ghost making its way towards him to exact revenge. Its plan was to sting his bare feet while he was cleaning his teeth at night. It could only be kept at bay if he made a point of glancing down and whispering, "Sorry."

His great and formative adventure had come earlier when he was eight. His father was central to it as a distant heroic figure. Unusually, Rosalind was absent. This was the first time that remote turns in international events intruded on his small world. His understanding of them was minimal. He would learn in his next school that arguments among the Greek gods had serious consequences for mere humans below.

Across the Middle East, Arab nationalism was a growing political force whose immediate enemy were the colonial and ex-colonial European powers. The new Jewish state of Israel, set on land Palestinians knew as their own, was also a goad. When President Nasser of Egypt nationalised the British-run Suez Canal in late July he became a hero to the nationalist cause. It was assumed that anti-British feeling would run high in neighbouring Libya. Once Britain and France in an alliance with Israel attacked Egypt to regain control of the canal, there were pro-Nasser demonstrations in Tripoli. The crowds also raised banners against King Idris, who was too well disposed to European and American interests. London and Washington decided to move all British and American families to safety until they could be evacuated.

What could Roland know of this? Only what his father told him, that the Arabs were angry. No time to ask why. All children and their mothers must proceed immediately to the nearest army camp for their protection. By chance, when the Suez crisis broke, Rosalind happened to be in England visiting Susan. There was trouble "at home" that Roland knew nothing of. Nor did he know who came into the white villa while he was at school to pack a bag of clothes for him. Certainly not the Captain, who was the officer in charge of the evacuation and was busy.

The bus that brought him from his primary school in Azizia barracks did not stop that day by the lane through the pomegranate orchard that led to the villa. It went on the extra mile to Gurji. There were sandbagged machine-gun nests by the guardroom, and light tanks parked by the road. Armed troops waved and saluted as their bus passed into the camp.

The big twenty-man tents were all the same but it was a given that officers' children were accommodated separately from the children of the other ranks. The wives banded together to manage an improvised kitchen, dining room and wash house. Nothing dramatic happened in the following week. Angry Arabs armed to the teeth did not attack the base in order to slaughter British children and their mothers. The camp was small, no one was allowed to leave and Roland had never been happier. He and two friends had the run of the place. They came to know well the smell of engine oil on hot fine sand. They explored the vehicle workshops, talked to the tank commanders, played football on the full-sized grassless pitch. They climbed up scaffold towers to be with the machine-gun crews. Either discipline was slipping or the expectation of an attack had vanished. The duty officers and soldiers—all young men—were friendly. A lieutenant took Roland on a whirl round the base on his 500 cc motorbike. Sometimes Roland wandered by himself, content to be alone. The army mums who supervised meals, bathed eighteen children one after another in a big tin bath and imposed bedtimes, were jolly and capable. Roland received extra sympathy because his mother was away. But maternal attention was just what he did not want.

Complaints and needs were directed at Captain Baines and his men. Sometimes he descended among the family tents to sort out a problem, service revolver strapped to his waist. He did not have time to speak to his son. That was fine. Roland was too young to account for his euphoria in those few days. The rupture of routine, the excitement of danger mixed with an exaggerated sense of security, hours of unsupervised play with his chums; and then, a set of absences: squinting at the blackboard at the Azizia school, release from his mother's anxious attention and sadness and from his father's iron authority. The Captain no longer vigorously Brylcreemed Roland's hair in the mornings before school and made a sharp parting with the tip of his comb; his mother no longer fussed over scuffs on his shoes. Above all he was free of the unspoken family problems, which had a power over him as pervasive and mysterious as gravity.

The families left the camp late at night and travelled to the RAF Idris airfield under heavy military escort, which included armoured personnel carriers. Roland was proud to see his father in charge, as ever with his gun, giving orders to the troops, delivering mothers and children safely to the steps of the twin-engine propeller plane bound for London. But there was no opportunity to say goodbye.

The episode, a taste of unreal freedom, had lasted eight days. It sustained him at boarding school, it shaped his restlessness and unfocussed ambitions in his twenties and strengthened his resistance to a regular job. It became a hindrance—whatever he was doing, he was pursued by an idea of a greater freedom elsewhere, some emancipated life just beyond reach, one that would be denied him if he made unbreakable commitments. He missed many chances that way and submitted to periods of prolonged boredom. He was waiting for existence to part like a curtain, for a hand to extend and help him step through into a paradise regained. There his purpose, his delight in friendship and community and the thrill of the unexpected would be bound and resolved. Because he failed to understand or define these expectations until after they had faded in later life, he was vulnerable to their appeal. He did not know what—in the real world—he was waiting for. In the dimensions of the unreal, it was to relive the eight days he spent in the confines of 10 Armoured Workshops, REME, at Gurji camp in the autumn of 1956.

Back in England Roland and Rosalind lodged for six months in the house of a builder in Rosalind's home village of Ash. Roland attended the same local school as his mother had in the early twenties, and where Henry and Susan went too. By Easter of the next year Rosalind and Roland travelled back to Libya, to a new development of villas close to the coast. Perhaps the separation had served his parents well, for life was easier, his mother was less tense and the Captain began to enjoy his adventures with his son.

In July 1959 a school was chosen and a visit was arranged for September, a few days before term began. Roland learned that he would be having piano lessons. The Captain himself played the mouth organ in a clever vamping style. His taste was for songs of the First World War. "It's a Long Way to Tipperary," "Take Me Back to Dear Old Blighty,"

"Pack up Your Troubles in Your Old Kit Bag." There were some Scottish songs, old Harry Lauder numbers he sang well. "A Wee Deoch an' Doris," "Stop Your Tickling, Jock!" and "I Belong to Glasgow." It was his keenest pleasure in life to be drinking beer with his army mates, to play or sing to the company and get them to join in. His greatest regret was that he never learned to play the piano, never had the opportunity. Roland must have what he had missed. The chap who could play the piano, he often told his son, would always be popular. As soon as he started on an old favourite everyone would gather round and join in.

The lessons were arranged with the housemaster, who wrote back pleasantly to say that all was in order and Miss Cornell, who had recently graduated from the Royal College of Music, would be Roland's tutor. The school took its music seriously and he hoped that Roland would take part in next term's opera, *The Magic Flute*.

A few weeks before the family left Libya for England, the Captain made another bold move. He arranged for an army three-ton truck to deliver to the house enormous wooden crates. A corporal and a private carried them round to the small garden at back of the house. Father and son nailed them together to make a "base" in the garden. Roland would crawl inside his labyrinth of boxes to conduct chemical experiments with random mixtures of household products—Worcestershire sauce, washing powder, salt, vinegar—along with hollyhock, geranium and date palm leaves. Nothing ever exploded as he hoped.

→→

There it was. In their different ways, they understood. The Palladian country seat on the far side of the cricket pitch marked the end of their triangular family. Its daily rhythms and currents of hidden feelings and conflicts had been intensified by being set in a distant outpost, one of the forgotten spoils of war. No one had anything to say about an end, so they walked on in silence. At last Roland let go of his mother's hand. His father pointed and they obediently looked. On the green, a tractor and trailer were bringing rugby posts. One H-shape was being raised in place by four men with ropes. The trees had obscured them before. There were no stumps on the cricket pitch and the scoreboard was blank. The end of summer. Now the driveway was taking them in a long curve past the stables and water tower. They had a glimpse beyond the main building of a balustrade, of ferns sloping away to woods, then the foreshore and the wide blue river again, drifting away from them in a broad straight road towards a far bend. Towards Harwich, the Captain said.

Roland did not know if this was his own idea or something he had once been told: nothing is ever as you imagine it. He fully grasped its startling truth. The scale, the space, the grandeur and greenness— how could he have known what lay ahead from their small house in Giorgimpopoli or from his desk before the blurred blackboard in his classroom at Azizia barracks or from the gentle sea and carefree heat of Piccolo Capri? Now he was too much in awe to feel anxious. He walked between his parents as though through a dreamscape towards the grand building. They entered by a side door. Inside it was cool, almost chilly. Within a narrow space before the entrance hall there was a telephone booth and a fire extinguisher. The staircase was steep and modest. These details were reassuring. Then they were in a larger reception space with an echoing high ceiling and three polished dark doors, all closed. The family stood uncertainly in the centre. Captain Baines was reaching again for the letter of directions when the school secretary was suddenly before them. After the introductions—her name was Mrs. Manning—the tour began. She asked some cheery questions of Roland which he answered politely and she announced that he would be the youngest in his year. After that he barely listened and she did not speak to him again—a relief. Her remarks were addressed to the Captain. He asked the questions while Roland and his mother walked behind, as if they were both prospective pupils. But they did not look at each other. What Roland did catch from their guide were the mentions she made of "the boys." After lunch, when it wasn't rugby, the boys put on their boilersuits. That did not sound good. She said several times how strange or peaceful or tidy it was without these boys. But she missed them really. His old anxiety returned. The boys would know things that he did not, they knew each other, they would be bigger, stronger, older. They would dislike him.

They left the building by a side door and passed under a monkey puzzle tree. Mrs. Manning pointed out a statue of Diana, the huntress, with what looked like a gazelle at her side. They did not go near, as he would have liked. Instead they stood at the top of some steps looking down at a gate which, she explained at length, was monogrammed in cast iron. Roland gazed at the immense river and drifted away in his thoughts. If they were at home now they would be getting ready for the beach. Rubber flippers and mask with their distinctive smell in the heat, trunks, towels. Sand grains from yesterday would be in the flippers and mask. His friends would be waiting. At night his mother would dab pink calamine lotion on his burnt and peeling shoulders and nose.

Now they were approaching a low modern building. Inside, upstairs, they inspected the dormitories. Here was the strongest evidence so far of the boys. Metal bunkbeds in rows, grey blankets, the smell of disinfectant, scarred cupboards Mrs. Manning called "tallboys" and in the washrooms rows of squat handbasins under small mirrors. No resemblance to the Palace of Versailles.

Later, tea and a slice of cake in the school office. Roland's piano lessons were paid for in advance. The Captain signed some papers and, after farewells, the walk back down the drive, a short wait under the immense tree for the bus into the centre of Ipswich, then to the stuffy school outfitter, where the oak-panelled walls soaked up most of the available air. It took a long time to work through the list. Captain Baines went to a pub. Roland put on a bristling Harris tweed jacket with leather patches at the elbows and leather trimming at the cuffs. His first jacket. His second was a blue blazer. The boilersuit came flat in a cardboard box. It was not necessary to try it on, the assistant said. The one item he liked was an elastic belt in blue and yellow, fastened with a hook shaped like a snake. On the Ipswich train to London, heading back to his sister's place in Richmond, surrounded by bags of his stuff, his parents asked him in different ways if he liked the school or this or that feature. He neither liked nor disliked Berners. It was simply, overwhelmingly there and it was already his future. He said he liked it and the look of relief on their faces made him feel happy.

Five days after his eleventh birthday his parents took him to a street near Waterloo station where the coaches were waiting. One was set aside for new boys. It was an awkward goodbye. His father clapped him on the back, his mother hesitated over an embrace then gave a restrained version of one which he received clumsily, sensitive to what the other boys might think. Minutes after, he witnessed many tearful noisy hugs, but it was too late to go back. Inside the coach there were a difficult fifteen minutes, with his parents on the pavement smiling and half waving and mouthing inaudible encouragement up at him through the window while next to him was a boy who wanted to talk. When the coach began to move at last, his parents walked away. His father's arm was round his mother's shoulders which were shaking.

Roland's neighbour put out his hand and said, "I'm Keith Pitman and I'm going to be a cosmetic dentist."

Roland had politely shaken hands before with many grown-ups, mostly his father's army colleagues, but he had never performed this ritual with someone of his own age. He took Keith's hand and said, "Roland Baines."

He had already noticed that this friendly boy was no bigger than he was.

In the first instance, the shock was not separation from his parents 2,000 miles away. The immediate assault was on the nature of time. It would have happened anyway. It had to happen, the transition into adult time and obligation. Before, he had flourished in a barely visible mist of events, careless of their sequence, drifting, at worst stumbling, through the hours, days and weeks. Birthdays and Christmas were the only true markers. Time was what you received. His parents supervised its flow at home, at school everything happened in one classroom and occasional shifts in routine were orchestrated by teachers who escorted you and even held your hand.

Here, the transition was brutal. The new little boys had to learn quickly to live by the clock, be its servants, anticipate its demands and pay the toll for failure: a telling-off from an irritable teacher, or a detention or, in the final resort, the threat of "the slipper." When to be up and making your bed, when to be at breakfast, then assembly, then first lesson; to gather up everything needed five lessons ahead; how to consult your timetable, or certain noticeboards for lists that might contain your name; to walk punctually from one classroom to another every forty-five minutes and not be late for lunch straight after fifth lesson; which days were games, where to hang and retrieve your kit and when to hand it in for washing; and on the afternoons when there were no games, when to be at class in the late afternoon, and when to be at class on Saturday mornings; when prep started and how long you had to complete your set tasks of memorising or writing; when to shower, when to be in bed fifteen minutes before the lights went out; which were the laundry days and at what time you must line up to present your dirty clothes to Matron—socks and underwear on certain days, shirts, trousers and towels on others; when the top sheet on your bed became the bottom and the new sheet went on top; when to queue for nit or nail inspection or haircuts or pocket-money distribution and when the tuck shop opened.

Possessions consorted tyrannically with time. They could disappear at the ends of your fingers. There were many things you were likely to lose or forget to bring at the start of the day—the timetable itself, a textbook, last night's prep, other exercise books, printed questionnaires and maps, a pen that didn't leak, a bottle of ink, pencil, ruler, protractor, compass, slide rule. If you kept all these small things in a case, you could lose that too and be in bigger trouble. PE was a separate, terrifying concern. Twice a week you carried your gym kit from class to class. The games master, Mr. Evans, a Welshman, was a bully who punished lateness or physical inadequacy with viciousness, mental and physical. In that first week he dug his thumbnail deep into Roland's ear for failing to sit cross-legged on the rugby pitch in the correct manner. As the pain increased he scrambled on the grass to find the right position. In Libya only Libyans sat on the ground, which was stony, hard and hot. In the gym, the games master's gym, the fat, the weak and the clumsy were the likely victims. After the first encounter Roland escaped attention.

Time, which had been an unbounded sphere in which he moved freely in all directions, became overnight a narrow one-way track down which he travelled with his new friends from lesson to lesson, week to week until it became an unquestioned reality. The boys, whose presence he had dreaded, were as bewildered as he was, and friendly.

He liked the warmth of the cockney accents. They huddled together, some wept at night, some wet their beds, most were relentlessly cheerful. No one was ridiculed. After lights out, they told ghost stories, or elaborated their theories about the world or boasted about their fathers, some of whom, he learned later, were non-existent. Roland heard his own voice in the dark trying and failing to evoke the Suez evacuation. But the story of the accident was a success. A man sailing through the air to his certain death, a woman blinded and bleeding, sirens, police, his father's bloodied arm. Another night, Roland repeated it by general request. He gained status, an element that had never been part of his life. He thought he was becoming a different person, one that his parents might not recognise.

After lunch, three afternoons a week, Roland's year group put on their boilersuits—simply done—and were sent out to play unsupervised in the woods and along the river's foreshore. Much that he had read about in the Jennings novels and dreamed of from dry Libya was at last fulfilled. It was as if they had received instructions from *Boy's Own* magazine. They built camps, climbed trees, made bows and arrows, and dug a dangerous unsupported tunnel and went through it on their stomachs for a dare. At four o'clock they were back in class. The hands that held fountain pens might be still streaked with black estuary mud or grass stains. If it was double maths or history, it was a fight to stay awake for ninety minutes. But if it was Friday, when the last lesson was English, the teacher thrilled them by reading aloud in a high nasal voice another episode of a cowboy story, "Shane." It occupied most of the term.

It took Roland several weeks to understand that most of the teachers were not fierce or hostile. They only appeared so in their black gowns. Largely, they were genial and some even knew his name, though only his surname. Many were shaped by their service in the war. Even though it had ended fourteen years ago—his entire lifetime plus almost a quarter—the world war remained a presence, a shadow, but also a light, the source of virtue and meaning, just as it was in Libya, in the Giorgimpopoli villa and in Gurji workshops on the edge of the desert. The Lee–Enfield .303 whose trigger he had been allowed to pull had belonged to the 7th Armoured Division, known as the Desert Rats, and it must surely have killed Germans and Italians. Here in rural Suffolk the hall and its land were requisitioned in 1939 for the army and later the navy. Their monuments were the Nissen huts on the edge of the woods sloping down towards the foreshore. Now the huts were used for Latin and maths. A short walk through those woods was the Berners concrete "hard," down which boats were carried or wheeled into the river. Close by was a wooden jetty built in the war by army engineers. From there, on 6 August 1944, a reinforcement group of 1,000 soldiers in forty landing craft set off down the River Orwell for the long haul to the Normandy beaches and the liberation of Europe. The war lived in the unfading stencilled lettering on the brick wall outside the sickbay—Decontam Centre. It was alive in most classrooms, where discipline was not imposed but assumed by ex-servicemen who themselves had once received orders in a grand cause. Obedience was a given. Everyone could relax.

Roland's terrible secret was revealed within two weeks. The new boys were sent in batches to the sickbay and stood stripped to their underpants, crammed together in the waiting room until their names were called. He presented himself before the fearsome Sister Hammond. It was said of her that she "took no nonsense." Without a greeting she told him to get on the scales. Then he was measured, his joints, his bones, his ears, even his testicles were inspected for abnormalities. Finally, the Sister put an eyepatch on him and, turning him by his shoulders, made him stand behind a line and look at a board of diminishing letters on the wall. In near nakedness he was about to be uncovered. His heart was thudding. Squinting couldn't help him, his right eye was no better than his left and all his guesses were wrong. He could not read past the second row. Unsurprised, Sister Hammond made a note and called the next boy.

Ten days after his visit to the Ipswich optician he was sent from his classroom to collect a stiff brown envelope. It was a warm autumnal morning, the sky was cloudless. He stopped before a tall oak tree to experiment before returning to class. He looked first to make sure there was no one nearby. He removed the case from the envelope, prised open the heavily sprung lid and took out the unfamiliar device. It felt alive in his hands, repellent. He opened its arms wide, raised it to his face and looked up. A revelation. He called out in joy. The great shape of the oak leaped as though through an Alice in Wonderland mirror. Suddenly every separate leaf of the many thousands that covered the tree resolved into a brilliant singularity of colour and form and glittering movement in the slight breeze, each leaf a subtle variation of red, orange, gold, pale yellow and lingering green against a deep blue sky. The tree, like the scores around it, had made a portion of the rainbow its own. The oak was an intricate giant being that *knew* itself. It was performing for him, showing off, delighting in its own existence.

When he shyly put his glasses on in class to test out possibilities of ridicule and shame, no one noticed. At home in the Christmas holidays, with the Mediterranean horizon restored to a sharpened blade, his parents made only neutral comments in passing. He noticed that dozens of people around him wore glasses. For two years he had worried about nothing and got everything wrong. It was not only the material world that had come into focus. He had caught sight of himself for the first time. He was a particular person—more than that, a peculiar one.

He was not alone in thinking so. Back at school a month later he was dispatched from the classroom on an errand to deliver a letter to the secretary's office. Mrs. Manning wasn't there. As he approached her desk he saw his name, upside down in an open file. He edged round the desk to read it. In a box marked "IQ" he read a number, 137, that meant nothing to him. Below it he read, "Roland is an intimate boy . . ." There were footsteps in the corridor outside and he came away quickly and returned to his class. Intimate? He thought he knew what it meant, but surely you had to be intimate *with* someone. When he was free in the afternoon he went to the library for a dictionary. He felt sick as he opened it. He was about to read an adult verdict on who or what he was. *Close in acquaintance or association. Very familiar.* He stared at the definition, his bafflement confirmed. Who was he supposed to be familiar with? Someone he had forgotten or had yet to meet? He never discovered but he kept a special feeling for the word that held the secret of his selfhood.

In his second week he had gone for his first piano lesson in the music block, close to the sickbay. For the previous ten days his life had consisted of unfamiliar events. This was just another, so he felt nothing as he sat swinging his legs in the waiting room. It was new, but everything was new. No sound of a piano. Only a murmur of voices. An older boy came out of the practice room, closed the door behind him and left. There was silence, then the sound of scales from a more distant room. Somewhere, a workman was whistling.

The door opened at last and a braceleted hand and part of an arm beckoned him in. The little room was filled with Miss Cornell's scent. She sat on the double stool with her back to the piano and he stood before her while she looked him over. She wore a black skirt and a cream silk blouse buttoned right up high on her throat. Her lips were painted deep red in a tight bow. He thought she looked stern and felt a first touch of anxiety.

She said, "Show me your hands."

He did so, palms down. She put out her own hand to touch and examine his fingers and nails. Unusually for his age, he kept his nails short and clean. His father's military example.

"Turn them over."

At the sight of his hands she shifted back slightly. Then she looked into his eyes for several seconds before speaking. He looked into hers, not because he was bold but because he was frightened and didn't dare look away.

She said, "They're disgusting. Go and wash them. And be quick."

He didn't know where the washroom was but pushed on an unmarked door and found it by chance. The cracked bar of soap was dirty and moist. She sent other boys in here. No towel, so he dried his hands on the front of his shorts. The running water had made him want to pee and that took up time. With a superstitious sense that she was watching over him, he washed his hands again, and again wiped them on his shorts.

When he went back, she said, "Where have you been?"

He didn't answer. He showed her his clean hands.

She pointed at his trousers. Her nails were painted the same colour as her lips. "You've wet yourself, Roland. Are you a baby?"

"No Miss."

"Then we'll begin. Come here."

He sat beside her on the stool and she showed him middle C and told him to put the thumb of his right hand on it. She showed him on the page in front of him how the note was written. And this was a crotchet. There were four of them in this bar and he was going to play them, giving equal value to each note. He was still flustered by her humiliating question and her use of his Christian name. He hadn't heard it since he said goodbye to his parents. Here he was Baines. When he had unfolded fresh socks that morning a wrapped sweet had fallen out, a toffee he liked put there by his mother for him to find. It was in his pocket now. A wave of homesickness came over him which he instantly suppressed as he played the note four times. The third sounded far louder than the first two and the fourth hardly sounded at all.

"Do it again."

The trick of keeping control of oneself was to avoid any thoughts of kindness his parents, especially his mother, had ever shown him. But he could feel the sweet in his pocket.

"I thought you said you weren't a baby." She reached across the piano lid and pulled a tissue from a box and pressed it in his hand. He worried that she might call him Roland again or say something comforting or touch his shoulder.

When he had finished blowing his nose, she took the tissue from him and dropped it in a wastepaper basket at her side. That might have undone him but as she turned back to him she said, "Missing Mummy are we?"

Her sarcasm was a deliverance. "No Miss."

"Good. Let's get on."

At the end she gave him an exercise book with stave lines. His prep was to learn and write out minims, crotchets, quavers and semiquavers. Next week he would clap them for her and she would show him how he would do it. By now he was standing before her as he had been at the beginning of the lesson. Even though she was sitting and he was not, she was taller. As she softly beat out a run of semiquavers her perfume grew stronger. When she had finished he thought he was dismissed and turned to go. But she indicated with a finger that he was to stay.

"Come closer."

He took a step towards her.

"Look at the state of you. Socks round your ankles." She leaned forward from the stool and pulled them up. "You'll go and see your matron and get a plaster on this knee."

"Yes Miss."

"And your shirt." She drew him to her, unfastened his snake belt and the top button of his shorts and tucked his shirt in, front and back. Her face was near his as she straightened his tie and he had to look down. He thought her breath was perfumed too. Her movements were swift and efficient. They were not about to make him homesick, not even her final touch, which was to use her fingers to brush his hair away from his eyes.

"That's better. And what do you say now?"

He struggled for an answer.

"You say thank you, Miss Cornell."

"Thank you, Miss Cornell."

And so it began—in fear, which he had no choice but to acknowledge, along with another element he could not think about. He appeared before her at his second lesson with clean, or cleaner, hands but his clothes were a mess as before, though he was no worse than the other boys in his form. He had forgotten about the plaster for his knee. This time she tidied him up before the lesson began. When she unbuttoned his shorts to straighten out his shirt the back of her hand brushed across his crotch. But that was accidental. He had done the work in the exercise book and he clapped the time value of the notes correctly. He had prepared well, not out of diligence or a desire to please her, but because he feared her.

He did not dare miss or arrive late for her lesson or disobey her whenever she sent him out to wash his hands, even though they were already clean. It never occurred to him to ask other boys who took piano with her how she treated them. His Miss Cornell belonged in a private world separate from friends and school. She was never maternal or affectionate with him so much as distant, sometimes contemptuous. From the beginning, by assuming authority over his appearance, especially when she unbuttoned his shorts, she established complete rights or control, mental and physical, though after those first two occasions she did not touch him in an unusual way. As the weeks passed, she bound him to her and there was nothing he could do about it. This was a school, she was the teacher and he had to do as he was told. She could humiliate him and make him tearful. When he repeatedly failed at an exercise and risked saying he could not do it, she told him he was a useless little girl. She had a frilly pink frock at home belonging to her niece and would bring it to the next lesson, confiscate his clothes and make him wear it to class.

All that week he lived in terror of the pink frock. At night he was sleepless. He wondered about running away but then he would have to confront his father, and he had nowhere to run to. He had no money for the train and buses to get to his sister's. He did not have the courage to drown himself in the River Orwell. When the dread lesson came round at last there was no evidence or mention of the pink frock. The threat was not repeated. Perhaps Miss Cornell did not even have a niece.

Eight months passed and he could play the simplified prelude. After the pinch, the smack with the ruler, her hand on his thigh, then the kiss, he had begun lessons in another building with the head of music, Mr. Clare. He was kindly and expert, the director and conductor of the school's production of *The Magic Flute*. Roland had helped with painting the flats and with the scene changes. The card that Miss Cornell had promised did not arrive in time and that was the reason, so he told himself, he did not bike to her house for lunch on the half-day holiday, even though he had not forgotten her clear instructions on how to find her cottage. He was still feeling relief at having left her behind. When her card had come two days later with its one-word message—"Remember"—he thought he could ignore her.

He was mistaken. Miriam Cornell appeared more and more frequently in arousing daydreams. These reveries were vivid and obliterating but there could be no conclusion, no relief. His young smooth body with its treble voice and a child's soft gaze was not yet ready. At

first she was one of a small cast—the others were girls in their late
teens, friendly, delightful in their nakedness, their faces remembered
from photographs in his mother's clothing catalogues. But by the time
he was thirteen, Miss Cornell had driven them out. She stood alone on
stage in the theatre of his dreams to supervise with her indifferent gaze
his first orgasm. It was 3 a.m. He got out of bed and went through the
dormitory to the washroom to examine what she had produced in his
palm.

He thought he was choosing her, but soon it was clear that there
could be no release without her. She had chosen him. In silent dramas
she drew him to her in the practice room. Often, as an overture, the
kiss was reimagined, deeper, hungrier. She would unbutton his shorts
all the way down. Then they would be somewhere else, both naked.
She showed him what to do. He never had a choice. He didn't want a
choice. She was cool and determined, even contemptuous. Then, at
the right moment, she gave him a deep look that suggested affection,
even admiration.

She had seeded herself into the fine grain not only of his psyche
but of his biology. There was no orgasm without her. She was the
spectre he could not live without.

One day the English teacher, Mr. Clayton, came into the class and
said, "I want to talk to you boys about masturbation."

They froze in embarrassment. To hear a master use the word was
excruciating.

"I've only two words to say to you." Mr. Clayton paused for
effect. "Enjoy it."

Roland did. One long boring Sunday he thought he would lay
the ghost of Miriam Cornell by summoning her six times in as many
hours. Pure indulgence, and he knew she would be back. For half a
day he was free of her, then he needed her again. He had to accept
that she was now embedded in a special region of fantasy and longing
and that was where he wanted her to remain, trapped in his thoughts
like the tamed unicorn behind its circular fence—the art master had
shown the class a picture of the famous tapestry. The unicorn must
never be free of its chain, never leave its tiny enclosure. Moving
between classes he sometimes saw her in the distance and he made

sure they never met. On long bike rides around the peninsula, he was careful to avoid her village. He would never go and see her even if she became seriously ill and was on her deathbed and sent a pleading message. She was too dangerous. He would not go to her even if the world was about to end.

# 3

A cloud of self-deception was general across Europe. A West German TV channel persuaded itself that the radioactive miasma would
contaminate not the West but the Soviet Empire alone, as if to take
revenge. An East German ministry spokesman referred to an American plot to wreck the people's power stations. The French government appeared to believe that the cloud's south-western edge matched
the Franco-German border, which it had no authority to cross. The
British authorities announced that there was no possible risk to the
public, even as they set about closing 4,000 farms, forbidding the sale
of 4.5 million sheep, impounding tons of cheese and emptying a sea
of milk down drains. Moscow, reluctant to concede an error, let its
infants and children drink irradiated milk. But soon self-interest pre-
vailed. There was no choice. The emergency had to be confronted and
that could not happen in secret.

Roland joined the retreat from reason. While Lawrence slept in
the evenings, he set about taping up the windows with plastic sheeting
to seal the house. But the cloud had missed London. Caesium 137 was
detected on Welsh pastures, in north-west England and in the Scottish
Highlands, and still he kept on. It was a long job, for the tape would
not hold unless the window frames were free of dust. The steplad-
der was rickety and too short. It swayed dangerously when he stood
on tiptoe on its summit to wipe the top of a frame with a filthy damp
cloth. Once, only a wild clutch at a curtain rail saved him from falling
backwards. He knew the project was unhinged. Daphne said so and
tried to talk him out of it. Other people were not securing their homes.

The weather was warm, a lack of ventilation would be unhealthy and unnecessary. There was no radioactive dust. It was madness. He knew that. His circumstances were mad and he could do as he liked. To stop now would be to concede he had been wrong all along. Also, a respect for order derived from his father insisted that what was started must be finished. It would have depressed Roland in his current state to go about the house today peeling off and binning the sheeting of yesterday. Finally, it was fortifying not to believe anything the authorities put out. If they said the cloud had gone north-west then it must be settling in the south-east. If they were isolating so many healthy sheep, then watch out. He would be a loner and a warrior. He ate from tins and paid attention to the date stamps on the lids. Nothing post late April. Lawrence joined in, making his first moves towards solids. His milk was of the best pre-Chernobyl spring water. Together they would survive.

It was not a good state, pretending to be out of his mind. Outwardly he was plausible enough, looking after and playing with the baby and bringing in more bottled water, doing the chores at rough speed, talking on the phone with friends. When he phoned Daphne another time—he depended on her in the weeks after Alissa's disappearance—he got Peter instead. Roland elaborated his theory that the Chernobyl disaster would mark the beginning of the end for nuclear weapons. Suppose NATO had launched a tactical device at Ukraine to halt a Russian tank advance—see how we all suffered, poisoned from Dublin to the Urals, from Finland to Lombardy. Blowback. A nuclear arsenal was militarily useless. Roland had raised his voice, another sign that he was not himself. Peter Mount, who then worked for the national electricity grid and knew about power distribution, thought for a moment and said that uselessness had never got in the way of war.

A few years earlier Peter had shown Roland round his workplace, the national control centre. Its peripheries resembled a military base, with high-security fences, electronically operated double barriers and two expressionless guards taking their time checking Roland against a list. The hub of the centre looked like a seedy copy of NASA's Hous-

ton control room: technicians silent before their consoles, a bank of
dials and gauges, a wide screen on a high wall. Here the essential business was to match supply to demand.

The trip was dull. Roland, with low interest in the management of
electricity, worked hard at paying attention. He was not excited like
Peter at the prospect of computers one day running the show. The
only memorable moment came in the early evening. Television moni-
tors high on the control-room walls were tuned to the popular soap
*Coronation Street*. Someone talked loudly into a phone in anglicised
French. As the advertising break approached, a voice over the PA
counted down from ten, to the moment when millions rose from their
sofas to power up their kettles for tea. Zero. Two hands on a heavy
black lever pulled down hard. Megawatts were flushed at the speed
of light along cables below the English Channel, purchased from the
uncomprehending French—what was *Coronation Street*? What was
the point of an electric kettle? Surely it was nothing so crude as a lever
that someone pulled. But Roland was to tell the story so often that he
came to trust his account.

The afternoon resembled a school trip. At the end they finished
up in a fluorescent-lit canteen. Peter, some colleagues and Roland
sat around a Formica table still wet from a heavy wipe-down. The
conversation turned to selling off electricity distribution to private
companies. Bound to happen, was the consensus. Serious money to
be made. But this too was not one of Roland's subjects. He gave the
appearance of full attention while he remembered a school trip to
the Ipswich Harris Bacon factory at the age of eleven, not long after
he failed to appear at Miriam Cornell's for lunch.

The idea was to watch what happened to the pigs he'd been feeding for the Young Farmers Club. Such misery at 5:30 a.m. Two heavy
pails of swill—meat scraps floating in custard—from the school
kitchens to be carried with a friend, Hans Solish, all the way to the
piggery. Not so easy at that age, in the damp autumnal pre-dawn, to
light a fire under a colossal iron bowl and tip the swill in to warm. As
it did, the pigs were frantic at the scent. The boys climbed into the
sty heaving the hot muck in pails with the pigs battering their legs.

The hardest part was pouring the swill into the troughs without being knocked to the ground.

Afterwards in the Ipswich bacon factory, as now at Peter's place, he sat with others at a Formica canteen table. Roland the child had been in a state of shock, refusing food or drink. The orange cordial in paper cups smelled of pigs' guts. He had seen slaughter and blood as in a nightmare. Squealing victims herded from a sealed truck, running in panic down a concrete ramp towards men in rubber aprons and gumboots inches deep in blood, in their hands electric stunners, the flash of knives slitting throats, naked bodies suspended by chains round ankles approaching massive doors swinging open to a white jet of roasting flame, then corpses spinning in boiling water scoured by revolving drums with steel teeth, whining power blades, heads with eyes and mouths open in stacks, tipped vats of gleaming viscera sliding down steep tin chutes towards roaring grinder machines making dog food.

Electricity was the cleaner business. But each left its mark. After Roland came away on the coach from the bacon factory, he did not eat meat for three years. Inconvenient at school in 1959. The housemaster sent a letter of complaint to his parents. The Captain, who had never heard of anyone not eating meat, disliked the letter's peevish tone and backed his son. He must be provided with alternative forms of nourishment.

Whenever, as now, Roland picked up an electric kettle, he thought of two hands, real or imagined, pulling a lever in the name of balance, supply and demand and magical convenience. Daily life in the city, from tea to eggs and bacon to ambulances, was sustained by hidden systems, knowledge, tradition, networks, effort, profit.

They included the postal services that had brought Alissa's fifth card. It lay picture side up on the kitchen table by the tulips. It was 11 p.m. He had sealed the last window and made a makeshift screen around the back door into the garden. The radio was murmuring the news—farmers were protesting against the restrictions on their flocks. Roland was drinking tea because he had given up alcohol. The decision was instant and easy, in part prompted by a call from Detective Inspector Browne. A liberation. To mark it he had poured a bottle and a half of Scotch into the kitchen sink.

The detective told him that on the day of her disappearance Alissa's name was on a list of foot passengers aboard the 5:15 p.m. Dover to Calais ferry. She spent the night in Calais at the Hôtel des Tilleuls, not far from the railway station. She and Roland had been there a few times together, had sat with their drinks in a dusty narrow courtyard where two lime trees struggled for the light. They liked these low-priced unassuming places with creaking floors, flimsy furniture, the unreliable shower with an ancient soap-stiffened plastic curtain. Downstairs, a fixed menu at thirty-four francs. These were various memories overlaid. A tall waiter with hollow cheeks and silver hair along the line of his cheekbones brought round the tables a silver tureen of soup. There was dignity in the way he presented it. Potato and leek. Next, a piece of grilled fish, one waxy boiled potato, half a lemon on the side, a white bowl of green salad, a litre of red wine in a bottle without a label. Cheese or fruit. It was the year before they married. They made love upstairs on a narrow jangling bed. Not right for Alissa to have gone there without him. He felt the desertion in a focussed moment of nostalgia. He cast the hotel as her lover and was jealous of it. But she may not have been alone.

The centralised system, Napoleonic and paranoid, of registering and collating all guests in French hotels was still in place. The following two nights, Browne told him, she stayed in Paris at the Hôtel La Louisiane on the rue de Seine in the *sixième*. They knew it well. More betrayal on the cheap. After Paris Alissa spent one night in the Hôtel Terminus in Strasbourg. She was welcome to that one, whatever it was. About Munich, nothing. West Germany took less interest in its visitors than France.

Browne's voice sounded distant. Behind it were murmuring voices, a typewriter and, repeatedly, a miaowing cat.

"Your wife is wandering about Europe. Her own free will. We've no reason to think she's in danger. For now that's as far as we can go."

No reason for Roland to mention her latest message. This affair was his own, as it should have been from the start. He pushed for an apology. "You don't think I faked the postcards. You don't think I murdered her."

"Not as things stand."

"I'm grateful to you for everything, Inspector. Will you bring back the stuff you took away?"

"Someone will drop it off."

"The pictures you took of my notebook."

"Yes."

"And the negatives."

The voice was weary. "We'll do what we can, Mr. Baines." Browne rang off.

Roland's grubby hands were around his tepid mug of tea. The wall clock showed 11:05. Too late to phone Daphne and discuss Alissa's latest card. Lawrence would wake within the hour. Best to shower now. But he didn't move. He took the postcard and stared again at the colour-enhanced picture of a sloping meadow backed by the Bavarian Alps. Wildflowers, grazing sheep. Not so far from her birthplace. As it happened, on the late news a Welsh hill farmer was explaining that city people could not begin to understand the bonds of affection that tied people like him and his wife to their sheep and lambs. But the animals in their care, certainly the lambs, were heading anyway towards some version of the Ipswich factory. Gentle justice. Despatched to oblivion by the ones who loved you. By the one who insists she still loves you. *Dear Roland, Away from you both = physical pain. I mean it. A deep cut. But I know mthrhd would've sunk me. And we were talking of a 2nd! Better pain now than longer pain/chaos/bitterness later. My only course + my path ahead are clear. Today kind people in Murnau let me be 1 hr in my chldhd bdrm. Soon heading north to parents. Please don't phone there. I'm sorry my love. A.*

In suffering's race she aimed to pull ahead. The abbreviations still got to him after several readings. She had more than an inch of clear space along the card's serrated bottom edge. Plenty of room to spell out motherhood. In the market town of Murnau, from her childhood bedroom tucked below a sloping ceiling, she had gazed out of the dormer window across the orange rooftops towards the Staffelsee and contemplated the span of her thirty-eight years with its sudden break, her breakout from the burdens of ordinary life, the regrettable miracle of Lawrence's existence, the ordinary fact of a less than brilliant husband. But her "path"? It wasn't her kind of word. She didn't believe in the preordained, which was what following a path implied. She was not religious, even in a diluted way. She was or had been a well-organised teacher of German literature and language who spoke highly of Leibniz, the Humboldt brothers and Goethe. He remembered her a year before, recovering from a dose of flu, sitting up in bed absorbed in a German biography of Voltaire. She was a benign sceptic by nature. He was ruling out New Age cults. No guru would tolerate her taste for gentle teasing. If she had stood for one hour in the bedroom she had once shared with the fraying teddy that now reclined in Lawrence's cot upstairs, then her path ran backwards into the past.

And if she was travelling north to see her parents Roland would be confirmed in this view. It was a difficult relationship. There were frequent storms. Apart for half a year, they got on each other's nerves at sight. Even though they were close, or because they were. Last time he and Alissa, four months pregnant, visited Liebenau was in April 1985. They had come to bring the parents the joyous news. A row broke out in the kitchen after dinner, brief but loud. Jane and her only child were washing the dishes together. The ostensible matter was the stacking of clean plates in a cupboard. In the next room, Heinrich and Roland were drinking brandy. In this household men were banished from all aspects of housework. As the voices rose in German to explode finally into English, the mother's tongue, Roland's father-in-law gave him a look, a what-can-you-do shrug and grimace.

The real issue came out at breakfast. Four months? Why was Jane among the last to know, long after all their London friends? How dare Alissa get married without inviting her parents. Was this the right way to treat those who had loved and cared for her?

Alissa could have told her mother that the child she was carrying was conceived in the bedroom upstairs. Instead she was instantly furious. What difference did it make? Why was her mother not rejoicing in her wonderful son-in-law and the prospect of a grandchild? Why didn't she appreciate that she and Roland had come all this way to deliver the news in person? She was due back in the classroom on Monday morning. Alissa spelt out the journey with great alliterative energy. By chance, it was a good part of Roland's old boarding-school route. London to Harwich, to the Hook of Holland, to Hanover, to here! It was tiring and expensive. She had expected a warm welcome. She should have known better! Roland's German was good enough for him to follow but not up to the right kind of calming remark. That was for Heinrich who said suddenly, as he had before, "Genug!" Enough! Alissa left the table and went into the garden to cool off. Next morning breakfast was taken in silence.

If she were there now in the neat brick and timber house standing in the centre of a half-acre garden, she must have some specific purpose. If she were to tell her parents she was deserting her child and husband the row would be like no other.

➤➤

Jane Farmer was born in Haywards Heath in 1920, the daughter of two schoolteachers of modern languages. After grammar school where she excelled at French and German, she did secretarial training—the question of university "never came up." She was a ninety-words-a-minute girl. At the beginning of the war she worked in a typing pool at the Ministry of Information and shared a tiny unheated flat in Holborn with a school friend. Under the influence of this flatmate, who went on to become a senior figure at the Courtauld in the sixties, Jane started reading contemporary poetry and fiction. Together the two went to poetry readings and started a book discussion club that lasted almost two years. Jane wrote short stories and poems, none of which was accepted by any of the small magazines that hung on during the war. She continued with various filing and typing jobs in different ministries and had affairs with men who had literary aspirations like herself. None of them ever broke through.

In 1943 she answered a classified ad for a part-time typist at Cyril Connolly's *Horizon* magazine. She did four hours a week. She later told her son-in-law that she was seated in an invisible corner and given the dullest correspondence. She wasn't beautiful or well connected and socially adroit like many of the young women who passed through the office. Reasonably enough, Connolly barely noticed her but occasionally she was in the presence of literary gods. She saw, or thought she saw, George Orwell, Aldous Huxley and a woman who may well have been Virginia Woolf. But, as Roland knew, Woolf had been dead for two years and Huxley was living in California. There was one glamorous high-born figure, an exact contemporary, who took a friendly interest in Jane and even passed on a couple of frocks she no longer needed. She was Clarissa Spencer-Churchill, niece of Winston. She later married Anthony Eden before he became prime minister. In 1956 she remarked famously that there were times when it seemed the Suez Canal flowed through her drawing room. Clarissa moved on. Jane remembered Sonia Brownell, who married Orwell, as a kindly presence. She gave Jane two books to review, but never ran either piece.

Jane was a marginal figure in the *Horizon* scene, coming in two afternoons a week after work at the Ministry of Labour. But cumulatively the place had an effect. By the time the war was over her literary ambitions were fixed. She wanted to travel across Europe and "report back." She had once overheard Stephen Spender talking about a brave group of anti-Nazi students, the White Rose, working out of the University of Munich. It was a non-violent intellectual movement which secretly distributed pamphlets listing and denouncing the regime's crimes, including the mass murder of Jews. In early February 1943 the main members of the group were rounded up by the Gestapo, tried in a "People's Court" and beheaded. In the spring of 1946 Jane managed to get Connolly's attention for five minutes. She proposed that she travel to Munich and look for survivors of the movement and get their story. They surely represented the best of Germany and the spirit of its future.

At *Horizon*'s inception in late 1939 the editor had taken an aesthete's view of the war. The greater defiance was not to bend to the madness of the moment but to stand aside and continue to uphold the best literary and critical traditions of the civilised world. As the war progressed Connolly became convinced of the importance of serious engagement, of reportage, preferably from the front line wherever that happened to be. He was kind and encouraging to Jane, amenable to her idea and offered £20 from the magazine's account towards her expenses. This was generous. He had in mind an additional project. After she was finished in Munich he wanted her to "pop across the Alps" to Lombardy and report on the food and wine there. The British diet, always a disgrace, had been made even more wretched by the war. Now was the time to start thinking about the sunny culinary traditions of southern Europe. Even before the war was over he had been to Paris to stay at the newly opened British Embassy and enjoy the food. Now he wanted to hear about farmhouse cooking, about *spiedo bresciano*, *osso buco*, *polenta e uccelli* and the wines of Brescia. He produced the £20 note from the petty-cash tin. The commission that would transform Jane Farmer's life and initiate Alissa's was agreed in the few minutes before Cyril Connolly left in a hurry for lunch at the Savoy with Nancy Cunard.

Twenty-six-year-old Jane Farmer left England in early September 1946 with £125, half of it in US dollars, cunningly spread about her person and luggage. Connolly signed a headed letter declaring her to be *Horizon*'s "European correspondent at large." In the summer of 1984, on Roland's first visit to Liebenau he sat in the garden with Jane. They had been talking literature earlier in the day and she had put on the table an old cardboard box. Jane showed Roland the yellowish headed note with the editor's signature. Connolly and Brownell had put themselves out. They may have felt sympathy for the office girl some referred to as "Farmer Jane." Through an ex-MI6 friend of Malcolm Muggeridge, Brownell supplied three names and possible Munich addresses of people who would know something of the White Rose. Through Connolly's contacts Jane also carried a couple of letters of introduction to British army officers who might help her out if she got into trouble crossing France. There was a haphazard whip-round. Cunard, always keen to honour a resistance movement, donated £30. Arthur Koestler gave £5 to someone to give to her. A few *Horizon* writers contributed ten-shilling notes. Most dropped half a crown or a two-bob bit in the White Rose Box kept in the office. Jane had inherited £50 from an uncle. She suspected that the £5 Sonia gave her came from Orwell.

On that summer's evening in the Liebenau garden, after showing

Roland Connolly's letter, Jane took from the box her seven journals. She tried to convey her sense of liberation on the journey she took from London to Munich via Paris and Stuttgart—the most thrilling episode of her life. No longer an obedient daughter or humble employee, or the social and intellectual inferior in the corner of an office and not yet a dutiful wife. For the first time in her life she had made a serious choice, she had initiated a mission and an adventure. She was in no one's care. She relied on her wits, and she was going to be a writer.

After three weeks in France she surprised herself by talking her way into an invitation to a dinner in an officers' mess near Soissons. She persuaded a reluctant Welsh sergeant to let her ride in his truck the last thirty miles to the German border. She fended off advances from various soldiers and civilians. An American lieutenant with whom she had a brief affair drove her from near Stuttgart to Munich in his jeep. She had decent school French and German and she soon improved in both. "I became myself!" she told Roland. "And then I lost myself."

The journals were a secret. Heinrich did not know of them. But Roland could show them to Alissa if he wanted. Jane left him alone in the garden while she went indoors to prepare supper. The first page of the first volume told him in neat copperplate that on 4 September 1946 she travelled third class on the reinstated Golden Arrow from London to Dover, and the Flèche d'Or from Calais to Paris. If she noticed her fellow passengers or gazed from the carriage window as she crossed the expanses of liberated Picardy, she made no record. She got started in Paris. "Seedy and glamorous by turns. Amazingly intact. Shops are empty." She worked on her journalistic skills describing her tiny hotel and its *propriétaire* in the Latin Quarter, a fight outside a baker's, a couple of the first few American tourists treated coolly in a *tabac* by the locals. She witnessed an argument in a bar between a British naval officer who spoke good French and "a sort of French intellectual."

A summary of their positions. Officer, a little drunk: "Don't tell me whose side France was on in the war. Your lot fought and killed our troops in Syria, Iraq and North Africa. Your battleships wouldn't sail from Mers-el-Kébir to Portsmouth to be with us, so we were forced to attack them. Now we learn that your gendarmes here in Paris marched 3,000 French children to the Gare de l'Est to be transported to their deaths. They happened to be Jews." Silver-haired intellectual, also a little drunk: "Keep your voice down, M'sieur. Someone might kill you for these sentiments. Your version is warped. Those ships would have stayed loyal to France. Later, when the Germans tried to take our ships in Toulon, we sank them first. My brother-in-law was tortured to death by the Gestapo. They killed nearly everybody in a village near my home town. The Free French were with you and fought bravely. Thousands of French citizens were lost in the liberation to the shells of your warships. The Resistance was the true spirit of France." At which everyone in the bar shouted *Vive la France!* I just kept on writing, pretending I'd heard nothing.

She let Roland keep the notebooks overnight. He read them after dinner and later that evening as they lay side by side in bed, Alissa started on the first, by which time he was reading the account of a "very amusing" evening with British officers in Soissons, in "a fine house with a park and a lake." What impressed Roland was the confidence and precision of the prose. More than that, she had the gift of brilliant and daring description. The page and a half devoted to the affair with the American lieutenant, Bernard Schiff, was a surprise. Jane Farmer had never encountered such a generous lover, so "extravagantly atten-tive to a woman's pleasure," a contrast to the Englishmen she had met so far with their "mealy in-and-out." Aware of his parents-in-law on the other side of a thin wall, he read in a whisper Jane's description of oral sex with Schiff. Alissa said, also in a whisper, "She must have forgotten it. She'd die if she thought I'd read it."

Two days later they had both read the Munich journals to the end. Before lunch they went for a stroll through Liebenau, along the banks of the Große Aue to the castle. Alissa was in an agitated state, excited by what she had read but baffled, even offended. Why had her mother never mentioned the notebooks? Why give them to Roland, not her?

Jane ought to publish them. But she wouldn't dare. Heinrich would never allow it. Within the family, the White Rose was his property, even though there were other survivors. A handful of scholars, historians, journalists had been to interview him. He hadn't been a central figure and never pretended otherwise. He was asked to give advice for a movie production. When he saw the result he was disappointed. They hadn't caught the reality. "The Scholls, Hans and Sophie, they weren't like that, they didn't look like that!" He said this even as he conceded he barely knew them. The newspaper articles, the scholarly essays, the books that began to appear didn't please him either. "They weren't there, they can't know. The fear! Now it's history it's no longer real. It's just words now. They don't realise how young we were. They can't understand that pure feeling we had. Journalists today are atheists. They don't want to know how strong our religious faith was."

There was nothing in any account that could ever satisfy him. It was not a matter of accuracy. It pained him that what had been a lived experience was now an idea, a hazy notion in the minds of strangers. Nothing could conform to his memories. Even if his wife's journals could have brought everything to life, they would have threatened him by displacing him in the story—this was Alissa's view and Roland thought she was right. Her father was a forceful man with old-fashioned views. Jane as an independent woman wandering around France and Germany having sex with strangers! Publication, even with a private press, was unthinkable. Jane would never go against his wishes. One mutinous concession she made was to permit her daughter and Roland to make a secret photocopy to take back to London. Publication of a sort. The day before they left they went to a print shop in Nienburg and spent the afternoon waiting for a copy on a slow and faulty machine. They concealed the 590 pages in a shopping bag. As they walked back along the river with it Alissa talked to Roland about her father. He was a kindly seventy-year-old, conservative, entrenched in his views. His memories of the White Rose movement and his opinions about it were fixed. He wouldn't want them complicated. As for the oral sex—at the thought of her father, a devout and upright churchgoer, acquainting himself with the energetic lieutenant of almost forty years before, Alissa began to laugh so hard she had to support herself against a tree trunk.

Roland was thinking about their stroll through Liebenau village as he picked up her postcard from the kitchen table and went upstairs to shower. Yes, that summer of 1984 she had been in a state of strange and fluctuating moods after reading her mother's journals. They had discussed them at length, then the subject faded. In the winter they moved to the Clapham house, the baby was on the way, Daphne and Peter were expecting their third and the two excited households saw much of each other—daily life swept all before it. The half-forgotten photocopy was wrapped in newspaper and stowed in a drawer in their bedroom.

He paused at the foot of the stairs. No sound yet from Lawrence. In the bedroom he dropped his clothes into the laundry basket. Radioactive from the Chernobyl dust. He could almost believe it. He stood in the bath under the improvised showerhead that hung precariously from an untiled wall, purging himself. Memories had a long half-life. As they hurried back through the centre of Liebenau to be in time for supper, he had wondered if the journals might allow Alissa to see her mother differently, admire her more, be less inclined to quarrel. The opposite was the case. During that last day they were impossible together. Like a bickering elderly couple who had long ago missed their chance of separating. Sixty-four-year-old Jane treated her daughter as a competitor who needed to be put in her place. As soon as they were back at the house Alissa was fighting her mother in the kitchen over the timing of supper. At table, they had a full-on row about the Christian Democratic Union and Helmut Kohl's *Erziehungs-geld*, his proposed childcare-allowance legislation. A clenched-fist thump on the table from Heinrich ended it. Later, in the garden, they wrangled over the sequence of events during a childhood family holiday in the Dutch fishing village of Hindeloopen. When Roland was getting into bed with Alissa that night he asked, as he had a few times before: what *was* it between them?

"It's the way we are. I can't wait to go home."

Later that night he woke to find her crying. That was unusual. She wouldn't tell him what it was about. She fell asleep on his arm while he lay awake on his back thinking of the young Jane Farmer's shocked arrival in Munich.

➤➤

Lieutenant Schiff had warned her. She had followed the progress of the war but had missed accounts of the seventy major bombing raids on the city. She climbed out of the jeep at an intersection by the remains of the main railway station. Munich was in ruins. She felt "personally responsible." A ridiculous sentiment, Roland thought. It looked as bad, she wrote, as Berlin. "Far worse than London's Blitz." She kissed Bernard Schiff goodbye "at length," with no pretence they would ever hear from each other again. He was a married man from Minnesota with three children and had shown her the happy photographs. He drove off, she picked up her suitcase and set off with a twenties Baedeker in her free hand. She stopped in some shade to look at a fold-out map. Impossible to know where she was when she could see no street signs. Around her was a wasteland, the day unseasonably warm. Masonry dust thrown up by the thin traffic—mostly American military vehicles—hung in the windless air. Near where she stood the buildings were without roofs. The windows were "great holes, vaguely rectangular." Sixteen months on from the end of the war the rubble had been collected up into "tidy mountains." She was surprised to see an old electric trolley gliding along, filled with passengers. There were a fair number of people on the street, so she abandoned the map and made use of her school German. Passers-by were not hostile at the sound of her accent. Nor were they particularly friendly. An hour and some wrong or misheard directions later she found a place, a boarding house off Giselastraße, by the university, close to the English Garden.

It amazed her, as it had all the way across France, that there were hotels and people to change the sheets and cook whatever could be found. So soon after total war. Elsewhere food was scarce. On roadsides, burned-out tanks were an unsurprising sight. The garbage of war was everywhere. In a French village the blackened wing of a fighter plane lay across the pavement. For reasons she could not discover, no one wanted to move it. The roads and the railway stations left standing were filled with displaced persons, Jewish survivors, ex-soldiers, ex–prisoners of war, refugees from the Soviet area of control. Tens of thousands were crammed into special camps. Everywhere, "homelessness, filth, hunger, sorrow, bitterness."

Two-thirds of this city were a ruin. But there were pockets of innocent normality where bombs had not fallen. Her tiny room on the third floor was dusty and smelled damp, but on the bed was a smooth plumped-up duvet, then an exotic item for the British. Standing at the window, angling her gaze to where she thought the river was, she could "almost persuade myself that the madness had not happened." The boarding house, as far as she could tell, had been taken over by American officers and civil administrators. As she descended the stairs from her room, she could hear typing behind closed doors. The smell of cigarettes leaked heavily into the stairwell.

Next morning she walked the short distance to the main university building on Ludwigstraße. She was directed to the first floor. She went down a long colonnaded corridor busy with students. More unexpected normality. She stopped outside the administration office to run through the German vocabulary she had prepared. Inside a rectangular room with high windows were a dozen secretaries or filing clerks. There was no obvious reception desk, so she spoke to the room in a loud voice in textbook German. Everyone turned to look at her.

"Entschuldigung. Guten Morgen!" She was writing an article about the White Rose movement for a famous London magazine. Could anyone help her with some names of people she might approach? She was ready for an unfriendly response. Six key members, Hans and Sophie Scholl, three close student friends and a professor, were sentenced to death and guillotined. Other executions followed. When news of the deaths spread, 2,000 students gathered to shout their approval. Traitors. Communist scum. And now? Too soon, too shameful perhaps for anything beyond an embarrassed silence. Instead, there was a friendly murmur. A couple of typists were standing from their desks and smiling as they came towards her.

Three years before, these clerks might have felt obliged to spit at the mention of the White Rose. In the new dispensation, the University of Munich wished to identify itself with the group, take pride in its courage and moral clarity. No other German seat of learning could claim such martyrs. The Scholls, Alex Schmorell, Willi Graf, Christoph Probst, Professor Kurt Huber were Munich's own. In the face of overwhelming and brutal state power their resistance had been purely intellectual. "Those kids were so young, so brave." Who would wish to dissuade a university, including its lowliest administrators, from claiming such figures as symbols of a return to its true purpose? Free thought! "This," Jane wrote, "was once the university of Max Weber and Thomas Mann—and so it is again."

The first to reach her was a plump lady in her sixties with glasses that magnified her eyes and gave her the appearance of "an amiable frog." She took Jane's elbow and turned her towards a filing cabinet. She took from it a thin sheaf of mimeographed papers.

"Hier ist alles, was Sie wissen müssen." Here is everything you need to know.

Copies of the original six White Rose pamphlets, each barely two pages long, were passed through Switzerland or Sweden to London. They were copied in quantity and dropped in millions across Germany by the RAF. Jane felt foolish in her ignorance. She had thought the leaflets were rare documents, long ago gathered up and destroyed by the Gestapo. Muggeridge or his contact must have known. Probably everyone in the *Horizon* office knew and assumed that she knew too.

Others in the Munich university office were writing down names and addresses. There were mild disagreements. She heard interjections of "She no longer lives there," and "He's a liar. He wasn't involved." The name of a sister, Inge Scholl, came up. She would be at the family home in Ulm. Someone said no, she was in Munich. The rumour was she was writing an account. She had spent time in a concentration camp and was still recovering. She might not want to talk. Others said she would. There was no anger in these exchanges. The mood, according to Jane, was of excitement and pride.

She spent an hour in the office. She was worried that a senior figure, a supervisor, would come in and give a general scolding for which she, Jane, would be responsible. But the supervisor was already in the room. He was "a shaggy figure in a dark suit two sizes too big for him." He was the one who explained to her the sequence of the leaflets—the first four produced in the summer and autumn of 1942 and secretly distributed around Munich and nearby towns. The final two were written early in the following year, after Hans Scholl, Probst and Graf had returned from the Russian front where they served as army medics. The very last was produced only a day or so before the Gestapo arrested the group. He told Jane that she would notice the difference in leaflets five and six.

She said her thanks and farewells and promised that she would send a copy of her article. On Ludwigstraße impatience overcame her. She stopped on a corner, took out the stapled sheets and read the title of the first: "Leaflet of the White Rose." Her German was good enough to see her through the first sentence without a dictionary: "Nothing is so dishonourable in a civilised nation as to permit itself to be 'governed' without resistance by a reckless clique that has surrendered to depraved instinct."

She devoted half a page of her notebook to her reaction on reading these words. Roland assumed that by the time she wrote the entry she had read all six leaflets.

> Nothing is so dishonourable in a civilised nation . . . It
> was as if I was reading a translation from the Latin of a
> venerable figure of antiquity . . . this opening declaration
> on such a grand note, written by a man, a student, still in his
> mid-twenties, with a passion for intellectual freedom and his
> sure sense of a precious artistic, philosophical and religious
> tradition under threat of annihilation. I felt a thrill, a sort of
> swoon . . . it was like falling in love . . . Hans Scholl, his sister
> Sophie and their friends, almost alone in the nation, raising
> their tiny voices against a tyranny, not in the name of politics
> but of civilisation itself. Now they were dead. Three years

dead and I grieved for them on a corner on Ludwigstraße. I so much wanted to know them, to have them here with me now. I walked back to the hotel full of sadness, like a bereaved lover.

She did not leave her room until she had reread and annotated the leaflets. How perilous, what courage, to call the Third Reich "a spiritual prison . . . a mechanised state apparatus lorded over by criminals and drunkards," and to write that "every word that Hitler utters is a lie . . . His mouth is the stinking gate of hell." And all set in such scholarly terms of reference. Goethe, Schiller, Aristotle, Lao-Tzu. She felt as though "I was receiving an education." She understood fully how a close acquaintance with writers like these could extend and enrich a love of freedom. She found herself "cross, even resentful" that her parents, without much thought and because she was a girl, had never offered her the privilege of the university education her brother had enjoyed. He was still in the army, a captain with the Royal Artillery. He'd had a distinguished war. She made the decision then, sitting up on the bed in her little room with its partial view of the English Garden, that once she was back, once she had turned in her article, she would get herself to a university. Philosophy or literature. Preferably both. It would be her own small act of . . . of what exactly? Of resistance, of homage. She owed it to the White Rose. She wrote out phrases from the leaflets. The government's "most despicable crimes—crimes that massively outstrip every human standard . . . Never forget that all citizens deserve the regime they are willing to endure . . . our current state is the dictatorship of evil." And from Aristotle, "the despot is endlessly disposed to stir up wars." At the very end of the first leaflet, after two elevated verses from Goethe's *The Awakening of Epimenides,* a simple, hopeful appeal struck her deeply with its pathos: "Please make as many copies of this leaflet as you can and distribute them."

". . . since the invasion of Poland 300,000 Jews have been slaughtered there in the most bestial manner." Hans Scholl and his companions longed with a passion to rouse the German people from their inaction, their apathy "in the face of these abominable crimes, crimes that demean the human race . . . the inane stupefaction of the German

people encourages these fascist criminals." Unless they took action
no one could be exonerated, because every man "is guilty, guilty,
guilty." In the final sentence of the fourth leaflet: "We will not be
silent. We are your bad conscience. The White Rose will not leave
you alone!" But there was hope, for it was not too late: "now that we
have seen them for what they are, it must be the first and only duty, the
sacred duty of every German to destroy these monsters." In the face
of total and vicious state power, all that was available was "passive
resistance." Quiet sabotage in factories, laboratories, universities and
in all branches of the arts. "Do not donate to public appeals . . . Do
not contribute to the collections of metal, textiles and similar."

In the last two leaflets the tone was heightened. The titles were
now "Leaflets of the Resistance," and "Fellow Fighters in the Resistance!" The fifth declared that with the United States rearming, the
war was approaching its end. Time for the German people to disso-
ciate themselves from National Socialism. But Hitler was "leading
Germany into the abyss. Hitler cannot win the war, he can only pro-
long it . . . Retribution is coming ever closer." "Correct," Jane primly
recorded in her notebook, "but a little too early."

The White Rose opposition seemed to have no political project
for the future. Then, in this last and shortest of all the leaflets, written
in January 1943, Jane read, "Only in broad co-operation between the
nations of Europe can the way be readied for reconstruction . . . The
Germany of tomorrow must be a federal state."

Sophie Scholl was caught distributing this sixth leaflet in the same
university building Jane had visited that day. A janitor saw her tipping
the sheets down the lightwell of the grand entrance. He reported her
and that was the end. By then German forces had been repelled at
Stalingrad. The slaughter there was on an unimaginable scale. This
was rightly identified as a turning point in the war. "330,000 Germans
have been pointlessly and recklessly driven to death and destruction
by the brilliant planning of our World War 1 Private First Class. Füh-
rer, we give you thanks." In the final paragraphs of the final leaflet,
a desperate plea for German youth to rise up, in the name of "intellectual and spiritual values . . . of intellectual freedom . . . of moral
substance." German youth must "destroy its oppressors . . . and set

up a new Europe of the spirit . . . The dead of Stalingrad beg us to act." Then the last ringing sentence: "Our people are ready to rise up against the National Socialist subjugation of Europe in an ecstatic new discovery of freedom and honour." And there it closed, in excitement and hope. There came in a quick succession after the arrests, a show trial with foregone conclusion, and the first of the executions. Three young heads brimming with goodness and courage sliced from their bodies. Sophie Scholl, the youngest, was twenty-one.

Jane lay on the bed for half an hour in a state of exhaustion and elation. It gave way, she wrote, to "an indulgent session of self-criticism." How small and ill-defined her own life seemed to her now. A shapeless mass of weeks were piled behind her. In a daze she had spent the war typing administrative letters. In all her years she had dared nothing beyond an illicit cigarette at the age of fourteen in a thicket of rhododendrons beyond the school playing field. Good luck had seen her through the Blitz, but that was no achievement. She had suffered it along with everyone else. She had never stood up to anyone or risked herself for an idea, a principle. And now? She didn't answer her own question. "Hunger got the better of me. I hadn't eaten all day." The hotel had no food that evening. She wandered through the university district looking for a cheap place to eat. "I felt different, on the edge of becoming a different person. I was at the start of a new life." At last she found somewhere selling "disgusting sausage on stale bread. But the mustard rescued it."

The immediate answer to And now? was to work through her list of White Rose contacts, write her piece, then set off for Lombardy. Among the ruins of Munich, her existence seemed to her "quite brilliant." She was casting herself as an honorary member of the group. She would continue its work, help build the new Europe they had dreamed of. Even a modest contribution would count, like improving English cuisine, she wrote in skittish mood, "by describing the art of *osso buco*!" A quarter of a century later, when she heard that her country had at last joined the European project she felt thrilled at the connection to a moment in her youth. Now, here, she devoted herself during the following ten days to a serious attempt at piecing together the story of the White Rose.

Her first mistake was to assume that the MI6 contacts represented privileged information. She did much walking across the city with her Baedeker only to draw three blanks. The first, a turn-of-the-century apartment block, was a ruin. In another, a small house in a narrow street in Schwabing was lived in by an Italian family who said they knew nothing. The third, also in Schwabing, was intact but it looked like much time had passed since anyone had lived there. In the chaos of war, then post-war, no one stayed in place for long. She did better with her university leads, though there were still many blanks. Her first success was an hour with a friend of Else Gebel who had been a political prisoner, a trustee whose job it was to register those arrested by the Gestapo. Gebel spent time with Sophie Scholl during those last days and even shared a cell with her for four nights. It was the truth at two removes but Jane trusted this lively intelligent woman, Stefanie Rude. Gebel was planning to write her own account that might perhaps be included in the book Inge Scholl was writing. Stefanie was certain that Scholl would be happy for Gebel to talk to Jane.

Sophie Scholl had told Else that she always assumed that if she was caught leafleting or daubing "Freedom!" on Munich walls that it would cost her her life. After her first all-night interrogation she came back to the cell calm and relaxed. When she was given the chance to say that she had been mistaken about National Socialism she refused. It was her captors who were mistaken. But when she heard that Christoph Probst had been brought in, her defences were down. He was the father of three young children. Later she rallied, sustained by religious faith and belief in the cause. She had persuaded herself that the Allied invasion must come soon and the war would be over in weeks. She remained convinced of the evil of National Socialism and insisted that if Hans, her brother, was to die, she must too. She was calm during the proceedings of the People's Court. After being sentenced she was driven to Stadelheim prison where her brother and Probst were taken too. The Scholls had a moment with their parents before their execution.

Everything Jane heard in this and other interviews was to pass into legend. The White Rose became the staple of the classroom, of bad poetry, of easy sentiment and sanctity, of dramatic movies and solemn children's books, endless scholarship and a cascade of doctoral theses. It was the story post-war Germany required as a founding narrative of the new federal state. It became a shining tale so well worn, so emphatically embraced by officialdom that in later years it would provoke cynicism or worse. Wasn't Hans Scholl once a group leader in the Hitler Youth? Wasn't the admired musicologist Professor Huber an anti-Semite and didn't his influence show in the second leaflet with its curious qualifier: "regardless of whatever position we take in relation to the Jewish question"? Sections of the German left accused Huber, a traditional conservative, of being an "anti-Bolshevik" just like the Nazis. Others wondered what difference these young Christian innocents made. Only the military might of the United States and Soviet Russia could have defeated Nazism.

But Jane believed that to read the story of lonely resistance while the country was in ruins and half the population was starving, and every German was still just waking from the nightmare to which they had all, or almost all, contributed, would be inspirational, a revelation, the beginnings of redemption. And here she was in the right time and place, ready to write and publish the first sustained account.

In a week, she spoke to a dozen people with various degrees of proximity to her subject. She was fortunate to get half an hour with Falk Harnack who happened to be visiting Munich. He had been a director at the National Theatre in Weimar. He was well connected to the scattered and uncoordinated elements of the German resistance. He had set up a meeting between Hans Scholl and a Berlin group of dissidents. The date agreed turned out to be that of Scholl's execution. From different sources Jane heard accounts of a famous formal occasion at Munich University when the assembled students, including maimed veterans, were addressed by a top National Socialist party hack, the gauleiter, Paul Giesler. In line with their policy of passive resistance, the Scholls stayed away. During a gross and leering speech, Giesler instructed the women students to get pregnant for the Fatherland. It was their patriotic duty. To those women who were "not attractive enough to find a partner" he promised to assign them to his adjutants. The students drowned him out with a crescendo of catcalls, foot stamping and whistling and began to leave—an unheard-of mass protest against the party. The White Rose was not so alone after all. Jane met Katharina Schüddekopf and later, too briefly, Gisela Schertling, Hans Scholl's girlfriend—that was the closest Jane came to the core of the group. Katharina showed her photographs of the Scholls, Graf and Probst. Both Schüddekopf and Schertling had served time in prison for dissident activities.

By now Jane had collected more than enough background material on the six key members of the movement, including Professor Huber. On the evening before her last two interviews, she wrote the opening paragraph of her *Horizon* article. The next morning she set off once more to Schwabing, this time to meet a mature law student at Munich University, Heinrich Eberhardt. He had been an enthusiastic painter of "Down with Hitler" and "Freedom" graffiti around Munich and had travelled to Stuttgart and other towns to distribute the fourth, fifth and sixth leaflets. Earlier, while serving in France he had been hit in the foot by a large-calibre bullet and had been granted non-combatant status and given extended study leave. He had met various people in the group, but he was never an intimate member. He knew one of the young lawyers, Leo Samberger, who had watched the Scholls–Probst trial in horror and shame. Jane thought he would be of interest.

She arrived punctually at ten. Unusually for a student Heinrich's ground-floor room was large, decently furnished and well lit with a glazed door onto a small garden. When he greeted her Jane felt a shiver of recognition. It was as if all her research had prepared her for this moment. Which was another way of saying that it had somewhat distorted and beguiled her judgement. The tall young man with the soft voice and slight limp who shook her hand and gestured her towards a chair was the incarnation of Scholl, Probst, Schmorell and Graf combined. Like them in their photographs he held a pipe in his hand, at that moment unlit. She saw in him Hans's energy and good looks, Christoph's open honest gaze, Alex's delicacy, Willi's dreamy profundity and the same abundant swept-back dark hair. Jane's impression was immediate—Heinrich was the White Rose. Even in that flustered moment she realised that she was in a strange, possibly deluded state, but it made no difference. She was enraptured. Her hands shook a

little as she settled herself in the chair and took her notebook from
her bag. In a grave tone that perhaps, she thought, concealed a good-
natured tease, he complimented her on her German. When he rose to
cross the room and make her a small cup of terrible coffee, she saw
the open law books heaped on his desk and a framed photograph of
what she took to be his parents. No sign of a girlfriend. She picked
up her coffee, taking care not to let the cup rattle against the saucer.
For a while she answered his polite questions about her journey from
England, the state of Paris, of London, of food rationing. She was
desperate to make a good impression.

After the preliminaries Jane guided the conversation to the trial.
What had Heinrich learned from his friend Samberger? With the
conversation now on the resistance Heinrich was more interested in
talking about the other groups that the White Rose had been in touch
with. He himself was originally from Hamburg, a city with an honourable tradition of hostility to Hitler. Hans Scholl had made connections there with a radical set interested in French Resistance—style
sabotage. There had been an attempt to procure some nitroglycerine.
Then there were the cells in Freiburg and Bonn. Stuttgart was a separate case. And then there was the Berlin group, directly influenced by
the White Rose. His voice was low and calm and she loved the sound
of it. But talk of other anti—National Socialist groups up and down
Germany made her impatient. It complicated the story. She was in no
position to squeeze into 5,000 words all the uncoordinated ineffective
dissident movements, especially those that sprang up after Stalingrad
and the relentless bombing of the Rhineland cities. She wanted only
the White Rose. She was bound to the subject. Why was Heinrich
leading her away from it? She persisted with her questions and finally
he began to tell her everything he had heard from his friend and other
sources.

His voice became lower and somewhat toneless. Jane leaned forward to hear him. Her journal recorded a mosaic of prison and court
gossip, some of it third-hand in untypical spidery writing. Strong
emotions may have made her hand shake. Everybody, even the prison
guards, even Robert Mohr, the Gestapo interrogator, was impressed
by the dignity and calm of the accused. Mohr was amazed by Sophie

Scholl's acceptance of her imminent death. The farewell letters to family and friends that Hans, Sophie and Christoph were advised to write were not delivered. Instead, the authorities filed them away. In court the Scholls' parents came in right at the end. The mother fainted, then she recovered. The judge, Freisler, was well known as a brute. In his eyes the three were dead before their trial began. Once sentence was passed Sophie refused to make the customary statement. Hans tried to plead for Christoph, who was the father of three children, one of them a newborn. But Freisler cut him off.

For the executions, the condemned were transferred to Stadelheim prison on the edge of Munich. The guards relaxed the rules and let the Scholls see their parents. Probst's wife was still in hospital, weak from an infection after giving birth. Sophie looked beautiful. She ate the little treat, a sweet thing, that her mother had brought and that Hans had refused. Sophie was taken away first and went without a murmur. When it was the turn of Hans, just before he laid his head on the block, he shouted something about freedom—accounts varied.

Heinrich paused. He might have noticed that Jane's eyes were moist. He told her by way of comfort of a rumour that Judge Freisler was killed in a bombing raid.

Then came the small gesture of kindness that was to transform their lives. Heinrich leaned across the table and put his hand on top of Jane's. In response, after several seconds she turned her hand and interlocked her fingers with his. They squeezed tight. What happened next was not described but Jane noted that she left Heinrich's room around nine that evening. Eleven hours later. The next morning she wrote a note to a colleague of Kurt Huber apologising for her failure to appear at her final interview.

Jane was not a professional journalist. If in her research she had been too close to her subject, now she was submerged and lost in it. It did not matter whether it was Heinrich she fell for or the White Rose. In a surge of powerful feelings she could not have told the difference. She needed them both. The tears that caused him to lay his hand on hers were prompted by her imagining how easily it could have been Heinrich led to the guillotine. The same beauty and intelligence, kindness and courage, terminated at a stroke.

Within a week she had moved out of her boarding house and into Heinrich's Schwabing room. There were some cold autumn evenings now but his place was warmer than anywhere she had known in London. Her life was changing at such a speed! She had never known herself so impetuous. Day and night, they were never apart. Heinrich set aside his work for law exams. Jane had no time for writing. She was not troubled, because when they roamed the city, she was still on the trail of the White Rose. Heinrich pointed out to her Hans Scholl's rooms and then the house belonging to Carl Muth, where the group and various friends often met. This was where Heinrich had first met Willi Graf and the Scholls.

Together they went out to the Stadelheim prison and to the Perlach cemetery nearby but they couldn't find the graves. Perhaps they were looking in the wrong places. Or the local authorities under Gauleiter Giesler had not wished to encourage martyr worship.

One evening, not long after she had moved in with him, Heinrich showed Jane his most valuable possession. It was under a pile of books, between folded moth-holed curtains and wedged between layers of cardboard. He had kept it hidden through the war. It was a first edition of the *Blaue Reiter Almanac*, published in 1912, a kind of manifesto of the group of expressionist artists active in and near Munich in the few years before the First World War. They were condemned by the National Socialists as "degenerate" and their paintings were looted and sold or destroyed or hidden away. Soon, Heinrich said, when the paintings of Kandinsky, Marc, Münter, Werefkin, Macke and many others were restored to the gallery walls, this publication would be worth a lot of money. It was a gift for his twentieth birthday from a well-off uncle who loved modernist art and had lost almost his entire collection. From then on, for Jane and Heinrich the Blaue Reiter was their joint pet project. From rose to rider, from white to blue, from war to peace, one intense movement happily succeeded another. Heinrich had a book of paintings dating from the late twenties and although nearly all the illustrations were in black and white, Jane began to share his taste for what was described to her as "non-representational colour."

On an unusually warm day in mid-October they rode south

sixty kilometres out of the city on a borrowed ancient motorbike to the small town of Murnau. It was an act of homage. The lovers Wassily Kandinsky and Gabriele Münter had come here in 1911 and been entranced. They rented a house which became a centre for the Blaue Reiter group. They claimed that the town and the countryside around it was a great stimulus to their art. Jane and Heinrich were also entranced as they strolled through the narrow streets. Perhaps they saw the bright autumnal colours of the surrounding trees and meadows through the eyes of Gabriele Münter. They had heard that she still had a house in Murnau. Much later they learned that like Heinrich, but on a far grander scale, she had hidden away from the National Socialist government many Blaue Reiter works, including several by Kandinsky. And so it was that after Jane became pregnant in January 1947, and when they were quietly married in the same month, the thrilling idea of moving to Murnau took form. They rented a house and moved in during the spring.

By the time they were unpacking their possessions in the three-storey chalet, Jane was coming to terms with the fact that she was never going to write her piece on the White Rose. She was in love, visibly pregnant and committed to a new existence. Heinrich had found work in the office of a country solicitor dealing in agricultural conveyancing. She was absorbed in setting up a home for the baby. With much guilt and many drafts, she wrote her letter of explanation to the *Horizon* office. Connolly had been so kind to her that she could not bear to address him directly. Instead she wrote to Sonia Brownell, explaining that conditions in devasted starving Munich had made it impossible to find out much about the White Rose. She could hardly say that she had married into it. For health reasons, she said, she was not able to travel to Lombardy. She undertook to pay back, in time, all the money she had been given. Once she had posted her letter she felt better. She experienced a pang when later that year, Inge Scholl's book came out. Jane could have been first into print. But she knew that the Scholl book was far better, more intimate and emotionally charged, more justified, than anything she could have achieved. Even so her regret lingered through a lifetime. Heinrich slowly shrank or solidified into himself—he was not and had never pretended to be a

Scholl, Probst or Graf. He became a small-town solicitor, a regular churchgoer, a man of sound and firm opinions and a locally active member of the CDU.

Jane resolved her destiny in the home. Soon all their pleasant Murnau neighbours had to agree that her German, her tuneful Bavarian accent, was almost perfect. She never went to university like her brother, never became a published writer, never "popped" across the Alps to relay the secrets of the ultimate *osso buco* to the unsensual English. It was not until she and Heinrich had moved north in 1955 that she began to accept that she had ended up with a safe life and a dull marriage. The same uncle who had provided the *Blaue Reiter Almanac* left Heinrich in his will a house in Liebenau, near Nienburg. Jane would have preferred to remain in Murnau but the prospect of living rent-free was, according to Heinrich, irresistible. Once there, they never lived anywhere else. For medical reasons that were never explained, Jane had no more children. Heinrich had completed his law degree in Munich in 1951 and eventually became a senior partner in a Nienburg firm. Jane hardly noticed how conventionally obedient she gradually became to her husband's wishes. Reciprocally, he had no awareness of his own domineering manner, his expectation that she should serve him in the home. Those who knew Jane well observed on some occasions a touch of sharpness, even sourness, of disillusion in her manner. Many years later at supper, describing to her son-in-law the trip she never took to the farmhouses of northern Italy, she proclaimed self-mockingly, "I could have been Elizabeth David!"

But that lay far in the future. According to the last page in her final notebook she was in a state of bliss in that fine summer of 1947. She decorated and arranged the rooms just so in the new house, planted out herb pots by the kitchen door, with vegetable and cut-flower patches further down the garden, and at weekends she swam in the calm waters of the Staffelsee with her handsome young husband, Heinrich Eberhardt, one of the few hundred Germans among millions to have resisted the Nazi tyranny.

Sometimes the couple saw from a distance the seventy-year-old Gabriele Münter in the street. On only one occasion, after some nervous discussion, did they approach her. She was standing alone outside a butcher's shop. They thanked her for her art, which had brought them not only enormous pleasure but had led them to beautiful Murnau. She said little and moved away but they took her gracious smile to be a form of blessing. In those sunny months Jane was less troubled by her abandoned projects than she would be later. She felt "more joyous than anyone deserved to be" in a country wrecked and impoverished by a disastrous war and there was surely more joy to come. On that high sentiment the journal ended. In October that year Alissa was born.

→→

He was startled from his thoughts by a single piercing cry in the darkness. It was not the ordinary sound of a baby waking and needing comfort. He knew he was capable of projection in this period of his life, but this feline wail sounded to him like despair. What must it be, to burst out of deep infant sleep into the shocking singular fact of existence. Everything unknown about the world, little to know it with. In that thin tapering sound, utter loneliness. A human shout. He was on his feet at the first instant, his own thoughts obliterated, as if he too had woken out of nothing. Wearing only a towel, he took a bottle of milk off the warmer. By the time he had his arms around Lawrence his cries had resolved into sobs, gulps too heavy at first to let him to drink. At last, he settled to it hungrily. By the time Roland had changed him and put him back under the covers the baby was almost asleep.

It was a pleasure to settle in the small armchair by the cot. The night visit could be a two-way arrangement—Roland was soothed by watching his son sleep, face up, arms thrown back, his hands barely reaching the full extent of his head. A big fat brain and its bone protection was such an encumbrance starting out. So heavy it wouldn't let Lawrence sit up during his first six months. Later it might think of other ways to be a burden. For now the high-domed almost bald head declared the baby to his father as a genius. Was it possible to find happiness and be a genius? Einstein did well enough, playing the violin, sailing, loving fame, finding pure joy in his General Theory.

But a messy divorce, battle for the children, distressing love affairs, paranoia that David Hilbert would steal his show, never making peace with the quantum, with the brilliant young men who owed him everything. Better to be stupid or run-of-the-mill? No one believed that. The stupid had their own routes to unhappiness. As for the contented mediocre, Roland was good counterproof. At school he was usually two-thirds the way down the class and exam lists, with termly reports of "satisfactory" and "could do better." He could have had a renaissance of the mind at fifteen but by then he belonged to Miriam Cornell. His intellectual moment was confined to the piano and could not translate into academic results. Since then no saleable skills, no success, not even much of a claim to bad luck. In his corner of south London, in a cramped dump of a house he had sealed up so tight that he and Lawrence could hardly breathe, living off state benefits, he was precisely and self-pityingly unhappy. What was a continent-wide radioactive cloud against his wife's vanishing? As for the indispensable transient joy of loving sexual union, he was further from it now than he had been on his sixteenth birthday.

When he woke his watch showed two thirty. Asleep for two hours and he was shivering. The towel had slipped down to his ankles. Lawrence had not changed position—his arms were still thrown up in a position of secure surrender. Roland went back to his room and took a second shower. Then he was on the bed again, clean, calm, near naked, uselessly alert at 3 a.m. He could no longer blame alcohol and he was in no mood for reading. He wanted to give himself a good talking to. Plan your life! You cannot continue to meander. Assume she is not coming back. Correct. Then what? Then . . . Whenever he reached this point there lay like a fog across his future the quotidian struggle with parenting and fatigue. There could be no conceivable plan, no uplift, when all he could do was stay close to the ground, keep going, keep Lawrence going, keep tending him and playing with him and taking the state support, then housework, cooking, shopping. The common tightly encircled fate of single mothers was his.

But there was a poem he had in mind, derived from a phrase he overheard while leaving a shop: *he had it coming*. Good title. And perhaps he did. So it would be personal, a demon he hoped to slay by describing it. But what use was poetry when he needed money? As if to mock his literary ambition, an old friend from his jazz days, Oliver Morgan, had phoned two weeks before with a proposal. Morgan by his own description represented the new spirit of Thatcherite enterprise. He was no longer a sax player. Instead, he set up companies, made them thrive, so he said, and sold them on. As far as his friends knew, he had never made money. At best, he broke even. The new venture was a greeting-cards business. The market, he told Roland, was saturated by trash, by sentimental pictures and words. Kitsch. Doggerel. Mostly bought, so research showed, by economic groups C and D. Fat chain-smokers, Morgan said. Little education, no taste, no cash. There was a neglected huge minority of educated young professionals, plus "professor types" in their fifties. Beautifully reproduced Indian erotic or European Renaissance art might be the sort of thing on the front. Creamy thick paper. For inside, Morgan wanted hip upmarket birthday verses. Cool about ageing, wry about birth, marriage and death. Obscene would be fine. Purchaser and recipient to be flattered by way of wide cultural reference. Roland would be perfect—housebound, time on his hands, knew about poetry. For the first six months he would be paid mostly in shares, so nothing to declare to the benefits people.

Roland, sleep-deficient and irritable, hung up, rang back twenty minutes later to apologise and their friendship remained intact. But Roland's sense of insult persisted. Morgan did not understand that he was a serious poet with more than half a dozen poems published in places of high culture. These were all university publications in tiny print-runs. But Grand Street could be next. On his desk four feet away was his latest revision. He was waiting to hear back.

Still warm from his shower he lay stretched out on a purple and orange bedspread of Indian cotton in a narrow beam of reading light that excluded from view the cramped over-stuffed bedroom. Over recent years the government had taught even its opponents that it was not shameful to imagine oneself rich. He tried to imagine himself in luxury. In a house four times the size, with a loving non-absconding wife, literary fame, two or three happy children and a cleaning lady like the one Peter and Daphne had who popped in twice a week.

"Popped," his mother-in-law's word from Connolly, would for-ever stand for all journeys not undertaken. As in, He popped over to Liebenau and persuaded his Alissa to return. He reached for her postcard on the bedside table and looked at it again. This could be the same steep meadow Gabriele Münter painted in 1908 of her Blaue Reiter colleagues Alexej von Jawlensky and Marianne von Werefkin at their ease on the grass. Strangely faceless. No sheep in view. A painting she might have hidden in her Murnau house along with many of Kandinsky's. They survived a few Nazi house searches. Discovery might have sent her to a concentration camp. Would Roland have had her courage? That was another subject. He pushed the thought away and turned the card over to read it again. Motherhood without the vowels no longer bothered him. Her meaning was clear. It would have sunk her and she needed to escape and "find herself." That was Daph-ne's theory. Motherhood might sink him too. At the time of writing she was heading to Liebenau. *Please don't phone there*. Unless her visit was brief, she was with her parents now. She had relieved him of the burden of phoning. It was always Jane, not Heinrich, who picked up. He would have had to tell the truth or lie to her without knowing what she already knew.

He had said nothing to his own parents. His father had extended his connection to the British army by taking a Retired Officer's job running a light-vehicle workshop in Germany. Those ten extra years were up, and Robert and Rosalind had settled down in a small modern house near Aldershot, not so far from the place where she was born and where they first met, in 1945, at the guardhouse, when Rosalind was a lorry driver's mate. Within two months of being "home," there had been a road accident. Major Baines, turning right onto the busy four-lane road that ran along the local hill ridge known as the Hog's Back, had looked the wrong way and edged into the path of a fast-moving car. It swerved and the collision was not full-on. No one was hurt but Robert and Rosalind were shaken up—in a state of shock that lasted weeks. She especially was forgetful, nervous, unable to sleep. Her hands and arms were covered in a rash, her mouth was ulcerated. This was not the time to tell them about Alissa.

He had reached that point—late thirties was common—when

one's parents set off on their downhill journey. Up until that time they had owned whoever they were, whatever they did. Now, little bits of their lives were beginning to fall away or fly off suddenly like the shattered wing mirror from the Major's car. Then larger parts came away and needed to be gathered or caught mid-air by their children. It was a slow process. Ten years later he would still be discussing it with friends round his kitchen table. Roland's big-hearted diligent sister Susan did the most by far. He had taken care of the accident insurance claim. Before that, the mortgage application, the poor drainage at the front of the new house, the programming of an unfamiliar new radio, then something that wouldn't open, something that wouldn't start—small stuff as yet. At Alissa's suggestion he bought for them a kind of clamp for removing the tops off jars and bottles. He demonstrated its use on a jar of pickled red cabbage. In their new kitchen his parents stood close by him to watch. It was a significant moment. Their hold was weakening. Now, in the eighties, the wartime generation was beginning its decline. It might take forty years, even more, for its last survivors to vanish. In 2020 it would still be possible for a centenarian to remember fighting through the entire duration of the war. As a foot soldier in the Highland Light Infantry, Private Robert Baines had seen slaughter of civilians and soldiers during the retreat along the crowded roads to the Dunkirk beaches. He had taken three bullets in the legs from a German machine gun. A French farmer called Roland had taken care of him and brought him to the Dunkirk beach. Back in England, after a long train journey to Liverpool, Robert spent months in Alder Hey hospital, the same ward where his father had been laid up with a shattered foot, serving the same regiment, fighting in the previous world war. Robert lost his brother in Norway in 1941. Rosalind lost her first husband outside Nijmegen four months after the Normandy landings. A bullet to the stomach. And he had lost his brother, a Japanese POW, buried in Burma.

It was common enough for Roland and his cohort as they turned adult in England to wonder at the dangers they never had to face. With free milk in third-of-a-pint bottles the state had guaranteed the calcium in young Roland's bones. It had given him some Latin and physics for free and even German. No one went to jail for modernism, for non-representational colours. His generation was also more fortunate than the one that followed. His lot lolled on history's aproned lap, nestling in a little fold of time, eating all the cream. Roland had had the historical luck and all the chances. But here he was, broke in a time when the kindly state had become a shrew. Broke, and dependent on what remained of its bounty—the whey.

But with two hours' sleep behind him, the bedroom warm, his limbs feeling good against the cotton covers, his thoughts vivid, a mood of rebellion was coming on. He could be free. Or pretend to be. He could go downstairs now, break his new rule and fill a glass, rummage in the back of a kitchen drawer for a plastic film canister of grass someone left behind six months ago. It might still be there. Roll one up, stand in the garden in the dead of night, step out of ordinary existence to be reminded, as he used to be in his twenties, that he was an insignificant organism on a giant rock rolling eastwards at a thousand miles an hour as it hurtled through the emptiness among the remote indifferent stars. Salute the fact by raising his glass. The pure luck of consciousness. It used to thrill him. It might still. Yes, he could do all that. He had done it before in the seventies with his old friend, Joe Coppinger, a geologist turned therapist. The Rockies, the Alps, the Causse de Larzac, the Slovenian mountains. At this distance, it also looked like freedom, when he used to pass into East Berlin at Checkpoint Charlie with semi-illegal books and records. He could go out into the garden now and pay tribute to his freedoms of the past, and raise a glass. But he didn't move. Alcohol and cannabis at four, when Lawrence would be waking before six and the day would have to begin? But that wasn't it. If the baby didn't exist, he still wouldn't stir. What held him back? There was an additional factor now. He was fearful. Not of the vastness of empty space. Something closer. It reminded him of what he had wanted to push away. Courage. An old-fashioned concept. Did he have it?

In Inge Scholl's White Rose memoir as summarised by Jane, Herr and Frau Scholl were permitted to go out to Stadelheim prison to see their children for a few moments of farewell before their execution. With wartime shortages, the little treat they brought with them was likely a tasteless substitute for chocolate. Hans refused it. Sophie accepted it cheerfully. She told her parents she hadn't eaten lunch and she was hungry. Roland doubted that. She must have thought that it would give her parents some comfort to see her eat the present they had brought, just before she was led away. Would he have been brave enough, moments before his beheading, to chew on an ersatz bar to reassure his parents?

He got up from the bed. It would be interesting to reread Jane's summary of Inge Scholl's account. Was Christoph Probst standing there with the Scholl family in those last minutes? His wife had given birth four weeks before but was too ill to leave her hospital bed. Was there no close family to say goodbye to him? Roland pulled open the bottom drawer where Alissa kept her sweaters. Folded in their neat piles, the blossomy scent of her perfume breathed on him again with affection. They had wrapped the 600 pages in an old edition of the *Frankfurter Allgemeine Zeitung*. So it took only seconds to establish that the photocopy had gone. But fine. It was hers to take. He had already established that she had taken with her the drafts of her two much-rejected novels. Her luggage would have been heavy.

He returned to the bed. As he remembered it Hans and Sophie Scholl were led out to their parents one at a time. Hans had his few minutes then it was Sophie's turn. They spoke to their parents across a barrier. Perhaps this was how the family wanted her remembered but it was probably true—Inge Scholl wrote that according to her parents her sister walked in proudly, relaxed, beautiful, her skin rosy, her lips a full natural red. Roland remembered too that afterwards the three accused were allowed a few minutes together. They huddled close. Christoph Probst, denied his wife and children, the child he would never see, at least had his two friends to embrace. Sophie was the first to be led to the guillotine. This was a tragedy played out on a stage constructed by men possessed by a wild and vicious dream. Their savagery had become the encompassing norm. In the face of it would he, Roland, have risen to Sophie and Hans's courage? He didn't think so. Not now. Alissa's departure had weakened him and the catastrophe of Chernobyl had made him fearful.

He closed his eyes. Across the north and western reaches of the country where soft limestone landscapes yielded to granite, on the uplands and the meadows, on all the blades of grass, within the plant cells, far down at the level of the quantum, the particles of poisonous isotopes were settled in their orbits. Strange unnatural matter. He conjured across Ukraine farm animals and pet dogs rotting by the thousands in bulldozed pits or tossed onto giant pyres, and contaminated milk flowing down gutters into rivers. The talk now was of the unborn children who could die of their deformities, of the fearless Ukrainians and Russians who suffered horrible deaths fighting a newfangled fire, of the Soviet machine's instinctive lies. He did not have what it took, neither the boldness nor the youthful gladness, to go downstairs and be alone under the sky in the dead of night and lift a glass to the stars. Not when man-made events were running out of control. The Greeks were right to invent their gods as argumentative unpredictable punitive members of a lofty elite. If he could believe in such all-too-human gods they would be the ones to fear.

# 4

In the third week after Alissa's disappearance Roland set about impos-
ing order on the overstuffed bookshelves around the table just off the
kitchen. Books are difficult to tidy. Hard to chuck out. They resist.
He set aside a cardboard box for charity-shop rejects. After an hour it
contained two out-of-date paperback travel guides. Some editions had
slips of paper or letters inside that needed to be read before they were
returned to the shelves. Others had fond dedications. Many were too
familiar to be handled without being opened and tasted again—on
the first page or at random. A handful were modern first editions that
asked to be opened and admired. He was not a collector—these were
presents or accidental purchases.

He made some progress while Lawrence was taking a late morning nap. In the evening Roland resumed after supper. The second
book he took from a newly exposed pile was a Berners Hall library
book. Inside were the London County Council markings and the
librarian's stamp, 2 June 1963. Unopened since then, it had survived
various house moves and a year's storage. Joseph Conrad, *Youth &
Two Other Tales*. Cheaper Edition, J. M. Dent & Sons Ltd, reprinted
1933, 7s 6d net. The pages were rough-cut. It still had its soft dust
cover in cream, dark green and red, a woodcut effect of palm trees,
a fully rigged sailing ship passing a rocky outcrop and distant mountains. An evocation of the tropical east, the prospect of which thrilled
the young man in the story. It excited Roland to have it now. It had
travelled with him unregarded. He had loved "Youth" when he was
fourteen, a time when he rarely wanted to read anything. He remembered nothing of the story now.

With the book in both hands, prayer-like, open at the first page, he lowered himself onto the nearest kitchen chair and did not move for an hour. As he was settling, a folded piece of paper slid out from between the pages and he set it aside. The narrator and four others are sitting round a polished mahogany table that reflects a bottle of claret and their glasses. Nothing is said of their surroundings. They could be in the wardroom of a boat, or in the private room of a London club. The table is smooth as calm waters. The five men are from different walks of life but they share "the strong bond of the sea." They all started out in the merchant service. It is Marlow, Conrad's alter ego, who will tell the story, and this is his first appearance. Famously, he will narrate "Heart of Darkness," the next story in the volume.

"Youth" is special because, as Conrad explains in his Author's Note, it was a "feat of memory." Marlow recounts the voyage he took at the age of twenty as second in command of an old ship, the *Judea,* that was to take a cargo of coal from a northern English port to Bangkok. It is a story of delays and mishaps. Leaving the Thames, the ship fights its way against a gale off Yarmouth and takes sixteen days to reach the Tyne. When the cargo is finally loaded, the *Judea* is accidentally rammed by a steamer. Days later, off the Lizard, a storm comes up. No one writes a storm at sea like Conrad. The boat ships water, the crew pump away for hours but are forced to turn back to Falmouth. They begin a long wait for repairs. Months go by, nothing happens. The ship and its crew become a local joke. The young Marlow gets leave, goes to London, comes back with the complete works of Byron. Finally repairs are made and they are off. The old ship lumbers towards the tropics at three miles an hour. In the Indian Ocean the cargo of coal begins to smoulder. Over the days, smoke and poisonous gas envelop the ship. After days of fighting the fire, then a colossal explosion, the captain and crew abandon the sinking ship and head off in three boats. Marlow is in the smallest with two able seamen. In effect, this is his first command. They row for hours northwards and make landfall at a village port in Java.

On that shiny table there must have been more than one bottle of Bordeaux. Marlow breaks his account regularly to say, "Pass the bottle." The point of his story and its title is that at every moment, however catastrophic, the young man, Marlow or Conrad, remains in a state of excitement. The tropics, the fabled East, is ahead of him and everything, however dangerous, physically demanding or dull, is an adventure. It is the demon, youth, that sustains him. Curious, resilient, savage in its hunger for experience. "Ah! Youth!" is the story's refrain.

The last words are given not to Marlow but to the narrator who had introduced him. As Marlow concludes, the narrator says, "we all nodded at him over the polished table that like a still sheet of brown water reflected our faces, lined, wrinkled; our faces marked by toil, by deceptions, by success, by love; our weary eyes . . . looking anxiously for something out of life, that while it is expected is already gone."

Roland read the last half-page twice over. It troubled him. Marlow says early on that the journey took place twenty-two years ago when he was twenty. That meant that when he tells his story to his friends, he and they with their lined, wrinkled faces marked by toil and their weary eyes, Marlow is forty-two. Old already? Roland was thirty-seven. Age and its regrets, its vanished youth and banished expectations—just steps away. He turned to the Author's Note. Yes, "Youth" was a "record of experience, but that experience, in its facts, in its inwardness and in its outward colouring, begins and ends in myself."

What did he, Roland, have that ended in himself? At the thought his hand touched on the table the square of paper that had been in the book. It was an old press cutting, cracked in places along the line of its folds. It was from *The Times*, dated Friday 2 June 1961 and headed "Community school with no restrictive conditions." Before reading it, he puzzled over the date. The library book was last stamped two years later in 1963, well before he left the school for good. The cutting must have been placed in the book by someone else and he had failed to notice it.

It was a well-meaning slightly dull article about the tenth anniversary of his school, which was "unjustly branded in the minds of many as the poor man's Eton." In fact it was a boarding grammar school, run by the London County Council, free of "the strangling traditions of many public schools," free too of "the problem boys of the approved school," with "beautiful grounds sloping down to a river," a school open to all who passed the eleven-plus exam, "a community of boys of every social background, sons of diplomats alongside sons of army privates . . . many go to university . . . generous sliding scale of fees . . . most parents paid nothing." There were many activities, much sailing prowess, a Young Farmers Club, opera productions and a "friendly atmosphere." What was most notable was "the easy air of the boys."

All of it true, or not untrue. By the time he was twenty Marlow had been at sea six years. He had been up the mizzen mast in rolling seas, furling the sails, shouting commands over the wind at men more than twice his age. Against that Roland had five years at boarding school among the easy air of the boys. He had sailed or crewed, crouching under the boom, pulling on a rope attached to a corner of the jib while an older boy called Young screamed at him for two hours. Back then it was thought that this was how sea captains should be. In Marlow's view such pottering about on a river was "only the amusement of life." His existence at sea was "life itself." Roland had once capsized on that River Orwell, a lovely blue from a distance, an open sewer up close. That was the essence of the *Times* piece—a distant view. What then, close up? What "inwardness"? He was not sure, and it was haunting him.

If he had still been drinking, this would be the occasion to pour a Scotch and contemplate the bridge of years. Marlow presented himself as well past halfway across. Roland was close behind. In your mid-thirties you could begin to ask what kind of person you were. The first long run of turbulent young adulthood was over. So too was excusing yourself by reference to your background. Insufficient parents? A lack of love? Too much of it? Enough, no more excuses. You had friends of a dozen years or more. You could see your reflection in their eyes. You could or should have been in and out of love. You would have spent useful time alone. You had a measure of public life and your relation to it. Your responsibilities would be pressing in, helping to define you. Parenthood must cast some light. The figure with the creased face standing just ahead was not Marlow. It was your forty-year-old self.

You would already have seen in your body the earliest signs of mortality. No time to waste. Now you might make out a self, apart and alone, to face your own judgement. And still you could be completely wrong. You might have to wait another twenty years—and even then be floundering.

What hope then for a fourteen-year-old schoolboy, living in a time and culture and crowded circumstances that did not encourage self-knowledge or even know about it? In a dormitory shared with nine others, the expression of difficult feelings—self-doubt, tender hopes, sexual anxiety—was rare. As for sexual longing, that was submerged in boasts and taunts and extremely funny or completely obscure jokes. Whichever, it was obligatory to laugh. Behind this nervous sociability was awareness of a grand new terrain spread before them. Before puberty, its existence was hidden and had never troubled them. Now the idea of a sexual encounter rose before them like a mountain range, beautiful, dangerous, irresistible. But still far away. As they talked and laughed in the dark after lights out, there was a wild impatience in the air, a ridiculous longing for something unknown. Fulfilment lay ahead of them, they were cocksure of that, but they wanted it now. In a rural boarding school for boys, not much chance. How could they know what "it" really was and what to do with it when all their information came from implausible anecdotes and jokes? One night, one of the boys said into the darkness, during a lull, "What if you died before you had it?" There was silence in the dormitory as they took in this possibility. Then Roland said, "There's always the afterlife." And everybody laughed.

One evening, when he and his friends were still new, eleven years old or so, they went by special invitation to the dormitory of some older boys. They were only a year ahead but they seemed a wiser, superior tribe, stronger and somewhat threatening. It was billed as a secret event. Roland and the other first-years did not know what to expect. Two boys, big muscular fellows, early developers, stood side by side in the aisle between the bunk beds. A large crowd, all in pyjamas, gathered round. Many were perched on the higher bunks. The smell of sweat was like raw onion. It was long after lights out. In memory, the dormitory was flooded with the gleam of a full moon. That might not have been so. Perhaps there were torches. The two boys removed their pyjama bottoms. Roland had never seen pubic hair before or a mature penis or an erection. At a shout the two began to masturbate in a frenzy, a blur of pumping fists. There were cheers and cries of encouragement. It was the din of the touchline at an important match. There was hilarity as well as awe. Most of the boys present were not sexually mature enough to have entered such a contest.

The race was over in less than two minutes. The winner was the one to orgasm first, perhaps furthest, and the matter was in immediate dispute. The competitors seemed to have crossed the finishing line together. Their two milky blobs on the linoleum floor appeared equidistant. But would they have been visible by moonlight alone? The contestants no longer seemed interested in victory. One of them began to tell a filthy joke that Roland could not follow. The voices and laughter at last brought in a prefect and they were all sent back to their beds.

Was Roland amazed, horrified, amused? There was no possible answer, no available history of inwardness as described by Conrad. The mind, the daily variations in mood of his young self were impenetrable at this distance. He never reflected on his mental states. One thing immediately displaced another. Classrooms, games, piano lessons, prep, shifting friendships, jostling, queuing, lights out. At school he lived the mental life of a dog chained to a constant present.

But there was one vital exception. In his thirties, Roland remembered all its details. Inwardness was preserved in a deep ocean trough of a boy's thoughts. When the dormitory talk trailed away into silence and the beginning of sleep he retreated into this special place. The piano teacher, who no longer taught him, did not know she led a double life. There was the woman, the real one, Miss Cornell. He saw her occasionally when he was near the sickbay, the stable block or the music rooms. She would be alone, walking to or from her little red car after or before a lesson. He never actually passed by her, he made sure of that. He would have hated the sort of conversation they might have had if she were to stop him and ask how he was "getting on." Worse if she walked past, not wanting to talk to him. Worse still if she failed to recognise him.

Then there was the woman of his nightly daydreams who did as he made her do, which was to deprive him of his will and make him do as she wished.

The outward colouring is mostly what remains of childhood. On a warm September afternoon when he had been at school two weeks he went with a party of boys on bikes across the peninsula to swim in the River Stour, wide and tidal like the Orwell, but cleaner. He followed the older boys down a track along a field to a beach of dried mud and small stones. He swam out further than the rest, showing off the strong strokes of his Tripoli years. But the tide was turning, drawing him away from the shore into deep cold waters. The muscles in his legs tightened into cramp. He could no longer swim or barely stay afloat. He shouted and waved and a big boy, whose surname really was Rock, swam out to him and towed him back to the beach. Fear, humiliation, gratitude, joy at being alive—no trace. They would have biked back to school in time to rejoin the tide of routine—four o'clock classes, then tea, then prep.

Periodically, there was a crisis, a moment of dark wrongdoing that bound the school in collective guilt. It usually involved theft. Someone's transistor radio, someone's cricket bat. Once, some lady's underwear vanished from a washing line outside the staff accommodation. The whole school would be summoned to the assembly hall. The headmaster, a genial, decent bumbling sort of fellow, a rugby blue, who was known to call his wife by the name of George, would appear on stage to tell the 350 boys that until the culprit came forward, everyone would sit in silence even if it meant missing a meal. It never worked, especially with the stolen knickers. The older boys knew to bring a book or a portable chess set when the summons came.

It was not only thefts that bound the school in such moments. Every spring there was a school trip to an open day at the American airbase at Lakenheath, which kept a fleet of giant B52 planes armed with nuclear bombs to deter or destroy the Soviet Union. Roland went along on the school bus with his friends. They queued for an hour to take a thirty-second turn at sitting in the pilot's seat of a jet fighter. There was a distant fly-past of the thunderous bombers. Their pocket money did not stretch to the barbecued ribs, steaks and fries with Coke in waxed-paper cups the size of flowerpots. But they watched.

That evening the school was summoned. The headmaster began the indictment. The commander of the base had phoned to bring to his attention the fact that certain boys, identified by their school blazers with the crest and motto, *Nisi Dominus Vanum*—Without the Lord All is in Vain—were observed getting off the bus at the base wearing the white-on-black badges of the CND. Such a display, the head announced, represented an abuse of hospitality, a gross rudeness to our American hosts. The boys responsible must declare themselves. Until they did school would sit in silence.

To the youngest boys at the front of the hall right below the stage, their heads level with the headmaster's heavily shod feet, the initials meant nothing. The Campaign for Nuclear Disarmament stood for whatever was shameful, perhaps even satanic, given the intensity of the occasion. It was a surprise when there was stirring at the back of the hall and half a dozen older boys stood up. The rest turned in their seats. The hall grew noisy as the names were identified—the school was small enough for everyone to be known. In single file the boys came onto the stage and stood close together facing the head. He stood still, tight about the jaw, staring at them with contempt. The murmur swelled as the realisation spread through the assembly—they were still wearing the forbidden badges on their lapels! One in the group, a sixth-form hero of the first fifteen, began to read a prepared statement. The assembly fell silent. The bomb was a threat to humanity, to life on earth, a moral abomination, a tragic waste of resources. The headmaster cut him off as he strode past to leave the stage. He would see them all in his study right away.

An evening of ethical defiance would have rounded out nicely if the group had reached the head's study and refused a caning. They were all big fellows. But three years would pass before the defiant spirit of the sixties reached along the muddy shores of the River Orwell. In April 1962 the honourable thing was to take your beating with a look of insouciance and without making a sound.

The small boys were encouraged to write home once a week. It was always Roland's mother who replied. If it had been preserved his correspondence might have given some access to his state of mind in 1959. But Rosalind the tidy housewife was in the habit of tearing up a letter as soon as she had answered it. Perhaps not much was lost, for he struggled over his reports home. His life, its routines and setting were so remote from his parents', and rural Suffolk was so utterly different from North Africa, that he had no idea, no beginnings, no terms of reference with which to express the quality of his new existence, of the noise, the rowdiness and fun and physical discomfort, of never being alone, of the necessity to be on time in the right place with the right stuff. As he remembered them he wrote lines like "We beat Wymond-ham 13–7. Yesterday we had egg and chips which was very good." His mother's letters had even less content. Her problem was greater than his own. Another of her children had been sent away without her pro-tests. She hoped he enjoyed the school trip. She hoped his team would win the next game too. She was glad it didn't rain.

Many years later Roland heard the four-year-old daughter of a friend declare to her father, "I'm unhappy." Simple, honest, obvious and necessary. No such sentence was ever spoken by Roland as a child. Nor did he frame the thought for himself until his adolescence. In adult life he sometimes told friends that when he arrived at boarding school he sank into a mild depression that lasted until he was sixteen, that homesickness did not make him cry at night. It made him silent. But was it true? He could equally claim that he had never been so free or so content. At the age of eleven he was roaming the country-side as if he owned it. With a good friend, Hans Solish, he found one mile south of the school a forbidden wood, thickly overgrown. They ignored the Keep Out signs and climbed a gate. Deep in a valley of pine trees they saw below them an immense lake. In a patch of sunlit windblown water a fish leaped from the surface. Probably a trout. It was an invitation. They scrambled down through the undergrowth to reach the shore where they built a rickety camp. Discounting the track that ran beside the lake the explorers persuaded themselves that they had discovered it first and agreed to tell no one of its existence. They went back many times.

Where else could he have been so free? Not in Libya where, he understood in retrospect, he belonged to a pale elite around which resentment was growing. White boys and girls did not roam the countryside unattended by adults. The beach they visited every day was forbidden to Libyans. They did not know that a building they passed on the school bus was the notorious Abu Salim prison. In a few years King Idris would be overthrown in a coup and a dictator, Colonel Gaddafi, would take his place. He would order the execution of thousands of dissident Libyans in Abu Salim.

Marlow, standing in for his creator and looking back twenty years, understood himself well—the inwardness, the outward colouring. To Roland in his mid-thirties the boy at Berners Hall was a stranger. Certain events were safely preserved in memory, but states of mind, like snowflakes on a mild day, were lost before they settled. Only the piano teacher and all the feelings he had for her remained. Once, when he was walking to a classroom with friends, he saw her in the distance, more than a hundred yards away. She was wearing a bright blue coat and was standing close to the tree where he had tested his new glasses. She seemed to notice him and raised her arm. Perhaps she was waving across the grass at someone else. He inclined his head towards his classmate, pretending to be intent on what he was saying. This inward moment was captured and laid down for life: as he turned away from Miriam Cornell, he became aware that his heart was beating hard.

➤➤

His school, like most, was held together by a hierarchy of privileges, infinitesimally graded and slowly bestowed over the years. It made the older boys conservative guardians of the existing order, jealous of the rights they had earned with such patience. Why bestow new-fashioned favours on the youngest, when they themselves had tolerated privations to earn the perks of greater maturity? It was a long hard course. The youngest, the first- and second-years, were the paupers and had nothing at all. Third-formers were allowed long trousers and a tie with diagonal rather than horizontal stripes. The fourth-years had their own common room. The fifth exchanged their grey shirts for drip-dry white which they scrubbed in the showers and draped on plastic hangers. They also had a superior blue tie. Lights-out time advanced by fifteen minutes each year. To start, there was the dormitory shared with thirty boys. Five years later that was down to six. The sixth form could wear sports jackets and overcoats of their own choice, though nothing colourful was tolerated. They also had a weekly allowance of a four-pound block of Cheddar cheese to be shared among a dozen boys, and several loaves, a toaster and instant coffee so they could entertain themselves between meals. They went to bed when they pleased. At the apex of the hierarchy were the prefects. They were entitled to take short cuts across the grass and shout at anyone lower down the scale who dared do the same.

Like any social order, it seemed to all but revolutionary spirits to be at one with the fabric of reality. Roland did not question it at the start of the academic year in September 1962 when he and ten others in his house took possession of their fourth-form common room. After three years' service this was their first significant step on the ladder. Roland, like his friends, was becoming naturalised. He had acquired the easy manner the school was noted for, with a touch of the nuanced loutishness expected of the fourth. His accent was changing from his mother's rural Hampshire. Now there was a touch of cockney, a smaller touch of BBC, and a third element difficult to define. Technocratic, perhaps. Self-sure. He recognised it years later among jazz musicians. Not posh and neither impressed by nor contemptuous of those who were.

His school marks remained average or below. A couple of teachers were beginning to think he might be cleverer than he appeared. He needed bringing on. After three years and two hours a week with Mr. Clare he was a promising pianist. He was working his way through the grades. After scraping through Grade 7, Roland was told by his teacher he was "almost precocious" for a fourteen-year-old. Twice he had accompanied hymns on Sunday when Neil Noake, by far the school's best pianist, was down with a cold. Among his peers his status hovered just above average. Being mediocre in sport and in class held him back. But he sometimes said something witty that was repeated about the place. And he had less acne than most.

The fourth-form common room had one table, eleven wooden chairs, some lockers and a noticeboard. A further entitlement they

had not expected appeared each day in their room after lunch—
a newspaper, sometimes the *Daily Express,* sometimes the *Daily Telegraph*. Discards from the staff common room. Roland once came into
the room to see a friend sitting with one leg crossed over the other,
holding in front of him an open broadsheet and he realised that they
were grown-ups at last. Politics bored them, as they liked telling each
other. As a group they went for human interest, which was why they
preferred the *Express*. A woman set on fire by her hairdryer. A madman with a knife shot dead by a farmer who ended up in prison, to
general disgust. A brothel unearthed not so far from the Houses of
Parliament. A zookeeper swallowed whole by a python. Adult life.

In that time, moral standards were high in public life and so, therefore, was hypocrisy. Delicious outrage was the general tone. Scandals
became part of the anecdotage of their sex education. The Profumo
affair was only a year away. Even the *Telegraph* carried photographs
of smiling girls in the news with bouffant hair and eyelashes as thick
and dark as prison bars.

Then in late October politics in the fourth-form common room
became interesting. Unusually, their two newspapers arrived together
on the table after lunch. Both were well-thumbed, dog-eared, the
newsprint softened by many hands and both showed the same photograph on their front pages. For boys who had recently visited Lakenheath, the nearby US air force base, on open day and had touched the
cold steel nose of a missile as some might a holy relic, the story was
compelling. Despite the absence of sexual interest, it offered unexpected pleasures. Spies, spy planes, secret cameras, deception, bombs,
the two most powerful men on the planet ready to face each other
down, and possible war. The photograph could have come from the
triple-locked safe of an intelligence mastermind. It showed low hills,
square fields, wooded terrain scarred white by tracks and clearings.
Narrow rectangular labels had helpful pointers: *twenty long cylindrical
tanks; missile transporters; five missile dollies; twelve prob. Guideline Missiles.* Flying their U2 reconnaissance jets at impossible heights, using
cameras with exciting telescopic power, the Americans had revealed
to the world Russian nuclear missiles on Cuba, only ninety miles from
the Florida coast. Intolerable, everyone agreed. A gun to the head

of the West. The sites would have to be bombed before they became operational, then the island invaded.

What might the Russians do? Even as the boys of the fourth-form common room affected genuine grown-up concern at this new state of things, the words "thermonuclear warhead" conjured for them like towering thunderclouds at sunset a thrilling reckless disruption, a promise of ultimate liberty by which school, routines, regulations, even parents—everything to be blown away, a world wiped clean. They knew they would survive and discussed rucksacks, water bottles, penknives, maps. A boundless adventure was at hand. Roland was by then a member of the photographic club and knew how to develop and print. He had clocked up some hours in the darkroom working on multiple versions of a view across the river, with oak trees and ferns, six inches by four, rather fine but for an annoying brown streak across the centre that he had failed to eliminate. He was listened to with respect as he examined the new U2 photos that appeared on the second day. This one had new labels: *erector launcher equipment; tent area.* Someone passed him a magnifying glass. He leaned in closer. When he discovered the mouth of a tunnel that the CIA analysts had missed, he was believed. One by one, they looked and saw it too. Others had important theories of their own of what should be done, of what must happen when it was.

Classes went on as usual. No teacher referred to the crisis and the boys were not surprised. These were separate realms, school and the real world. James Hern, the stern but privately kind housemaster, did not mention in his evening announcements that the world might soon be ending. The somewhat put-upon matron, Mrs. Maldey, did not speak of the Cuban Missile Crisis when the boys handed in their socks, underwear and towels, and she was usually irritated by any threat to her complex routines. Roland did not write about the situation in his next letter home. It was not that he did not want to alarm his mother, for she would surely know about the danger from the Captain. President Kennedy had announced a "quarantine" around Cuba; Russian vessels with their cargo of nuclear warheads were heading towards a flotilla of American warships. If Khrushchev did not order his ships back they would be sunk, and the Third World War could begin. How was that to make sense alongside Roland's account of planting nursery fir trees with the Young Farmers Club on boggy land behind the house? Their letters crossed and hers were as innocent as his. The boys had no access to TV—that was for the sixth form only on certain days. No one listened to or knew about serious radio news. There were some breezy announcements on Radio Luxembourg, but essentially the Cuban missile affair was a drama confined to their two newspapers.

The first rush of boyish excitement began to fade. The official school silence was making Roland anxious. He was affected most when alone. A moody stroll through the oaks and bracken beyond the ha-ha didn't help. For an hour he sat at the foot of the statue of Diana the Huntress, looking towards the river. He might never see his parents again or his sister Susan. Or get to know better his brother Henry. One evening after lights out the boys were discussing the crisis as they did every night. The door opened and a prefect came in. It was the Head of House. He didn't tell them to quieten down. Instead, he joined their conversation. They began to ask him questions, which he answered gravely, as if he himself was just back from the Crisis Room in the White House. He claimed insider knowledge and they believed everything he said and were flattered to have him to themselves. He was already a full member of the adult world, and he was their bridge to it. Three years ago he had been one of them. They couldn't see him, only hear his low certain tone coming from the direction of the door, that school voice of softened cockney touched with bookish or scientific confidence. He told them something startling, which they should have worked out for themselves. In an all-out nuclear war, he said, one of the important targets in England for the Russians would be the Lakenheath airbase, less than fifty miles away. That meant that the school would be instantly obliterated, Suffolk would become a desert and all the people in it would be—and this was the word—vaporised. *Vaporised.* Several boys echoed the word from their beds.

He left, the dormitory talk continued. Someone said that he had seen a photograph of Hiroshima after the bomb. All that remained of one woman was her irradiated shadow on a wall. She had been vaporised. The talk slowed and stumbled into the night as sleep took hold.

Roland remained awake. The word would not let him sleep. Then it was death. It made sense. Mr. Corner, the biology teacher, had told the class not so long ago that their bodies were 93% water. Boiled away in a white flash, the remaining 7% coiling in the air like cigarette smoke, dispersed on the breeze. Or whipped away by the bomb blast's hurricane. No heading north with his best friends, rucksacks loaded with survival rations, fleeing like Daniel Defoe's citizens escaping London in the plague year. Roland had not believed in the survival adventure anyway. But it had stopped him dwelling on what really might happen.

He had never contemplated his own death. He was certain that the usual associations—dark, cold, silent, decay—were irrelevant. These could all be felt and understood. Death lay on the far side of darkness, beyond even nothing. Like all his friends he was dismissive of the afterlife. They sat through the compulsory Sunday evening service in contempt of the earnest visiting vicars and their wheedling and beseeching of a non-existent god. It was a point of honour with them never to utter the responses or close their eyes, bow heads or say "amen" or sing the hymns, although they stood to open the hymnal at a random page out of a residual sense of courtesy. At fourteen they were newly launched on splendid truculent revolt. It was liberating to be or feel loutish. Satire, parody, mockery were their modes, ludicrous renderings of authority's voice and stock phrases. They were scathing, merciless with each other too, even as they were loyal. All of this, all of them, soon to be vaporised. He did not see how the Russians could afford to back down when the whole world was watching. The two sides, protesting that they stood for peace, would, for pride and honour's sake, stumble into war. One small exchange, one ship sunk for another, would become a lunatic conflagration. Schoolboys knew that this was how the First World War began. They had written essays on the subject. Each country said it didn't want war, and then they all joined in with a ferocity the world was still discussing and trying to understand. This time there would be no one left to try.

Then what of that first encounter, that beautiful dangerous mountain range? Blown away with the rest. As he lay waiting for sleep he remembered his friend's question: what if you died before you had it? *It.*

The next day, Saturday 27 October, was the beginning of half-term. No Saturday lessons, no games was the extent of it. School would resume on Monday. Some of the London boys had parents coming down. A sixth-former had a copy of the *Guardian* and let Roland look. In the Caribbean the Americans had allowed through a Russian oil tanker bound for Cuba. It was assumed it contained only oil. The Russian ships carrying missiles brazenly strapped to their decks had slowed or stopped. But Russian submarines were reported in the area and new reconnaissance photos showed that work was continuing on the Cuban sites. The missiles were ready for firing. There was a build-up of American military forces in Florida, at Key West. It looked likely that the plan was to invade Cuba and destroy the sites. A French politician was quoted as saying that the world was "teetering" on the brink of nuclear war. Soon it would be too late to turn back.

To mark the so-called holiday the kitchen produced fried eggs. Because some boys hated them or the grease they floated in, Roland was able to eat four. After breakfast he sought out the assistant housemaster, a man the boys esteemed because they had decided he had a dozen girlfriends, carried a gun and went on secret missions. It was true that he drove a convertible Triumph Herald, oozed the scent of tobacco through his skin and was called Bond. Paul Bond. He lived in nearby Pin Mill with his wife and three children. Permission was granted for a bike ride. Mr. Bond, still quite new, was impatient with the rules. He forgot to stipulate a return time and didn't bother to mark Roland's departure from the site in the book.

His bike was on a raised pavement behind the school kitchens, a rusty old racer with twenty-one gears and a slow leak in the front tyre he could never be bothered to fix. As he pumped it up he felt a touch of nausea. When he bent over to tuck his jeans into his socks there was a taste of sulphur on his breath. One of the eggs was bad. Perhaps all of them were. The day was almost warm and cloudless. Clear enough to watch missiles sailing in from the east. He came down the slope towards the church at speed, holding his breath against the smell of warmed pigswill from the sty. He turned left out of the school gates towards Shotley. After Chelmondiston village he was looking out for his short cut, a farm track on his right that would bring him across flat fields, past Crouch House, along Warren Lane to the duck pond and Erwarton Hall. Every boy at school knew that Anne Boleyn was happy there visiting as a child and that the future King Henry came to court her. Before she was beheaded in the Tower of London at his command, she asked for her heart to be entombed in Erwarton church. It was supposed to be in a little heart-shaped box buried underneath the organ.

At the hall Roland stopped, propped his bike by the ancient gatehouse, crossed the road and walked up and down. Her house was only minutes away. He wasn't ready. It was important not to arrive sweaty and out of breath. He had spent so much time thinking about and avoiding Erwarton that he felt as if he too had spent his childhood here. He was staring at the duck pond wondering why there were no ducks when he heard a voice behind him.

"I say. You."

A man in a flecked yellow tweed jacket and deerstalker was standing by the gatehouse, feet well apart, arms crossed.

"Yes?"

"Is this your bike?"

He nodded.

"How dare you lean it against this magnificent building."

"Sorry sir." It came out before he could stop himself. A school habit. He therefore slowed his pace as he went back across the road and added some swagger and blanked his expression. He was fourteen and not to be messed with. The man was also young, spindly and pale, with bulging eyes. Roland stopped in front of him.

"What did you say?"

"Your bike."

"So what?"

The man smiled. "Quite right. You're probably quite right."

Disarmed, Roland was about to give way and set his bike down on the grass but the man clapped a hand on his shoulder and, pointing, said, "You see that little house way down on the right?"

"Yes."

"The last person ever to die of the plague in England lived right there. 1919. Isn't that something?"

"I never knew that," Roland said. He suspected that the man was a mental patient of some kind. "But I'd better get going."

"Jolly good!"

Within minutes he was passing the church, then the scattered houses of the village and soon after he was outside her cottage. He knew it by her red car parked on the grass. There was a white picket gate and a brick path that led with a slight curve to her front door. He propped his bike against the car, pulled his trousers free of his socks and hesitated. He felt watched, though there was no movement at the two downstairs windows. Unlike the other cottages around, this one had no net curtains. He would have preferred her to come out to him. Greet him and do all the talking. After a minute he pushed open the gate and went slowly towards her door. The borders that ran along the path had the ruined look of a forgotten summer. She hadn't yet dug out the dying plants. He was surprised to see old plastic flowerpots on their side and sweet wrappers trodden into the dead leaves. She had always seemed a neat and organised person, but he knew nothing about her. He was making a mistake and should turn back now, before she saw him. No, he was determined to tie himself to his fate. His hand was already lifting the heavy knocker and letting it fall. And again. He heard rapid muffled thumps as she descended the stairs at speed. There was the sound of a bolt withdrawn. She pulled the door open so fast and wide that he was instantly intimidated and couldn't meet her gaze. The first thing he saw was that she was barefoot and her toenails were painted purple.

"It's you." She said it neutrally, without hesitation or surprise. He lifted his head and they exchanged a look, and for a confused moment he thought he may have knocked at the wrong house. Sure, she recognised him. But she looked different. Her hair was loose, almost to her shoulders, she wore a pale green t-shirt under a loose cardigan, and jeans that ended well above her ankles. Her Saturday clothes. He had prepared something to say, an opening, but he had forgotten it.

"Almost three years late. Lunch is cold."

He said it quickly. "I had a long detention."

She smiled and he blushed with helpless pride in his smart reply. It had come from nowhere.

"Come on then."

He stepped past her into a cramped hallway, with a steep run of stairs in front of him and doors to the left and right.

"Go left."

He saw the piano first, a baby grand squashed into a corner but still taking up a good part of the room. Piles of music on two chairs, two small sofas facing each other over a low table, also stacked with books. Today's newspapers were on the floor. Beyond, a door through to a tiny kitchen that gave onto a low-walled garden.

"Sit," she said, as if to a dog. A joke, of course. She sat opposite and looked at him intently, seeming vaguely amused by his presence. What did she see?

In later years, he often wondered. A fourteen-year-old boy, average height for his age, slender build but looking strong enough, dark brown hair, long for the times under the distant influence of John Mayall and Eric Clapton. During a brief stay with his sister, Roland had been taken by his cousin Barry to the Ricky Tick club at Guildford bus station to hear the Rolling Stones. It was there that Roland's look had been consolidated, for he was impressed by the black jeans that Brian Jones wore. What other changes might Miriam have noted? Voice newly broken. Long solemn face, full lips that sometimes trembled, as though he was suppressing certain thoughts, greenish-brown eyes behind National Health Service specs whose plastic rims he had prised off long before John Lennon thought of doing the same. Grey Harris tweed jacket with elbow patches over a Hawaiian shirt with palm-tree motif. Drainpipe grey flannel trousers were the closest substitute for tight black jeans that the Berners dress code would permit. His winkle-picker shoes had a medieval look. He smelled of a lemony cologne. That day he was free of acne. There was something indefinably unwholesome about him. Something lean and snakelike.

Where he sprawled back uneasily on the sofa, she was upright and now she tilted forwards. Her voice was sweet and tolerant. Perhaps she pitied him. "So, Roland. Tell me about yourself."

It was one of those adult questions, impossible and dull. Only once had she ever used his first name. As he politely pushed himself up into a position more like hers he could think of nothing other than his piano lessons with Mr. Clare. He explained that he was getting an extra hour and a half a week for free. Lately, he told her, he had been learning—

She interrupted him and as she did so, she pulled up her right leg and tucked it under her left knee. Her back was far straighter than his had ever been. "I hear you got your Grade 7."

"Yep."

"Merlin Clare says your sight-reading is good."

"I don't know."

"And you've come all this way on your bike to play duets with me."

He blushed again, this time at what he thought was innuendo. He also experienced the beginnings of an erection. He moved a hand across his lap in case it was visible. But she was on her feet and going towards the piano.

"I've got just the thing. Mozart."

She was already sitting at the piano and he was still on the sofa in a daze of embarrassment. He was about to fail and be humiliated. And sent away.

"Ready?"

"I don't really feel like it."

"Just the first movement. It'll do you no harm."

He could see no way out. He rose slowly, then squeezed behind her to take the left side. As he passed he felt the warmth coming off the back of her head. When he was sitting down, he became aware of a ticking clock above the fireplace, as loud as a metronome. Against it, keeping time in a duet would be a challenge. Against both would be his agitated heart. She arranged the music before them. D major. A Mozart four-hander. He had played some of it through once with Neil Noake, perhaps six months before. Suddenly she had a change of mind.

"We'll swop. More fun for you."

She stood and stepped away, and he slid along to his right. As she sat down again she said in that same kindly voice, "We won't take it too fast."

With a slight tilt of her whole body and raising both hands above the keyboard and dropping them, she brought them in, and off they went at what seemed to Roland a hopeless pace. Like tobogganing down an icy mountain. He was a fraction behind her on the opening grand declaration, so that the piano, a Steinway, sounded like a bar-room honky-tonk. In his nervousness he gave a snort of smothered laughter. He caught up with her and then, too earnest, he was slightly ahead. He was clinging to a cliff edge. Expression, dynamics were beyond him—he could do no more than play the right notes in the right order as they careened across the page. There were moments when it sounded almost good. As they tossed back and forth a little figure in an extended throbbing crescendo she called out "bravo." What a din they were making in the tiny room. When they reached the end of the movement she flipped the page over. "Can't stop now!"

He managed well enough, picking his way through the lilting melody while she played a gentle Alberti bass that bore him along. She pressed against him, leaning to her right as they lifted into a higher register together. He relaxed a little when she almost fumbled over a run of notes, a private game of mischievous Mozart. But the move-ment seemed to last hours and at the end the black dots that signalled a repeat were a punishment, a repeat jail sentence. The weight on his attention was becoming unbearable. His eyes were smarting. Finally the movement sank away into its final chord, which he held for a crotchet too long.

Immediately she stood. He felt close to tears with relief that they were not going to play the allegro molto. But she hadn't spoken and he sensed he had disappointed her. She was right behind him. She put her hands on his shoulders, leant down and whispered in his ear, "You're going to be all right."

He wasn't sure what she meant. She crossed the room and went into the kitchen. Watching her bare white feet, hearing their scuff-ing sound on the flagstones, made him feel weak. A couple of min-utes later she came back with glasses of orange juice, actual crushed oranges, a novel taste. By then, he was standing uncertainly by the low table, wondering if now he was expected to leave. He would not have minded. They drank in silence. Then she put her glass down and did something that almost caused him to faint. He had to steady himself against the arm of a sofa. She went to the front door, knelt and sank the heavy door bolt into the stone floor. Then she came back and took his hand.

"Come on then."

She led him to the foot of the stairs where she paused and looked at him intently. Her eyes were bright.

"Are you frightened?"

"No," he lied. His voice was thick. He needed to clear his throat but he didn't dare do it in case it made him sound weak or stupid or unhealthy. In case it woke him from this dream. The staircase was narrow. He held on to her hand as she went before him and towed him up. On the landing there was a bathroom straight ahead and, as downstairs, doors to the right and left. She pulled him to the right. The room excited him. It was a mess. The bed was unmade. On the floor by a laundry basket was a small heap of her underwear in various pastels. The sight of it touched him. When he knocked she must have been organising her washing for the week ahead, the way people did on Saturday mornings.

"Take your shoes and socks off."

He knelt before her and did as he was told. He did not like the way his pointed shoes had formed a deep crease on the uppers and rose up at the tips. He pushed them under a chair.

She spoke in a sensible voice. "Are you circumcised, Roland?"

"Yes. I mean, no."

"Either way, you'll go in the bathroom and have a good wash."

It seemed reasonable enough and because of that his arousal drained away. The bathroom was tiny, with pink carpet, a narrow bath and a glass-fronted shower cubicle at a slight lean, and on a chrome rack, thick white towels of a kind that reminded him of home. On a shelf above the basin he saw a curvy bottle of her perfume and its name, rosewater. Aware that this was not the first time she had sent him away to wash, he was thorough in his preparations. Displeasing her in any way was what he dreaded most. As he was getting dressed he peered out of a small leaded window under the gable. He had a view across wide fields to the Stour nearing low tide, with its mud-banks emerging from the silver water like the humped backs of monsters, and seagrasses and circling flocks of seabirds. A twin-masted sailing boat was in mid-channel running out with the flow. Whatever was happening here in this cottage the world would go on anyway. Until it didn't. Perhaps within the hour.

When he returned she had tidied the room and turned back the covers. "That's what you'll do every time."

Her suggestion of a future excited him again. She gestured him to sit beside her on the bed. Then she put her hand on his knee.

"Are you worried about contraception?"

He did not answer. He hadn't given it a thought and was ignorant of the details.

She said, "I could be the first woman on the Shotley peninsula to be on the pill."

This too was beyond him. His only resource was the truth, what was most obvious at that moment. He turned to face her and said, "I really like being here with you." As the words left him they sounded childish. But she smiled and drew his face to hers and they kissed. Not for very long or very deeply. He followed her. Lips then, glancingly, tips of tongues, then just lips again. She lay back on the bed against the pillows and said, "Get undressed for me. I want to look at you."

He stood and pulled his Hawaiian shirt over his head. The old oak floorboards creaked under him when he stood on one leg to pull off his trousers. Tapered by his mother to keep him in fashion, they were tight over the heels. He was in good shape, he thought, and not ashamed to stand exposed in front of Miriam Cornell.

But she said sharply, "All of it."

So he pulled down his underpants and stepped out of them.

"That's better. Lovely, Roland. And look at you."

She was right. He had never known such anticipation. Even as she frightened him he trusted her and was ready to do whatever she asked. All the time he had spent with her in his thoughts and, before that, all the intimidating lessons at the piano were a rehearsal for what was about to happen. It was all one lesson. She would make him ready to face death, happy to be vaporised. He looked at her expectantly. What did he see?

The memory would never leave him. The bed was a double by

the standards of the time, under five feet across. Two sets of two pillows. She sat against one set with her knees drawn up. While he was undressing she had taken off her cardigan and jeans. Her knickers, like her t-shirt, were green. Cotton, not silk. That t-shirt was a large man's size and perhaps he should have worried about a rival. The folds of the material, brushed cotton, seemed to him voluptuous in his heightened state. Her eyes were also green. He had once thought there was something cruel about them. Now their colour suggested daring. She could do anything she wanted. Her bare legs had traces of a summer tan. The round face, which once had the quality of a mask, now had a soft and open look. The light through the small bedroom window picked out the strength of her cheekbones. No lipstick this Saturday morning. The hair she had worn in a bun for lessons was very fine and strands of it floated up when she moved her head. She was looking at him in that same patient, wry way she had. Something about him amused her. She pulled her t-shirt off and let it fall to the floor.

"Time you learned to take a girl's bra off."

He knelt beside her on the bed. Though his fingers shook, it turned out to be obvious enough, how to lift the hooks from the eyes. She pushed the blankets and sheets away. She was holding his gaze, as if to prevent him from gaping at her breasts.

"Let's get in," she said. "Come here."

She lay on her back with her arm stretched out. She wanted him to lie on it, or within it. With her free hand she pulled up the covers, turned on her side and drew him towards her. He was uneasy. This was more like a mother and child embrace. He sensed he should be in a more commanding position. He felt strongly he shouldn't let himself be babied. But how strongly? To be enveloped like this was sudden unexpected bliss. There was no choice. She drew his face towards her breasts and now they filled his view and he took her nipple in his mouth. She shuddered and murmured, "Oh God." He came up for air. They were face to face and kissing. She guided his fingers between her legs and showed him, then took her hand away. She whispered, "No, gently, slower," and closed her eyes.

Suddenly she pushed the bed covers away and rolled on top of him, sat up—and it was complete, accomplished. So simple. Like some trick with a vanishing knot in a length of soft rope. He lay back in sensual wonder, reaching for her hands, unable to speak. Probably only minutes passed. It seemed as if he had been shown a hidden fold in space where there was a catch, a fastener, and that as he released it and peeled away the illusory everyday he saw what had always been there. Their roles, teacher, pupil, the order and self-importance of school, timetables, bikes, cars, clothes, even words—all of it a diversion to keep everyone from this. It was either hilarious or it was tragic, that people should go about their daily business in the conventional way when they knew there was this. Even the headmaster, who had a son and a daughter, must know. Even the Queen. Every adult knew. What a facade. What pretence.

Later she opened her eyes and gazing down at him with a faraway look said, "There's something missing."

His voice came faintly from beyond the cottage walls, "Yes?"

"You haven't said my name."

"Miriam."

"Say it three times."

He did so.

A pause. She swayed, then she said, "Say something to me. With my name."

He did not hesitate. It was a love letter and he meant it. "Dear Miriam, I love Miriam. I love you Miriam." And as he was saying it again, she arched her back, gave a shout, a beautiful tapering cry. That was it for him too, he followed her, just one step behind, barely a crotchet.

>>

He went downstairs ten minutes after her. His head was clear, his tread was light and he took the steep stairs two at a time. The clocks had not yet gone back and the sun was still high enough. It was not even one thirty. It would be a delight now to be on his bike, taking a different route to school, the Harkstead way, at speed, passing close by the pine wood that contained the secret lake. Alone, to prize the treasure that no one could take from him, to taste it, sift it, reconstruct it. To get the measure of the new person he was. He might extend the ride, take the farm tracks to Freston. The prospect was sweet. First, a goodbye. When he arrived in the sitting room she was bending down to gather up the papers from the floor. He was not too young to sense a shift of mood. Her movements were quick and tense. Her hair was tied back tight. She straightened and looked at him and knew.

She said, "Oh no you don't."

"What?"

She came towards him. "You absolutely don't."

He started to say, "I don't know what you mean," but she spoke over him. "Got what you came for and heading off. Is that it?"

"No. Honestly. I want to stay."

"Are you telling me the truth?"

"Yes!"

"Yes, Miss."

He looked to see if she was making fun of him. Impossible to tell.

"Yes, Miss."

"Good. Ever peeled a potato?"

He nodded, not daring to say no.

She brought him into the kitchen. By the sink, in a tin bowl were five big dirty potatoes. She gave him a peeler and a colander. "Did you wash your hands?"

He tried to sound curt. "Yes."

"Yes, Miss."

"I thought you wanted me to call you Miriam."

She gave him a look of exaggerated pity and continued. "When they're done and rinsed, chop them into four and put them in that pot."

She stepped into some clogs and went into the back garden and he started work. He felt trapped, bewildered, and at the same time he felt he owed her a great debt. Of course, it would have been wrong, appalling bad manners to leave. But even if it had been right he would not have known how to withstand her. She had always frightened him. He had not forgotten how cruel she could be. Now it was more complicated, it was worse and he had made it worse. He suspected he had brushed against a fundamental law of the universe: such ecstasy must compromise his freedom. That was its price.

The first potato was slow. Like woodcarving, at which he had always been useless. By the fourth he thought he had the hang of it. The trick was to ignore the detail. He quartered and rinsed his five potatoes and put them in the pot of water. He went to the kitchen's half-glazed door to see what she was up to. The light was golden. She was dragging a cast-iron table across the lawn towards a shed. Pausing, then dragging a few inches at a time. Her movements were frantic, even angry. The terrible thought came to him that there might be something wrong with her. She saw him and waved at him to come out.

When he got to her, she said, "Don't just watch. This thing is bloody heavy."

Together they stored the table in the shed. Then she put a rake in his hands and told him to sweep up leaves and put them on the compost heap at the bottom of the garden. While he raked beech leaves from next door's tree, she was busy in the borders with her secateurs. An hour passed. He was dumping the last of the leaves on the compost. Across the open space he could make out a slice of the river, part of an inlet, tinted orange. He could step over the low fence into the field, walk round the front of the cottage, retrieve his bike and be off. Never come back. It would hardly matter if the world was ending. He could do all that. But it was simple—he couldn't. His urge to leave surprised him as much as his inability to. It was a matter of courtesy to help out, to stay for lunch. He was hungry, the leg of lamb he had seen in the kitchen would be far superior to anything at school. It helped, or simplified matters minutes later, when Miriam told him to rake the front garden also. He had no choice. As he turned to obey she pulled him back by the collar of his shirt and kissed him on the cheek.

She went indoors to prepare lunch while he pushed a wheelbarrow with his rake down a side passage and set to work out front. It was harder. The leaves were massed between and behind thorny rose shrubs along the borders. The rake's head was too wide. He had to go down on all fours and scoop the leaves out with his hands. He col-

lected up the empty plastic flowerpots, sweet wrappers and other rubbish that had blown in. Just beyond her front gate was her car and his
bike leaning against it. He tried not to look at it. Perhaps it was hunger
that was making him irritable. That and the fiddly nature of the job.

When he was done at last and had returned the rake and wheelbarrow to the shed, he went indoors. Miriam was basting the lamb.

"Not ready yet," she said, and then she saw him. "Look at the
state of you. Your trousers are filthy." She took his hand. "You're all
scratched. You poor darling. Get your shoes off. Into the shower with
you!"

He let himself be led upstairs. The backs of his hands were indeed
bloody from the rose thorns. He felt cared for and just a little heroic.
In her bedroom he undressed in front of her.

Her tone was warm. "Look at you. Big again." She drew him
towards her and fondled him while they kissed.

The shower was not a good experience. The water came out in a
dribble, with a hair's breadth turn of the tap between icy and scalding.
When he returned to the bedroom, towel round his waist, his clothes
were gone. He heard her coming up the stairs.

Before he could ask, she said, "They're in the washing machine.
You can't go back to school covered in mud." She passed him a grey
sweater and a pair of her beige slacks. "Don't worry. I'm not lending
you my knickers."

Her clothes fitted well enough, though the slacks looked girlish
around the hips. There was an odd little loop that was supposed to
go under his heel. He let it drag. As he followed her down the stairs
the thought that they were both barefoot pleased him. At their very
late lunch she had a glass of white wine, which she said she preferred
at room temperature. He did not know the rules of wine but he nodded knowingly. She poured him some home-made lemonade. At first,
they ate in silence and he was nervous, for he was beginning to understand how quickly her moods shifted. It was also worrying that he
was without his clothes. The washing machine was turning, making
little moaning sounds. But soon he did not care because he had a plate
of roast lamb, pink, even bloody in places, which was new to him.
And seven large roast potatoes and much buttery cauliflower. When it

was offered he had another plate of meat and then a third and a total of fifteen roast potatoes and most of the cauliflower. He would have liked to pick up the half-full gravy boat and drink it all because it was surely going to be thrown away. But he knew his manners.

Finally she raised the subject, the only real topic. Since it had been the cause of his visit he had automatically assumed the matter buried.

"I don't suppose you read the papers."

"I do," he said quickly. "I know what's happening."

"And what do you think?"

He thought carefully. He was so full of food, and he was also a new person, a man in fact, and at that moment he was not really bothered. But he said, "We might all be dead tomorrow. Or tonight."

She pushed her plate aside and folded her arms. "Really? You don't look very scared."

His present indifference was a heavy weight. He forced himself to remember how he had felt the day before and the night before that. "I'm terrified." And then, suddenly feeling the rich aura of his new maturity, he returned her question, in a manner that would never have occurred to a child. "What do you think?"

"I think Kennedy and all of America are behaving like spoiled babies. Stupid and reckless. And the Russians are liars and thugs. You're quite right to be frightened."

Roland was astonished. He had never heard a word against the Americans. The president was a godly figure in everything Roland had read. "But it was Russians who put their missiles—"

"Yes yes. And the Americans have theirs right against the Soviet border with Turkey. They've always said that strategic balance was the only way to keep the world safe. They should both pull back. Instead, we have these silly dangerous games at sea. Boys' games!"

Her passion astonished him. Her cheeks were red. His heart was racing. He had never felt so grown up. "Then what's going to happen?"

"Either some trigger-happy idiot out at sea makes a mistake and it all blows up, just like you fear. Or they do the deal they should have done ten days ago like proper statesmen instead of driving us all to the brink."

"So you think a war might really happen?"

"It's just possible, yes."

He stared at her. His own position, that they might all die tonight, was largely rhetorical. It was what his friends and the sixth-formers said at school. There was comfort in having everybody say it. But hearing it now from her was a shock. She seemed wise. The newspapers were saying the same kind of thing, but that mattered less. Those were stories, like entertainments. He began to feel shivery.

She placed a hand on his wrist, turned it and found his fingers and interlocked them with hers. "Listen, Roland. It's very, very unlikely. They might be stupid, but both sides have too much to lose. Do you understand?"

"Yes."

"Do you know what I'd like?" She waited for his answer.

"What?"

"I'd like to take you upstairs with me." She added in a whisper, "Make you feel safe."

So they rose without letting go and for the third time that day she towed him up the stairs. In the fading light of the late afternoon it happened all over again, and again he wondered at himself, how earlier in the day he had been so eager to get away, to regress and become a kid on a bike. Afterwards he lay on her arm, his face level with her breasts, feeling a growing drowsiness begin to smother him. His attention drifted in and out of what she was quietly saying.

"I always knew that you'd come . . . I've been very patient, but I knew . . . even though you didn't. Are you listening? Good. Because now you're here you should know. I've waited a very long time. You're not to speak about this to anyone. Not to your closest friend, no boasting about it, however tempting it is. Is that clear?"

"Yes," he said. "It's clear."

When he woke it was dark outside and she had gone. The bedroom air was cold on his nose and ears. He lay on his back in the comfortable bed. From downstairs he heard the front door open and close and then a familiar ticking sound that he could not place. He lay for half an hour in loosely associated daydreams. If the world did not end then the school term would, in fifty-four days. He would make the journey to Germany to be with his parents for the Christmas holidays, a prospect of comfort and boredom. What he liked was to think about the stages of the journey, the train from Ipswich to Manningtree, where the River Stour ceased to be tidal, change there for Harwich to get the night boat to the Hook of Holland, walk across the railway lines on the quayside and climb up onto the train to Hanover, at all stages checking the inside pocket of his school blazer to make sure his passport was still there.

He dressed quickly in the clothes she had lent him and went downstairs. The first thing he saw was his bike propped against the piano. She was in the kitchen, finishing the washing-up.

She called to him. "Safer in here. I spoke to Paul Bond. Did you know, I teach his daughter. It's fine for you to stay overnight." She came towards him and kissed his forehead.

She was wearing a blue dress of fine corduroy with darker blue buttons down the front. He liked her familiar perfume. Now it seemed that for the first time he really understood how beautiful she was.

"I told him we're rehearsing a duet. And we are."

He wheeled his bike through the kitchen into the garden and propped it by the shed. It was a night of stars and the first touch of winter. Already the beginning of a frost was forming on the lawn that he had raked. It crunched underfoot as he moved away from the kitchen light in order to see the smudged forked road of the Milky Way. A Third World War would make no difference to the universe.

Miriam called to him from the kitchen door. "Roland, you'll freeze to death. Get inside."

He went immediately towards her. That evening they played the Mozart again and this time he was more expressive and followed the dynamic markings. In the slow movement he tried to imitate her smooth and seamless legato touch. He thundered his way through the allegro molto and the cottage seemed to shake. It hardly mattered. They laughed about it. At the end she hugged him.

The next morning he slept in late. By the time he came downstairs it was even late for lunch. Miriam was in the kitchen preparing eggs. The pages of the Sunday paper, the *Observer*, were spread across an armchair and the floor. There was no change, the crisis continued.

The headline was clear—Kennedy: No deal till Cuba missiles are made useless. She gave him a glass of orange juice and made him play another Mozart duet with her, this time the F major. He sight-read all the way. Afterwards she said, "You play the dotted notes like a jazz musician." It was a rebuke he took as praise.

When at last they sat down to eat and she turned on her radio for the news, the story had moved on. The crisis was over. They listened to the deep voice, rich in authority, issue the deliverance. There had been an important exchange of letters between the leaders. The Russian ships were turning back, Khrushchev would order that the missiles be removed from Cuba. The general view was that President Kennedy had saved the world. The prime minister, Harold Macmillan, had phoned his congratulations.

It was another cloudless day. The low afternoon sun, well past the equinox, blazed through the glazed upper half of the kitchen door into the little sitting room and spilled across their table. As he ate his omelette, Roland felt again the insidious desire to be off, hurtling along the route he had in mind. Out of the question. He had already been told that while she ironed his clothes he would be washing the dishes. She had earned the right to tell him what to do. But she had it from the beginning.

"What a relief," she kept saying. "Aren't you happy? You don't look it."

"I am, honestly. It's amazing. What a relief."

But she read him well. Somewhere below a layer of decorum, barely available to himself, was a sense he had been cheated. The world would go on, he would remain unvaporised. He needn't have done a thing.

→-

Mr. Clare, head of music, busy with his production of *Mother Courage,* for which he had written an original score, told Roland he would be taking future lessons from Miss Cornell again.

"She knows about your progress, the sight-reading and the rest. She'll be delighted to see you. She'll also take you for your extra ninety minutes. The school will pay for that. My hands are full. I hope you'll understand. Good lad."

It was obvious whose initiative this was, though she had not mentioned it to Roland. She informed him that they would be playing the Schubert Fantasia and a Mozart duet in a concert in Norwich. A week later he saw a poster. It advertised the school Christmas concert on 18 December. Under Brandenburg Concerto No. 5 was Mozart and under him was his name and Miriam's. Sonata for two pianos, D major, K448.

"You'd have refused if I'd told you. I'm the teacher, you're my pupil and these concerts are what I want you to work towards. Now, enough of that. Come here."

They were in bed at the time. It was 6 a.m. He sometimes crept out of the dormitory at five, pedalled like a maniac through the dark, along the muddy tracks. He had the journey down to fifteen minutes, then fourteen. Her front door would be ajar, an exciting crack of yellow light. He would race back, post dawn and merge unnoticed with the boys going into breakfast at 7:30. Where young Marlow had his mizzen mast in high seas, Roland had his bike. He went to Erwarton on free afternoons, and weekends when he wasn't playing in a match. He took his prep in a carrier bag on his handlebars to her house but rarely touched it when he was there. On Sundays he was usually with her for lunch. He now told the housemaster where he was going—piano lessons and rehearsals were their badge of respectability. Whenever he left her she made a strict arrangement for the day and hour of his return. She kept him close. He often set out from school reluctantly as November turned to December and the trees were stripped leafless by a wind which was said to blow in from Siberia unhindered by a single hill. He hung about less with friends, he cancelled sessions in the darkroom. His reputation among his year was that of a dedicated and therefore boring pianist. No one was curious about his absences. He was late handing in work. His essay on *Lord of the Flies*, which he had intended to be twice the required length, was a poor and hurried thing, barely three pages in large well-spaced handwriting. C minus minus in red biro was the reckoning of Mr. Clayton, the inspirational English teacher. "Have you read it?" was his only remark.

It was hard to drag himself away from the centrally heated fug of his house and the schoolwork he needed to do. Hard to set out into the bitter driven rain. The cottage had only a coal fire and two small electric heaters. For his journeys she bought him a skiing jacket and a woolly hat. It had a bobble on top which he cut off with his penknife. But the problem was not only the power she had over him. He was a problem to himself. Even before he rode out of the school gates onto the Shotley road, he would be pedalling with half an erection. But he had to accept that there would not be sex every visit. He did not dare express disappointment. He reckoned he was lucky half the time. She was energetic with her jobs around the place and would want him to help. She might insist on a long piano lesson. Then it would be time to send him back to school. Sometimes she said she was simply glad he was there with her and not anywhere else. But when she did take him upstairs it was an experience beyond the remotest reaches of joy. At school, in the dormitory after lights out, he listened to the false boasts of his friends and knew that they would never have what he had now. He was in love, a beautiful woman loved him and was teaching him how to love, how to touch her, how to build slowly. She spoiled him with her praise. He was "the genius sight-reader with his tongue." He discovered that he was averse to having his cock in her mouth. He couldn't explain why it made him tense. She said that was fine by her. When they slept, she cuddled him like a child. She often treated him as one, correcting his manners, suggesting he wash his hands, reminding him what to do next.

When, early on, he objected she said, "But Roland. You *are* a child. And don't get sulky. Come here and kiss me."

So he went and kissed her. That was the point—he could not resist her, not her face, her voice, her body or her manner. Obeying her was the toll he paid. Besides, she outmanoeuvred him, she could frighten him with a rapid shift of mood. Dissent, and especially dis-obedience, could provoke her instantly. The obliterating tenderness would be withdrawn.

He turned up one Sunday morning and for an hour they played duets and rehearsed for the concert, as far as it was possible with-out two pianos. When they were done, she went into the kitchen to make herself coffee—she did not allow him to drink it—and when she returned he took out something from his carrier bag to show her. He had bought it new for two shillings, the sheet music of Thelonious Monk's "'Round Midnight." As she sat down beside him she glanced at the cover and murmured, "That rubbish. Put it away."

It was a risk, but he had to stand up for what he liked. He said, not very loudly, "No, it's really good."

She snatched the music from him and put it on the stand and began to play. She meant to wreck it and she did. Played exactly as written it sounded thin, simple, like a nursery song. She broke off. "OK?"

"But that's not how you play it."

This was a dangerous thing to say. She stood up, took her coffee across the room, into the kitchen and out into the garden, and while she went he played it to her. That was madness but he was keen to show her that he had already worked out how to do it with Monk's heavy pretend-clumsy syncopation. Now he saw how wise he had been to keep his secret from her. He was planning to set up a jazz trio with two older boys. Both drummer and bass player were good.

He watched her go down to the bottom of the garden and look out over the fields while she warmed her hands around her cup. Then she turned and walked back at a decisive pace. He stopped playing and waited. No question, he had gone too far.

When she was by the piano, she said, "Time for you to be going."

Half an hour before, she had made hints about upstairs. When he started to protest she spoke over him. "Off you go. Take your bag." She was by the front door. Now she was holding it open. The matter was so far gone that he had nothing to lose by showing that he could be angry too. He took the music, picked up his bag, grabbed his ski jacket and walked past in silence without looking at her. His front tyre was down but he was not going to pump it up in her sight. He walked his bike down the road. They had made no arrangement for his next visit.

He suffered a week of remorse, uncertainty and longing. He did not dare to turn up at the cottage uninvited and risk a definitive rejection. His unsent attempt at a letter of apology was insincere. He still thought she was wrong about "'Round Midnight." Could they not agree to have different tastes? All he wanted was that she take him back. He had no idea how this was to be arranged when he could not decide what to apologise for. His crime had been to tell her that was not how to play it. It couldn't be unsaid. And it was true. Jazz written down was only half the story, merely a rough guide. You couldn't just play it like a chaconne by Purcell.

He loitered by the little phone kiosk under the stairs in the main building. He had coins for a local call in his grip. If they talked, it could go badly, it could be terminal. Still, he went in, put his pennies in the slot, almost dialled, pressed button B for the return of his coins and came out. He walked down through the grounds, past the ha-ha, along a path through the rusty collapsing bracken to the foreshore where he and his pals used to play in their boilersuits. There, under a bare oak on a little grassy promontory overlooking the shoreline's first muddy pools he allowed himself the luxury of crying in hopelessness. There was no one around, so he let go, he blabbed, then he filled his lungs and shouted in frustration. He had brought the disaster upon himself. He could have kept quiet about Thelonious Monk. There was no need to challenge her. A magnificent edifice toppled, a palace of sensuality, music, homeliness—in ruins. It was no longer about sex. This was the homesickness for which he had never shed tears.

And yet. And yet that week he rewrote his *Lord of the Flies* essay and within two days it came back from Neil Clayton. A+. Roland's best grade yet. *OK, redeemed. Smart use of* Civilisation and Its Discontents. *But don't go too far with Freud. He's not reliable. Remember that beyond allegory, Golding was a schoolmaster once, dealing all day with horrible little boys.*

The jazz trio had its first session. The drummer and bassist were withdrawn lonely figures, not unhappy taking direction from a boy two years younger. Their first attempts were messy. The bass could only read tablature, the drumming was far too loud. Roland suggested brushes next time. He himself fumbled with their simple three-chord blues. Afterwards they told each other that they had made a good start. He played a fine game of tennis in the cold against his summer doubles partner and almost won. He hung about with his friends again. They lolled against the radiators outside the dining room—by convention, these radiators were reserved exclusively for the fourth form. Roland was agreeably teased for being a piano swot who even got up before breakfast to rehearse. He told them the truth. He was having a passionate affair with an older woman. They all laughed. But even as he made this hiding-in-plain-sight joke, he felt a stab of despair. Also, that week he came fourth in a physics test about the coefficient of friction and got a good mark for a translation in class without dictionary of five paragraphs from Georges Duhamel's *Le notaire du Havre*. All his prep that week was handed in on time.

On the Saturday an exceptionally small and neat boy with a pointed nose like a little mouse approached him with a folded scrap of paper. He was one of her pupils, Roland assumed. The note said only, Sunday 10 a.m. Now dread and hope displaced despair. That afternoon he played away against Norwich. For eighty minutes, while he ran up and down a sodden pitch dominated by the cathedral, he did not think about her. Norwich was known for its generous post-match teas. For a further twenty minutes she was absent from his thoughts as he sat with his team and the opposition and ate a dozen sandwiches. It was a long ride back in the school coach. He was moodily on his own at the front, ignoring the usual filthy chatter. He had recently heard the term "chinless wonder," clearly one of abuse. Now as the bus headed south in the dark back towards Suffolk, he saw his reflection in the window and began to suspect that he did not have much of a chin. When he ran his forefinger from his lower lip to his Adam's apple he confirmed it was a flat line. What kindness in her, never to have mentioned it. Repeatedly, he traced and probed with his finger. He tried to catch his profile in the vibrating bus window. Not possible. His prospects were poor. Better, perhaps, to stay away. He could not imagine how it would be when she opened the door to him. They would need to have the Monk conversation. He was prepared to give way on everything. If she knew about the trio and wanted him to abandon it, then he would.

Towards the end of the journey he settled on the idea of a present for her, a token that would say everything without him having to find the words. In the art class he had made a pot, the only one of his not to have crumbled in the kiln. He had painted it in green and blue hoops. Below his house was an allotment tended by his gifted friend, Michael

Boddy, who made exquisite watercolours of his plants. He would not miss one little specimen. But would a present mitigate the effect of Roland's deformed appearance?

He was first off when the bus stopped outside the main building. One minute with a borrowed hand mirror and the wide mirror in the dormitory bathroom restored his chin. At no other time in his life would an urgent personal problem be so easily resolved. He had to accept that he was in a peculiar state.

The next morning after breakfast, he wheeled his bike down to Boddy's plot and chose the most insignificant flowerless plant, barely four inches high. There were plenty more of the same. A couple of handfuls of soil and it was nicely potted. He protected it in his carrier bag with balled up wastepaper. At the right turn off the main road, past Chelmondiston onto the farm track, he realised that if she rejected him the journey along this route would be his last. He slowed down, trying to see it, the featureless flat fields, a line of telegraph poles against a smooth grey sky, as though from memory, from many years ahead, when he was old and had forgotten almost everything.

By the time he had slid the bag off his handlebars and dumped his bike on her front lawn she had opened the door. There was nothing in her expression that helped him gauge her mood. Before they had exchanged a greeting, he took out his present and put it in her hands. She stared at it for several seconds.

"But Roland. What does this mean?"

It was a genuine question. He said, "It's a present."

"Is your severed head in here? Am I meant to be pining away for you?"

His look was blank. "I don't think so."

"You don't know Keats's poem, 'The Pot of Basil'? Isabella?"

He shook his head.

She drew him into the house. "You'd better come in and get an education."

That was it, that was all. They simply resumed. She brought him into the living room where a fire was burning and the table set for breakfast—he could always eat a second breakfast. She explained the poem, she told him about Frank Bridge's setting of it. She said she had a piano version of it somewhere, an interesting piece which they might look at together. While she spoke she combed his hair out of his eyes with her fingers, like an affectionate mother. But she also touched his lips and dropped her hand to his waist and played with the snake clasp of his elastic belt, though she did not release it. They ate cereal and poached eggs and talked about the missiles being removed from Cuba, and stories in the newspapers about a tunnel that might be built under the English Channel to France. Upstairs, when they were in bed, she made him tell her about his week. He told her about the rugby, the tight tennis game, his physics and French tests and what Mr. Clayton had said about his Golding essay. When they made love she was so tender and his relief was so great that at the crucial moment he could not help himself, he let out a shout that was not so different from his cries of despair on the foreshore.

Afterwards, as he lay in her arms with his eyes closed, she said, "I've something important to say to you. Are you listening?"

He nodded.

"I love you. I love you very much. You belong to me, and to no one else. You're mine and you'll stay that way. Do you understand? Roland?"

"I understand."

When they were downstairs, she described driving to Aldeburgh to hear Benjamin Britten give a talk about string quartets. Roland said that the name meant nothing to him. She drew him closer to her and kissed his nose and said, "We've got a lot of work to do on you."

That was it, and that was how it was going to be. This was what the far-off belligerent gods, Khrushchev and Kennedy, had arranged for him. He did not dare jeopardise a reconciliation by bringing up the matter between himself and Miriam. When she was enfolding him so sweetly, it would have been self-destructive folly. She would banish him again. But the questions remained. Why send him away, why bring down unnecessary pain and deny their pleasure in each other for the sake of " 'Round Midnight" or even for the entire concept of jazz? He was too cowardly to confront her, too self-interested. What mattered was that he had been forgiven. She was taking him back and she loved him. She had been upset and angry and now she was not. That was enough for her, and so it was for him. He was too young to know about possession, to understand that his interest in jazz had threatened to remove him from her sphere of command. At fourteen, how was he to know that, at twenty-five, she too was young? Her cleverness, her love and knowledge of music, literature, her liveliness and charm when he was securely hers masked her desperation.

Through November and most of December he worked with her for the concerts and his Grade 8 piano—a tough exam and he was young to be taking it on, everybody said, especially when he passed with distinction. He now played his part in the Mozart and Schubert duets with what she called the "three Ds," dexterity, delicacy and dash. Their concert in the Norwich assembly rooms was in mid-December. It was a large audience and they seemed to Roland extremely old and stern. But as the two pianists rose from their stools to stand in front of the full-sized Steinway grands, the applause for the Mozart and then the Schubert thrilled him. Miriam had rehearsed him well in taking a bow. He would never have guessed that mere clapping could produce in him such a swooning sensation of pleasure. Two days later she showed him a review in the local paper, the *Eastern Daily Press*.

A truly remarkable, if not historic, occasion. Miss Cornell had the generosity and foresight to allow her pupil to take lead position. Precocious young players in classical music are not unusual, but fourteen-year-old Roland Baines is a sensation. I'd be a proud man if I'm the first to say that he has a great future. He and his teacher dazzled us in Mozart's exhilarating K381. The Fantasia however is a masterpiece and a far more demanding work. It was one of Schubert's last compositions and poses a serious challenge for any player at any age. Young Roland played his part not only with technical mastery, but with a barely credible emotional maturity and formidable insight. I predict that within ten years the name of Roland Baines will resound in classical circles and beyond. He is simply brilliant. The audience knew it, loved it and rose to its feet. The ovation must have been heard right across the Market Square.

At the school Christmas concert five days later he had a moment of panic before going on stage. One of the side arms of his glasses came off and they wouldn't stay on his face. Miriam was calm and fixed them with sticky tape. They played the piece better than they ever had. Later, Mr. Clare would tell them that he was amazed by the beauty of their performance and that he choked up during the slow movement. At the end, when teacher and pupil stood from their upright pianos to great cheers and, hand in hand, took their bows, the little mousey boy came out from the wings to present a single red rose to Miriam and to Roland a large bar of milk chocolate. Ah! Youth!

# Part Two

# 5

How did Berlin and the renowned Alissa Eberhardt come into his life? In settled expansive mood Roland occasionally reflected on the events and accidents, personal and global, minuscule and momentous that had formed and determined his existence. His case was not special—all fates are similarly constituted. Nothing forces public events on private lives like a war. If Hitler had not invaded Poland and so diverted Private Baines's Scottish division from its planned tour of duty in Egypt to northern France, then to Dunkirk and his serious leg injuries, he would never have been designated unfit for combat and posted to Aldershot to encounter Rosalind in 1945, and Roland would not exist. If the young Jane Farmer had done as she was asked and popped across the Alps for Cyril Connolly in his bid to improve the nation's post-war diet, Alissa would not exist. Commonplace and wondrous. In the early thirties, if Private Baines had not taken up the mouth organ, he might not have been so keen for his son to take piano lessons to enhance his personal popularity. Then, if Khrushchev had not placed nuclear missiles on Cuba and Kennedy had not ordered a naval blockade of the island, Roland would not have biked to Erwarton, to Miriam Cornell's cottage that Saturday morning, the unicorn would have remained chained in its enclosure and Roland would have passed his public exams and gone to university to study literature and languages. Then he would not have drifted for more than a decade, successfully driving Miriam Cornell from his thoughts to become in his late twenties an ardent autodidact. He would not have taken German conversation lessons in 1977 at the Goethe-Institut in

South Kensington with Alissa Eberhardt. Then Lawrence would not exist.

Roland arrived late for his first lesson and the conversation had already started. There were five others in the group, two women, three men. They sat on folding chairs in a horseshoe facing her. She nodded curtly at Roland as he took a seat. He had picked up enough German at school to have entered himself in the low-intermediate class. The teacher's English was perfect. Barely a trace of an accent. Her teaching style was precise, exacting, with a touch of impatience. She made sure everyone spoke in turn. She was compact and energetic, unusually pale, with extremely dark eyes that were not made-up. She had an interesting habit of glancing away to her right and upwards whenever she gathered her thoughts. There was something dangerous or unruly in her manner, Roland decided. Immediately, he felt himself to be in competition with the three men. The conversation was about children on holiday. Now, her gaze was on him in an intense look of expectation. He had not been listening closely, but he understood he was supposed to say something like, It's my turn.

He said, "Ich bin dran."

"Sehr gut. Aber," she glanced down at her list of names, "Roland, *with the new toys.*"

He had missed that part. He hesitated. His heart had made a pleasant lurch at her "very good." He had come to learn but he wanted to show off what he knew. Needing to impress her, to show her he was above the rest, he proceeded with caution.

"Ich bin . . . an die Reihe mit dem neue Spielzeug."

Her correction was patient, her enunciation was exaggerated for the benefit of a dimwit. Ich bin an *der* Reihe mit dem *neuen* Spielzeug.

"Ah. Of course."

"Genau."

"Genau."

She moved on. The toys were boring, the day was sunny, the children were hungry, they liked fruit. They also liked swimming, especially when it was raining. When she came back to Roland he made three basic errors in one sentence. She corrected him briskly and the class ended.

Two weeks later, at the end of the third lesson someone asked her in faltering German to say a little about herself. Roland listened carefully. She spoke slowly for their benefit. They learned that she was twenty-nine and had been born in Bavaria to an English mother and German father. But she grew up in the north, not so far from Hanover. She had just completed her MA at King's College London. She liked hiking, movies and cooking—and something else he didn't catch. She would be married next spring. Her fiancé was a trumpet player. The class, minus Roland, murmured its approval. Then one of the women asked their teacher to tell them her greatest ambition. They had just been practising that word. *Der Ehrgeiz*. Miss Eberhardt told them without hesitation that her ambition was to be the greatest novelist of her generation. She said it with an ironic smile.

Her marriage prospects simplified matters. He could concentrate on being fascinated and nothing else. Besides, for the past six months he had been happy with Diana, a medical student just starting her clinical year at St. Thomas's, whose family was from Grenada. A constraining factor was her sixty-hour week, sometimes more. But she was delightful, witty, played the guitar and sang, wanted to specialise in eye surgery—and said she loved him. At certain moments he felt the same about her. But she went further. She was in favour of marrying him. Her parents, both teachers, were for it too. They welcomed him, promised to show him one day the beautiful island they had left behind. They invited him to Grenadian feasts in their house near the Oval. Diana's younger brothers and sisters were also keen on this marriage and kept saying so. Roland smiled and nodded and began the inevitable withdrawal. Here was yet another if–then. If Colonel Nasser had not nationalised the Suez Canal, and if British elites were not still immersed in dreams of empire and determined to take back their short cut to the Far East, then Roland would not have spent a rapturous week of play in a military camp. Though his wild travels were over, a notion of impossible freedom and adventure still spoiled him for the present where most of life's satisfactions were located. It was a habit of mind. His real life, the boundless life, was elsewhere. During his late teens and most of his twenties he banished Miriam from memory and rock music became his passion. For a while he was an occasional keyboard player with the Peter Mount Posse. He alternated manual or menial labour in England with journeys with friends, with carefully planned mescalin and LSD adventures in high places—the Rockies and Cascades, the Dalmatian coast, the desert south of Kandahar, the Alps, the Tramuntana, Big Sur. Wasted time in beautiful places, lingering joyfully just inside the gates of paradise with the world's colours aflame, always regretting the setting sun and the call home, the Edenic expulsion into the next day and its usual concerns.

For all the big-hearted rambling on spectacular ridges, he still was not free. One friend, Naomi, who worked in a bookshop, and who took him to hear Robert Lowell at the Poetry Society, received the news that Roland was ending their affair with dismay, then bitterness. Coldly, she set it out for him. There was something wounded about him, something faulty. "You could never tell me what it was, but I know this much. You'll never be satisfied."

He thought that what he did in the actual world—his serial free-lance careers, his friends, entertainments, his self-education—were distractions, light relief. He avoided salaried employment in order to be available. He had to remain at large—in order not to be. The only happiness and purpose and proper paradise was sexual. A hopeless dream lured him from one relationship to the next. If it had come real once, it could, it must do so again. He knew that life at its best was rich and plural, obligations were inevitable, it *was* impossible to live only in and for blanketing ecstasy. That he had to tell himself this proved to Roland how lost he was. But what he knew to be true he also expected to be disproved. He could not stop himself. Here was a bass note, a ground, a drone of disappointment. Diana disappointed him, so did Naomi, and others did too. His torment was in knowing how eccentric he was. Or perhaps even mad, as grandly mad as Robert Lowell, whose poetry came to obsess him. Later, parenting, its double helix of love and labour, should have delivered him. In the actual world, he *was* delivered. For years ahead, his commitment as a father was clear. There should be no hope now. But he could not suppress his hopeful thoughts. What he once had, he had to have again.

A mosaic of memories helped form the half-fictional vision he often summoned: speeding down wintry Suffolk lanes, weaving among farm-track puddles, skidding and drifting round tight corners, letting the bike fall on the lawn, seven paces up her short garden path, his signature taps at the door—crotchet, triplet, crochet, crochet—for she never let him have a key. Her form precise against the tiny hall's yellow light, the cottage exhaling its warmth in his face. Always midwinter, always the weekend. They didn't embrace. She preceded him up steep narrow stairs, towing him towards obliteration, his and hers. Then again, and after supper, again.

At school he was fine, playing rugby, running cross-countries, messing about with friends, learning a new piece. But certain tasks—memorising, listening in class, writing the first line of an essay, especially reading a set book—would set him drifting, dwelling on the last time, fantasising the next. Within half a paragraph, the swell and ache of an erection would dull his concentration. He would come across an unfamiliar French or German word, reach for his dictionary. Five minutes later, it would still be in his hand, unopened. By the time his schooldays were over, he had got through no more than a dozen pages of *Les trois aveugles* or *Aus dem Leben eines Taugenichts*—appropriately, Memoirs of a Good-for-Nothing—or the first two books of *Paradise Lost*. Memorising ten new German nouns could take him all evening. Usually, he didn't bother. He received warnings from his teachers. Neil Clayton, the English teacher, his supporter, sent for him three times in a term to remind him how bright he was, how exams were approaching and there would be no sixth form for him unless he passed at least five.

Did Roland have regrets at the time and wish that he had never had a piano lesson, never heard of Erwarton? The question did not occur. This was his brilliant new life. He was flattered by it, he was privileged and proud. Where his friends could only dream and joke, he was receding from them, crossing the horizon, then the invisible one beyond, and the horizon after that. He believed he had entered a transcendent state that most of them would never know. Schoolwork he could sort out later. He believed he was in love. He presented Miriam with small gifts—some flowers selected from an arrangement in the assembly hall, her preferred chocolate bar from the tuck shop.

Something reptilian, single-minded and greedy, had been aroused in him. If he had been told he was pathologically addicted to sex as others were to drugs, he would have owned up gaily. If he was an addict, he must be an adult.

Many years later, when he was able to talk of his teens and early adulthood, he was hiking above a remote Norwegian fiord with Joe Coppinger, by then working for a clean-water charity. They were walking side by side along a high ridge, each with a glass of wine in his hand, a pleasant convention they had established long ago.

"If I'd come to you for advice, back in the days when you did clinical work, what would you have said?"

"Something like, you long to make love night and day? So do we all. It can't happen. It's the price we pay for order in the streets. Freud knew that. So grow up!"

Dead right, and they laughed. But in his teens Roland had already read *Civilisation and Its Discontents*. It hadn't helped.

If he was damaged by his past, it showed itself obliquely. He didn't follow women down the street or make blatant propositions or grope women on the Tube—grotesquely common in the seventies. He did not come on hard at parties. Unusually for the time he was serially faithful in all his affairs. His was a dream of crazed monogamy, total mutual devotion and dedication to a common pursuit of the sexual and emotional sublime. In fantasy its backdrop, the dreamscape, had a borrowed or clichéd look—a hotel in Paris, Madrid or Rome. Never a midwinter cottage by a Suffolk estuary. High summer, lazy traffic outside, through half-closed shutters, bars of fierce white light on the tiled floor. Also on the floor, all the bedclothes. An aftermath of sweat, cool showers, calls down to reception for iced water, snacks, wine. As interludes, strolls along the river, a restaurant, while someone changed the sheets, tidied the room, renewed the flowers and the coffee machine. Then resume. Who was to pay for all this? No jobs to go to? Not relevant. A conventional enough daydream of a long weekend. The magical or silly element was that he wanted it forever. No way out, no wish for one. Locked in, driven, fusing their identities, trapped in bliss. They never tire, nothing changes in their monastic life, when it is always August in the half-deserted city, where this is all they have—each other.

The early days of each of his affairs summoned the ghost of a promise of such a life. The great monastery door opened half an inch. But soon, his attitude, his craving would begin to be tiresome. She might have seen it before in other men, a banal insistence on more time together than she had inclination for. The demon would not desert him and eventually things must go one of two ways. Unless they went both at once. She would retreat from him, surprised, annoyed, perhaps suffocated, or he moved on, victim once more to disappointment then, increasingly, to shame he tried to conceal.

Alissa Eberhardt's course at the Goethe-Institut ran for twelve sessions. When it ended he was ready to sign up for more but she had gone. No goodbye, not to the class, not to him. It was four years before he saw her again.

➤➤

He also signed on for classes at the City Lit, encouraged by Daphne, who thought he should commit to a five-year educational plan. She helped him draw it up. English literature, philosophy, contemporary history and French grammar. By the time he started at the Goethe-Institut, he had been playing piano for six months in the tea room of a second-rank central London hotel—"munch music," the assistant manager called it, old favourites discreetly rendered so as not to disturb tranquil chat over Earl Grey tea and crustless sandwiches. The hours were good—plenty of time for his reading lists. Two ninety-minute sessions, late afternoon and early evening, seven days a week. He earned enough. In the mid-seventies, despite the political turmoil or because of it, one could live cheaply in London. And if he played "Misty" languorously, someone might come over and leave a pound note on the piano. One American lady who did, told him he looked like Clint Eastwood.

He had already been a photographer. Soon he would be leaving the hotel to become, so he thought, principal coach for a chain of brave non-sectarian tennis schools. The trip round Northern Ireland led nowhere, as did other projects in London. He ended up as an instructor at the public courts in Regent's Park. His pupils were mostly adult beginners. A large minority found it exasperating, connecting racket to ball. Tapping it over the net twice in succession was something to aim for. A few were in their mid-eighties looking to learn something new. Twenty contact hours a week. Grinding work, being kindly and encouraging all day.

After two years he left the courts. He had read and made notes on 338 books, according to his notebook. More than he would have got through at a university. From Plato to Max Weber by way of David Hume was the way he described it early on to Daphne. She had cooked him dinner to celebrate his "magnificent" essay on John Locke. It was a memorable evening. Peter was out that night at a school reunion and came back drunk and accused Roland of trying to steal Daphne from him. Not completely untrue.

Now, Roland had new ways to describe his progress. From Robert Herrick to Elizabeth Bishop by way of George Crabbe. From the rise of Sun Yat-sen to the Berlin Airlift. Time to put away the trainers and tracksuit. He could read a book for ninety minutes without folding into reveries. Maturity. He was plausible, his disguise was in place. Time had worked its tricks. He was ready to become an intellectual or, at least, a journalist. But it was hard. No one had heard of him, no one would commission him. Finally, through the son of one of his tennis pupils, he was sent to review a fringe production—bloody, naked, much shouting—for the London listings weekly, *Time Out*. It was a thumbnail piece, 120 words of wry dishonest praise that earned him more commissions. But within two months he had tired of the empty night buses home from Morden and Ponders End. He wrote a short profile of the Leader of the Opposition for a radical left weekly. He received a polite letter from her office declining an interview, which she had personally signed. His piece was sceptical, but it concluded with the observation that if Margaret Thatcher became prime minister, which he was beginning to accept as inevitable, it might, just possibly, advance the cause of women's empowerment. At least he had finally made an impression. The angry letters in the following edition filled a whole page. She's a woman, was the general drift, but not a sister.

He had been a Labour Party member since 1970. Slowly, it became an awkward association by way of a special set of accidents. In June that year, 1979, he started to see Mireille Lavaud, a French journalist living in Camden. Her father was a diplomat, recently posted to Berlin. Mireille wanted to visit him, her stepmother and young half-sister in their new apartment and was proposing that Roland come too. He hesitated. The usual cracks had not started to appear, but they had known each other only two months. His reluctance amused her.

"I'm not *presenting* you to them, if that's what you mean. We won't be staying there—the apartment's too small. Un p'tit dîner, c'est tout! I have friends in the East. You said you want to improve your German. Oui ou non?"

"Ja."

They hired bikes and over two days cycled the length of the Wall, then the perimeter fences that enclosed West Berlin from the rest of East Germany. For young West Germans, living in West Berlin granted exemption from military service. The unconventional—would-be poets, painters, writers, filmmakers and musicians and the counterculture at large—piled in. The city seemed empty, a backwater. Away from the centre there were high-ceilinged apartments available at low rent. The generally despised Americans guaranteed the security and freedom of the Western sector against the expansivist ambitions of the Soviet Union. The Wall, an embarrassment to so many left-leaning artists, was best ignored. Twenty years had turned it into a negligible fact of life. Mireille, who had studied for one year at the Free University as a postgraduate, had various friends remaining in the city. She took Roland around. The evenings, in French, German and English, were disputatious and fun—impromptu living-room concerts, even the occasional poetry reading.

One afternoon they walked from their hotel off Friedrichstraße to stand in line at Checkpoint Charlie. Mireille had a special pass for the families of diplomats, but it made no difference. It took ninety minutes to get through. When she showed the guard the bag of coffee she was bringing in, he shrugged. They took a taxi ride through quiet run-down streets to Pankow, to a clump of eight-storey apartment blocks. Mireille's friends, Florian and Ruth Heise, lived on the seventh floor. The small flat was crowded with people waiting for them round two Formica tables pushed together. There were cheers as the Westerners came in. The air was grey with smoke. Half a dozen children were running in and out of the room. Several people stood to offer the visitors a chair. Florian went to the window to look down at the road to check if they had been followed. There were more cheers when Mireille produced her Colombian coffee beans. Ruth went round the table, making the introductions. Stefanie, Heinrich, Christine, Philipp . . . Roland's German was weaker than his French. It was going to be hard. He was relieved to be introduced to Dave from Dundee.

The conversation resumed. Dave had been asked to summarise conditions in his country. Philipp gave a running translation.

"As I was saying. In Britain, we're at breaking point. Mass unemployment, inflation, racism, an openly anti-socialist government just installed—"

Someone said, "Gut Idee." There was quiet laughter.

Dave continued. "People in the UK are organising. They're on the move. They're looking to you."

Florian said in English, "Thank you. Not to me."

"Seriously. I know you have your problems. But objectively, this is the world's only truly viable socialist state."

There was silence.

Dave added, "Think about it. Daily life can blind you lot to your own achievements."

The East Berliners, all of them under forty, were too polite to say what they thought. Later, Roland learned that three months before, a neighbour from their building had been shot in the leg during a poorly organised escape attempt. She was in prison hospital.

It was Ruth, their hostess, who rescued the moment. She spoke in strongly accented English. "So they say, trust the Germans to go and make the only viable socialist state." Philipp translated.

There were sighs. That joke had long worn thin. But it shifted attention from Dave's exhortations. Or had it? It may have been a rebuke when someone produced two mimeographed sheets of paper.

They had been smuggled in, a German translation of a poem by Edvard Kocbek, a Slovenian writer persecuted by the communist authorities. The first part referred to the moon landing, the second summoned the memory of Jan Palach, the student who set himself on fire in 1969 in Wenceslas Square in protest at the Soviet invasion of Czechoslovakia. *A burning rocket named Palach / Has measured history / From bottom to top. / Even black glasses have read / The smoky message.* As this was read out and translated, Roland was looking at Dave. It was the strong earnest face of a decent man. At the end he said mildly, "Black glasses?"

Embarrassed for him, Roland said quickly, "Worn by security agents."

"Got it."

Roland was not sure he had and avoided him for the rest of the evening.

The significant moment came while Mireille was deep in conversation with Ruth, and Florian took Roland into the bedroom. The children were making a camp out of the bedclothes. After shooing them out Florian took from under the bed a flimsy suitcase which he unlocked to show off his record collection. Dylan, the Velvet Underground, the Stones, the Grateful Dead, Jefferson Airplane. Roland went through them. The stack was not so different from his own. He asked what would happen if the authorities found them.

"At first, perhaps not so much. They would take them, sell them. But it could go on my file. They'd take more interest in me. Could be used against me later. But we play them quietly." Then he said mournfully, "Is he still a born-again Christian?"

"Dylan? Not over it yet."

Florian was on his knees, securing the case. "In another box I have them all except the latest. With Mark Knopfler."

"*Slow Train Coming.*"

"That's it. And all the Velvet Undergrounds except for the third."

As Florian stood up, dusting his hands, Roland said without thinking, "Make me a list."

The young German looked at him steadily. "You're coming back?"

"I think so."

Two months later, after a coffee at the Adler he stood in line at Checkpoint Charlie, waiting to enter East Berlin. In his hold-all were two LPs ready for inspection. *Slow Train Coming* and the Velvet Underground's third album were in disguise. The sleeves were genuine and second-hand—Barshai conducting Shostakovich—but the labels on the new albums were impossible to steam off. Instead, Roland had defaced and aged them. Also in his bag was a paperback *Animal Farm,* in English, with a false cover, Dickens's *Hard Times.* He need not have been so cautious. He had asked around. Separately, two journalists, old Berlin hands, had assured him that it was easy enough to take books and records in. Worst case, they would be confiscated, or he would be sent back and told to return without them. Preferable, he was told, not to take books in German. His false LP covers were unnecessary.

He should have been relaxed as the queue shuffled forwards. But his vision was throbbing in time to his heart. The evening before he left London Mireille had come to his place and they had rowed. He was beginning to think she may have been right. There were only four people in front of him now. But he wasn't leaving the line.

Roland had cooked dinner for two. Before they ate he showed her his contraband.

"Orwell? Madness! If they let you through it's because they'll follow you there."

"I'll walk. I'll keep checking."

"Do you have their address?"

"I've memorised it."

She pulled a record out. She was not impressed by the dust he had blown across the vinyl.

"Seven tracks on each side! Do you think that's how a Shostakovich symphony sounds?"

"Enough. Let's eat."

"What are you going to say? That the GDR needs to discover Shostakovich?"

"Mireille, I've spoken to people who've crossed scores of times with books."

"I lived there too. They might detain you."

"I don't care."

He was irritable, but she was in command of a superior Gallic fury. If only her English had not been so precise. He heard her voice now as he stepped up to present himself to a border guard.

"You're putting my friends at risk."

"Nonsense."

"They could lose their jobs."

"Sit down. I've made a stew."

"Just so you can feel virtuous. So you can tell the world that you're *doing* something." She was on her feet, on her way out of the room, out of the house, flushed, splendid. "Quelle connerie!"

The guard took the open passport. He was about Roland's age, Florian and Ruth's age, thirty or so. His uniform looked tight and cheap, a pretence, like his regulation stern manner. A chorus member of a low-cost modern-costume opera. Roland waited and watched. The face was pale and long, with a mole on a cheekbone, the lips were thin and delicate. Roland wondered at the chasm, the wall that divided himself and this man who, in another dispensation, could have been a tennis partner, a neighbour, a distant cousin. What lay between them was a vast and invisible network—its interlacing origins mostly forgotten—of invention and belief, military defeats, occupation and historical accident. The passport came back. There was a nod in the direction of the bag. Roland opened it. Now that it was happening he didn't feel much at all. The possibilities seemed neutral. A sleep-deprived spell in Hohenschönhausen, the Stasi prison. There were rumours of Chinese water torture. There was known to be a circular black rubber-lined cell kept in absolute darkness for purposes of dis-orientation. *I don't care.* The guard lifted the two records, put them back, picked up *Hard Times* and some boxed socks, let them drop, took out a bottle of Valpolicella and set it back gently. Then he gestured him through. Roland, fastening his bag, resisted as a matter of honour the urge to thank him. Then, too late, regretted it.

So, if Mireille was right, he was being followed. He didn't believe it, but he could not shake her off. Her voice pursued him down quiet side streets, through one clumsy, self-dramatising doubling-back and the next. If at one point he thought he had confused himself and was lost, there was the occasional glimpse of the pale unmarked Wall to his left. At last, he emerged onto Unter den Linden and found a taxi to Pankow.

It was all the jollier that Florian and Ruth were not expecting him. Neighbours showed up, bringing with them ingredients for a make-shift dinner. They drank the wine he had brought, and lots more, they listened to the Velvet Underground album many times at fearless full volume. "So different, this one," Florian kept saying. "So close!" Late at night the company wanted to hear over and again Moe Tucker singing "After Hours." "It's so beautiful that she can't sing," some-one said. Finally, with everyone drunk, they sang along to "Pale Blue Eyes"—*If I could make the world as pure* . . . They knew the words by now. Arms round each other's shoulders, they rose lustily to the refrain, *linger on . . . your pale blue eyes,* and turned it into an ode to joy.

In all he made nine trips in fifteen months between '80 and '81. Mireille was wrong, it was never dangerous. His missions didn't have the seriousness and dash of the Jan Hus Educational Foundation's work in Czechoslovakia. He merely did the shopping for his new friends. On the second trip, emboldened, he took the album covers with the Shostakovich symphonies inside. Florian was keen to unite his new Dylan and Velvet Underground with their sleeves. After that it was only books—the usual list. No German translations. *Darkness at Noon, The Captive Mind, Bend Sinister* and, several times, *Nineteen Eighty-Four.* He often stayed a few nights and slept on the black plastic sofa. He made friends with the children, five-year-old Hanna and her sister, Charlotte, aged seven. They gleefully corrected his German. These were playfully confiding girls. He loved it when they cupped a hand round his ear to whisper in a roar *ein erstaunliches Geheimnis,* an amazing secret. They sat three in a line on the sofa to give each other language lessons. He brought them exciting undidactic picture books from London.

Their mother taught maths in a *Gymnasium.* Florian was a low-level bureaucrat in a ministry for agricultural planning. He was barred from promotion because of participation as a second-year medical student in a raucous piece of absurdist theatre. In the afternoons the girl's *Oma,* Marie, picked the children up from school and looked after them in the apartment until one of the parents was back. On a few occasions, when Marie had an appointment at the hospital, Roland met them at school and played with them at home. Otherwise he wandered around the city, visited museums, shopped for dinner, or he stayed alone in the apartment, reading or rereading the books he had brought in. He learned from Ruth that a certain woman acquaintance performed an illegal community service by making rapid English-to-German translations to be quietly handed around. She worked in longhand. Others did the typing. A typewriter was kept somewhere away from any apartment. Florian once gave Roland a glimpse of a smudged carbon copy of Orwell's *Farm der Tiere* before he passed it on.

This was Roland's other world, as remote from his London existence as a distant planet. He found Ruth's and Florian's lives hard to describe. Economically pinched, generally constrained, wary rather than fearful, but warmly domestic and fierce in their friendships and loyalties. Once you had children, Ruth told Roland, you were bound to the system. A bad step by the parents, a moment of unguarded criticism and the children might find the path to university or a decent career barred. A friend of theirs, a single mother, made repeat applications for an exit visa—against all advice. The result was the state threatened to take her son, a shy thirteen-year-old, into care. Those institutions could be brutal, which was why the mother never made another application. That was why Ruth and Florian lived "within bounds." Yes, there was the music and the books but that was a tolerable and necessary risk. She took care, she said, to keep her husband's hair short, despite his protests. A hippie-ish look—that of "a normal deviant" in official terms—could attract interest. If an informer report suggested that Florian had "an asocial lifestyle" or belonged to "a negative group" or was prey to "egocentrism," the trouble would begin. He'd had enough already. It had taken him a long time to accept that he would never become a doctor.

The evenings with Mireille's circle in West Berlin came to seem trivial. No one there was ever asked to give an account of "conditions" in their country. That would not have been cool. The West Berliner bohemians declared themselves oppressed by the system but it was one that left them alone to think, say and write what they wanted, to play the music they preferred and write poems in any style. Repressive tolerance they would have called it. At Florian and Ruth's gatherings on the seventh floor of a mean apartment building the system was an active enemy. Gauging its condition, discussing how to survive within it and not go mad or be crushed was the common currency of conversation, which was urgent, deep, sincere. Also funny. The hypocrisies and monstrous intrusions of the state had to be tamed with humour of the blackest sort. That things were worse elsewhere in the Warsaw Pact countries was a jokey form of consolation.

Each return to London from Berlin brought bitter confrontations. Roland was arguing with too many of his friends and with the left wing of the Labour Party. Here was the awkward association. He was a member in good standing, had leafleted and knocked on doors for Wilson in '70 and '74 and had borrowed a car to get the old and disabled to the polls for Callaghan in the spring of '79. Now, just back from Berlin, he went along to his local party meetings. In the general discussion Roland spoke of gross abuses in the GDR and, by report, of violations of basic human rights across the Soviet Empire. He reminded the room of the psychiatric "treatment" of Russian dissidents. He was booed and shouted down. There were cries of What about Vietnam! There were many furious evenings. A couple he had known for years came to his place for dinner. He was living in Brixton at the time. They had remained members of the Communist Party of Great Britain out of old loyalties. After two hours arguing over the invasion of Czechoslovakia (they insisted that Soviet forces went in at the "behest" of the Czechoslovakian working class), he told them wearily to leave. In effect, he threw them out. They left behind an unopened bottle of Hungarian wine, Bull's Blood, which he could not bear to drink.

Friends who belonged to no party were also unsympathetic. But how did the atrocities of Vietnam make Soviet Communism more loveable? he kept asking. The answer was clear. In the bipolar Cold War, communism was the lesser of two evils. To attack it was to sustain the grisly project of capitalism and US imperialism. To "bang on" about abuses in Budapest and Warsaw, to remember the Moscow show trials or the imposed Ukrainian famine was to "align" himself with political undesirables, with the CIA and, ultimately, with fascism.

"You're sliding rightwards," one friend told him. "It must be age."

For a while Roland took refuge in a small group—"middle-class intellectuals"—within the Labour Party that supported the democratic opposition across Eastern Europe. He wrote two articles for their magazine, *Labour Focus,* went to lectures by the historian E. P. Thompson and joined European Nuclear Disarmament. It campaigned against the apparent intentions of the two superpowers to station limited nuclear weapons across Europe, East and West. Europe was to be the battleground of a proxy nuclear war.

One afternoon Roland had a call from Mireille and everything changed. By then they were no longer lovers but they kept up a close friendship. Her voice was flat. Her father had phoned from Berlin to tell her. Six weeks before, the Stasi had come to Florian's workplace and arrested him as he sat at his desk. A colleague in the Agricultural Ministry had filed a complaint about a remark he had made. Four days later they took Ruth. While the terrified little girls watched, the Stasi searched and trashed the apartment. They found nothing significant, though they took away the record collection. Hanna and Charlotte were sent to be looked after by their grandmother, Marie. She tried without success to find out where Florian and Ruth were being held. She didn't dare push her enquiries too hard. But now—Mireille's voice failed her and Roland had to wait—the children may have been transferred to the Institute for Youth Welfare in Ludwigsfelde. A court could have ruled that the parents were "incapable of raising the children to become responsible citizens." Hanna and Charlotte were to be taken into care. Worse, they might be placed in separate state institutions. M. Lavaud had said he was a little sceptical and would make further enquiries.

Roland arranged to go to Berlin the next day. It was that or paralysing misery at home. On the way to Heathrow he went by his bank to plead for a modest overdraft. In Berlin he took a bus and crossed at Checkpoint Charlie. This time, the guard who looked in his overnight bag was his friends' tormentor. He hated him. When he rang the familiar Pankow apartment bell a young woman in heavy make-up with a baby on her hip answered the door. She was friendly but said she did not know the name of Heise. Behind her, he could see Ruth and Florian's furniture. Their lives had been stripped, their possessions reassigned.

It was a ten-minute walk to Marie's place, a six-storey pre-war block. No one came to the door. On his way down the communal stairs, he met a neighbour coming up. She told him Marie was in hospital but she didn't know which one.

He was reluctant to leave the neighbourhood, to give up on the family. There was no choice. That smothering silence and darkness peculiar to East Berlin was settling on the apartment buildings around him. He took a bus heading into the centre and on an impulse got out at Prenzlauer Berg. He felt overheated, damp round the collar and didn't care what happened to him, which was why he strode the twenty minutes to Normannenstraße, to the Ministry of State Security. It should not have surprised him that he was barred from entry by the armed guards on the door.

Back in the West he ate in the street—sausage, potatoes and gherkins in a cardboard tray. No good calling in on M. Lavaud for more information. Mireille had said her father was in Paris for the week. After some dithering Roland took the cheapest room available, in his usual hotel off Friedrichstraße. It was a high-ceilinged broom cupboard with a porthole window. He slept no more than an hour that night. He groaned aloud at the thought of sweet-natured inventive Hanna and Charlotte, so vulnerable, bewildered and isolated, torn from their enclosed loving worlds, abandoned to an incomprehensible regime. He groaned when he thought of their parents in their separate cells, in agonies of despair and anxiety for their girls and for each other. He loathed himself. The books and records he had brought in would have helped the state's case. His self-loving exercise in virtue. Mireille was right. He should have listened. Trying to escape his own demons. And today's pointless errand—mere displacement. Did he think the feared Minister for State Security, Erich Mielke, would welcome him into his office, phone the prison and the orphanage, reunite the family for the benefit of one Herr Baines, an indignant nobody from the West trying to diminish his shame?

But he went back to Normannenstraße, the next morning. This time different guards turned him away with a brisk explanation. He had no letter, no appointment and he was not a citizen. He went around a corner of the square to get clear of the building. He needed to think. He'd had one final pointless plan—to travel to the Institute for Youth Welfare in Ludwigsfelde. But at his hotel that morning he had learned that this was not a district of Berlin as he had thought, but a separate town several miles to the south. Travelling there required a visa. He had run out of options. He walked back to Checkpoint Charlie, ate a sandwich at the Café Adler, then took a bus to the airport.

Back home he wrote letters. He had to keep from sinking. He had lost the trick of sleep. In the mornings he sat on the edge of the bed, dazed, half-dressed, thinking of nothing. Or trying to. He didn't see Mireille. He was sure she held him responsible, though she had accused him of nothing. He wrote letters about the family to Amnesty International, to the Foreign Secretary, the British Ambassador in Berlin, the International Red Cross. He even wrote a personal letter to Mielke, pleading clemency for the family. Lyingly, he evoked Florian and Ruth's frequently declared love of their country and the party. He described the Heises' plight in an article he submitted to the *New Statesman*. It was turned down there and elsewhere. Eventually, the *Daily Telegraph* ran it in reduced form. He returned his Labour Party membership card. He avoided the friends he had argued with. He could not even face the Labour Focus people. One evening, trying to numb himself in front of the TV, it was his bad luck that a BBC documentary came on, determined to demonstrate how the GDR had overtaken Britain in quality of life. There was no mention of 200,000 political prisoners—Amnesty's estimate.

Mireille phoned with the news a month later. Her father had a contact at the GDR Ministry of Justice who had passed on some information. It was just a scrap, she warned. Florian's crime was to have written for a banned publication. His history in absurdist theatre counted against him. Ruth's crime was to have failed to report her husband, even though she had read what he had written. The possible good news was that the article was not political, it contained no criticisms of the party. It was about Andy Warhol and the New York music scene. But there was no official word of the little girls.

So Florian had not gone down for possessing certain LPs or books. On the phone Roland concealed his relief. Two weeks later Mireille phoned again, delirious with the good news. The sentence had been two months only and they were already out and reunited with Hanna and Charlotte! They had not been taken into care. When their grandmother had gone into hospital, an aunt had looked after them in nearby Rüdersdorf. This, after all, was not Czechoslovakia or Poland, Mireille's father had told her. Threatening to take away the children of dissidents was common practice in the GDR, but these days never acted on. On the phone now Mireille began to cry. Roland was choked up, unable to speak. When they were both calm, she told him the rest. The Heises were forbidden to live in or near Berlin. They had been assigned to the town of Schwedt in the north-east, close to the Polish border, well away from the depravities of the West.

"Sweat?"

She spelled it out for him.

Ruth was not permitted to teach. She was a cleaner. Florian was working in a paper factory. They were required to report monthly to a local party official to give an account of themselves. But . . . but, Mireille and Roland kept telling each other, they were out. M. Lavaud had been to the town two years before, after a coachful of French tourists had crashed into a river. The place was a dump. A giant refinery complex taking oil pumped from Russia, pulping mills, factories, bad air, low-grade prefabricated apartments—Plattenbau. But . . . but they would be with the girls. They could love and protect them. Hanna and Charlotte would be barred from university. That mattered less. The Heises were together. The local Stasi and neighbourhood informers would keep close watch on them. But they were together.

By the end, just before Mireille and Roland had talked themselves out, they conceded the fact—the state remained the family's jailers. It was not good. It was less bad by a very long way. Afterwards, he consulted his four-volume encyclopaedia. There was no entry. He found the town in his atlas and stared at the little black dot until it began to pulse. In a twenty-five-minute conversation, Roland thought, they had measured the moral circumference of the German Democratic Republic through the journey of one family. From catastrophe to mere bleakness. *Schwedt.*

The shift in mood was responsible for a minor decision that would transform his life and begin another. The following morning, to cheer himself up—he was drinking coffee in his Brixton "studio," the new word for a bedsit—he concentrated his thoughts on the girls. Delivered from hell. For now, they would feel safe. They would be less concerned than their parents that their new home was smaller, the surroundings uglier. If the authorities gave her permission, their grandmother might visit. He could possibly send them some colourful picture books. Charlotte and Hanna had each other again. The scars could begin to heal. He glanced up and happened to see in front of him on the table the listings magazine, *Time Out,* opened at a half-page advertisement for a concert. Bob Dylan at Earls Court. He had seen it before and thought nothing of it. He had other concerns. To go, he now decided, would be to honour the parents. A symbolic act of solidarity. As if he was taking Florian and Ruth with him. And he hadn't seen Dylan on stage since the Isle of Wight in '69.

He spent a morning waiting in line at a bucket shop in Leicester Square and was lucky to pick up two returns. Friends had told him a year before, when these tickets were about to go on sale, that people had slept overnight on the pavement outside Chappell's in Bond Street. They had been woken in their sleeping bags by a Sunday morning Salvation Army band.

He asked along an old friend, Mick Silver, a rock journalist, photographer and Dylan buff. On that night in late June 1981 they were as far from the stage as was physically possible. At Mick's suggestion they had brought binoculars. Before the concert began Roland became aware of two long rows of Jesus Army people sitting in front of him. Another army. He had not come to hear about Jesus and it was not looking good when Dylan opened with "Gotta Serve Somebody." Do you? Do I? Roland kept wondering. The Jesus heads were nodding in time. It got worse with the next number, "I Believe in You." Then abruptly it was better. Dylan called up the old songs, joyous, bitter, some with a nasal tone of wounded sarcasm. "Like a Rolling Stone," "Maggie's Farm." Where the old melody lines were once beautiful, he snatched at them, he tossed them away until only the harmonic progressions remained. He wasn't standing still for anyone. The Army heads stopped bobbing. Mick was also immobile, eyes closed, attending closely. "Simple Twist of Fate" began and spoke directly to Roland, sending him into a reverie—of the Heise family again, this time of Florian, banished from his circle of literary and musical friends, from his harmless record collection under his bed, from his dreams of escaping, from his romantic notion of New York—all of it to be buried under a life of dull labour. A simple twist of fate, to be born in the GDR. If only Florian could be beamed down here, just for one hour.

After the prolonged applause for the third encore, after hopes had faded for a fourth, Roland and Mick shuffled out of the hall in a long file of cheerful people. Outside, where the crowd began to thin out, they were walking at a near normal pace towards the Tube. Mick was recalling the June '78 concert, comparing the guitars of Billy Cross and Fred Tackett. Suddenly a figure appeared before them. They had a moment to take him in. Early twenties, bright pink face, stringy, short leather jacket. Perhaps he wanted money. He tilted his head back, as if to make a pronouncement, then brought his forehead down into Mick's face. It was a sharp soundless movement. As Mick rocked back on his heels, Roland caught his elbow. The man glanced off to his left, possibly to check that the act had been witnessed by friends. Then he ran off into the crowd. Roland helped Mick to the ground, and they sat together while Mick nursed his face. People were gathering above them.

"Did you pass out?"

The reply was muffled. "For a second."

"Let's go to A and E."

"No."

They heard a woman's voice. "I saw it. Poor man. That was a terrible thing."

He knew it well enough, that tentative German inflection. In his confusion, he thought of Ruth, beamed down at his command. He looked up and found the face among a half-dozen peering at Mick with concern. It took him a moment. The German conversation teacher from the Goethe-Institut. He couldn't remember the name. Four years, after all. But she remembered his.

"Mr. Baines!"

The solicitous passers-by had walked on. Mick was a strong fellow and a stoic. Within minutes he was on his feet and saying mildly, "I didn't actually need that." He was sure his nose was not broken. When Roland asked him to name the prime minister he straight away said, "Spencer Perceval."

The one who was assassinated. So Mick was OK. Roland introduced him to the German woman, who considerately said her name. She in turn introduced them to her Swedish friend, Karl, as they walked to the Tube. Alissa said she was working as a classroom assistant at Holland Park School. The kids were terrific. But the place experienced "every day a new riot."

"We don't have this in Germany. Even happy riots."

"What about your novel?"

She was pleased. "It keeps getting longer. But it's coming!"

Karl, well over six feet, blond ponytail, chestnut tan, was a sailing instructor based in Stockholm. Roland told Alissa he was a freelance journalist. He did not say he was contemplating a new life as a poet. In such company, tennis coach might have sounded better. At the station they found they were heading to different platforms. He and Alissa had a routine exchange of phone numbers and addresses in the ticket hall. Surprisingly, she kissed him on each cheek in farewell. As they watched the couple walk away Mick said that he did not rate Roland's chances against the Swede.

That was perceptive. For a few weeks she was occasionally in his thoughts. That pale round face, enormous eyes that this time had looked purplish black, the compact body that appeared to struggle to contain wild impatience. Or mischief. The trumpeter fiancé had been displaced by the sailor. And by others, surely. Roland recalled how fascinated he had been. Now, until the Earls Court encounter began to fade, she crossed his mind from time to time and then he forgot about her entirely.

➤➤

Two years passed, the Falklands War was fought and won, some-where, beyond most people's awareness, the foundations of the Inter-net were laid, Mrs. Thatcher and her party won a 144-seat majority in Parliament. Roland turned thirty-five. He had one poem published in the *Wisconsin Review* and was making an adequate living, writing pieces for in-flight magazines. His life as a patient serial monogamist continued. He remained privately fixated on a life he knew he would never have.

When, finally, a version of that life presented itself, nothing was required of him, no scheming, no striving. The goddess of happiness waved a hand, the monastery door swung open. The doorbell of his Brixton place rang one late Saturday morning—it was early Septem-ber and hot. A J. Geils Band cassette was playing loudly. He had spent an hour tidying up his one large room plus bathroom on the second floor. He went down barefoot, and there she was, in a patch of fierce sunlight, smiling. Tight jeans, white t-shirt, sandals. She had a canvas shopping bag in one hand.

This time it took only a couple of seconds. "Alissa!"

"I was passing, I still have your address, so . . ."

He held the door open wide, she came up, he made her coffee. She had been food shopping in Brixton market.

"Not very Germanic."

"Actually, I looked a long time into a barrel of pigs' feet. Very German. I was tempted."

They got by for half an hour talking about their work, their cir-cumstances. They compared rents. He remembered to ask about her novel. Still in progress. Still getting longer. Two days before he'd had his second poem accepted by the *Dundee Review*. He held back on that, but he was still feeling buoyant.

Into a pause he said, "Tell me really. Why did you come all the way from Kentish Town?"

"When I bumped into you last year—"

"The year before."

"You're right . . . I thought you were interested in me."

Their eyes met and she cocked her head slightly and gave him a minimal smile. Take that.

"You were with your sailor."

"Yes. It didn't . . . That was sad."

"I'm sorry. When did it—"

"Three months ago. Anyway. Here I am." She laughed. "And I'm interested in *you*."

He let a silence settle as he met her gaze again. He cleared his throat. "It's uh sort of thrilling to hear you say that."

"You're excited?"

"I am."

"Me too. But first . . ." She reached into her bag and brought out a bottle of wine.

He stood to reach for some glasses and passed her a corkscrew. "You had everything ready."

"Of course. And I have a meal to cook here. For afterwards."

Afterwards. An innocuous word had never sounded so laden.

"If I hadn't been in?"

"I'd go home and eat alone."

"Thank God I'm here."

"Gott sei dank," she said, and raised her glass to his.

And so it began, his place, her place, days, rowdy dawns, a delirium of repetition and renewal, greed, obsession, exhaustion. Was it love? They hardly thought so at first. It couldn't last, they both thought and admitted later, this level of idiot addiction. Until it ended, they had to have more. Why waste it when soon the slow dwindling would begin, or an eruption, a hurricane of a row would blast everything apart? Sometimes they reeled away, almost sickened by the sight and touch of the other, desperate to be alone, outside somewhere. That could last a few hours. Then there were the elements that had been too dull and inconvenient to incorporate into his fantasies—work, obligations to others, minor administrative tasks. But all soon left behind.

He returned to Brixton one afternoon to pack a suitcase in preparation for his permanent move to Kentish Town. She had two rooms to his one. He observed himself in amazement. Here it was for real, one of the dream components—gathering up socks and shirts, washbag and a couple of books he was unlikely to read. An act of erotic abandonment. He cherished the feeling that he had no choice. He was throwing everything away. Delicious. He locked the place and ran the half-mile with his case to the Tube. It was madness. Even the words "Victoria Line" carried an erotic charge. This could not last.

Whenever he came back to his room to turn in an article or collect something, the whole place and every object in it accused him of desertion. He could take it. Even his guilt thrilled him. The junk-shop spindle chair he had repaired, the framed thirties photographs of Glasgow street children he had bought, the cassette stereo player he had carried back from the Tottenham Court Road—this used to be his life. Independent and intact. Addiction had stolen it from him. There was nothing he could do. It wasn't indifference that inured him. It was the thrill of compulsion.

The weeks became a month, then months, and still it went on. They saw nothing of their friends, ate in cheap restaurants, stirred themselves now and then to spring-clean her first-floor flat in Lady Margaret Road. They pieced together something of each other's backgrounds. He heard the name of her village, Liebenau, for the first time, and of the White Rose and her father's part in it. She was interested in his story of the Heise family—he still had not heard from them. Nor had Mireille. It surprised him, how little Alissa knew of the Eastern portion of Germany and how little she cared to know. She thought that the Heises were unfortunate and untypical. He had heard versions of her views during his Berlin days: unlike the Federal Republic, the GDR had purged Nazis from public life, it provided well for its citizens, had firm ideals of social justice and was environmentally clean. Unlike the West.

Their conversations, even this one, were interludes rather than journeys in themselves. That the emotional bond between them remained frail was one part of the excitement. It was thrilling to be strangers or, as gradually happened, to pretend to be. But the world outside the sash windows—they were warped and would not open—was pressing in. It refused to allow them to waste more of their time in bed. (He disliked this bed, with its orange pine headboard and biscuit-thin hard mattress.) The school summer holidays ended and she had to get up early weekday mornings to be at Haverstock School by 8:15. Their weekends were ecstatic. He also had obligations, a short-lived promotion, standing in for a regular who was sick—journeys for Air France and British Airways to Dominica, Lyons and Trondheim to write soft travel pieces. Their reunions were also ecstatic. But they began to let in the air. They introduced each other to certain of their friends. They went to a movie. The conversations deepened. She told him his German was improving. They stayed in a hotel on the Northumberland coast, though they barely stepped outside. At last, back in London, they had a row, not a hurricane but forceful enough and bitter. It made up for all they had avoided. Roland was astonished by the strength of his anger and at how hard she pushed back. She was tough in argument. As it was bound to, their dispute concerned the GDR. He tried to tell her of what he knew about the Stasi, about the party's penetration into private lives, of what it meant, not to be free to travel, to read this or that book, or hear certain music and of how those who dared criticise the party risked having their children taken away and being denied their choice of occupation. She reminded him of the Berufsverbot, the West German law that barred perceived radical critics of the state as well as terrorists from the public sector, including teaching. She spoke of racism in America, its support of fascist dictators, of NATO's vast armoury, of unemployment and poverty and poisoned rivers across the West. He told her she was changing the subject. She told him he wasn't listening. He said the issue was human rights. She said poverty was an abuse of human rights. They were close to shouting. He left in a fury to spend the afternoon at his own place. Their reconciliation that evening was joyous.

Eight months passed before they yielded to the facts and conceded that they were in love. Not long after, they took a walking holiday on the Danube delta and made love outdoors—three times in a single afternoon's outing—behind a barn, then on a jetty hidden among the reeds, then in an oak wood. On the first anniversary of the morning Alissa came to Brixton and, so Roland said, "fried me then cooked a meal," they took the night train from Euston to Fort William and set off north in a rented car. They found an uncomfortable hotel outside Lochinver that stood alone down a track, set against a fine view of the magnificent mountain, Suilven. Here they took shelter in their chilly room during a September gale and near-horizontal rain. They lay on the pink candlewick bedspread while he read to her celebrations of the landscape, of the mountain they could almost see, by the poet Norman MacCaig. The storm raged on into the early evening. It made sense to undress and get under the covers. And it was here, mid rapture, that they decided to get married. Another beautiful page from his ancient scripture—to be bound to her, no going back, a commitment so thrilling it was almost like pain. Eventually he got dressed and went downstairs to confront the hotel owner, a man of unfriendly silences, and ask for a bottle of champagne in a bucket of ice. It did not matter, coming away with a litre bottle of white wine at room temperature. That was low enough. They scrubbed out two toothbrush mugs and sat at the window to watch as the storm began to move away. It was almost 9 p.m. and as bright as midday. They took the bottle and mugs down a path to a burn and sat mid-stream on a boulder and toasted each other yet again.

They decided they must have fallen in love from the start without recognising the fact. How brilliant of her to turn up with a bag of groceries when they hadn't seen each other in two years and then, hardly at all. How knowing he had been to welcome her immediately, without question. How much it said for them and their future, their easy and delightful lovemaking on first acquaintance.

The progress of their love towards a public existence had begun earlier that summer when Alissa took Roland to Liebenau and Jane showed him her journals. Then in the autumn it continued when Roland took Alissa to meet his parents in their modern semi-detached house near Aldershot. While Rosalind prepared one of her elaborate roasts, the Major, already expansive on three pints of lager, told his Dunkirk stories for the benefit of a German visitor. These were well-worn and vaguely comic. Alissa listened with a frozen smile, uncertain if she was being indicted for the sins of the fathers. Roland tried to tell his father about the White Rose and Heinrich Eberhardt's role. But the Major, somewhat deaf, was in too good a mood to be listening, especially to new information. He wanted to talk and he wanted to get everyone drunk. Several times he urged Alissa to down her second glass of white wine and take another. She refused him with polite shrugs. Rosalind rose regularly from the floral sofa with frowns and a sigh to check on the progress of the meat, gravy, Yorkshire pudding, roast potatoes and three vegetables, warm plates and hot gravy boat, the carving, the serving. Roland observed the old tensions that had shaped his life with them. Even now, they still touched him, still had the power to revive the suffocation that became unbearable in his teenage years. To step into the garden now, see the night sky, call up a taxi to the station and leave. He followed his mother into the kitchen. Her frets over the meal were only the outward face of her fear. The Major, lifted by their marriage news, was already well ahead of his nightly drinking schedule. Rosalind was too loyal to speak of it. Things could turn nasty. At best, they would have to be managed. There could be embarrassment ahead—in front of a stranger set to become a family member. Roland's sister thought their mother should have left the marriage twenty-five years ago, when he went to boarding school. "You weren't happy there," Susan told him once, "but you were safe. Out in Tripoli he was hitting her, but she wouldn't leave him."

When he asked his mother now if she needed help, she said quickly, "You go back in and be with your father."

The dining table, set with the best plates and glasses with long green stems, was at one end of the sitting room, opposite the kitchen serving hatch. It was the image of his mother in later life Roland could never forget—her in the kitchen stooping to frame her anxious face in that hatch as she passed the serving dishes through. Alissa, assuming the daughter-in-law role, received the dishes and set them out. The Major stood to finish up his fourth pint and open the wine. The meal started in near silence. Only the chink of serving spoons on dishes, murmured thanks, the gurgle of poured wine. Roland opened a topic he knew to be safe. He asked his mother about her small garden at the back of the house. She had bought new roses in the spring. How were they doing? She started to answer but his father spoke over her. He told Alissa that his responsibility in the garden was the lawn. He had needed a new lawnmower. Roland saw a helpless look on his mother's face. Major Baines had seen an ad for a second-hand machine. The address was just a few streets away. It was a woman whose husband, a sergeant in a signals regiment, had died. The mower was too heavy for her to handle. She wanted fifteen pounds. She showed him into the garden shed where it was kept.

The Major now directed his story at his son. Something only another man would understand. "She was waiting outside. So I knelt down, son, and found the screw on the fuel feed, gave it a couple of turns. Then I tried to start it. Of course, it wouldn't go. She was watching. I tried a few more times. Examined it, tried again. I told her it needed a lot of work. Offered her five pounds. She said oh, I suppose it hasn't been used in a while. So there you are, son. Brought it home, almost new. Works a treat. Five pounds!"

There was silence. Roland could not bear to look in Alissa's direction. He set down his knife and fork, took his napkin off his lap and wiped his clammy hands. "Let me get this straight."

"What was that?" his father said abruptly.

Roland raised his voice. "I want to understand this. You cheated. You tricked this woman who had lost her husband. A widow of a serving soldier, if that makes any difference. And you're proud of yourself, you—"

He felt a light touch on his forearm. Rosalind said quietly, "Please."

He understood. There would be a row, and when he and Alissa had left, she would face the consequences.

"Never mind, son," the Major was saying in the voice he reserved for jokes. "That's how it is today. Everyone for himself. Isn't that right, hen?" He was trying to fit a few drops of wine into her glass, filling it so the meniscus swelled over the rim. She said nothing.

After dinner the Major got out his mouth organ and played his songs for Alissa. "I Belong to Glasgow." "Bye Bye Blackbird." The songs that had brought Roland to his piano lessons. Nobody felt like singing along. Rosalind went into the kitchen to do the dishes. Alissa followed her. The mouth organ was back in its case. A heavy silence lay between father and son. Every now and then, between long pulls on his after-dinner beer, the Major repeated, "Never mind, son." He wanted the whole business forgotten.

On the train back to London the next day Roland was silent.

Alissa took his hand. "Do you hate him?"

It was the only question. He said, "I don't know. I just don't know."

After a while and more silence, she added, "Don't hate him. It will make you unhappy."

➤➤

In January of the new year, 1985, they were walking by the River Aue along a path concealed by eight inches of compressed snow. The low winter sun had failed to lift clear of the alder trees along the riverbank and was sinking back. It was still, brilliantly cold. Icicles hung from the too-frequent, regularly spaced litter bins, from fences and from the gutters of nearby houses. This was Liebenau's favourite strolling route. They passed solemn toddlers towed along on sheeps' fleece thrones mounted on toboggans and dodged through the middle of a snowball fight between shrieking groups of little girls in pigtails. The snow had softened at midday and now, at 3 p.m., was freezing hard and was loud underfoot. They were talking parents—again. What else was there when, on the first full day of their visit, Alissa had bickered then rowed in English with her mother while Roland watched on, as Alissa had at the November dinner of the Major's self-betrayal.

"She's jealous of me. She got wartime London then marriage and childcare. I got the German economic miracle, two universities, the pill, the sixties. You heard her. School teaching isn't good enough. When you weren't there, she said marriage would obliterate me."

"Both of us, I hope."

They stopped and she kissed him. "Was your mind ever off sex?"

"I remember it well. Just before my ninth birthday I fell off a—"

"Genug!"

But the welcome to the neat Eberhardt house had been warm. They had hardly put their suitcases down before they had thin glasses of *Sekt* in their hands. Roland now knew a little more about Cyril Connolly's *Horizon* magazine and spent an easy hour with Jane on the forties literary scene. In preparation he had read Elizabeth Bowen, Denton Welch and Keith Douglas. When he told how much he admired her journals, which he had read twice over the preceding summer, she didn't seem inclined to talk about them. So far, most of his time in company had been spent alone with Heinrich, trying to match him in beers with shot glasses of schnapps on the side. The women went out of earshot on short fractious walks around the suburban houses and came back flushed and silent. Even on the third schnapps, Alissa's father was not easy to draw out on the White Rose. Two weeks before, he had spoken to camera for a long unprompted ninety minutes. There was hunger for the redemptive testimony of "good" Germans during the war. The race was on to catch them all before they died.

He spoke slowly for the benefit of his guest. "I feel embarrassed Roland. I was on the margins of the movement. I came into it late. No, no. It's worse. I feel ashamed. There were others, you see. Heroes in the factories. Armaments, trucks, tanks. Little acts of sabotage. Shells that wouldn't explode, piston rings that cracked, screws that wouldn't fit. Little things. Things that could get you tortured and shot. Thousands of heroes, tens of thousands. We don't have their names. Undocumented. No history. I tried to tell the television people, but no, they wouldn't listen. They only want to hear about the White Rose."

Heinrich's manner and convictions were remote from Roland's but he warmed to the older man, who wore a tie at all times and sat stiffly upright in even the softest chairs. He was an active member of the Christian Democratic Union, a lay reader in the local church and had given his life to the law as it impacted on the lives of farmers in the surrounding countryside. He approved strongly of Ronald Reagan and believed that Germany needed a figure like Mrs. Thatcher. And yet he thought rock and roll was good for what he grandly called the "general project of happiness." He didn't mind men with long hair or hippies so long as they caused no harm to others, and he thought that homosexual men and women should be left in peace to live their lives as they wished.

He had a good heart, Roland thought. So when Heinrich spoke of national redemption by way of constructing a history of anti-Nazi sabotage, his prospective son-in-law did not say what he thought— that nothing, not a score of White Rose movements, a million saboteurs, a trillion ill-tooled screws, could redeem the industrialised savagery of the Third Reich and the tens of millions of citizens who knew and looked away. Roland thought the only redemptive project was to know everything that happened and why. And that could take a hundred years. But he didn't say that. He didn't even want to. He was Heinrich's guest, getting warmly drunk by a log fire three nights in a row, while somewhere out in the cold his future wife was doing battle with her mother.

Now, on the banks of the river, Alissa said, "I've been thinking more about your father's lawnmower."

This was not a change of subject. Her mother, his father, her father, his mother. In their mid-thirties shouldn't they be beyond all this now? On the contrary. In their new maturity, they had fresh insights.

She said, "In an unconscious way he was telling that story against himself because he wanted your forgiveness."

They stopped. He rested his hands on her shoulders and looked into her eyes—deepest black against the bright surroundings. "You're a generous spirit. I've had another thought about it. In my first ten years, in Singapore, in England between postings, then Tripoli, I had half a dozen primary schools and as many homes in different countries, with the same army-issue stuff, from sofas and curtains to cutlery and carpets. Then boarding school, which was not a home. Then I left school early and drifted through scores of jobs. I'm rootless. In our household there were no beliefs, no principles, there were no ideas that were valued. Because my father had none. Army drill and standing orders, regulations instead of morals. I see it now. And because she was frightened of him, Rosalind had none, or showed none. My sister Susan loathes him, she hates her stepfather. So does my brother Henry. They won't talk about it and they never show it. I must have been shaped by all that."

They stepped off the path to let a woman pass by with a clutch of dogs on leads. They walked across the grass to a copse, but it was fenced off and they could see no way of getting in among the trees. They headed back towards the path.

Alissa said, "We have to forgive the fathers or we'll go mad. But first we have to remember what they did." She had stopped to say this.

"We haven't got very far. There were Jewish families in the villages round here, now there are none. Their ghosts are in the streets. We live among them and pretend they don't exist. Everyone would rather think about a new TV."

They were walking the four kilometres back towards the Eberhardt home. Feeling intense love and trust, Roland began to tell her what he thought he would never tell anyone. As they trod through the snow, as their feet became numb, he described his time with Miriam Cornell. How driven he was, obsessed, and how it seemed an entire lifetime to him then. It took him almost an hour to describe the affair, if that was what it was, and the school, the cottage, the two rivers. How strangely it ended. How it never crossed his mind that her behaviour was depraved, despicable. Even for years afterwards. He had nothing to judge her by, no scale of values. No proper measure. When he finished, they did not speak for a while.

They stopped outside the low wooden gate to the Eberhardt garden. Roland said, "Try not to fight with her tonight. It doesn't matter what she thinks. You'll make your own decisions anyway."

She took his hand. "It's so easy to forgive other people's parents."

Her ungloved warm hand was a comfort. The broad lawn under snow was smooth and pure and turning yellow-orange in the late afternoon light. They kissed and fondled each other, but they were reluctant to go indoors. They longed to make love but it was not easy in the guest room. After a while she said wonderingly, "Fourteen years old . . . and you still want it, again and again."

He waited.

"This piano teacher . . ." Alissa paused before her pronouncement. "She rewired your brain."

Precisely because this was so unfunny and appalling they began to laugh as they went across the garden, leaving the path to make a detour through the untrodden snow. They were still laughing as they stamped their boots clear in the vestibule and stepped into the warmth of the scented polished hallway.

➤➤

A couple of months later, soon after they were married, Roland and Alissa took the final step towards a public existence when they bought the shabby two-storey Edwardian house in Clapham Old Town which Daphne had found for them. A year before, she and Peter had bought a place nearby. Not long after they had moved in, Alissa gave Roland the astounding news. There was no reason to be surprised. They counted back the weeks. They had made love just once during their five-day Liebenau stay. The silence in and around the house, the bed that creaked at every turn, Heinrich's cough coming through the party wall in ragged detail—all too much, even for Roland. So that was surely the night, after their walk by the river. In September of that year, 1985, in St. Thomas' Hospital, London, Alissa gave birth to Lawrence Heinrich Baines.

# 6

Detective Inspector Browne was finding an apology difficult. Ostensibly, the policeman had dropped in to return Roland's stuff—Alissa's postcards, the photos of his notebook, the negatives, her sweater. Three years late, after phone calls, angry letters and worthless threats of legal action, Browne had turned up with nothing. These items remained in the police station, in a wire basket, as Roland imagined them, inside a version of a lost-property depot. The empty-handed policeman was working his way around an explanation in swerves and feints. He seemed determined, Roland thought, to fit the stereotype of the dim copper.

"When you've been in the Force as long as I have—"

"Where's my—"

"—you'll discover that nothing moves more slowly than—"

"Where's my stuff?" he asked again. Roland, richer than he had ever been in his life, was in combative mood. He didn't care that the kitchen where he and the detective sat was unchanged. The same crammed bookshelves, the unflown kite pale with dust on a top shelf, the irrepressible litter of daily life spread across the table. He was in funds. His leaf-green button-down cotton shirt was newly out of its wrapper. He was wondering about buying a car. His underlying condition was good and he was in the right. His possessions should have been returned. He and Douglas Browne were older than Conrad's Marlow. They were contemporaries, equals. When he was talking to Browne, he wasn't talking to the state.

They were sitting as before, facing each other across the table. This time the detective was in uniform. He was on his way, he said, to the funeral of a colleague. His hat was on his knee. The same blood-hound look. The massive hands with their scribble of knuckle hair were clasped in front of him, betraying the apology he found so hard to give. He didn't seem to have aged and he hadn't been promoted.

He fumbled the question again. "All perfectly safe."

"But where is it?"

"You get these young guys—"

"Jesus!"

"—kids really. Fresh in, hungry, looking to impress, far too keen."

"If you're not going to tell me, you may as well leave."

Browne unclasped his hands. Innocent, nothing to conceal. "You ought to know. I've been fighting your corner."

"I don't have a corner."

The policeman brightened. "Ah, I'm afraid you do."

"Just tell me where my stuff is. I'll go and get it myself."

"Very well. It's on or in a desk somewhere at the offices of the Director of Public Prosecutions."

Roland's little gasp of laughter was genuine. "I'm under suspicion?"

"Some young Turk—"

"But you traced her to the ferry and a string of hotels."

"Could have been your accomplice, travelling on her passport."

"Oh for God's sake!"

Browne no longer seemed so dim and Roland, a little shaken, therefore trusted him even less, especially when he leaned forward and lowered his voice.

"I'm not making their case. I'm on your side. You haven't heard from her in, three years, is it?"

"When she went to her parents. A big bust-up, according to them. But who's my accomplice? Why would I have one? This is just silly."

"Exactly what I said. In terms. Some fresh-faced kid finds the papers under a pile. They shouldn't have been at the DPP anyway. Gets excited, takes it to his boss, who's also looking for a step-up. Then—"

"Excited?" Roland's indignation lent a hint of a yodel to the word.

"The problem here is your notebook." He was taking a pad from the pocket of his jacket. The movement stirred his short-wave radio into life, into a crackle and a distant female voice. Dispatching men to places where things had gone wrong. Browne turned it off.

"This is what's got them all excited. Let me see . . ." He turned some pages, cleared his throat, read out in the toneless voice policemen prefer. As a list. "Um, *When I brought it to an end she didn't fight me* . . . erm . . . *murder hung over all the world* . . . *lay buried* . . . let's see, um, *dirt of the grave in her hair* . . . *She won't go away* . . . *when I need calm* . . . Oh yes, and this last one . . . *She must remain dead*."

Not worth a rebuttal. This was what happened when idiots read your notebook. Roland rested his chin in his hands and stared at the table, at the upside-down newspaper he had been reading before Browne arrived. Ordinary people, whole families, walking through the parted barbed wire of the Hungarian border, parted like the Red Sea, making their way through Austria to Vienna. Anti-Soviet demonstrations in Poland, East Germany, Czechoslovakia. Millions intent on larger mental spaces. But here the room was growing smaller.

Browne said, "They sent me back to you. Not my idea. Things they want to know, plain and simple."

"Yes?"

"The uh location of this grave."

"Oh come on."

"OK."

"It wasn't about my wife."

"Some other lady you buried." The detective was faintly smiling.

"That isn't funny. It was about a long-ago affair. I thought it was dead and buried. It came back to haunt me. That's all."

Browne was writing. "How long ago?"

"Sixty-two to sixty-four."

"Name?"

"I don't remember."

"Not in touch with her."

"No."

The detective went on writing while Roland waited. Thinking of her name and not saying it, naming the years, evoking their finite quantity, had an effect. He was not upset but he felt a little blurred in his thoughts. *When I brought it to an end*. There was too much packed into a simple half-sentence. In twenty-five minutes he would walk to pick up Lawrence from nursery. Deliverance, back into the ordinary routines of his day. He was beginning to think he'd been overplaying his reactions to the policeman, whipping himself up. No need. This was farce. Around him was the fortress wall of his innocence. The street-level forces of law and order were long ago typed into the culture as Shakespeare's Dogberry. This visit would be an exquisite tale, one that Roland would work up and tell, as he had before. Somewhere in West Germany, between Hamburg, Dusseldorf, Munich and West Berlin, Alissa was in ruthless pursuit of her new life. The grave containing her remains did not exist. Why even tell himself this?

Browne snapped shut his notepad. "I tell you what." He seemed about to propose a treat. "Let's take a quick look upstairs."

Roland shrugged and stood. At the foot of the stairs, he gestured for the detective to go first.

When they were standing together on the small first-floor landing, Roland said, "Are you still with that lady?"

"Nah. Back with the wife and boys. Never been better."

"Glad to hear it."

As Browne glanced into Lawrence's room, at the single bed and Thomas the Tank Engine duvet, Roland wondered why this answer suddenly lowered his spirits. Not envy. More, the grind, the labour of private lives, keeping the little ships on course. For what?

They went into the main bedroom. Browne nodded towards the desk in the window. "You got one of those."

"Word processor."

"Takes a lot of getting used to."

Roland said, "Sometimes I want to throw it at the wall."

"Do you mind?" As he asked, Browne was pulling open one of the oak leaf and acorn drawers, the top one, and taking a look at Alissa's underwear.

"There," Roland said. "The intimate apparel of my accomplice."

Browne closed the drawer. "Think she'll come back?"

"No."

They went downstairs and the detective prepared to leave.

"I think the sergeant told you some of it. We heard back from the Germans. Took them eighteen months. They spoke to her father. Nothing. Not a trace. If she ever crossed the border at Helmstedt to get to Berlin, she used another passport. Banks, tax, rentals—nothing."

"It's a big counterculture," Roland said. "Easy to disappear."

So Jane had not told Heinrich of Alissa's visit. He opened the front door. The street was a well-established rat run. The robinia, thriving on the fumes, was well over twenty feet. He raised his voice against the din. "What are you going to say to them?"

Browne was replacing his hat with great care, making small adjustments, repeating them. "You married a free spirit who buggered off."

He took several steps before he paused and looked back. Outdoors, he had drawn himself up to his full height and stood as if at attention—the uniform, especially the peaked cap with its chequered band, had a Ruritanian look. It needed to be worn with defiance.

He called out, "They might not believe me."

➤➤

Roland thought it over as he walked to the nursery. It was not merely a cinematic cliché, the good cop–bad cop routine. Browne had no reason to protect him from the prosecution department. At that moment he would have liked to talk to someone. Someone serious. To tell the story of the notebook entry he would have to include Miriam Cornell. Everything. Of his friends only Daphne would do but he was not prepared to tell her that history. He would never tell anyone again. Besides, she would have practical advice, which was what he did not want.

They walked home hand in hand. Roland carried a Tank Engine–themed lunch box containing a single apple core. Sometimes on these journeys Lawrence was silent. Today, he gave a measured account. He played with his friend, Amanda. They took turns with a watering can. Gerald cried during rest time. A big black and white spotted dog came in and Lawrence patted it. He wasn't afraid like Bisharo. One of the helpers called him Lennie by mistake and everyone laughed.

At the end, after a silence, Lawrence said, "Daddy, what did you do today?"

Roland, still a beginner parent, still a doting father, often marvelled at the mere fact of his son's existence, at how he could run, think, speak, at the precise enunciation of his words and their lyrical intonation, the skin and hair beyond the fantasies of the cosmetics industry. A new intelligence had leaped from two cells merging and daily wove itself into greater complexity and surprises. The eyes were clear and thickly lashed. The unconditional love, sense of humour, embraces, confidences, the tears, the meltdowns, the 5 a.m. starts—all of it still surprised him. As they waited to cross the road the boy held his father's forefinger in a tight grip.

Roland said, "I wrote four poems." He had found four poems and written them out.

"That's a lot."

"Do you think so?"

"I think so."

"After I came home from dropping you off I made a cup of coffee—"

"Revolting!" His new word.

"Delicious! Then I wrote one poem, then another—"

"Then another and one more. Why did you stop?"

"I ran out of ideas."

For a small child, an obscure concept. And it was not quite true. He had paused to read the newspaper and was interrupted by Browne's visit. Lawrence never ran out of ideas. They came to him in a continuous stream. He wouldn't even know them as ideas. Roland guessed they flowed or spilled as an extension of selfhood.

Lawrence slowed as they approached a newsagent. "What about a lolly?"

"Please?"

"Please."

He indulged his son as he himself had once been. It didn't happen every day. The treat was in the shape of a rocket, rainbow-coloured. Sucking it demanded complete attention and Lawrence did not speak until they were home. As they arrived at their front door, purple, reds and yellows were spread across his hands, wrists and face. He showed the bare stick to his father.

"This could be useful."

"Yes. But what for?"

"Counting ants."

"Perfect."

If a friend wasn't over for a playdate, the routine was simple and unvaried. They ate tea together, Lawrence had his daily dose of TV, limited to forty minutes, while Roland returned to his desk. They prepared supper together—with Lawrence's thoughtful help, a slow business. After they had eaten they played. Lawrence was the kind of child who needed to sleep early. Somewhere between seven and seven thirty he could lose his reason. His day was long. Left too late, petulance, wild fluctuations of mood, uncontrollable anger would overwhelm him. Worse was his occasional descent into unapproachable sorrow, a desperate keening, as though he was mourning a death. Whichever it was, the teeth-cleaning rituals, the bedtime stories, the end-of-day chat would be disrupted. Roland had learned after many errors that timing was everything.

The stories could be a challenge, at least to the adult reader-aloud. The illustrations were fine, sometimes even beautiful. Lawrence spent much time gazing at them. But the words—predictable rhymes, unambitious little fables barely disguising the counting lessons they were determined to impart. No thrill in the language, no commitment to or talent for the soaring imagination. A handful of writers appeared to have cornered the market for the under-fives. Some were making millions. A lot of these books, he decided, could not have taken more than ten minutes to write. One evening he read "The Owl and the Pussy-Cat." It was like bursting through a screen. Lawrence instantly wanted it again. Then again. He was right. This was the pure poetry of nonsense. A beautiful impossible adventure. No shadows of condescension, no remorseless counting or dull repetition. He had it every night for almost a year. He liked to shout the refrain at the end of each of the three verses. *What a beautiful Pussy you are, / You are, / You are! / What a beautiful Pussy you are!* He was fascinated to be shown how the third line in each verse had an internal rhyme. They wondered together what a runcible spoon was. Or a bong tree. From the local supermarket Roland bought jellied quince, which they ate in slices. Lawrence knew the poem by heart.

After a banana sandwich Lawrence sat on the floor, staring up at the TV, listening while a young woman with a patient, sing-song voice described a day in the life of a building site crane operator. "It's 7 a.m. With his tea and sandwiches in his backpack, Jim is mounting the ladder, higher and higher towards his little cabin in the sky." Roland watched from the doorway. The angles and shots had a woozy look. He felt for the cameraman who was climbing right behind Jim, a hundred feet up zigzagging steel ladders coated in early morning ice. Lawrence was impassive. The documentary was only as real as cartoons in which characters tumbled from cliffs and landed safely on their heads.

Upstairs, in the bedroom, Roland sat down at the desk that made him rich. Relatively rich. Rich for a poet. But he was no longer one, he was an anthologist-thief, a sometime manufacturer of very light verse. Oliver Morgan of Epithalamium Cards had scaled the rungs of entrepreneurship, had become, to the amazement of his friends, a young hero of the new business culture. A greeting-card corporation had offered a buyout but so far Morgan clung on at the top, surveying his next move, letting the company grow. Like the dizzy cameraman, Roland had struggled up the ladder on his patron's heels, for months pouring out wised-up doggerel—on behalf of birthdays, anniversaries, newly-weds, retirees, recovering drug addicts and alcoholics, ingoing hospital patients, outgoing neonates. His first creative act had been to give Morgan's company its name. At the start, he was paid in promises, in a 1% share in the enterprise and an agreed royalty of 0.5% on each card. They cost around £2. Three years on, the cards of thick creamy paper and tasteful artwork were everywhere. Two million sold in what Morgan called the anglophone domain.

After twenty-six months it came in a single payment, £24,000. It should have been uncomfortable for a left-of-centre voter like Roland that courtesy of Mrs. Thatcher the top rate of tax was at 40%. Down from 83% under Labour. More awkward was the matter of his pride. His integrity as a poet was in ruins. Since Grand Street returned his

revised submissions without comment he had written nothing. One
more failed career to add to the list. Daphne was aggrieved on his
behalf. He was able to tell her he was no longer a burden on the state.
What he couldn't confess to anyone was his lightness of being. To
have money! Why had no one told him, it was a physical thing? He
felt it in his arms and legs. Especially in his neck and shoulders. Mortgage paid off, son brightly clothed, two weeks together on an overlooked Greek island reached by a three-hour speedboat dash across a
flat cerulean sea.

There was a limit to how much doggerel one man could turn out.
Oliver agreed that Roland could ransack the world's literatures for
out-of-copyright aperçus on life's transitional moments, all correctly
attributed. His cut remained in place. He had made mistakes. One was
to have included Yeats's "The Chambermaid's Second Song" (*His rod
and its butting head / Limp as a worm*) in a birthday card for eighty-
year-olds. Lawyers for the estate wrote to Morgan to point out that
the poem was protected by copyright until 2010. A science-fiction
date. And Yeats, a monument, so long dead. Twenty-five thousand
cards were pulped.

On the floor in stacks near the desk were anthologies of translated
Iranian, Arab, Indian, African and Japanese verse. There were more
downstairs. On the desk was a note from a kind, accomplished and
attractive woman, Carol, his fifth lover since Alissa left. *Given the circs
I'm minded to call it a day. What about you? No bad feelings. On the contrary, much affection, Carol*. She was right, the circs were constrained.
She was a single parent too, of two-year-old twin girls. She lived six
miles away, north of the river, in Tufnell Park, a great distance in a
crowded city. At roughly midpoint in their nine months—she was
right, it was over—the idea had been floated of both selling up and
merging households. It had gone that far. But in prospect, the disruption, the effort, the commitment was too great. Once they had agreed
on that it was bound to wind down. What also held him back he could
not confide to her: the possibility of Alissa's return. He wasn't waiting
for her. But if she ever turned up he wanted his options open. Which
was another way of saying he was waiting.

He could hear the TV downstairs now broadcasting the orchestral clatter of a cartoon. In twenty-five minutes he would go down and fry some fish fingers. He wrote a note to Carol, equally friendly and brief, casting his vote with hers. As soon as he had put it in an envelope he had a moment of doubt. With his succinct reciprocal message he may have been throwing away an entire happy existence. Existences. For several weeks he had been drawn to the idea—a good mother for Lawrence, who was fond of Carol. That would soon have turned to love. And love for the playful twin sisters Lawrence now would never get to know. For himself, a loving partner he could trust, funny, good-hearted, educated, beautiful, a supremely competent TV producer. Her adored husband had died in a plane crash and she had fought to make family and work thrive. His nerve had failed him. Hers too. She might have caught a whiff of failure about him. His various careers, the wife who may have deserted for good reason. Before Roland closed the envelope, he read her note again. *Much affection.* This time he thought he sensed sadness in her quiet plea. *What about you?* She was open to persuasion. He wrote the address, stuck down a stamp and sealed the envelope. If this was an error, he would never know its full ridiculous extent. To post tomorrow. Or not.

As Roland understood it from a book he had read parts of, from what friends had said, it was important not to close down Lawrence on the subject of his mother. She was often on his mind, sometimes for days on end, then nothing for weeks. He liked sorting through photographs of her. His questions used to be manageable even though they were, in adult terms, impossible.

"What's my mummy doing now?"

"It's a hot day. She must be having a swim."

A year ago, when his language was just cohering into whole sentences, that would satisfy him. But lately there were follow-ups. A swimming pool or the sea? If it was a pool it must be the one he knew, since he didn't know of others. She's there now. Let's go and look. If the sea, they could go on the train. His more general questions put his father on the defensive.

"Where did she go?"

"On a long journey."

"When is she coming back?"

"Not for a long time."

"Why didn't she send me a birthday present?"

"I told you already, darling. She asked me to get you a hamster and that's what I did."

Towards the end of October that year Lawrence got into his bed at 4 a.m. and asked, "Did she go away because I was naughty?"

Hearing this, Roland, half asleep, emotionally wide open, felt tears. He himself needed guidance. What he said was, "She loves you and she never ever thinks you're naughty." The boy slept. Roland lay awake. It was helpful that half the children at the nursery were raised by single parents. Lawrence himself had observed in neutral tones that while he did not have a mummy, Lorraine didn't have a daddy, nor did Bisharo, nor did Hazeem. But soon he would see through the evasions. The questions would keep coming. If Alissa had talked to Roland about a hamster, why couldn't she talk to Lawrence? Keeping Alissa alive in the child's thoughts could be a form of unintended cruelty. But if Roland had consigned her early on to a plane crash, and then she turned up—what then?

He arranged an evening with Daphne. It was easily done. The youngest of the Mounts' three children was an intense and freckled little boy, Gerald, joint favourite with Amanda as Lawrence's best friend. They went to the same nursery, had sleepovers in both households, and had spent family holidays together in the Cévennes in a big farmhouse that Peter Mount found, far from the sea and therefore cheap.

Roland and Lawrence arrived at six so that the boys could play before bedtime. A Norwegian au pair gave the four children supper. Peter was out and would join them later. According to Daphne he had a "fun" proposal to put to Roland. She led him into the small front room, a corner of the house from which, by an old-fashioned arrangement, children and their toys and games were banned. Roland was beginning to see the point of it.

Each time he visited the Mounts' house, not much bigger than his own, he noticed an improvement, a shift to greater comfort, even opulence. A man-sized fridge, recovered oak floorboards, bergère sofas, a bigger TV sitting above an improved video tape recorder, the once fashionable stripped and waxed doors painted over in muted white. A Vanessa Bell drawing hung above the fireplace. Daphne worked for years in the local council's housing department. The popular sell-off of council flats and houses, the Right to Buy, disgusted her. After years trying and failing to obstruct the process, she resigned. She had set up a housing association and did good work for twice the salary, finding decent places to live for the hard-pressed. Peter had also resigned. After twelve years at the Central Electricity Generating Board he was part of a consortium preparing to form itself into a private electricity company. American and Dutch money was involved. The Electricity Act had already passed that year. Peter had input into the drafting of the bill, the economic calculations, the regulatory body, consumer protection, the shareholders' slice. Daphne, like Roland, disliked and on occasions loathed the Thatcher government but, like him, she was prospering under its edicts. They often discussed the contradiction, but they would never resolve it. They had voted for Labour and its higher tax rate, but their side had lost. Their consciences were clear. Peter had the more coherent position. He had voted for Mrs. Thatcher from the start.

Daphne poured two glasses of Riesling. During the months after Alissa left, she had been Roland's main support and guided him as Lawrence worked through the scary rota of early childhood illnesses. She had also featured strongly in his thoughts—and still did. She was big, not overweight but big-boned, strong and tall, with blonde hair she wore in the sixties style, centre-parted and long. The pink complexion gave her the look of a countrywoman, but she was a child of the city, of quite a few cities. Only child of a doctor father and teacher mother, Daphne had the most stable background of all Roland's friends. She had absorbed her parents' passion for public service. She was restlessly energetic, a great organiser of things, events, children, friends. Her memory for people was long and deep. Her connections were extensive in that zone where academics and politicians overlapped. She had introduced her husband to Stephen Littlechild, a coming figure in electricity supply. If you lost your passport in rural Burkina Faso you would address your telegram to her. If she didn't know the Foreign Secretary, she would know people who could help. She knew Alissa well, had heard nothing from her and was amazed.

He wondered sometimes if she knew more about the disappearance than she pretended. But she was good with awkward advice. Last month she told him it was time to "snap out of it." He had the Epithalamium money. It was not only Lawrence who needed new clothes. Roland, she said, was still living like a student, a depressed student. Whether Alissa was coming back or not, brighten up. Move on. She had advised him to make a home with Carol. If necessary, marry her. Daphne had cooked meals for her and liked her. They discussed the governance of television, how to open it up in the public interest, not just to commercial opportunity. Daphne had connected Carol to some of her future-of-broadcasting friends who were pushing to set up a production company on Charlotte Street. The entrepreneurial spirit had seized the centre-left.

Now Roland and Daphne talked through their usual subjects— the latest from Solidarity in Poland. East Germans were being permitted to pass through Czechoslovakia into West Germany. Roland reminisced about his Berlin days of the late seventies. Labour had a nine-point lead over the Conservatives, the Chancellor of the Exchequer had resigned, the flashily renamed Liberal Democrats had announced themselves. One of the released Guildford Four had made a fine speech. Roland told the story of the policeman's visit. He was no longer in the mood to make a comedy of it and he was vague about his notebook entry.

She murmured, "I wouldn't worry about the DPP."

The conversation meandered. She described how she had taken the children to the Chilterns at the weekend to watch a friend and her team release a dozen huge carrion birds, red kites, into their new environment.

They paused. She poured a second glass. It wasn't even seven o'clock. From somewhere in the house they heard a child crying. Roland started to get up but Daphne stayed him.

"If it's serious they know where we are."

So he told her about Lawrence's plaintive question at 4 a.m. Did his mother leave because he was naughty? "I'm pretending she's a presence. When he looks at her photos, he talks to her. I'm protecting him with lies. Here he is, just four and his questions are getting harder."

"He's generally happy."

It wasn't a question, but Roland nodded. He had come for advice but now he didn't feel like hearing it. Lawrence was not the problem. *He* was. He knew it could be pleasurable, handing out wise counsel. Receiving it could be suffocating when you've moved on. Where exactly? Backwards, twenty-seven years, to the core. Alissa's vanishing had left open ground to the past. Like trees felled to clear the view. In rare moments like this, he could see the origin, a point of light in sharp focus, of all that troubled him and those who came close to him. The piano teacher haunting him that first night was often on his mind. Was it time to find and confront Miriam Cornell? It was a sudden big thought but outwardly he showed nothing.

Daphne was staring into a corner of the room where Peter's unplayed guitar rested on its stand. He was once the lead in the Peter Mount Posse. Between unskilled jobs and travels—his lost decade— Roland played Hammond organ and electric piano, Billy Preston-style, for the Posse. He was brought in by the drummer, a friend from school who had been part of the short-lived jazz trio. That was how Roland met Peter and through him, Daphne. The band never made a record but they had a college following and played pacey rock, much under the influence of Greg and Duane Allman. Then punk blew their project away in 1976. Peter cut his hair, bought a suit in Burton's and took a job in an Electricity Board showroom selling stoves and fridges. He rose fast, gained experience in the provinces, then was summoned to HQ where he flourished.

At last she said, "If he keeps pressing, I think you should tell him exactly what it is."

"Which is?"

"A mystery. One you can share. One day, when he was little, she went away. You don't know why. You're as puzzled as he is. You'd love to hear from her too. He can adapt. The main thing is he doesn't blame himself."

"I think he's decided she's coming back."

"Perhaps he's right."

Roland looked at her. Did she know something? But her pale blue eyes met his full on and he decided she didn't.

She shrugged. "Or perhaps not. You can tell him. You're in this together. Side by side. You just don't know."

It was a noisy sociable evening, putting the children to bed and reading to them in different shifts. Roland and Daphne cooked together and drank more at the kitchen table. Much like their French farmhouse evenings in the high Cévennes, without the evening warmth. Outside, a thick autumnal mist came down suddenly. Daphne turned up the central heating a notch. In the fug of the tiny kitchen, a party spirit developed. For old times' sake they listened to the first Balham Alligators album. Who in Britain could play a Cajun fiddle better than Robin McKidd? They turned up the volume on "Little Liza Jane" and during that song Peter came in with a bottle of champagne and his news, the fun that Daphne had hinted at. There was an American backer for the planned electricity company. He wanted the consortium to meet up. He had a private jet and would be in Europe soon— not sure where just yet. It could be Malmö or Geneva or somewhere else. In the next week or so. He would fly Peter and his colleagues to wherever he was. And this was the point—there was a spare seat. Roland could come along for the ride, entertain himself during their meetings, join them in the evenings for dinner. Lawrence could stay here for three nights. Daphne would be around, and Tiril, the au pair, would take care of the nursery run. Gerald would be delighted. Simple! It will do you good, Daphne and Peter insisted. Say yes!

He said yes.

During dinner they argued about Mikhail Gorbachev. He was an innocent fool to believe that with his glasnost and perestroika he could liberalise to a minimal controllable extent the tired old tyranny and still have the party in command. This was Peter's view. Or, as Roland and Daphne argued, he was a genius and a saint who understood, ahead of his colleagues, that the entire communist experiment, its violently imposed empire, its instinct for murder and implausible lies, had been a grotesque failure and had to be ended. The champagne propelled them to a boisterous state. They argued extravagantly. As he sided with Daphne against her husband Roland thought that this was as close as he would ever come to an affair with her. Unusually, brandy brought them to a more genial state at the close of the evening. Together they cleaned up the kitchen backed by the Alligators' "Life in the Bus Lane" at full blast. A Welsh, Scots and English version of Cajun, itself a bastard form, dreamed up by the French far from home, pushing 2,000 miles south, deep into Louisiana. The world was agreeably diffuse. Peter reminded Roland that in the Posse days they had one number with a hint of Cajun sound. Roland thought it was more zydeco than anything else. They agreed there were touches of both. Who cared? Murmurs of apartheid's end in South Africa, democracies breaking out across South America, China opening up, now the great Soviet ship of empire springing leaks. Roland's grand conclusion as they were about to leave the kitchen was that in the new millennium, only eleven years away, humankind would have reached a new level of maturity and happiness. A good note to end on as they raised their glasses.

It had been decided earlier that he would take Lawrence home with him. The boy slept on as Roland lifted him from his bed in Gerald's room, wrapped him in a blanket and carried him downstairs. The three said their goodbyes in the Mounts' miniature front garden, where the fog, tinted by orange street light, swirled about their shoulders. It was a short walk along deserted streets. Lawrence's forty pounds were nothing in his arms. The prospect of a three-day break, the absurdity and romance of a private jet, even a touch of tipsy guilt at the thought of leaving Lawrence behind, elated him as he strode without effort down streets crowded with parked cars and modest terraced Edwardian houses. For the moment, Miriam Cornell did not trouble him. He would deal with all that. Now, escape! He was enjoying the coiled strength in his legs, the taste of wintry city air in his lungs. Wasn't this how he used to feel, or wanted to feel, most of the time, fifteen, twenty years ago, in his teens and twenties, light on his feet, eager for the next thing? Whatever Conrad's Marlow said, Roland's youth was not gone from him yet.

➤➤

The year before, in late August, Roland and Lawrence had travelled to Germany. It was in part a familial duty, a response to pressure
down the phone from Jane. She and Heinrich had not yet met their
only grandchild and Lawrence deserved as much family as he could
get. Roland was easy to persuade. He wanted to hear at first hand
about Alissa's visit in 1986, the great bust-up, her last known appearance. He was not looking for her, he told himself. He just wanted to
know.

An enveloping high-pressure system had settled over Europe.
London was already baking—a good moment to take a quick holiday before the summer's end. Jane offered to pay the airfares. Each
stage of the journey delighted the little boy. He was almost three,
entitled to his own seat, the window seat, on the flight from Gatwick.
He approved of the train from Hanover to Nienburg and kept his
nose close to the window the entire sixty-five minutes. The taxi to
Liebenau fascinated him, especially the loudly clicking meter and the
driver, in thick leather jacket despite the heat, who made a fuss over
him. It was during a routine chat with the man that Roland discovered
how much his German had fallen away. He struggled for the nouns
and their genders. He mumbled his way round the accusative forms
of the definite articles. Prefixes came loose from their verbs to land
in the wrong place. The word order, which he once thought he had
mastered, now appeared prickly with rules—time precedes manner
precedes place. He was obliged to think through each sentence before
he spoke it. Not easy in small talk. He decided before they arrived in
the village that German, like Alissa, belonged in an abandoned past.

Heinrich Eberhardt, the stolid burgher, turned out to be the ideal
grandfather. As Roland and Lawrence came through the wooden gate
in the high hedge and onto the broad lawn, now baked brown, Heinrich was standing with a hose in his hand, filling the plastic dinosaur-
themed paddling pool he had just bought. Lawrence ran straight over
to him and demanded to be undressed. Without a greeting, just a
murmured "So . . . ," his grandfather knelt to the task with the Vel-
cro shoes. Then he stood back, arms folded, grinning as the little boy
climbed into the few inches of lukewarm water and began to dance

and splash about, consciously showing off. His pleasure in being naked, Heinrich said later, was proof of his German heritage.

It got better. Indoors, after Jane had tried to embrace Lawrence and given him a cool apple juice, he and Heinrich started the game they would keep up for the next five days. Lawrence sat on the old man's lap in order to teach him English. In exchange, Heinrich would teach his grandson German. Already, the boy had learned to point and say, "Opa, was ist das?" Heinrich would look hard, pretend to consider and then say slowly, in a deep, clear voice, "Ein Stuhl." Lawrence would repeat the words, put his face close to Heinrich's and pronounce, "A chair." Heinrich said it back. He pretended to have no English, which was almost true.

Lawrence was slower to make friends with his grandmother. He was shy before her, struggled free of her welcoming hug and refused to thank her for the juice. When she spoke to him he retreated behind Roland's legs. He may have been suspicious of a woman whose face reminded him, however vaguely, of the figure in the photographs at home. She had the sense, the delicacy, to hold back. Half an hour later, when they were sitting in the garden in the shade of a willow, he approached cautiously and put his hand on her knee. In the spirit of the game he had started she pointed first at Heinrich, then at herself and said very slowly, "Das ist Opa. Ich bin Oma."

He got it. Still naked, he stood before them and pointed, and pronounced in what sounded to Roland like perfect German, "Ich bin Lawrence. Das ist Opa, das ist Oma." The immediate applause and laughter so thrilled and energised him that he ran off and capered about on the lawn. He jumped in the paddling pool and began to yell and kick up water, keen, as his father knew, to keep their attention and have more praise, more success.

Jane said, "He's a beauty."

The innocent remark reminded them of what was broken, what was missing. They sat silently for a while watching Lawrence until Heinrich rose with a heavy grunt from his wicker chair and said he would fetch some beers. Later, after his supper, Lawrence let Oma take him upstairs for a bath and a bedtime story. Heinrich was in the tiny room he used as an office. Roland sat in the garden with a gin and tonic. The sun had set but the thermometer nailed to the trunk of the willow showed twenty-six degrees. He had always found the neat house and garden oppressive. Much like his own parents' place. Too obsessively managed, too many things in exactly the right place. Now the tidiness, the order and gleam in the rooms in both houses seemed to him a liberation. The grandparents in Liebenau, as in Ash, were eager to help with Lawrence. Roland leaned back in his garden chair. He was barefoot. The vast complicated continent was overheating. The sound of crickets, the feel of warm dried grass on the soles of his feet and the scent of baked earth pleased him. The big thick glass was icy in his hands. When he set it down, the tinkle of the ice cubes sounded personal. He closed his eyes and indulged a lazy fantasy. He and his son would move here, migrate as if into the heat of southern Spain, take the studio room over the garage beside the house and he would work on his German, teach English in a local school, live an orderly life with a warm family setting and when Lawrence was older go fishing with him along the banks of the Aue, a river that teemed with red-spined perch, and they would take a boat southwards down the Weser, leave England behind, his private version of it, be free, everything taken care of . . . take Alissa's place, become a German, a good one.

When he woke the sun was going down. Jane was sitting opposite him, smiling. On the table before her were two candle lanterns.

"You're worn out."

"Must have been the gin. And the heat."

He went inside to get two large glasses of water.

When he returned she told him that Heinrich had gone to a committee meeting. Money had to be raised for the church roof. So she and Roland would have the conversation, the first of three, over the five days. In memory their sessions became inseparable. As a prelude, as though drawing breath, they sat quietly for a minute drinking water. The evening air was smooth and still warm. The crickets paused their racket, then resumed. From further away came a repeated high-pitched call. Mournful frogs by the river. Jane and Roland looked at each other and looked away. The weak light from the lanterns barely showed their faces. In the past, she had encouraged him to speak German. She corrected his mistakes without making him feel stupid. After a few minutes, he said, "Erzähl mir, was passiert ist." Tell me what happened. Even as he said it, he had his doubts. Was it *mich* rather than *mir*?

She understood and started without hesitation. "Of course, we thought she was in London with you, so it was a shock when she rang one afternoon from a phone box. From Murnau, of all places. She said she was coming to see us for one night. I asked her if she had the baby with her. When she said no, I knew something was wrong. Perhaps I should have phoned you. Instead, I waited for her. Two days later she appeared. One tiny suitcase, everything different. Hair cut short like a boy's and hennaed. Almost orange! Black jeans, black boots with silver studs, tiny black leather jacket. Even as she was getting out of the taxi I thought it looked like trouble. She always loved skirts and dresses. She had this little cap, a Lenin sort of thing, at a jaunty angle. Ridiculous! And pale! I thought it was pancake. But no, when we were indoors, I could see she was on the edge of total exhaustion. Her eyes, her irises were pinpricks. Isn't that something to do with drugs?"

"I don't know," Roland said. His pulse had moved up. He didn't want anything bad happening to her. Even two years ago.

"It was three in the afternoon. I offered to make her a sandwich. She just wanted a glass of water. I said her father would be back in a couple of hours and he was dying to see her. Stupid to say that. But he was worried sick. But she said she only wanted to talk to me. We went upstairs to the spare bedroom. She closed the door. In case we were interrupted, she said. I was sitting on a chair, she sat on the edge of the bed, facing me. I was very nervous and when she saw that it made her calm. Then she let me have it. She had been to our old house, the chalet in Murnau. The people there let her take a look at her bedroom. They left her alone. She told me she sat on the floor and began to cry as quietly as she could. She didn't want the couple coming up to see if she was all right. And she wasn't all right. She told me that several times, over and over. 'I wasn't all right, Mutti. I wasn't back then and I'm not all right now. It was never all right.'

"I sat there, frozen. Some damning accusation was coming my

way. I could do nothing but wait for it. Then she said it. The sort of sentence you recognise straight away as prepared, polished, worked on through nights of insomnia or hours of therapy. Was she having therapy?"

"No."

"She said, 'Mutti, I grew up in the shadow, the chill of your disappointment. My whole childhood was lived around your sense of failure. Your bitterness. You didn't become a writer. Oh, how terrible that was. You didn't become a writer. What you got instead was motherhood. You didn't hate it. You put up with it. But you barely tolerated it, this second-rate life. You think a child doesn't notice? You certainly never wanted another baby, did you? And the man you thought you married turned out to be someone else. Another disappointment and you couldn't forgive him. You were marked out for something better and it didn't happen. It made you sour, ungenerous, suspicious of anyone's success.'

"She went quiet for a bit, and I sat there waiting. Her eyes were wet. Then she said that all through her childhood and teens she had never seen me happy, really happy. I never let go, according to her. Never embraced our lives together. I never could because I thought I'd been swindled by life. That's what she said. *Betrogen.* I could never let go and be joyful and love the life I had with my daughter. And because she loved me, because she was so close she could never allow herself to be happy either. It would have been a second betrayal. Instead, she followed me, copied me, became me. She too was sour on life. Couldn't find a publisher for her two books. She too failed to become a writer. She too . . ."

Jane stopped and rubbed her forehead with her forefinger. "I don't know if it's right to tell you."

"Say it."

"All right. She too deceived herself in marriage. She thought you were a brilliant bohemian. Your piano playing seduced her. She thought you were a free spirit. Just the way I thought Heinrich was a hero of the resistance and would go on being one. You misled her. 'He's a fantasist, Mutti, he can't settle to anything. He's got problems in his past he won't even think about. He can't achieve anything. And nor can I. Together we were sinking. Then there was the baby and we sank faster. Neither of us were ever going to achieve anything. You taught me, a baby is second best. Not even second. But we even talked about having another because an only child is the saddest thing in the world. Isn't it, Mutti?'

"At this point, she stood up, so I did too. She said, 'This is what I've come to tell you. Try and think of it as good news. I'm not going to sink. I'm leaving him. And the baby. No, don't say anything. Do you think it doesn't hurt? But I have to do this now before it becomes impossible. I'm also leaving you. I refuse to follow you.'

"Now she was almost shouting at me. 'I am not going to sink! I'm going to rescue myself. And in the process I might even rescue you!'

"Then I said something stupid. I couldn't have said anything less useful to her at that moment. Trying to be nice and maternal, I suppose. The words were out before I could stop myself. I said, or I started to say, something like, 'Darling, you do realise, lots of mothers get very depressed in the baby's first few months.'

"She raised both hands, you know, in surrender, or to shut me up. She was horribly calm. She said, 'Stop. Please stop.' She came towards me. I thought she might even hit me. Very quietly she said, 'You haven't understood a thing.'

"She was edging her way past me to get to the door. I was trying to say I was sorry. Wrong thing to say. But she was out of the room and going down the stairs at speed. I followed her but I'm slow on the stairs and by the time I was down she was already outside, crossing the lawn. I had a glimpse of her through the window. She had her suitcase. I went out and called after her but she wouldn't have heard me as she slammed the gate behind her. I ran out onto the pavement. I couldn't see which way she had gone. I called her name over and over. Nothing."

Again, they sat in silence for a while. Roland tried not to dwell on her insults. A fantasist. Can't achieve anything. He let other details crowd in. Short hennaed hair. That he could imagine. He was about to ask his mother-in-law about the German police when they heard a cry from Lawrence. His room overlooked the garden and his window was open. Roland jogged towards the house. The evening could be lost if Lawrence woke to a strange room and got himself in a state. But when Roland got to his bedside the boy was asleep. He sat with him a few minutes. By the time he was back with Jane he had forgotten his question.

She had one of her own. "Don't tell me anything you don't want to but was she right, is there something in your past?"

"Nothing in particular. Usual gripes. No one's parents are perfect." Then, preferring to move the conversation on, he said, "It's there in your journals. You were frustrated. Didn't she have a case?"

"There was a grain of truth. One and a half perhaps. My fault, I did miss out on something. But Alissa had everything. See it from the point of view of our war generation. She was blessed. History was kind to her. So was the government. Nice schools, free dance and music lessons. Each year everything getting slightly better. Compared to what went before, tolerance everywhere. And we doted on her." She paused, and then, as if to clarify, "*Your* generation."

"What do you think she meant when she said she might rescue you?"

Before she spoke, she gave him a long look. A beautiful face had become commanding with age. In low light the confident gaze, the fine straight nose, the accentuated cheekbones gave her the air of a powerful woman in charge of some mighty enterprise, of an important country.

She said, "Ich habe nicht die geringste Ahnung." I have simply no idea.

➤➤

As he walked up and down the VIP lounge he was thinking of that conversation—those three evening conversations in the garden. He had reason to reflect, and time on his hands. Little by little the romance had drained out of private jet travel. The journey from London to Bristol airport had taken four hours because of an accident on the motorway. In their luxury coach they reassured themselves that their jet would be waiting for them. It wasn't. They were met by an anxious young woman in pencil skirt and starched white blouse. She collected their passports and told them that their flight to Malmö had been delayed by another two hours. The exclusive lounge was in a temporary building surrounded by a chain-link fence in a far corner of the airfield beside a long-term car park. Roland and Peter Mount and his colleagues had the place to themselves. There was a tea urn with paper cups, teabags and one bottle of milk. No coffee, nothing to eat. The terminal and its cafés were across the runway, two miles distant. There were four units of steel-framed chairs grouped around low plastic tables. Peter and his electricity friends were content to hunch together and refine their business plan. Roland sat at another unit. His reading material, snatched from the shelves as he left the house, was *Cousine Bette* in an English translation. He was aware of the voices of the next table—Peter was doing all the talking. He had developed a habit of talking over others and raising his voice whenever he thought he was about to be interrupted. Now he was taking charge of the group's agenda though they were supposed to be equal partners. It was a reminder of the Posse days when Peter, aged twenty-two, a decent lead guitarist, exulted in bossing everyone around, from roadies to venue management to fellow musicians.

Ninety minutes later the woman returned. They never discovered where she retreated to. Their plane had been diverted to collect its owner, James Tarrant III, from Lyons. Two hours passed. The update came that Mr. Tarrant was reunited with his plane. He had taken it not to Malmö but to Berlin. It would refuel there and come to collect them. In the most difficult circumstances, hotel accommodation had been secured in the city and their host would be waiting for them. The next message in the late afternoon was no surprise. Tegel airport in Berlin was having trouble with the unusual volume of traffic. Their private jet would come to collect them at nine o'clock tomorrow morning. Transport was on its way to take them to the Grand Hotel in Bristol.

It made sense. Everyone wanted to be in Berlin. Anyone with a plane of his own was heading there. So was anyone with a plane ticket. Every news organisation in the world was sending its reporters, fixers, camera teams. Foreign ministries were despatching diplomats. Military planes were crowding the skies and had priority. He had read a

hundred pages of *Cousine Bette* and could read no more. He wanted
the news. There were no papers in the lounge, no TV, no radio. The
electricity meeting had broken up long ago. After an hour the bus
came. As he was finding a seat Roland heard someone say, "I could
have told my grandchildren I was in Berlin two days after the fall of
the Wall. Now it will have to be the day after that!"

They were a noisy group at the hotel check-in. The prospect of
food and drink put Peter's lot in a jolly mood. Meeting each other,
they had been re-energised by the possibility that within a few years
they would be exceedingly rich. Roland made his excuses and went
to his room. He wanted to speak to Lawrence before his bedtime. It
was the au pair who picked up. The young Mounts and his son were
at supper. Phone conversations with Lawrence generally proceeded
by interview.

"How was it at nursery today?"

"Spiders don't bite."

"Of course they don't. Did you play with Jai?"

"We're having ice cream."

By this distracted drift Roland assumed his son was in good spirits, not missing him. It sounded like the phone had fallen to the floor.
There was laughter and one of the older kids was singing. Lawrence
shouted, "My daddy can eat swords." Then the phone was retrieved
and the line went dead.

He watched TV reports from Berlin and the studio analysis while
he ate a room-service dinner. Checkpoint Charlie was the symbolic focus. In Washington, President Reagan was triumphant. Mrs.
Thatcher, fresh from her big speech to the UN on climate change,
was circumspect. One of the talking-heads said he thought she was
troubled by the prospect of a united and resurgent Germany.

Next morning, success and limited luxury. Their plane was waiting by the VIP lounge. On board, the seats, though small and tightly
packed, were of the softest leather. Because of delays and disruption
of supplies, there was nothing to eat. At Tegel airport a bus came to
the foot of the aircraft's steps. As they boarded, a security official
checked their passports with a glance. Roland noticed that the rest of
the group, hungover and subdued from an evening in Bristol pubs,

had cases bulky enough for changes of shirts, shoes and suits. He was travelling with a small backpack—underwear, a different sweater, two thick shirts. He was wearing summer hiking boots and jeans. If the hotel was grand enough, it might not let him in. Daphne was right, he lived like a student.

As they headed in heavy traffic towards the centre he decided not to check in to the hotel just yet. Peter's group was committed to lunch with Mr. Tarrant and an afternoon of presentations. Roland asked to be set down by Potsdamer Straße, from where he walked east with the flow of the crowd. Almost nine years had passed. What luck, to be here, not Malmö. He felt an immediate easy familiarity, even though the mood was high and everything looked new. Coming the other way was a steady line of East Berliners. Lads in groups with football scarves, elderly couples, families with children, and babies in push-chairs. Roland assumed they had missed their way from Checkpoint Charlie and were heading for the bright shops of the Kurfürstendamm with their one hundred Deutsch Mark "welcome money" from the West German government. They faced cries of Willkommen! and even embraces. The TV reports of the night before made much of how the "Ossis" were easily identified by their cheap clothes, their ill-cut denim jackets. But Roland didn't see that. What they had in common was a certain dazed and tentative look. They suspected this could not last. Soon they would be summoned back East to some form of reckoning. It was inconceivable that the authorities could be so suddenly deprived of their reach into private lives.

As he walked, Roland told himself that he was scanning the crowds for the Heise family and that he was not looking out for Alissa. A divided Germany had meant less to her than to him. Even if she had come, the possibility of spotting her among tens of thousands was minute. And he did not wish to see her. Potsdamer Straße curved gently east to confront the Wall. Ahead, on a broad expanse of wasteland broken by birch trees and lamp posts, was a massive crowd. Roland passed a group of bemused West Berlin police with flowers stuffed in the buttonholes of their green jackets. He went close by the high viewing platform where visiting dignitaries were often brought to gaze across no-man's-land into the Eastern sector. Now it was so overladen with people and film crews that it looked ready to topple. As he pushed further into the crowd a great cheer went up. A crane, stark against the featureless pale sky, was beginning to lift an L-shaped section of wall, barely a metre wide. It dangled for a while, one side white, the other brightly graffitied, and slowly gyrated as if to demonstrate two domains in crazed collusion. Then, to general applause, the section was lowered into no-man's-land, where other sections had been placed upright—standing stones, Stonehenge monuments to a vanishing culture.

Roland went deeper into the crowd and soon he was carried forward by it. He couldn't stop himself scanning faces as he was carried towards the thirty-foot gap in the Wall. The youngest and fittest had scrambled up, or had been hauled up, and were sitting astride the curved concrete summit. They stretched for 200 metres, a great line of legs. One lone figure with a vague resemblance to Buster Keaton was bold enough to stand up to balance, overlooking the breach. He turned eastwards, raised both arms to make a peace sign. It was unlikely that anyone on the far side could see him.

Roland had imagined that he would be standing to one side, witness to joyful East Berliners crossing west. Instead, he was being borne by a triumphant crowd flowing east into the giant sandy meadow of no-man's-land. At last he abandoned himself to the moment. Some part of the history of the divided city, of the divided world, was his. In the crossings he had made in the late seventies, he never could have imagined a scene like this, one of such boundless significance and symbolic weight—and yet it was in the hands of beneficent crowds. They—he—were making the moment. To be standing here, treading this forbidden militarised space was as extraordinary as standing on the moon. Everyone felt it. Roland had always been sceptical of the labile moods of crowds but now he felt himself dissolved into the general joy. The grim settlement of the Second World War was ended. A peaceful Germany would be united. The Russian Empire was dissolving without bloodshed. A new Europe must emerge. Russia would follow Hungary, Poland and the rest to become a democracy. It might even lead the way. It was not so fantastical to imagine driving one day from Calais to the Bering Straits and never showing a passport.

The Cold War's nuclear menace was over. The great disarmament could begin. History books would close with this, a jubilant mass of decent people celebrating a turning point for European civilisation. The new century would be fundamentally different, fundamentally better, wiser. He had been right to say so to Daphne and Peter the week before.

He was being carried deeper into the obvious, easily forgotten fact—the Wall was mostly two parallel walls separated by the Death Strip. They were crossing it by means of a broad corridor bound left and right by chain-link fences. The space had been cleared of land-mines and mantraps. Through the fences he could see East German border guards, the Vopos, standing about in groups, most of them barely older than teenagers. Days before, their standing orders were to shoot at sight anyone venturing onto this earth. Now they had a sheepish look. He noticed how they wore their revolvers in the small of their backs. Fifty metres beyond the Vopos were multitudes of rab-bits nibbling the grass. Their golden age was coming to an end. One day soon, the developers would be moving onto their terrain.

A safety request came through a megaphone on the west side for people to spread out if they could. The good-natured crowd instantly obeyed. Roland was searching again. Could Florian and Ruth have made it here with the girls? He knew that getting out of Schwedt so soon would have been impossible. But he wanted them here. They deserved to be here. For five minutes on end, keeping apart from the flow across the abandoned land of last summer's grasses, weeds and flowers, he forgot where he was and looked only at faces.

The thrill of being in a once-forbidden place was beginning to fade. After twenty minutes of standing about in the field in wonder and taking snapshots, much of the crowd that had poured through the gap in the Wall in excitement, began to move back west. Roland followed them. It was cold if you didn't keep moving. Like the rest he had experienced the alien thrill of being on the cusp of a significant historical transition and now he wanted it again in fresh form, some-where else along the old border. Much of the remainder of his evening was a restless wandering in search of fresh evidence or enactment of the momentous event. He was always moving with the tireless crowd against a flow of people coming the other way to see what he had just seen. But he could not stop himself looking out for Alissa.

As he passed back through the gap in the Wall he was greeted with cheers and applause. Newcomers had arrived and were mistaking him and those around him for East Berliners crossing to freedom. A stooped elderly man pressed a pack of chewing gum into his hand. No point trying to give it back. Today historical consciousness was highly attuned. In 1945 a GI or a British squaddie might have tossed the same treat to this man from the turret of a tank or three-ton truck. A newly arrived film crew stopped Roland. Over the din a reporter with a microphone asked him in a mellifluous Welsh lilt if he spoke English. He nodded.

"It's a fantastic day. How do you feel?"

"I feel fantastic."

"You've just crossed no-man's-land, the notorious Death Strip. Where have you come from?"

"London."

"Jesus! Cut!" The reporter smiled pleasantly. "Sorry mate. No offence."

They shook hands and Roland turned north, keeping the Wall on his right. With thousands of others he wanted to see what was happening at the Brandenburg Gate. The light was fading by the time he arrived. A far greater crowd, and here the Wall, masking the lower portion of the monumental gate, remained intact. Standing on top of it was a line of Vopos vividly picked out by TV lights. Something comic about them, Roland thought. As though a theatrical revue was about to begin. To one side, down on the ground, was their commanding officer, smoking nervously, striding this way and that. The crowd was pushing closer to the Wall and looked ready to take it from the guards. But when someone hurled a beer can at them a great cry went up of "Keine Gewalt!" No violence! Roland pushed forwards with the rest. The soldiers looked as nervous as their officer. There were thirty of them and thousands in the crowd, easily capable of overwhelming them. Then there were boos and catcalls and slow handclaps. For several minutes no one in Roland's part of the throng could see what was happening. In a sudden surge and eddy, a motion flowing through the packed bodies, he was carried sideways and it became clear. A line of West Berlin police now stood in front of the Wall, facing the crowd, protecting the Vopos. Somewhere up the chain of command there must be deep anxiety. An incident could escalate. For years it had been predicted that the Third World War would begin with some accidental confrontation at the Wall. The communist authorities might attempt to restore the status quo. Tiananmen Square was on every mind. Memories of April's Hillsborough disaster were troubling Roland. Scores crushed to death by the helpless weight of bodies. It only needed one person to stumble. He had to get out.

He turned his back on the scene and began to make a path towards the rear, then to the side. It was not easy. The press of bodies was constant, mindlessly eastwards. In the crush, his backpack annoyed people but there was no space to take it off. It took him half an hour of shoving and muttering "entschuldigung" to get free. He found himself close to his entry point, on the south side so it made sense to wander back in the direction he had come. He needed to pee and there were trees along the way.

He returned to the Potsdamer section to find that darkness had not dispelled the crowds. People had climbed up the birch trees and hung there in the shadows like enormous bats. Why was he here again? Because he was looking for her, not just glancing at passers-by but actively searching. He had convinced himself that it was impossible that she was not here. He leaned by a support strut of the viewing platform while people pushed past. TV lights gave him sufficient illumination. He felt stupid, irresolute, with no idea of what he wanted or would say if she appeared. Should he call out her name, touch her arm? It didn't feel like love. He was in no state for recrimination. He just wanted to *see* her. Meaningless. She was at home somewhere, watching it on TV. But no, he couldn't shake her off.

After half an hour he thought he had seen every version of the human face, every variation on a limited theme. Eyes, nose, mouth, hair, colour. But still they kept coming, each infinitesimal shift promoting vast difference. Did he know what he was looking for? Short hair grown long, still hennaed? It wouldn't matter. He would know her by her presence.

At last he gave up and moved on. Soon he was walking by the Wall, along Niederkirchner Straße. In white paint a graffito read, *Sie kamen, sie sahen, sie haben ein bisschen eingekauft*—they came, they saw, they did a little shopping. In historical Berlin, Caesar would certainly be remembered. Roland slowed by the remnants of the demolished Gestapo headquarters. There was nothing left above ground. He stopped to look down. A row of white-tiled basement cells glinted in the semi-dark. Here, Jews, communists, social democrats, homosexuals, countless others spent their final moments in agony and terror. The past, the modern past, was a weight, a burden of piled rubble, forgotten grief. But the weight on him was at one remove. It barely weighed at all. The accidental fortune was beyond calculation, to have been born in 1948 in placid Hampshire, not Ukraine or Poland in 1928, not to have been dragged from the synagogue steps in 1941 and brought here. His white-tiled cell—a piano lesson, a premature love affair, a missed education, a missing wife—was by comparison a luxury suite. If his life so far was a failure, as he often thought, it was in the face of history's largesse.

He arrived at Checkpoint Charlie in a better state of mind. The opposing tides of jubilation and the pointless searching had brought him to some stillness and neutrality. He could stop scanning faces. The scene here was as shown on TV—cheering, applauding crowds greeting pedestrians and Trabbies with their exultant passengers spraying *Sekt* out the windows, the patient lines for welcome money. He too had once passed many dull hours queuing here. What he saw in addition was the frustration of film crews trying to capture the brilliant moment without other film crews in shot.

He was moved by what he saw and joined the applause but stayed only fifteen minutes. The Café Adler was close by and he was thirsty and feeling the cold.

He had often come here in his Berlin days. The place was in the old East European style, spacious, high-ceilinged, with an air of ancient self-assurance. The waiters were real waiters, bred from birth, not aspiring actors and graduate students. Tonight it was packed, and overloaded with winter coats and scarves piled on chairs. No more room for them elsewhere. It was clamorous with urgent conversation, the warm air was moist with excited breath. Instantly his glasses steamed up. He had nothing to wipe them with so he waited for them to clear while he stood by the door. The din of raised voices, a vague, not unpleasant sense of exclusion, put him in mind of parties he had been to where he had known no one. But here it was not the case. As his lenses warmed and cleared he saw her, thirty feet away perhaps, at a small round table. On it were two coffees. She was in conversation with a man about her age. Roland approached them slowly. She was turned towards her companion, listening closely. Roland was only seconds away and she had not seen him yet.

# 7

He knew that it was illusory, the silence that fell on the Café Adler crowd as he made his way between the tables. No one noticed him and they all went on talking. But the illusion was vivid, a form of narcissism or, closely related, paranoia. The meeting or confrontation ahead would be momentous, but only for him and perhaps, so he hoped, for Alissa. When he stopped in front of her table the restaurant roar and clatter seemed to surge back into life like a radio abruptly switched on at reckless volume. A world-historical moment needed to be loud. For several seconds he had observed unseen Alissa and her friend and he had drawn conclusions. But Roland still did not know what he wanted. To demand an explanation, satisfy his curiosity, level charges, expose his wounds? None of these. Not even to propose a reasonable formalised separation? His needs were vague. More like an unbroken habit of wanting her, a longing that included but went beyond the erotic. Something childlike about it, innocent, fierce. Probably love. In the seconds before she saw him he felt that fundamentally little had changed between them. He had a right to be here. She was his wife, after all, even though he had abandoned hope of getting her back. He was right to approach her even if he did not know what he wanted. It was his right to want nothing.

She looked well—as much as ever, more than ever. No sign of the studded leather and cropped hennaed hair that surprised her mother three years before. Alissa's chin and cheek were lightly cupped in her hand and she was turned towards her friend, fully engaged. She wore a loose thick sweater that drooped in swags about the elbows, tight jeans, dark red fashion-hiking boots. Her hair, mid-length, looked expensively cut. She had money. Well, so did he. But he was dressed like a student hitch-hiker, with backpack to match. Between her and her companion, between the coffee cups, was a face-down book, a thick paperback. The man at her table was slender, artificially blond, with a miniature gold peace sign in his left earlobe. He was the first to look up. He stopped talking and placed his hand on Alissa's wrist. But he did not let it linger there, Roland noted. Lover's guilt. She made no movement but simply glanced to the side and upwards, and only then did she slowly turn her head to align it with her gaze and fix it on Roland's. What struck him was that her shoulders seemed to sag as her breath left her in a quick sigh. His impression was of her disappointment. Roland Baines, just when she needed him least. He thought his own expression was to the warm side of neutral as he made a faint nod of greeting. But on her he did not see even the palimpsest of a smile. He lip-read her murmured, "Das ist mein Mann."

Her friend did better. He immediately stood and extended his hand. "Rüdiger."

"Roland."

Rüdiger pulled out a chair, Roland sat down.

"The waiter is hard to find today. May I get you something?"

His manner was softly courteous. Roland asked for a large coffee. It was inevitable, obvious, but still, he was amazed to be sitting directly opposite his wife. As Rüdiger set off across the room, Roland regretted that he would be left alone with her. There was so much to say that nothing came to mind. She was looking past his shoulder, not meeting his eye. The sudden familiarity of her overwhelmed him. Different emotions came in succession—anger, sorrow, love, then anger again. He had to suppress them but he was not sure he could.

He knew her well enough. She would not let herself be the first to speak. He sounded feeble in his own ears when at last he said, "What incredible events." The end of the Cold War was their small talk.

"Yes. I came as quickly as I could."

He was about to ask where from but in the same breath she added quickly, "How is Larry?"

He missed the sorrow that lay behind her lightly posed question and heard only a trivial enquiry. It startled him, the sudden force of his own feelings. This was what he carried with him all the time and barely knew it. He leaned back in his chair to increase the distance between them. He was determined to sound level, unhurt, but his voice was hoarse.

"What do you care about Lawrence?"

They were looking straight at—straight into—each other. They knew too much. To his naive surprise, he saw the tears swelling over pupils and irises, left eye, then the right, and spilling down her cheeks. So copious. With a cry, she lifted her hands to her face just as the waiter, an old man with a penitent face-down scoliosis, arrived with a tray of three coffees. Right behind him was Rüdiger, who helped the waiter set out the cups, paid him and, still standing, said to both, "I'm so sorry. Should I leave you now?"

Roland and Alissa were already lost, after only five minutes. Again, he didn't want to be left alone. Having someone there, even her lover, would keep them both within bounds.

Raising his voice above the din, he said, "Bitte bleib." Please stay.

Rüdiger sat. The two men drank their coffee without speaking. Alissa recovered slowly. Roland felt queasy in anticipation of the moment when his rival put an arm around her shoulder or whispered some comfort in her ear. But Rüdiger stared straight ahead, warming his hands round his coffee. Alissa stood abruptly and said that she was going to the bathroom. This was awkward too, to be left alone with the boyfriend. Roland regretted coming to the Adler. He felt incapable, clumsy, absurd. Rüdiger seemed at ease or, at least, patient, and leaned back in his chair. After he had finished his coffee, he took from his pocket a small paperback and began to read. Roland glimpsed the cover. Heine. Selected poems. The line came to him, and it was as if someone else was speaking it. It was a cliché, familiar to every German schoolchild, like Wordsworth's daffodils or Larkin's Mum and Dad. He didn't care. The words simply left him. "Ich weiss nicht, was soll es bedeuten . . ." I don't know what it might mean . . .

Rüdiger looked up and smiled. "Dass ich so traurig bin . . ." That I am so sad . . .

Roland started on the third line, "Ein Märchen . . ." But he immediately felt a stupid lump in his throat and, inconveniently, he could not go on. Ridiculous. He didn't want the other man to see. Sadness and exasperation, self-pity, tiredness, he would never know. This was a poem Jane Farmer had shown him. Perhaps it was nostalgia for the days of unbroken family.

Rüdiger leaned forward. "So you like Heine."

Roland took a deep breath and found his voice. "The little I know."

"I should tell you something, Roland. In order to be clear."

"Yes?"

"In case you think it. I'm not Alissa's close friend. Lover, or how you say it. I'm her, uh, scheisse, Verleger?"

"Publisher?"

"I mean Lektor, editor. Lucretius Books, Munich." To Roland's blank look he added, "She didn't tell you her news? I suppose she didn't. So." He made a loose hopeless gesture with his hand.

"So?"

"Then it's for her to tell you. She's coming now."

They watched as she approached. Roland knew that walk. She would be brisk and want to leave. He did too. He was tired of the clamour of celebration, the breath and bodies and coats around him, hour after hour of other people. He also feared more confrontation. Two minutes was enough.

She said as she arrived, "I'd like to get out of here."

Rüdiger stood immediately. They stepped aside for a quick conversation. In the seconds he had to himself, Roland imagined being somewhere cool and treeless, Scotland, Uist, Muck, a rocky coast, an ultramarine sea. Alone. He picked up his backpack. Rüdiger and Alissa briefly embraced and as he walked away, he raised a hand towards Roland in casual parting.

She turned and said, "There's something I have to say to you. But not here."

He followed her out. The crowds were pouring towards them from the open checkpoint. Many had their welcome money and were eager for sightseeing. There were scores, hundreds of children in a state of high excitement, skipping and bouncing over the pavement. Alissa was heading against the flow towards Kochstraße into what they would have to learn to call the old East. Roland was a couple of paces behind. Neither could bear another attempt at small talk as they went along. They went down a narrower street that seemed to have no name. She stopped just as it started to rain slightly. Here, under a bare plane tree, they would have their conversation. Then she saw across the road an alley.

They went down it a little way. It was barely ten feet wide, partly cobbled, before it turned to mud and the summer's dead weeds where the cobbles had been lifted. There was a block of yellow light from a window above and they stood just near its edge, almost within its glow. Finally, they had silence. She leaned back against the wall. Facing her, he did the same—and waited. They ignored the cold rain on their bare heads. He knew that giving a speech was not her style. After a while he said softly, "So, something you have to tell me."

He said it, even though he would have preferred not to hear her, anticipating a stream, a river, of accusation. When he was the injured party. But he did not feel like complaining or saying anything. He was in a state of helpful numbness. Unreal indifference. He might regret it later. But whatever was said here, nothing would change. She would continue with her determined business. He would go home. His life would go on as before. Lawrence was happy enough, long used to life with a single parent. The world was about to become a better place. He remembered and rehearsed his moment of optimism in no-man's-land. Only three hours ago. Already it was expected that the satellites of the Soviet Empire would turn West, stand in line for the Common Market, for NATO. But what need of NATO? He saw it clearly—Russia, a liberal democracy, unfolding like a flower in spring. Nuclear weapons negotiated downwards to extinction. Then mega-tides of spare cash and good intentions flowing like fresh water, cleansing the dirt of every social problem. The general well-being refreshed, schools, hospitals, cities renewed. Tyrannies dissolving across the South American continent, the Amazon rainforests rescued and treasured—let poverty be razed instead of trees. For millions, time for music, dancing, art and celebration. Mrs. Thatcher had demonstrated it at the UN—the political right had finally understood climate change and believed in action while there was time. On this, all could agree and Lawrence, his children and their children were

going to be fine. Berlin, Roland saw clearly, had sustained him back
in the seventies and today gave him a perspective on the petty sor-
rows and indignities of his personal life. Now that he had seen her,
Alissa had shrunk to life-size, to one more person struggling to make
sense, as vulnerable as he was. He could leave now, take the U-Bahn
to Uhlandstraße, find his hotel, at the bar raise a glass to the future
with Peter and his electric pals. Perhaps they had made their deal. But
he felt he owed Alissa something. What did she owe him?

She remained silent as she stood against the streaked concrete wall
of the alley. The faint rain continued. She took her tote bag from her
shoulder and settled it between her feet.

"Come on, Alissa. Say it, or I'm leaving."

"OK." She reached in her bag for a cigarette, lit it and drew on
it hard. This was new. "I've imagined saying this to you for three
years. It always came easily, it flowed. But now . . . all right. When
Larry was around three months old, I had an important realisation.
Perhaps it was obvious to everyone else who knew me well. To me it
was a revelation. We took the baby for a walk in Battersea Park in the
afternoon. When we came back he slept. You wanted sex. I didn't. We
had a sort of row. You remember?"

He shook his head before he realised that he actually did not
remember. But it sounded true.

"I went upstairs and lay on the bed, too tired even to sleep. That
was when it came to me, I was living my mother's life, retracing its
pattern exactly. Some literary ambition, then love, then marriage,
then baby, the old ambitions crushed or forgotten and the predictable
future stretching ahead. And bitterness. It horrified me, how her bitterness would become my inheritance. I could feel her life dragging at
mine, pulling me down with her. These thoughts wouldn't go away. I
kept thinking of her journals. The story of how she almost became a
writer, how she failed and how her failure was what I grew up with.
Over the next few weeks I realised that I was going to leave. Even
as we were talking about having another child I was making plans.
I was two people at once. I had to make something in my life, something more than a baby. I was going to achieve what she couldn't or
wouldn't. Even though I loved Larry so much. And you. At first I

thought I should explain everything. But you would have fought me, you would have talked me out of it. I felt so guilty, it wouldn't have been hard . . ."

The words faded on her lips and she was staring at her feet. Was she accusing him of failing to persuade her to stay? He was struggling again with his confusion. Ah, the great consumer marketplace of self-realisation, whose lethal enemy was the selfishly mewling baby in league with the husband and his absurd requests. He had crushed ambitions of his own, had put in the nights and days with the neonate. But they were not here in a wet alley to conduct a post-marital row. His equanimity, or the appearance of it, was still on top, just. He said, "Go on."

"I've lost you already. I can tell. It's not worth the bother."

She knew him well. He said, "I'm listening."

After a pause she said, "Perhaps I was wrong. I thought that it had to be total and it had to be quick. It was cruel and I'm sorry. Really sorry . . . It was always bad enough, your sex-every-day problem. But the baby . . . his needs, he was annihilating me. The two of you . . . I was nothing. I had nothing. No thoughts, no personality, no wishes except for sleep. I was sinking. I had to get out. The morning I left . . . walked to the Tube, it was . . . but I'm not going to describe it. You're a good father and Larry was tiny and I knew he'd be OK. And that you would be too, sooner or later. I wasn't OK but I'd made my choice and I did what I had to do. This."

She was reaching into her shoulder bag again, taking out the book he had seen in the café. She took a couple of steps and gave it to him.

"It's the English proof. It's coming out the same time as here. In six weeks."

He slipped it into his backpack and got ready to go. "Thank you."

"Is that all you're going to say?"

He nodded.

"Do you remotely understand how difficult it's been historically for women to create, to be artists, scientists, to write or paint? My story means nothing to you?"

He shook his head and began to walk away. A grown man in a sulk? Pathetic. So he changed his mind and went back to her. "I'll tell you your story. You wanted to be in love, you wanted to be married, you wanted a baby, and it all came your way. Then you wanted something else."

The rain was starting again and falling heavily. He turned to leave but she held on to his sleeve. "Before you go. Tell me something about Larry. Please. Anything."

"It's just like you said. He's OK."

"You're punishing me."

"Come and see him. Anytime. He'd love that. Stay with us, or with Daphne and Peter. I mean it." Suddenly he wanted to take her hand. Instead, he said it again. "Alissa, I really mean it."

"You know that's not possible."

He looked at her and waited.

She said, "I'm just starting another . . . a book. If I saw him, it would be all over."

He had never known such a mix of intense and contrary feelings, one of which was sadness, for he suspected that they would never meet again. Another was anger. A shrug was the least appropriate signal of such turmoil, but that was all he could manage. He paused a moment to check if there was anything more he could give or if she had more to tell him. But they were mute, there was nothing, so he set off into the rain.

➤➤

He was in no mood for the confines and crowds of the U-Bahn so he walked back through the checkpoint, took a long circuitous route towards the Tiergarten, then turned west to his hotel. The bar was deserted and it was only ten o'clock. The concierge confirmed that his English friends were out. All the excitement was further east. For an hour he sat on a high stool at the bar and slowly drank a beer while he traced the long day in his thoughts, a day that had started in a temporary building on the far side of Bristol airport. He was feeling good, glad, even proud, to have seen the breaches in the Wall and the crowds pushing through. He told himself he was feeling better now for having met Alissa. It was as though he had been cured of a prolonged illness, only known or understood when it was relieved. Like a background sound that suddenly ceases. He believed he was no longer in love. Most vivid among the things she had said was that the force of Lawrence's needs and his own had caused her to feel she was sinking. Yes, his desires . . . But. But hers were lusty and urgent at the time and she had other needs too, which he had tried to meet. Helped her with her two books in English, typed up two drafts of the second, made a thousand suggestions, most of which she took, got involved with the rewriting of the first. He had struggled with her alienated prose, the staccato verbless sentences, her heroine's obscure motivations. They had shared the pressure of Lawrence's needs, which were total. All three were new to the experience, all three had needs. But it was time to get beyond this indignant voice in the head. It was over. He decided at the bar that he had laid a ghost. She had explained why she vanished. Her friends, including Daphne, who had been critical of her would be interested to know. And he was free now. He might begin to teach himself to admire from a distance her commitment to writing. Even as he thought it he felt the bitterness return. He was not there yet.

He went upstairs to his room, a suite far grander than anything he was used to. How kind of Mr. Tarrant. Roland sat on the edge of the bed and ate all the courtesy chocolates, kiwis, physalises and salted nuts and drank a litre of carbonated water. Then he took a long shower, put on a clean t-shirt and lay on the bed. After hesitating, he took out her book and felt its weight in his hands. It was heavy. He studied its title on the plain cover, *The Journey*—a little dull, he thought—and the novelty of her name in large capitals. Alissa J. Eberhardt. He glanced at the end. Seven hundred and twenty-five pages. And the dedication? Did he imagine it would be him? It was to her parents. Good. He turned the page. She had translated it herself. He turned another and read the first paragraph. He paused, read it again, and groaned. He read five pages and stopped, went back and read them again—and groaned. He started from the beginning and read to the end of a section, sixty-five pages. An hour and a half had passed. He let the book fall from his hands and lay still, staring at the ceiling. This was what she had left him for. Start again. See the world as if for the first time. He had confidence these days in his judgement. Something was happening to his body. A tingling, a sensation of lifting off. Even now, after one chapter, he could see the problem—the problem for himself.

The setting was 1940, the aerial bombardment of London, the Blitz. The first paragraphs describe a 500-pound bomb penetrating the roof of a terraced house in the east of the city. An entire family on its way too late to a shelter is killed. Observing the aftermath, among the firemen, ambulances, neighbours, police and onlookers, is a young woman, Catherine. She turns away and walks towards her lodgings. She works in the typing pool at a government ministry. She also puts in a few hours a week in the office of a literary magazine. No one there notices her much. She watches and listens to various writers as they pass through the office. Many of them bear the weight of great fame. They are self-declared or generally acknowledged as geniuses. She keeps a notebook and has quiet ambitions of her own. The London she inhabits is dusty and dim, and fearful. The food is vile, her little room in Bethnal Green is cold. She misses her parents and brother. She has a brief affair with a man she suspects is a criminal. The sex they have is closely described and oddly joyful.

All this should have been a depressing start for the reader, but it was not and this was his problem. He could feel it line by line, everything he had thought and felt was coming apart. The prose was beautiful, crisp, artful, the tone from the first lines had authority and intelligence. The eye was exact, unforgiving, compassionate. In some of the starkest scenes there was a near-comic sense of both human inadequacy and courage. There were paragraphs that rose from Catherine's limited perspective to provide a broad historical awareness— destiny, catastrophe, hope, uncertainty. An invasion has been averted in the summer in the great aerial battle. But the possibility lingers in the evening shadows as Catherine hurries home from the ministry to cook her meagre supper. It was a world once evoked by Elizabeth Bowen, but the writing here was more finely turned, more conscious of its surface, which was dazzling. If there was an influence, a guiding spirit hidden in the folds of the prose, it was Nabokov. It was that good. He could not relate these pages to Alissa's previous two novels written in English. Their solipsistic disassociated methods had been abandoned in favour of realism, personal, social, historical.

He read on until 4 a.m., to the end of a chapter on page 187. She had found something new. There had been a promise of grandeur in the overture. Now he knew it was going to be fulfilled. The novel was big in several senses. She might have set out to write her mother's story from the journals. But Alissa was moving far beyond it. In 1946 Catherine meets an American lieutenant in occupied France and, needing his help, has sex with him for two nights. The reflections that follow, the narrator's rather than the heroine's, represent a set piece in high style on compromise and moral necessity. There were many such asides—how language, German, English, French, Arabic, shape perception, how culture shapes language. There was another set piece, a comic scene by a lake near Strasbourg that made Roland laugh against his will and laugh again when he turned back to reread it. Later she meets a young French woman who has been tarred and feathered. There follows a long aside on the nature of retribution. She has an affair with an Algerian Muslim who fought for the Free French. Their love ends in a comedy of misunderstanding. In a barracks prison in Munich she has a long conversation with a high-ranking Gestapo officer awaiting trial in Nuremberg. He speaks freely to her. He has nothing to lose because he mistakenly believes he will be hanged. This gives rise to a meditation on the nature of cruelty and the imagination. The description of Munich in ruins has a hallucinatory quality. In a departure from the source, it looks like Catherine will make it across the Alps to Lombardy and it will be a dangerous journey. She will lose a trusted new friend. As early as chapter five it is hinted that the White Rose movement lies in Catherine's future. Roland saw Jane Farmer in Catherine, and he saw Alissa too. In none of the men encountered along the way so far had he seen himself. He was relieved, but his vanity kept him alert to the prospect.

He got up from the bed and went to the bathroom to brush his teeth. Then he stood at a window looking down into an empty side street. Still a long way from the November dawn. Then, to his surprise, he saw a family, parents, three children, surely from the East, coming slowly along the pavement. Dreamlike steps. How much easier it would have been if she had deserted her son and husband to write a mediocre novel. Then he could set loose his contempt. But this . . . He thought of their sorry little house in Clapham Old Town, two up, three down, leaking, damp, crammed with books, papers, useless portions of household items waiting without hope to be repaired and reunited, clothes and shoes that could be of use but never would be, electric leads for lost or abandoned devices, light bulbs, batteries, transistor radios that might still work—but who would ever set aside the minutes to find out? Nothing could be discarded. Two adults, a baby, broken nights, excrement and milk, laundry piles, a small shared table in the bedroom to work on, otherwise the kitchen table piled with its immovable litter. Face it. Would she, could she, have written *The Journey* there? The lapidary prose, the high-flying digressions offered up to the ghost of George Eliot, whom Catherine admires, the fine painfully attuned consciousness of the heroine, the hovering watchful eye, the ever-generous tolerant narrative self-consciously organising, as if in slow motion right before the reader, the vast body of its material? No, impossible, no one could conceive a book of such ambition and execution in that house. Unless she was alone there. Or rather, taking the other view, yes, it was more than possible—it was her duty to write in whatever place, in whatever situation, including motherhood, her own grown-up decisions had landed her. But that was unreal. He knew Auden's famous line. He must forgive her for writing well. As unbearable as not forgiving her. Had she not been self-serving and cold in withdrawing her love? But now, in this bound proof she offered unlimited creative warmth. Paragon of humanist virtue! What a deception. Permitted only in fiction.

Dangerously, it was down to this—he loved her novel already and he loved her for writing it. All that steady thinking at the bar downstairs was undone. No ghost was laid and he should write to her. Forget everything that passed between us. It's probably, no, it *is* a masterpiece. He had to tell her, before anyone else did. But he wouldn't. He had failed to ask for her address—a weak excuse! What stood in his way was his ridiculous pride.

➤➤

A little before 5 a.m. on a Saturday in mid-February, Lawrence brought two stuffed toys into his father's bed and, eager for the day, sitting upright in the cold bedroom, began to recite the stream of his thoughts, some of it spoken, some chanted—recent events, story fragments, rhymes, and a run-through of names, the entire cast of his busy life, which included his friends, teachers, four grandparents, Roland's friends, certain soft toys, Daphne, the neighbour's dog, Daddy and Mummy. Roland lay listening, not charmed, waiting, hoping for Lawrence's energies to run down. Demanding it was pointless. After half an hour the boy subsided and, with no school, they slept until well after seven thirty. At breakfast Lawrence sat on Roland's knee working away at a piece of a building set that had fascinated him this week—a plastic bolt, nut and washer. He screwed the nut onto the bolt until the washer locked in place with a satisfying snap. He unscrewed the nut, turned it over, screwed it down against the washer—in place with a different click. What engaged him was that there were two ways of getting it right. Roland was opening a letter from his old school. The secretary was responding to his query of a month ago. The typing was neat. A word processor. Nearly everyone he knew had one now but he and they complained about them, about printer "interfaces," and having to learn coded instructions. People, Roland included, urged the laggards to get one. It would save time, they said. Then they complained about lost work, wasted hours, bitter frustration. It might have made sense to resist. Sometimes he thought he might look out his old portable typewriter. It was in its case, somewhere under a pile of books.

The school secretary had looked through the files and regretted that she could be of little help. Miss Cornell had left the school in 1965, twenty-five years ago. The forwarding address was Erwarton. The bursar, who had lived in the village all his life, thought Miss Cornell had moved to Ireland but was not sure of the date. She left no address with the neighbours. The secretary closed by wondering if Roland was aware that the school would be shutting down for good in July.

Their Saturday was like many others. Ritual tidying up the house, for which Lawrence gave willing token assistance. Scooting on Clapham Common, lunch at the Windmill pub with friends who had children Lawrence's age. In the afternoon, a play at the children's puppet theatre in Brixton, tea at the house of Lawrence's current best friend, Ahmed, then home. Supper, bath, a thrilling game of snap, stories, bed.

That evening Roland copied out a couple of translated Arabic poems in celebration of wine and love for Epithalamium Cards. He suspected from Oliver Morgan's evasive attitude lately that the enterprise was coming to an end or was about to change. That would be fine. He was tiring of it. He reread the letter from school. It had been on his mind during the day. He was surprised by the tension in his stomach at the sight of the familiar device at the top of the letter, a wolf's head in profile with the Latin inscription underneath. Berners Hall. Five years of his life. All the routine, the deprivation, his turning away from friendships, his flight from her. It stirred him strangely to see her name in print as if in a book, and the name Erwarton. Moving to Ireland, without him. He stood up from the desk in his bedroom, peeped in at Lawrence and went downstairs to sprawl on an armchair. Yes, he felt the reverberation of old longings. The desperation. He had not seen her in twenty-six years and it had crept up on him, a hollow sense of being bereft. He indulged it. Why not? It was harmless. So was his indignation. She had left him behind. Where in Ireland, why, and doing what, and with whom? Another schoolboy perhaps.

In the summer holidays of 1964, he was staying with his sister and her first husband near Farnborough. Roland wanted a job—not easy in Germany, where his father, now the Major, had been posted. He was in his bedroom after work when he opened with shaky fingers the brown envelope that contained his O level results. He sat on the bed staring at the list, trying to make one particular letter look different. Eleven subjects and *he hadn't scraped through one.* The flimsy printed slip with "F" by every subject was a physical shock. Even English. Everyone said you had to be a moron to fail English. Even music. He hadn't bothered to learn the right kind of stuff. No sixth form then, no English, French and German A levels, no university. He had always thought he'd get through a half-dozen O levels on his wits. Eleven times "F," machine-printed like a telegram, delivered to inform him eleven times over what a Failure, a Fraud and a Fool he was. He was almost sixteen. The examiners had not been impressed by his precocious sexual experience.

That summer he had been working as a labourer for a landscape-gardening company. He was getting half the adult wage. He hated it. The boss, the man they called the gaffer, frightened him. Now it could become his sort of life. With these results the school would not accept him in the sixth form. Most boys clocked up nine or ten passes. He was out.

It was fortunate that his parents had both left school at fourteen and would not grasp the scale of his disaster. His father had lied about his age to join the army at the age of seventeen. He was a great believer in starting at the bottom. Rosalind went straight from school into service as a chambermaid. In the wider family no one was expected to stay on at school past sixteen. No one ever had. The shame was all his own. He couldn't even tell his sister. Susan would have been cheerful and consoling, full of practical advice. The only contemporary he could have told would have been the boy with a worse result. That was not possible. He knew what he had to do, and it was making him sick with anticipation because he knew what she would say. The phone box was half a mile away. He reversed the charges as usual. As soon as she picked up he told her.

Miriam said simply, "They won't take you back."

"No."

"So what now?"

"I don't know."

"You don't have a plan?"

"No."

"Then you'd better come and live with me."

He felt his legs go weak. He slumped against the side of the kiosk. His heart hurt from thumping. If someone had tapped on the glazed door and offered him eleven grade "A" passes, he would have had to refuse.

"I'd have to get a job."

"No you don't. Just come. I'll look after you. You'll be fine."

He was silent, as if thinking this through. But she already knew his answer.

The next day he was back to digging drainage ditches with two older men, well into their forties. They were working on a patch of weedy land under the flight path of the Farnborough airfield. All day, fighter jets and lumbering transport planes screamed or thundered above him. Too close. At first he had instinctively ducked as they came in. It was impossible not to stop digging and watch them. But it became possible because the gaffer, Mr. Heron, shouted at them afterwards. In terms as loud as the fighters he reminded them that they were not paid to be plane spotters.

The previous month all the papers had carried the new pictures of the moon sent back by an American spacecraft. A thousand times better than any image seen through a telescope. The sharp images of craters and their shadows had excited him. Everyone involved must have had far more qualifications than he would ever have. So too did the pilots dropping bombs on north Vietnam. Even some of the Beatles, still triumphant across America, had been to art college. Mick Jagger had been to the LSE. All weekend Roland luxuriated in premonitions of doom, even as he knew he was deceiving himself. The reality was overwhelming in its simplicity. He had no other choice. He had been condemned to a life of erotic bliss.

On Monday after work, he found another letter, handwritten, postmarked Ipswich. Good news. Mr. Clayton, the English teacher, was writing to explain that he had intervened with the headmaster. At first he had made no headway. Then the physics teacher, Mr. Bramley, had pitched in. Next, Mr. Clare had told the tone-deaf head that Baines was a "one-in-a-million" pianist and had shown him the Norwich press cutting. Reluctantly, an exception was granted. It was agreed that Baines was a bright boy whose potential was obscured by his exam results. He was permitted after all to join the sixth form in September. "You're going to have to work hard," Clayton wrote. "You'd be a bloody fool not to. Peter Bramley, Merlin Clare and I are out on a limb here pleading your case. Don't you dare let us down. I've written to your parents to tell them we're expecting you. Don't worry. I've assumed you haven't told them your results."

Roland took the letter upstairs, removed his boots and lay on the bed. Two years ago, for just ten minutes, he had impressed the physics teacher. Not since. He had approached him after class. His question was genuine. If he tied a piece of string to one end of a twelve-inch ruler and pulled gently, but not enough to overcome the friction between the ruler and the table it rested on, then something must be happening between the front of the ruler where the string was attached and the far end. Some force or tension was running from front to back. And if he pulled a little harder, the ruler would start to move, all of it, front and back at the same time. So information of a sort must be instantaneously transmitted along the ruler. And yet Mr. Bramley had told the class that nothing could travel faster than the speed of light.

He had been too interested in the cleverness of his question to remember the explanation the physics teacher had given. Two years later Roland wished he had kept his mouth shut. And what had he ever done to impress Mr. Clayton? It must have been his *Lord of the Flies* essay. As Roland lay on the bed, gaze fixed on one polystyrene ceiling tile, he accepted that he had truly deceived himself. His terrible exam results had promised a grand adventure. A beautiful break with routine, a wild sortie, a liberation, a Gurji camp at the time of Suez. Now, without his permission, the adventure had been cancelled and a weight of expectation, of duty and boring scholarly labour had been laid on him. He had been devising a simple explanation for his parents. He had been about to tell them he did not want more school. He wanted to get on with life. His father would have understood and his mother had no voice in the matter. After a personal letter from his teacher they would be proud of him staying on, and naturally insistent.

When he told Miriam on the phone she was angry with everyone. He knew she would be. She was also seductive.

"That Clayton's an idiot. I know him. Always interfering. It's none of his business."

"I know."

"You're old enough to be making your own decisions."

"I'll still be coming to see you. It'll be just like before."

"I want you here all the time."

"Yes."

"I want you to leave school. I want you in my bed."

He supported himself against the kiosk door. His head was light. It was getting hard to breathe in the narrow space.

"All night, do you understand? And in the morning. Waking up together every morning. Can you imagine that?"

"Yes." He said it faintly and she didn't hear him. He repeated the word, the delicious fateful assent. To the night, to the morning.

"So you're leaving school."

"OK. I will . . . but I can't. Look, I'll think about it."

"You'll phone me again in one hour."

This continued over many calls. When he listened to her he was ready to obey. He was almost sixteen and he was free to choose. She was right. He had to be with her. All night, every night. The rest was trivial. When he came away from the phone box he was back in the real world, with real people and what they were doing for him and wanting from him. He had already written a letter of thanks to his English teacher. He had confirmed to his parents that he would be staying on at school for his A levels, English, French and German. Another two years. But Miriam was also the real world and she was the only one actually talking to him.

It took courage to say to her during one conversation, "But what am I going to do all day while you're out teaching?"

She didn't hesitate. "You'll stay in your pyjamas and wait for me. I'll lock your clothes in the shed."

They both began to laugh. He knew that this was a tease. That really, she expected him to be back at school. But he was powerfully drawn to the idea of himself in pyjamas all day with just one purpose in life. Finally they reached a compromise. He would come to her well before term started and then . . .

She said it softly over the phone. "My darling, we will see."

Rather than confront Mr. Heron, Roland walked out on the job, sacrificing a week's wages. He had saved sixty pounds in one-pound notes, a thick wad inside his buttoned-up back pocket as he followed a porter with his trunk and saw it loaded into the guard's van of the Liverpool Street train to Ipswich. She was waiting on the platform for him. In greeting, they hardly touched each other or spoke. That was for later. In silence they hauled his trunk over the footbridge. Roland was pleased that when he showed his child's ticket to the inspector at the gate, he wouldn't believe he was under sixteen. He was ready for that and showed his passport.

Miriam said, "See. He's not a cheat. You should apologise."

The man, not so old, but short and shrivelled, spoke quietly to her. "Just doing my job, ma'am."

She put her hand on his arm and said warmly, "I know you are. I *know* you are." As they crossed the gloomy concourse, they had a fit of giggles. He admired the way she had parked right outside the station, half on the pavement, right under a "no parking" sign. For him. A joyous sensation of freedom hit him hard, right in his chest. Of course, he wasn't going back to school. What reckless folly that would be. With an effort they squeezed his trunk onto the back seat of her car. The rear door would not close. She took some string from her handbag and passed it to him. He threaded the handles of the trunk and door together, secured them with a reef knot. He felt not only liberated but capable, more so when he sat beside her and they kissed at length with no thought for the scores of passengers coming out of the station entrance. Kissing in a car! In his swoon he felt he was in a movie, that this was Paris, not Ipswich. He should take up smoking, however much—to his shame—tobacco repelled him. They had not seen each other in five weeks. Even in his most dedicated fantasies, he had forgotten so much. The warmth, the feel of her, now the touch of her hand on his nape, and then her tongue. He was in the early approaches, the long ice-slide of an orgasm, right here in her car. That never happened in Truffaut movies. Wisely, gently, he pulled away from her. She reached down in one smooth movement to turn the ignition key and flick the car into gear and bump off the kerb and into the flow of traffic. She was so much more in control than he was. He must learn to be cool.

But ten minutes later, as they turned onto the narrow road by the boatyard and went along the foreshore, he experienced some churning minutes of excitement and dread. This was the familiar route he had first taken with his parents on the 202 bus on a warm day like this. Now, the big blue space of river and sky belittled him, pulled him back into bewildered childhood. There was nothing in this landscape which did not anticipate the destination and his immediate future. Berners Hall. The oak trees on the far bank were school trees. Likewise the telegraph poles and their dipping wires, the uncommon pastel green of the roadside grass, the warm air that carried the rotten salt mud tang of the foreshore. A school smell. All of it belonged to school, and so did he.

"You've gone quiet," she said. They were passing the concrete water tower at the Freston crossroads. Another school item.

"Beginning of term feeling."

She put her hand on his knee. "We'll see about that."

They carried his trunk up the garden path, into the house and set it down in the sitting room. His name stencilled on the lid announced his proud return.

She stood close to him, kissed him lightly, unzipped his jeans and fondled him as she spoke. "It can't stay there, can it?"

"No."

"We'll put it straight in the shed."

He laughed.

She turned from him and gripped a handle.

"Lift your end."

They carried the trunk through the kitchen and into the garden. They put it down while she unfastened the padlock on the shed door. While he waited it seemed to him that he was hundreds of feet below murky water, that light and sound were denied him and desire was the pressure of many tons. He would do anything she asked. They pushed the mower aside and heaved the trunk in among the spades, hoes and rakes. When she had shut the door and snapped the padlock onto the hasp, she kissed him again and plucked at his shirt. "These are coming off anyway. Upstairs."

They were standing close in the centre of the small lawn, looking into each other's eyes. A small tree cast some broken shade over them. Her eyes appeared to bulge and there were tiny scraps of colour he had never seen before, fragments of yellow, orange and blue, mere pinpricks around her pupils. It came to him, a passing treacherous thought, that she was indeed mad, like some boys said. She was completely mad and was keeping it a secret from him. Even as the idea frightened him, it also thrilled him that she might be out of her mind, beyond self-control and he would have to go with her, go down with her into some hellish paradise. This was his adventure, his journey. Most would be too scared to go on it. Others wanted dull and reliable partners. He put his hand under her skirt and as his finger moved lightly over her, as she had taught him, she murmured a long sentence in a low monotone, most of which he did not catch. The repeated word "have" was all he heard. He would have felt an idiot, asking her to say it all over again.

They went indoors. Roland took her hand and led her up the stairs. The bedroom was in perfect summer order. The windows were open to the late afternoon sun. The tide was full on the River Stour. The bedcovers were neatly stripped back from the laundered and ironed sheet. He undressed her where she stood, on the faded yellow rug, guided her to the bed, spread her legs and with his tongue performed for her in respectful silence what they called in one of their private jokes, Prelude No. 1. Then he went into the bathroom to wash. The little pink room with the sloping floor was also full on to the sun. As he took off his shirt he saw himself in the mirror. Weeks of digging trenches for Mr. Heron had served his torso well. He looked amazing, he decided. Fierce light from one side enhanced the effect. It needed to be inscribed in memory, he thought, how good he felt, how his every action had a discrete and beautiful flow as though he moved to the sound of an orchestra. The theme from *Exodus*. And such glorious anticipation of what was about to happen. He raised one arm to tense his biceps and turned to catch sight in the mirror of the muscles across his back. Cool. She called his name impatiently from the bedroom.

They made love for what seemed like an hour but it was hard to tell. Later she lay on his arm and murmured, "I love you . . ."

His eyes were closing. He grunted in assent. It pleased him, how manful he sounded. They dozed for twenty minutes. He woke to the sound of the bath she was running for him. He lay in it a long time, admiring how the rich light of the setting sun transformed his pallor, promoting him to a race of honey-skinned supermen whose intellectual capacities could never be measured by mere exams.

He went naked into the bedroom and saw that his clothes and shoes had gone. She had made the bed. By the pillow on his side was a folded pair of yellow cotton pyjamas. He spread them out. There was pale blue piping around the cuffs and lapels. She hadn't been joking. She was brilliant—and mad. He put them on. They fitted loosely but well, though his erection showed ridiculously. He went to the window and looked at the river, a stream of molten gold, to distract himself.

Downstairs, she was making a salad with shrimps. She put her knife down and stood back to admire him. "Gorgeous. I got you two other pairs. Blue and white."

"Oh God," he said. "You really mean this." He went to kiss her. She hitched up her skirt. She wasn't wearing knickers. Everything was planned. They fucked standing against the flimsy kitchen counter. That forbidden word was the right one, he thought as it started, not "made love." They didn't speak, there was no tenderness. They were energetic, as if showing off before an invisible presence. Homely cups, saucers and teaspoons in the stainless steel sink tinkled comically and they tried not to hear. It didn't matter—it was over in minutes.

Now he felt like a god. She told him to open a bottle of wine. He had never opened one before but he knew how to do it. She took down two glasses. He filled the first, then she stopped him.

"Not to the brim, child. Half. Never more than two-thirds."

She tipped some of the first glass into the second and gave it to him. "To your new life," she said. They touched glasses.

Before supper they played a duet, one of the Mozart pieces they knew well. He hadn't practised in weeks. There were no pianos where he had been. But he fumbled his way through, he winged it. He was a god after all, a winged god. They ate outside on a rickety wooden table. She refilled his glass while he told her about his summer. Two weeks' stay with his parents in the officers' married quarters at a huge dull army camp near the little town of Fallingbostel. The Captain was now a major in charge of a tank repair workshop. He also conducted courts martial against disorderly or criminal soldiers. His mother was attentive to Roland, bringing him breakfast in bed and cooking roasts every evening. His father drank heavily at dinner, became merry first, then cantankerous.

In the day there was nothing to do—"Except think about you," Roland said. It was an understatement. He was supposed to be reading his set books for school—*Mansfield Park*, *Les faux-monnayeurs*, *Der Tod in Venedig*—but he could not concentrate. He could not keep his mind off Miriam. In the long July afternoons the very titles, the weight of a book in his hand, made him want to sleep, which was what he did. Some evenings he went to the army cinema, the AKC, with his mother. They saw Marlon Brando in *Mutiny on the Bounty*. Oh to be there, in that century, with Miriam, even on that troubled ship far from the nearest school. Walking home with his mother, companionably arm in arm, she talked to him about his father, how Roland was "the apple of his eye." On another evening she told him that the Major sometimes hit her after he'd been drinking. Roland did not tell her that he already knew this from Susan. It had always been hard to imagine. Rosalind was frail, barely five foot three, while the Major in his late forties was as strong as ever. He could have killed her with a punch. Susan had tried to persuade Rosalind to leave the marriage the day that Roland started at boarding school. On that hot bus ride along the foreshore, on the upper deck with his parents, he had known nothing. But the memory was altered.

He was on his third glass and talking freely. He was no longer bothered about his pyjamas. The thin cotton was well suited to the warm evening of late August. He was telling Miriam that what he had seen during his stay in Germany had happened, with variations, three times. The dinner was over. He was helping his mother carry plates and dishes into the kitchen. His father came in and clapped Rosalind hard on the back and complimented her on the meal. Once, and then again. It was a real blow, barely concealed behind a show of affection.

"Robert, I wish you wouldn't do that." It was brave of her, saying this much.

"Ach, Rosie. Just praising your cooking. Isn't that right, son?"

And he did it again, clapping his hand down hard on her shoulder so that she buckled slightly at the knee.

It was not affection but the pretence was there, just enough of it, a raw challenge that made it impossible to know what to say.

"I've asked you so many times. You know it hurts."

Then he became petulant. "Is that all I bloody well get for being kind?"

In such a mood he was adept at a blend of sulk and fury. The exchange prompted his shift from wine to a beer-and-chaser. Rosalind stayed in the kitchen, clearing up, then went straight to bed, while Roland sat in the living room with his father, who was conscious of the awkwardness in the air and said, as he always did when he wanted to move on and have Roland move on with him, "Never mind, son. Never mind."

That night, as they were preparing for bed, Miriam gave Roland a replacement washbag with toothbrush and razor.

"I want you naked in bed. Pyjamas are for daytime."

It was as exquisite as she had promised, to sleep in each other's arms. They made love before they got up. That morning she was driving to Aldeburgh to teach all day at a piano summer school. His job, she told him just before she went out to her car, was to be ready for her return. As she stepped out of the house she added, "Shed key is with me so don't turn the place upside down."

Today he was wearing white. He sat at the piano a while trying to improvise around some jazz standards. The music she hated. Then he invented freely and after several minutes played himself into a melody he rather liked. He found some manuscript paper and jotted it down and for most of the rest of the morning tried out different harmonies until he was satisfied and wrote out the new version. He was beginning to make a discovery about himself. Or it was a discovery about sex? In the immediate aftermath of making love to Miriam his thoughts expanded outwards, away from her into the world, into ambitious plans which entailed bolder versions of himself. His thoughts were cool and clear. Then slowly, over an hour or two, with narrowing focus his thoughts turned back to her, into delicious acceptance, which soon became a selfish hunger. He only wanted her. Everything else was pointless. This was the rhythm, inwards, outwards, like breathing.

So it was that during breakfast and after she had left, he knew very well that they were indulging in a sexy game with his stuff locked away and he loved her for it. It was playful and silly. Mortifying, if anyone he knew found out about it. His return to school, only a week away, was inevitable. There was a momentum set by others. The rugby season was starting and he expected to be asked to captain the second fifteen or even make it into the first. Now that the gifted Neil Noake had left, Roland was by far the best pianist in the school and would be depended on to accompany the hymns at the Sunday evening assembly. He was due on the first day of term to meet Mr. Clayton for a pep talk. The physics teacher also wanted to see him. In the shed, in his trunk, were the books he should be reading. Not only the untouched novels, but Dryden's *All for Love*, Racine's *Phèdre*, Goethe's *Selected Poems*. He had noticed a steel poker by the fireplace. He guessed it would be easy enough to prise the hasp off the shed door. Also, the tune he was writing was interesting, it had a sweet, melancholy lilt. It needed words. The Beatles might sing it. He could be rich.

He went outside. It was another warm day. If he had lived in the tropics, this was how he would be dressed. A reassuring scrap of a D. H. Lawrence poem came to him. They had to write about it, back in the third form. *And I in my pyjamas for the heat.* He was by the shed, looking for a way he could get in under the hasp and lever it off. It was not as straightforward as he had thought. The ironware was counter-sunk into seasoned hardwood. He was still looking when he heard the over-the-fence neighbour, the very chatty Mrs. Martin, open her back door. Almost certainly, about to hang out her washing, most certainly eager to chat with Roland. She hadn't seen him in weeks. What was he doing in his pyjamas with that poker in his hand? He moved swiftly back into the house. This was when the process began to reverse, the exhalation was on the turn and Miriam, her body, her wild possessiveness rose before him, though not so powerfully, not yet.

Upstairs, he had a good view of Mrs. Martin. She was setting out a deckchair in the shade of her Victoria plum tree. On the grass beside her were two magazines. He turned. Here was the bed, with its smoothly stretched counterpane and at its foot his third pair, in case he was in need, blue with green piping. He could not go out the front. People walked past from time to time. He was confined to the house and now Miriam, thirty-five miles and six or seven hours away, was right before him, her voice, her face, everything. And everything not her was receding. The tide, his tide, was racing out. He couldn't get into the shed and what did it matter? He wouldn't read the books anyway. No concentration. Pyjamas were his only clothes, if that was the word. His money was in his locked-away jeans. The world that included teachers, rugby, the Beatles and all European literature was not available to him and he didn't care. There was nothing he could do about any of it. What he wanted was coming towards him, but so slowly. He had to wait.

He returned to the piano. His tricky little melody had shrunk. It was trite, derivative, embarrassing. Impossible to improve it when the entire area around his groin ached—almost pleasurably—and he kept yawning. He couldn't even hold himself to playing right through the easiest of the Two-Part Inventions. He abandoned the attempt and went into the kitchen to look in the fridge. If only he was hungry it would take up some time. He made himself eat anyway. It was a mess, his attempt at frying eggs. Cleaning the place up he left for later. In the sitting room he patrolled her bookshelves. Biographies of composers, music theory, guidebooks to Venice, Florence, Taormina and Istanbul, fat nineteenth-century novels and many poets, too many poets. He was about to take down a book, any book, then he couldn't be bothered. The world was brimming with pointless endeavour. Besides, he was supposed to be reading Dryden.

He wondered if Miriam's was one of the few homes in the country that did not have a television. He found instead a little pink transistor radio with the name Perdio in silver scroll on the front. Too early in the day for Radio Luxembourg and no one cool at Berners listened to it anyway. It played only releases from the big record companies that sponsored the shows. The thinking man's station was Radio Caroline, broadcast from a ship anchored not so far away, beyond where the Orwell, the Stour and the North Sea met. The ship lay just outside the three-mile limit, the DJs were renegades, rebels, and the authorities were in a panic—a section of the nation's youth had set up just beyond its control. For a while he listened, usefully distracted, to a whole programme dedicated to the Hollies. He lay on the sofa, radio pressed to his ear because the battery was running down. Close three-part harmonies in pop music interested him. If he had the energy he could write something for them. He could go to the piano now. But he didn't move, and then Cliff Richard came on. No right-minded boy at school tolerated him beyond "Move It." He snapped the radio off and fell into a light doze.

The hot afternoon passed in a haze. When he went upstairs Mrs. Martin was still on her first magazine. At her side now was a low table and a pot of tea. Back in the kitchen he ate a half-pound cube of Cheddar cheese. He couldn't be bothered with bread. A buzzing fly had to be tracked down. Eventually, he crushed it against a window in the folds of the cheese wrapper. He went back to the piano, tried improvising and was soon irritated by his limitations. His classical training was a burden. He lay on the sofa and reckoned it would be the work of a minute or two, to give himself, *donate* was the word that came to him, an orgasm and free his thoughts. But he was waiting for Miriam, he didn't want to be free. Or could he get away with it? In answer, he went back upstairs to stare at himself in the bathroom mirror. Who was he? Captain of the second fifteen? An abject housebound halfwit in his pyjamas? He didn't know.

The boredom of a fifteen-year-old can be as refined as Portuguese gold filigree, as the spiral orb web of the Karijini spider. Painstaking, skilful, static, like the embroidery that Jane Austen's women persuaded themselves was work when nothing else was permitted. Slowly, with care, he cleaned up around the chaos of his fried eggs. The kitchen wall clock stopped along with his existence. He hovered over it, his life, supine on the sofa, with nothing left for him but to long for her. And when at six thirty, he heard her car and saw her coming up the garden path and she breezed in after her busy day, embraced him tightly, kissed him deeply, the time behind him collapsed into a vanishing point of amnesia, and when she asked as they were on their way up the stairs if he had been unhappy, he told her, "No, no, I was fine. Completely fine."

The three days passed like those hours of the first, a clever torture that left no mark. In a state of deep excitement he kissed her goodbye in the morning and rediscovered the sweet pain of waiting through the day. The heatwave yielded to cold winds from the east and then steady rain. She washed and ironed his pyjamas. One day she was in Bury St. Edmunds for the premiere of a choral piece by an old friend. She spent the other two days at the summer school. In the evening they made love as soon as she returned and ate the suppers she cooked.

Three days before his birthday there was to be a celebration dinner. She would be working late on the day of his sixteenth, she had said. She came back earlier than usual. He lay in the bath after their reunion while she was busy in the kitchen. He was to stay upstairs until she was ready to call him down. He put on freshly ironed pyjamas, the white ones again, and sat on the bed waiting for her summons. His thoughts were agreeably clear. School would be starting soon. His plan was to go to the sixth-form library in the evenings and catch up on the set books during the first week of term. He was a fast reader and would take notes. Mr. Clayton had taught them how to "gut" a book. All that was needed, Roland decided, was focus.

She called his name softly up the stairs, as if asking a question, and he went down. There was a tablecloth, two lit candles, champagne in an ice bucket, his favourite meat, roast lamb. At table they clinked glasses. She was wearing a low-cut red dress and, a playful touch, had put in her hair a red rose from her garden, one of the last of the summer. She was more beautiful than ever. He didn't tell her that he had never drunk champagne before. Like lemonade, but sharper. She passed him his present, a thick brown envelope tied up with white ribbon. She raised her glass again and he took his.

"Before you open it, just remember. You'll always belong to me."

He nodded and drank deeply.

"Sip it. It's not fizzy pop."

It was a wad of papers held together with a paper clip. On top were two railway tickets to Edinburgh, on the express, first class. The day after tomorrow. He looked at her for an explanation.

She said softly, "Keep going."

The next sheet was a letter acknowledging her booking of a suite at the Royal Terrace Hotel. They would be there the night before his birthday.

"Fantastic," he murmured. The next page confused him. He read it too quickly, saw some kind of official form, already filled out. There was a heraldic device at the top in blue. He saw his name in block capitals, and hers. Then the address of a registry office.

"*Marriage?*" The absurdity of it was so extreme that he began to laugh.

"Isn't that exciting darling." She was refilling his glass, watching him intently, with a sweet half-smile. Her eyes were wide and glazed.

The absurdity faded. Now it was fear in the form of a tumbling sensation. He was going to need strength and he wasn't sure he had it. Or wanted to have it. But he needed it. An hour ago they had been making love. In the bath he had been whistling his Beatles song and had seen how it could be rescued, heard some better harmonies in his thoughts. The world beyond Miriam, the domain of gutted books. But now he was on the borders, drifting back towards her domain. After all, it was seven thirty and he was in his pyjamas. He looked at the form again. A lifetime of nothing but making love. It was a colossal effort, but there remained to him some dwindling resources of clarity, a broader sense of the real. To be her *husband,* to assume the condition of . . . his parents! Insanity. He had to resist before he started to persuade himself that insanity was a bold adventure. Perhaps it was. It was an effort but finally it was the captain of the second fifteen who spoke. He fumbled but it was the captain.

"But we haven't . . . we haven't even talked about it."

She was still smiling. "What are we going to talk about?"

"Whether that's what we both want."

She was shaking her head. Her confidence frightened him. Perhaps he was wrong. "Roland, we don't have that kind of arrangement."

She waited for him to speak and when he didn't, she said, "I know what's best for you. And I've decided."

He could feel himself yielding. He didn't want to seem ungrateful or spoil the occasion. Was it possible, to throw his life away in order to be polite? He had to say it now, quick. "I don't want it."

"What?"

"It's too soon."

"For what?"

"I'll be *sixteen.*"

"That's why we're going to Scotland. It's legal."

"I don't want to. I can't."

She pushed her chair back and came round to his side of the table and stood over him. Her breasts were close to his face. "I think you'll do as you're told."

He knew that voice from his first piano lesson. But this could be a game they were playing. If he nodded, even faintly, they would soon be upstairs, and how he longed for that now even though he knew it could destroy him. Once they were together on the bed he would say yes to everything. Afterwards when his mind was clear, he would regret it and it would be too late. He had to keep going. The main thing was to get out from under her. While she was so close he could not think, as she knew well. It was awkward, standing up without touching her. He crossed the room so that the sofa, where he had lain for days, was between them. It might just protect him.

She regarded him steadily. "Roland, what do you think this has all been about?"

"Loving each other."

"And what does love mean? Where does it lead?"

He still believed that whenever she asked a question he was obliged to answer it.

He said, " It doesn't lead anywhere." He had a brilliant idea, something half-remembered. "It's a Ding an sich, a thing in itself."

She smiled sadly and shook her head as she corrected him. "No, it isn't, darling. It's a commitment, to each other, to the future, a commitment for life. That's what love is."

"Not necessarily." This was weak and it was too late to call it back.

She was coming towards him, smiling faintly. There was nowhere for him to back into. She said as she approached, "Come here. We shouldn't be arguing. I want to kiss you."

He took a step towards her and they kissed. At the same time she touched him through the thin white cotton. She would have felt him instantly swelling in her hand. He broke away, pushed past her roughly and went to stand by the dining table. The untouched roast was going cold.

She pointed. "Look at you. What's that saying?"

"It's saying I love you and I don't want to get married." He was pleased with this reply.

They were silent. Her expression did not change but he knew from experience that something was about to happen and he had better be ready. As always, she surprised him. From an armchair she picked up the satchel she took to Aldeburgh and bent over it to rummage among her sheet music. When she straightened he saw that she was flushed. To his horror he also saw tears in her eyes. But her voice was clear and steady.

"All right. Too bad. You'll spend the rest of your life looking for what you've had here. That's a prediction, not a curse. Because I don't wish it on you. Love is all about chance and good luck. You happened to meet the right person for you when you were eleven. You were far too young to know it, but I did. I would have waited longer, but you showed up and it was obvious why. I should have sent you away but I wanted you as much as you wanted me. I had plans for us. They would have thrilled you. Now you're backing out and I'm sorry. So get out. Take your stuff and leave and never come back."

She threw the garden-shed key at his feet. When he started to protest she spoke over him louder than before, but not quite at a shout. "Do you hear me? Get out!"

While she accused him, as long as there was anger in her voice, he felt usefully unaroused. He picked up the key and, prompted by a vague notion of decency or gratitude, gathered from the table his birthday present, the envelope and papers. Without looking in her direction he turned and went through the kitchen. Outside it was still just light enough and raining steadily. He walked barefoot across the waterlogged lawn to the shed door. He needed both hands to turn the key. His trunk was not locked. The clothes he had worn when he arrived were on top. He dressed hurriedly in the doorway of the shed. The cash, his precious wad, was still in his back pocket. The pyjamas he screwed into a ball and tossed them out onto the lawn. A parting note. They would be sodden in the morning. She would be sorry when she had to carry them into the house, out of Mrs. Martin's sight. He put the envelope in the trunk, closed it, lifted one end and dragged it across the lawn, round the side of the house, across the front lawn and through the gate. He knew from sending it by British Road Services that his trunk weighed around fifty pounds, a weight he could have carried but it was too big, too awkward. He set off along the road towards the pub. There was a grass verge and the trunk slid along it easily. By the pub car park was a phone box but he had no change, only pound notes. He went into the public bar and ordered a half-pint of bitter. The cigarette smoke, garbage from the lungs of others, was suffocating in the damp air and he was glad to be out again.

There was a one-man taxi service in Holbrook village and after he had spoken to the driver he waited with his trunk by the kerb. The rain kept on, but he did not mind—he had been indoors too long. From time to time he looked along the road towards the cottage. He was feeling the first touches of regret. If she had come out looking for him and had been persuasive he might have gone home with her and taken his chances. But it looked like the weather was keeping everyone inside tonight and in ten minutes his taxi arrived.

He asked to be taken to Ipswich railway station. While he was helping the driver lift the trunk onto the back seat he had no plan, no idea where he was going. But as they descended the hill past Freston water tower and went along the darkened foreshore, it came to him. Pack a carrier bag with a change of clothes and his books, deposit the trunk at the left luggage and check in to the Station Hotel. It looked run-down and cheap enough. He would hole up and read his set books and arrive on the first day of school well prepared for the sixth form. That plan fell apart as soon as he was standing on the pavement, watching his taxi draw away. A London train was just in, people were brushing past him, traffic on the main road was unusually heavy, there was tinny pop music playing from somewhere. He drew strength from this bustle. He was in the real world again. It was plain what he had to do. Last time she threw him out she had taken him back within days. A hasty note, a summons without explanation, delivered by the boy who resembled a mouse, and whose name was actually Thomas Meek. Next day, there was Roland on his bike, pedalling in a frenzy to her cottage, delivering himself up to her for lunch. It would happen again, she would come to claim him. He could never resist her. There was only one way to be free.

He had to act quickly, before he changed his mind. A friendly boy his own age helped him carry the trunk to the ticket office. His request was proud—a full-fare adult ticket, one-way. A porter took his luggage on a trolley to the guard's van. Roland tipped him two shillings and sixpence. Probably too much but this was his new existence, the one in which he was in command. Before his train pulled out he had time to buy a newspaper. On the way to London he read about preparations for the grand opening of the Forth Road Bridge in Edinburgh, the city he had escaped from. He was too late into town to make an onward connection. The place he found near Liverpool Street station was even seedier than the one in Ipswich. He had never checked in to a hotel before. The feeling it gave him confirmed that he was doing the right thing. The next morning, before he took a taxi across the city to Waterloo station, he phoned his sister.

She was on the platform to meet him at Farnborough station. Her car was the same make as Miriam's, so he knew how to fit his trunk in. Susan was not surprised about his change of plan. As Roland put it—like her and their brother Henry, like their parents and their parents, he would benefit from the minimum schooling the authorities required of him. He was done with classrooms and timetables. She stopped outside his old place of work and waited while he walked the quarter-mile to where Mr. Heron was supervising the digging. It was clear from the mud on his boots and jacket and the sweat on his face that he was short-handed. The gaffer seemed to have shrunk. Roland was fearless. He asked for the wages he was owed, and he offered— he did not ask—to work again. When he got the nod Roland set out his condition. He could work faster and harder than the forty-year-old chain-smoking fellows. He must be paid at the full adult rate or he would go elsewhere. As Mr. Heron turned away he agreed with a shrug.

After they had brought in his trunk from the car and heaved it upstairs to his bedroom, Roland and Susan had a cup of tea and settled on four pounds a week for his keep. Over the weekend it was beautiful weather again and he helped his sister in the garden. While she made a bonfire Roland went back into the house to bring out his books. Camus, Goethe, Racine, Austen, Mann and the rest. He dropped them one by one onto the flames. It would have been satisfying to believe that *All for Love* was consumed faster than the rest. But everything burned with equal ferocity. He wrote to his parents about his decision, assuring them he was earning good money. Over the following week, worried letters came from school, from Mr. Clayton and Mr. Bramley. A day later there was one from Mr. Clare, who urged him to return and continue the "vitally important lessons with Miss Cornell. You have a stupendous talent. Roland, it can be nurtured here—for free!" He ignored them all. He was already busy working extra hours at time and a half, and he had met a lovely, sweet-natured Italian girl, Francesca, in an Aldershot pub.

# 8

By mid-1995 Roland was out of funds, though hardly impoverished. Alissa forwarded the Child Benefit that had helped sustain her while she was writing *The Journey*. This weekly allowance of £7.25, hard-fought for by campaigners, went straight from government to all mothers, rich or poor, and now came from her London to her German bank to his London bank. She added a decent £250 a month for Lawrence's maintenance. She passed a message through Rüdiger that she would send more if Roland wanted her to. He didn't. There was enough to eat and drink, almost enough for clothes and school trips. Repairs, holidays abroad, a car, spontaneous presents and the piano tuner fell off the list. The bank overdraft was closing in on £4,000. He could not face a return entanglement with social services and join fellow supplicants slumped on steel benches screwed to the floor. He and Lawrence had lived well for two years, the rest went on tax at the new low rate. The household survived by Roland collating some of his earlier freelance careers. He wrote a little journalism, he taught tennis seven hours a week, he played lunchtime munch music at a superior small hotel in Mayfair. How could he be poor when he and Lawrence lived on an income just above the national average? Because poverty was not an absolute, so he had read, it was relative, and his friends, many of them graduates, were doing well in the professions, in science, TV and print. One couple, evangelists for a digital future, had opened an Internet café in Fitzrovia. They were flourishing.

There was an interesting term going about that he liked and used to console himself. Social capital. How could he complain when he was soon to be married? When he had a loveable interesting child, friends, music, books and health, when his son was not at risk from smallpox or polio, or from snipers hidden in the hills above Sarajevo? But he would have preferred social capital plus capital, and if his life was safe, it was also too safe. He rarely left London these days. Look what others of his generation were doing. He had not left home to publicise the Sarajevo siege and its atrocities as bold Susan Sontag had, by staging *Waiting for Godot* in the city's National Theatre.

He and Daphne had decided to merge households. The four children were keen. Peter, down in Bournemouth in a peeling seafront apartment with his new friend, didn't mind Roland living with the woman he had left. Roland had formed a suspicion that Peter had hit Daphne on occasions, but she refused to talk about it. It turned out that she and Peter, pushing against convention in their youth, were not actually married. Whatever had happened, the bitterness of their parting was largely spent. That was a bullet Roland and Alissa had dodged. He had signed papers prepared by German and English lawyers, paid for by Alissa. Now, with Daphne, the plan was clear. Find a big house and garden where Lawrence and his best friend Gerald, and the two girls, Greta and Nancy, would be happy and free. Roland was counting on Daphne's genius for organisation. They had long been confidants, now they were lovers. It had started out wonderfully, had faltered a while and now was well again. Or well enough. At last he understood that there was no liberating elsewhere beyond the sandbag defences of Gurji camp, that on the other side of the best orgasm he'd ever had, a better one was not waiting.

He was just over three years short of his fiftieth birthday. His tennis clients were mostly decent players in their thirties wanting to "hit." After a long session on court he noticed dull aches around his hips and electric twinges in his right elbow. He had his heart checked out—a bit ragged, some of the beats, but not so bad. At his doctor's suggestion he submitted to a camera journeying around his large colon in search of polyps—nothing so far. A humiliating process but one of the drugs, fentanyl, gave him a taste of the old days. Thinking seriously for the first time in his life about his health and his inevitable deterioration added to his certainty that it was time to arrange a different kind of existence. Too late for Sarajevo. The future he had in mind was solid, secure, friendly, ordered, and he was coming to it after many delays and denials.

Months had passed since they had elatedly made these plans. But Daphne worked a fifty-hour week and was raising three children. Her au pairs came and went often. The public housing stock was pitifully diminished. The demand for affordable London homes to rent was overwhelming her mid-sized housing association. Roland's hours were spread all over the day and he was needed at the school gates by 3:30. In six months, they had seen eleven places, all hovels or over-priced or both. For now, they lived in two small houses in Clapham.

Epithalamium Cards had not collapsed—it had been sold on to a big mainstream concern for a sum that was never disclosed to Roland. The money owed to him was on its way, the elusive Oliver Morgan had been telling him for four years. Certain legal and financial issues were being resolved. He was not to worry—his portion was increasing in value all the time. Roland's recycled birthday and condolence verses were now on sale everywhere with a company said to be bigger than Hallmark. At school long ago he had read several pages of a set book, a novel by Georges Duhamel, *Le notaire du Havre*, enough to get the general idea. A hard-pressed family was waiting to receive a generous inheritance. The fortune was always about to arrive. Frustrated hope was slowly destroying these poor people. The money never came. Or perhaps it did. He didn't read far enough to find out. It was a cautionary tale.

He could go weeks and the matter hardly crossed his mind. He was too busy and he reckoned he was more resilient than the family from Le Havre. But occasionally, waking in the small hours, his brooding insomniac mind would go searching for a cause. Then he would hear Morgan's reassuring voice from a recent conversation. *Roland, just be patient. Trust me.* Lying in the dark on his back he attended to unspooling dramas—written and directed by someone else. He had no responsibility for the hiring of the East End thugs who snatched Oliver Morgan from his car and brought him to an abandoned bacon factory in Ipswich, where soon he, along with some senior executives from Krazikards Inc., dangled naked, upside down, their ankles secured by the chains of a moving belt transporting them towards the steel doors of a giant blast furnace. At their approach those doors slid open, a roaring jet of white flame rose twenty feet high. The bound men, writhing on their chains, squealed like pigs for mercy. By chance it looked like Oliver would be going in first. Time for Roland to intervene, to pause the conveyor belt. He spoke into Oliver's upside-down ear. There were certain conditions. With what ease and speed the money was in his hands. But now the bedclothes were too hot and his noisily beating heart would not let him sleep.

It was during those early days, when the old friends became lovers, that Daphne explained her theory of domestic order. The centre of the modern home was no longer the sitting room, the parlour or the study of the paterfamilias. It was the kitchen, and the heart of the kitchen was its table. This was where children learned basic manners, including the unspoken rules of conversation, and how to be in company and where they would absorb for a lifetime the vital rhythm and rituals of regular meals and begin to take for granted their first simple duties in helping to clear away. It was where the post was opened, where friends sat around talking and drinking, while their host prepared their supper. And it was where, she pointed out, at his table they were squeezed up at one end because of the mountain of crap that occupied almost all the space. Under there was a nice old pine table. Clear it and the effect on the rest of the house would follow. It took him a weekend. Most of the mountain he binned, the rest he distributed around the house. She was wrong, there was no effect on the other rooms but the kitchen was fundamentally improved. As a new convert Roland worked hard to keep the table clear. It became a kind of hearth. Even Lawrence noticed.

Round this table various friends gathered during 1995. It could accommodate ten at a squeeze. If Daphne was not working too late she could get across by nine thirty. Her girls took Roland's spare room and Gerald doubled up with Lawrence. Roland had limited cooking skills and ambitions. One course only: lamb chops, roast potatoes, green salad. To feed ten, he would count on forty chops. They made little impact on his overdraft. The wine was taken care of by the guests. They formed a shifting, ill-defined group. Many worked in the public sector—teachers, civil servants, a GP. Joe Coppinger came with

Sofia, the doctor he was about to marry. There was also a cello maker, an independent-bookshop owner, a builder and a professional bridge player. The average age was around forty-five. Most were parents, none was rich, though everybody earned more than Roland. Most were heavily mortgaged, many had been married twice and had complicated families and complex weekly arrangements. Almost all had been educated by the state. There was a fair national and racial mix. The two schoolteachers were third-generation Caribbean. The bridge player was of Japanese extraction. Occasionally, Americans, French and Germans passed through. Two, Mireille and Carol, Roland's previous lovers, came with their husbands, one of whom was from Brazil. Some were people Roland had met through tennis. The gatherings overlapped with other groups in other houses where the food was more sophisticated. On any given occasion about half would know each other.

They were all still young enough for the subject of ageing to be a running joke. It remained paradoxical that they now found themselves older than senior policemen, than their doctors, than their children's head teacher—and now, senior to the Leader of the Opposition. A related and emerging topic was the care of elderly parents. These grown-up children were at that hinge of life when parents must begin to shrink and fold. The decline of mobility, reason fading in and out like short-wave radio, the trickle of minor ailments that fed a deeper river—the subject was vast and not all of it was unfunny. They could smile at comedies of misunderstanding when a vague parent came to live with a busy family in a house that was too small, the children too noisy, the weekly timetable too complex, when the family's supper was fed in error to the cats while everyone was out.

The conversation embraced the logistics as well as the guilt and sadness of moving a parent from home to care home. One friend said she loathed her mother almost as much as her mother loathed her. But she was shocked by the way she felt when she had to "put my mother away." The subject was mortality and therefore limitless. They looked ahead to their not-so-distant fiftieth birthdays and knew they were discussing their own future decline. Some were already contemplating knee and cataract operations or forgetting a familiar name. There were good selfish reasons to be kindly to the old.

That apart, there was much optimism about, though twenty-five years later it would be hard to recall. Politically, the median position was not very far left of centre. There were no revolutionaries here. They suffered somewhat from like-mindedness. Much that was predicted the night the Wall fell had come about. Germany was united, the Soviet Union had vanished. Already, eight nations of its Eastern European empire had joined the European Union with a couple more to follow. Military spending was down, though nuclear weapons remained. There was an academic consensus that democracies never invaded other countries—and that was cited around the table. After centuries of war, ruin and torture, Europe had found a permanent peace. First the dictatorships of Spain and Portugal in the seventies, now the rest, tumbling into a condition of openness and future prosperity. There was a Democrat in the White House. Bill Clinton was seeing through benign welfare reform and children's health insurance. His administration was showing a budget surplus—all good for a second term.

Recent by-elections predicted that the president's British colleague, the new Labour Party leader, Tony Blair, would sweep away the tired fractious government of the embattled Tory prime minister, John Major. Some round the table had connections with various Labour groups working on policy. The Conservatives had been in power sixteen years. Labour had to become electable again. At Roland's table and in other houses, in different combinations they dissected and welcomed "the third way." Equality, always unattainable and incompatible with liberty, was to be replaced by social justice—equality of opportunity. The old Labour ambition, no longer taken seriously, to nationalise all the major industries—to be junked. The Bank of England to become independent and depoliticised. "Tough on crime, tough on the causes of crime"—no voter, left or right, could argue with that. Education and health would be central. Human rights to be brought into British law. A minimum wage. Free nursery places for all four-year-olds. The creative energies of properly regulated capitalism would drive and fund these projects. Fixed-term parliaments. Peace in Northern Ireland. A Welsh Assembly. A Scottish Parliament. Lifelong Learning. Internet-based National Grid for Learning. The right to roam the countryside freely. Incorporation of the European Social Chapter. A Freedom of Information Act. All this in a plausible future. The evenings were long, the mood was high. At two in the morning one friend said as she was leaving, "It's not only rational. It feels so *clean*."

On occasions the like-mindedness broke down. A faction under the influence of the sociologist Anthony Giddens insisted that commerce, the market, could never promote social justice until the financial sector was cleaned up and made socially responsible. To some, that was utopian. To others, a quibble. One evening, early on, sitting at an end of the table so that he could be near the roasting chops, Roland stayed out of the conversation. He had spent a sleepless night and shopping, tidying and cooking had been arduous. Now it was a relief to be sitting down, removed from the cross-currents of conversation. Earlier in the day he had read a poem by Keats, "Ode to Psyche," long ago urged on him by his ex-mother-in-law. Despite his tiredness it had left him with a tranquil inward feeling.

The topics round the table narrowed to a single issue—targets. Everyone approved. A policy working group had just completed a paper. If Labour came to power, the public sector was to be made efficient and humane by being set clearly defined outcomes. Fear of failure would raise performance. Fulfilling targets would lift morale. The public interest would be met. To be targeted and increased: appendix removals and breast screenings, apprenticeships, ethnic minorities visiting national parks, kids from disadvantaged backgrounds at universities, literacy levels at ages seven, ten and fourteen, crimes solved, rapists tried and imprisoned, people moved out of unemployment. To be targeted and reduced: numbers of homeless, suicides, schizophrenics, air pollution, Accident and Emergency waiting times, lonely old people, infant mortality and child poverty rates, class sizes, street muggings, traffic accidents. Clear ambitions. In the name of transparency, success and failure would be set before the public for its judgement.

Roland was drifting away—it felt like upwards—and entered a state of detached contentment. He looked down the table. These were good and serious men and women. Intelligent, hard-working, intent on social justice. If they had privileges, they were determined to share them. The world, so his mood allowed, was full of such people. All was well. He remembered himself around Lawrence's age, watching two ambulances pull away with their accident victims as he concealed his tears of joy at a revelation: how good people were at heart and how well organised and decent things were. His father had acted heroically. It was clear, then as now. Every problem was solvable. Even in the murderous Balkans, even in Northern Ireland. Roland drifted further away. He was in an unreal and sentimental state. Mushy was his word for it. As if someone had slipped a psychotropic substance into his drink. Now, as the voices around him rose, he was going further as he entered a condition—hopeless to have tried to explain it—in which he took pleasure in mere existence. What luck, just to *be*, to have a mind, an asset never entered in the credit columns of social-capital ledgers. He remembered a fragment from the "Ode to Psyche": *the wreath'd trellis of a working brain*. That was anyone's privilege and Roland's patrimony—low on cash but he had a working brain. A mushy one. As intricate as a mature rose trellis.

At which point he snapped out of it, filled his glass and joined the conversation, whose level, unfortunately, had sunk. Roses are barbed. The heartless sport of the moment was to celebrate the travails of John Major, the prime minister, a decent put-upon man, trapped between, on one side, a cult of parliamentary right-wing cranks determined on the fantastical project of taking the country out of Europe; and on the other side, from every faction of the party, a sequence of ministerial peccadilloes, splashed everywhere to much glee, just when—this was how the press construed it—the PM had urged on the nation the cold blessings of chaste family values.

→>

Months later Lawrence sat at the same cleared table on a Saturday afternoon in September, three days after his tenth birthday, arranging newspaper pages, scissors, paste and the folio-sized scrapbook he had asked for as a present. Daphne was at work. Her children were in Bournemouth with their father, meeting twenty-four-year-old Angela for the first time. Roland sat across the table from Lawrence. They had less time together alone, these days. In a certain mood Roland studied his son's face and saw only Alissa's, and felt an old love stir, or the memory-shadow of love. He could almost recall what it was like to love her. The pallor, the large dark eyes, the straight nose and that habit of glancing away before speaking. Then, brewed out of what both parents had donated on that furtive night in Liebenau, all that was Lawrence's own. An unwieldy head too big for his frail shoulders—when he agreed intently, it wobbled rather than nodded. The lips were in the classic form of a Cupid's bow. Daphne said that one day someone kissing that boy would die of pleasure. And the head again, already so full of thoughts, too many of them unspoken. It was a relief, a joy, when Lawrence sidled up, took Roland's hand and confided a thought that implied much contemplation, much study behind it.

Five years before, he and Lawrence had stayed with friends in their country cottage. Their daughter Shirley was five, same as Lawrence. There were some older children too. The two youngest were encouraged to play together and the adults kept telling them how they were just right for each other. When a ride on a pony trap was arranged, they sat together, up with the driver and took turns holding the reins. In the evening, they shared the bathtub, then a bedroom. Just after 3 a.m. Roland was woken by a gentle tap on his shoulder. Lawrence was standing close, silhouetted against a moonlit wall.

"Can't you sleep darling?"

"No."

"What's up?"

The grave head tilted forward and he spoke to the floor. "I don't think Shirley is the girl for me."

"That's all right. You don't have to *marry* her."

There was a silence. "Oh . . . OK."

By the time Roland carried the boy back to his bed he was asleep. The following evening, adults and children were standing in the garden together to watch the moon rise from behind a stand of oaks and ashes. As it coyly peeped clear of the highest branches, Lawrence, determined to be conversational, tugged at the arm of their host and made the solemn pronouncement that passed into family legend.

"Do you know, in my country we also have a moon."

The tenth birthday, anticipated daily for many months, had deep significance for Lawrence. Double figures at last, but something beyond that. Almost like adulthood. The boyish presents were all around the kitchen. From Daphne and family, inline skates and street-hockey clobber. But also, as requested by him, an introduction to mathematics for adult beginners, a grown-up two-volume encyclopaedia and the scrapbook. A while ago, in answer to more questions from Lawrence about his mother, Roland had shown him a folder of press cuttings Rüdiger had sent over the years. Perhaps it was a mistake. But the boy's pride was intense. He stared at her photographs a long time. Her fame amazed him.

"Is she as famous as . . . Oasis?"

"No. Book famous is a lot less than that. But still famous, and more important."

"*You* think."

"I do. But you're right. Lots of people would disagree."

The heavy head moved slightly side to side as he considered. "I think you're right. More important." Then the familiar question. "Why doesn't she come and see me?"

"You could write to her. I don't know where she lives but I know someone who does."

"I think Oma knows where she is."

"Perhaps."

His letter, written over many evenings after school, covered ten pages in his extravagant loopy hand. He described his school, his friends, his house, his bedroom and his last holiday, on the Suffolk coast. At the end he told her he loved her and added in terms of an intimate personal secret that he also loved maths. Roland knew that Jane would not forward the letter. He marked the envelope "persönlich" and sent it to Rüdiger with a covering note. Two months passed— nothing. Roland was not surprised. Since their meeting in Berlin, he had written to her three times without a reply, encouraging her to be in touch with Lawrence. He had spoken to Rüdiger when he was in London. They met in the bar of his hotel near Green Park. The publisher said he was sympathetic, he understood, but he knew it would be more than his professional life was worth, to try and intervene in his author's private affairs. "She doesn't want to talk about it."

But Lawrence was not deterred. He was intent on compiling "The Book of Alissa Eberhardt"—so the scrapbook was now headed in gold crayon. He explained that the articles were to be in chronological order, English to be followed by German. Scissors, gluepot, marker pen and a damp cloth he arranged in a line. He sorted through the folder until he found an English review of *The Journey*. It was a single column, which he cut around and pasted onto the first page. It was neatly done.

He was right about his grandmother. Since publication of the first novel, Alissa and her mother had been reconciled. Jane was under instruction not to give Roland her daughter's address. He was irritated by this and on a visit, after Lawrence was in bed, they had argued. He told her she owed a duty to her grandson to put him in touch with his mother. Jane told Roland he failed to understand the complexities. Of families, of literature. Had he actually read *The Journey*? It was beneath him to reply. She convinced herself that he was too jealous of Alissa's success to bother with her extraordinary book. How petty of him. After that things went cool, until they didn't speak or write at all. It made sense when she failed to invite him to Heinrich's funeral. The vengeful son-in-law would have turned up with Lawrence to embarrass Alissa.

He discussed this with Daphne. Her view never varied. "She could be the second Shakespeare for all I care. She should write to her son." And two evenings ago: "She needs a good kick up the backside." One woman clearing the decks of another? No, far more than that. But there was symmetry in these upheavals. Lately, he had been referring to Peter as a "fuckwit," a term that was pleasing on the tongue.

Daphne may have been right about Alissa's need of a metaphorical kick, but it wasn't helpful, Roland kept telling her. His animus against his ex-wife was consigned to the basement of his thoughts where it wrestled with his admiration for her work. The higher matter was Lawrence. His awareness had expanded to this point—his mother was glamorously alive, not so far away in familiar Germany and she did not wish to know him. What to do? It could have been a mistake to show him her press. It formed a pile six inches deep. Whenever Rüdiger sent the latest Eberhardt cuttings, Roland read through them and put them in his folder. He too was intrigued by her fame.

While Lawrence leaned over the scissors to concentrate on a precise cut, Roland took a page off the pile. After five years it was yellowing at the edges, the long review by an esteemed critic in the *FAZ*, the *Frankfurter Allgemeine Zeitung*, that had set the tone for *The Journey*'s ecstatic reception in Germany, Austria and Switzerland. Rüdiger had clipped a translation to the cutting. Roland skipped the extensive plot summary and read again the closing paragraphs.

At last, a leader with a commanding voice has emerged from among the generation born after—and born of—the war. Untainted by the arid experimentalism, the solipsistic, existential anomie of our subsidised literary culture, she bursts into our presence, a writer who understands her responsibilities to the reader and yet remains in complete control of an exquisite literary prose and the boldest imaginative ambition. Only her title escapes her capacity for brilliant invention.

Alissa Eberhardt is not afraid of our recent past, or of history itself or of a gripping narrative, of full and deep characterisation, of love and the sorry end of love, and of profound and informed moral speculation that sometimes makes a respectful curtsey to *The Magic Mountain* and even to the magic of Montaigne. There seems to be nothing that she cannot evoke, from the ruins of bombed-out Munich to the wartime criminal underclass of Milan to the spiritual desert of the post-war economic miracle as experienced in an obscure little town in Hesse.

Tolstoyan in sweep, with a Nabokovian delight in the formation of pitch-perfect sentences, Eberhardt's novel

delivers without lecturing us a quietly powerful feminist
conclusion. Her heroine, even as she fails, exhilarates by what
she illuminates. There can be nothing left to say beyond the
obvious—this novel is a masterpiece.

*Ein Meisterwerk,* Nabokovian, winner of the Kleist and Hölderlin
prizes and Roland was first, he was right, even about the title. He
should have written the letter. If he had, she might have been preparing now to spend Christmas with her son, who was holding up "The
Book of Alissa Eberhardt" with a proud smile to show his father the
first page.

"Brilliant. Nicely arranged. What's next?"

"Something in German."

"This was one of the first. Have a look."

Lawrence set to work on the *FAZ* page. He was not interested
in trying to read the translated articles. He wanted to arrange them
and tame the mystery of his mother within his own book. Roland was
looking now at a magazine piece in English. In a full-sized colour
photograph she was in a white summer dress, cinched at the waist in
the style of the forties, sunglasses pushed back above her forehead.
The styled hair was cut in a bob without a fringe and tucked behind
her ears. She leaned against a stone balustrade. In the panoramic background were conifers and a distant wisp of river. The smile looked
forced. Ten interviews a day. Beginning to loathe her own voice, her
repeated opinions. She never came to London for publication. Coverage in the book pages saved her the bother. The copy, six months old,
was an extended caption in breathless prose.

Like awesome Doris Lessing before her, glamorous Alissa
Eberhardt made the sort of scary leap many women only
dream about. She abandoned baby and husband and high-
tailed it into the Bavarian forest, see above, where she lived
on leaves and berries (just joking!) and wrote her famous first
novel, *The Journey.* The book world pronounced her a genius
and she's never looked back. Her latest, *The Running Wounded,*
is our Book of the Month. Watch out, Doris!

This one, Roland decided, he would keep back from his son. It was as far as the well-known story ever went. Alissa never elaborated, never named her abandoned family, never spoke about the scary leap and its absolute nature. An energetic British press could have found Roland easily. What luck, the left-behind were not interesting. So far, three novels and a collection of stories. Whenever he read her, he looked for the character who embodied some elements of himself. He was prepared to be indignant if he found him. The kind of man her heroine might hole up with for many sensual months. The pianist, tennis player, poet. Even the failed poet, the sexually overdemanding man, the restless unfulfilled man of no settled work that a reasonable woman might tire of. The husband and father that a woman character deserts. What he found instead were, among many others, two versions of the big Swedish sailor with the ponytail, Karl.

As five short years passed, the books and prizes in Germany and around the world accumulated. She rewrote and brought to life one of the novels that Roland had typed up and publishers in London had rejected. She published a collection of linked stories about ten love affairs. She was astute, even hilarious about the contradictory demands of her clever heroines. There could have been room for him in there. In her novel about London her heroine worked for a stretch at the Goethe-Institut. But he wasn't the student she fell in love with. He wasn't even in her class. Another character lived near Brixton market but not in Roland's old flat. The Eberhardt mode was defiantly realist, it addressed a world that was collectively known and felt. There was nothing, material or emotional, that she could not vividly depict. And yet, for all the intensity of their time together—the Lady Margaret Road tryst, the emotionally wrought visits to Liebenau and the walks by the river, the outdoor thrills of the Danube delta, their little shared house and above all, their child—nothing, not even disguised or displaced. Their shared experience bulldozed from her creative landscape, including her own vanishing. He had been expunged. So had Lawrence—there were no children in her fiction. The break in 1986 was total. He had prepared himself for indignation. Now he was coming at it from another direction.

He read the profiles for evidence of Alissa's lovers but she never spoke of her private life. "Next question," was the calm response, even if she was blandly asked which part of Germany she lived in. An unposed picture in a magazine showed her at a happy restaurant table. No one around it looked like a possible lover. The German press was not as doggedly intrusive as the British. But because she didn't visit and therefore belonged to no literary circle, had no known affairs, was never seen in favoured restaurants or at red-carpet openings and was almost forty-eight, she was poor material for the gossip columns. Selected British journalists travelled to Munich and met her in her publisher's office. They were mostly bookish types, respectful, even awestruck.

As the years stacked up behind them, their time together shrank, at least by the calendar. A mere three years, '83 to '86. But the emotional span was greater and Lawrence was its embodiment. Also, the Goethe-Institut in '77 and four years later, meeting outside the Dylan concert when Mick Silver got nutted. Then Berlin, the Adler, the alley in the rain. That span extended when he wrote to her about Lawrence and received no reply and extended further when he quietly admired her latest book and noted again his absence. Whenever he saw her photograph, a fine thread was reconnected to a distant past. Eighteen years on, it seemed unchanged, the face of the woman who had once declared her literary ambitions in slow and simple German for the benefit of her class.

An anti-monarchist friend, hit and killed by a motorbike ten years back, had once told him that by their intense media presence, certain young members of the royal family were constantly invading his privacy.

"Stop reading about them," Roland had replied. "I never do and they never bother me."

Now he saw what was meant. Alissa occasionally bothered him. He had to read each book as it came. He had to sift through the press Rüdiger sent. She wouldn't leave him alone, she refused to stop writing well even as she ignored him in her novels. After so many years, he didn't much mind but it would have helped if her face, artfully lit in quality magazines, had faded from his view. But even if it had, it would linger, not only in their son's eyes and that habit of glancing away, but in his consuming seriousness. Above all, that was what Lawrence and his mother shared.

→←

Two years later the Clapham households still had not merged. Talk of marriage was not dropped. It faded. They were busy, house prices were rising unevenly across the postal districts, and it was less perilous somehow to have two places barely a mile apart. Daphne's children were spending every other weekend with their father. That caused an imbalance, for Daphne valued her four days a month alone. That was fine. Roland was long used to and liked time alone with Lawrence. The families overnighted in each other's places. The parents babysat for each other. It was messy sometimes but his and Daphne's four kids liked each other and living this way was easier than taking a big decision that would be hellish to undo—they never felt like spelling it out. Some love affairs comfortably and sweetly rot. Slowly, like fruit in a fridge. This might be one such, Roland thought, though he was never quite sure. The sex, increasingly sporadic, remained intense. They talked easily, profoundly when it was possible. Politics bound them and there was much excitement as the general election approached. So, all six of them, all the "stakeholders" as New Labour economists now said, lived in an agreeable fog of arrangements too settled or interesting to be easily dispersed. Inertia itself was a force.

In the spring of '97 there was a death in Roland's family. Once, no one advanced far through childhood without confronting a dead person. But in the prosperous West, after the mass carnage of two world wars, to live without death became the peculiar privilege and vulnerability of a protected generation. Loud and hungry for sex and goods and much else, it was squeamish about extinction. To Roland it seemed proper to forbid eleven-year-old Lawrence from coming with him. He travelled alone to his first close encounter with a corpse.

He arrived early by train. To settle his thoughts, he took a circuitous route from the station through the town. Aldershot looked like it had been beaten up the night before by drunks. Soldiers or civilians. In the centre, by the market, there were scatterings of bottle glass on the pavements and gutters, and spilt blood or tomato ketchup diluted by rain. It was round here that his brother Henry, then eighteen, had bumped into their mother in 1954 and she had failed to recognise him. That old mystery, why Rosalind sent Henry and Susan away in 1941, would never be solved. She insisted that she was too hard-up to raise them but no one was convinced. She was no poorer then than she was before the war. The question was so old they had stopped thinking about it.

Roland came out by Woolworths where, as a three-year-old, he had been in awe of a dark red colossus just inside the swing doors—an I-speak-your-weight machine. Near it, he had once lost his mother by absently following the wrong skirt. Coloured dots on a white background—just like Rosalind's. When an unfamiliar face looked down at him he went numb with horror. When he was reunited with his mother he wept. In memory, the acetate flavour of his grief was that of the Pick 'n' Mix sweeties piled on a nearby counter. Pear drops.

He crossed the road by Woolworths and passed two large free-standing cinemas side by side. In one of them he had sat through two consecutive showings of Elvis Presley's *Blue Hawaii*. He was thirteen years old. He must have been on holiday from Berners. His parents had left Tripoli and were waiting for the next posting. First Singapore, then Libya, soon it would be Germany—their life of exile, of Rosalind's buried homesickness. As if they were fleeing something. That long afternoon in the ABC, Roland could not bear to leave Elvis's sunny beaches and beautiful friends to join the drabness outside. His father had turned up unexpectedly to collect him and was furious at having to wait around in the foyer. Eventually he came into the cinema with an usher, whose torch beam found Roland in the front row. Father and son walked back in silence through the rain to where they were staying with Susan.

Now, Roland retraced part of their route across a deserted car park and went towards a dismal part of town where married soldiers and their families were once quartered in late Victorian, two-storey terraces, cramped, unheated, damp. Susan had lived there with her first husband and their two children when they were babies. Roland had stayed in Scott Moncrieff Square occasionally. In Parliament it had been referred to as a slum. Cold buildings of sooty brick surrounded a grassy mound around which the women hung out their washing. The terraces were knocked down in the late sixties when everything Victorian was an abomination. But the quarters were solidly constructed. Better to have refurbished them, for now the cheap replacements were ready for demolition too.

He looped back towards the centre of town, then up a hill towards the Cambridge Military Hospital where he was born. A fine Victorian edifice with a locally famous clock tower whose bells were spoils of the Crimean War. Closed two years before, destined, he had heard, to become luxury apartments. The windows had the smudged blind look of an abandoned wreck. Somewhere in there, separated from him only by a thin wall of time, he had been slung upside down, naked and bloody and, in the fashion of the day, welcomed into the world with a brisk slap on the buttocks. He took a wide detour, dropped behind Aldershot Football Club ground with the floral clock outside, still telling the time. He crossed the road and slowed as he approached Bromley & Carter's establishment in a parade of shops. His father was waiting for him. No silent fury this time, no usher's torch. He went on past, then, a hundred yards further, walked back, hesitated, and rang the bell.

The news had come early in the morning when he was at work, playing tennis on a Portman Square court. His opponent and client was a thirty-year-old, working himself back into his game after breaking a leg in a skiing accident. He was a wiry county-level player with a whip-like forehand. Roland was a set and three games down and trying to look as though it was part of his teaching method. Encouragement through victory. His job was to keep the rallies long and interesting but that demanded more running than he was used to. When his new little Nokia phone rang from the bench he raised a hand in apology and was grateful to take the call. As soon as he heard his sister's voice, its flat tone, he knew. For the next hour a blank indifference settled on him—useful in a competitive game. He took the set and allowed himself to be beaten in the third.

Lawrence's love for his grandfather was simple. The Major was a craggy ogre who made comic but frightening growling noises and played the mouth organ or made a hilarious wailing sound on a set of miniature bagpipes. As the boy grew older the ogre was free with his one-pound coins and made sure the neat house on a modern estate near Aldershot was well stocked with lemonade and chocolate. The ogre became more exotic when he acquired an oxygen tank to keep at his side, with a tube from it running into his nose with a gentle hiss. From early childhood Lawrence was interested in a grotesque figurine that the Major had brought back from Germany. It sat hunched on a windowsill, a bald gnarled gremlin with a long curved nose, leaning on a stick. The Major made a custom of presenting it to Lawrence as soon as he arrived. As a five-year-old he handled it with delicacy. The slow realisation that the monster could not harm him endeared it to him. The fearful could be contained, even loved. The gremlin may have been a surrogate for his grandfather.

That evening the two households were eating together at Roland's place. When he arrived from his afternoon session the children were doing their homework at the kitchen table while Daphne cooked. The girls, Greta and Nancy, were at one end, Gerald and Lawrence at the other. Between clients Roland had phoned Daphne with the news. Now he had to find the right moment to tell Lawrence. Losing Grandad Heinrich had been baffling and abstract. Being at the Liebenau funeral might have helped. Grandad Robert was another matter.

After Daphne he had made the more difficult call to Rosalind. Her voice was distant and he had to ask her to move the phone closer. The Major had fallen against her, trapping her against the kitchen worktop. There was blood spilling from his mouth. As she struggled to get out from under his weight, his head had dropped forward and fell hard against the counter. "I killed him," she kept saying faintly. To reassure her, he pretended to medical insight. "Put that thought away. If there was blood coming out of his mouth, he was already gone."

"Say that again," she said. "I want to hear it again."

He sat down among the silent children. It touched him, the way their heads were bent so studiously over their writing. In fifteen minutes all four would be loud again. His feet were throbbing, his knees and right arm ached. Daphne brought him a mug of tea. As she left him, she laid a hand on his shoulder. The sounds from the kitchen as she prepared a shepherd's pie were soothing. The table remained clear of junk. Here it was, the tranquil bliss of domesticity, orderly, secure, loving. Certain of his friends evoked it when they encouraged him to marry Daphne. Often, as now, he could see the point—the unasked-for tea, the murmuring radio news from the kitchen transistor (a chemical weapons ban would soon come into force), the children on their assignments, the scent of their freshly washed hair. He could let go, sink himself in the warmth. To suffer and drown? There had been some stronger hints lately of problems between Daphne and himself. No, it was singular, his problem, the old one. He couldn't help himself. She had said in a tight voice that he could and must.

He glanced across at Lawrence's work. Maths again. The book he had wanted for his birthday had made an impression. He had developed an understanding of differential equations, $dy$ over $dx$, by means of which he had left his father behind. When Greta asked Lawrence, as Roland had wanted to, what the point of these sums were, he replied after a thoughtful moment, "They're all about how things change and how you can get right inside the change."

"What change?"

"There's speed, then you sort of . . . *fold* and there's acceleration." He couldn't explain more but he could solve the equations. His understanding was immediate, almost sensual. His teacher thought he should go to a maths summer school for gifted under-twelves. Roland believed in holidays and was sceptical. Enough school! There was also the question of money. He didn't want to ask Alissa. Daphne had offered to pay. The matter remained undecided.

While he was taking a shower, he decided to break the news to Lawrence at supper in a kindly familial setting. Gerald, Greta and Nancy had lost a grandmother eighteen months ago. They would understand. And Daphne was very tender to Lawrence. How could he, Roland, resist merging his life with hers? Too difficult to think about now. He dressed and went downstairs. As soon as they had finished eating he told the children that he had some very sad news. When he delivered it, he spoke directly to his son. The large head was still, the boy's eyes were darkly fixed on him and Roland, the messenger, felt himself accused.

Lawrence asked quietly, "What happened?"

"Aunt Susie told me. They had just finished lunch. Granny was clearing away the plates. Grandad followed her carrying a bowl—"

"The orange bowl?"

"Yes. Just as he came into the kitchen he collapsed on the floor. You know how his lungs weren't much good, so his heart had to pump extra hard getting oxygen around his body. His old heart was worn out." Roland suddenly could not trust his voice. His own altered version had detached a splinter of sorrow. It felt artificial, more to do with storytelling and that loaded word *heart* than the fact of a painful death.

Lawrence's gaze was still on him, waiting for more, but Roland could not speak. Nancy put her hand on Lawrence's arm. She and Greta were starting to say something sympathetic. They were more expressive than their brother, who sat rigidly, and than father and son. With a wagging movement of a forefinger Daphne stilled the girls. The table was silent, expecting Roland to continue.

Lawrence may have seen the brightness in his father's eyes. It was the boy who would comfort the man. He said in a tone of gentle encouragement, "What did they have for their lunch?"

"Chicken, potatoes . . ." He was going to say peas. The bathos of the question had made him want to laugh. He cleared his throat noisily and stood up, crossed the room and went to the window to stare into the street while he got himself under control. It was fortunate that the girls were irrepressible. They were out of their chairs, making cooing noises. Their hugs and commiserations were useful cover. Even Gerald was joining in.

"That's really bad luck, Lawrence."

This caused the girls to giggle, then Daphne and Lawrence joined in. Laughter all round. Such a relief. The muscles of Roland's throat relaxed and now here it was again, a sentiment he had failed to banish earlier in the afternoon. It had come back to him riding the Northern Line to Clapham, standing in the crush, tennis gear over his shoulder. And again on his short walk home through the Old Town and down Rectory Grove, a terrible inappropriate thought. Liberation. He stood under a bigger sky. You are no longer your father's son. You are the only father now. No man stands between you and a clear run at your own grave. Stop pretending—elation is proper, as well as sorrow. He was a novice at death but he knew to be suspicious of first feelings. Surely, they were proof of a reasonable derangement and they would fade. With his back to the room, watching the slow procession of traffic, he reckoned up the options. You buried your parents, or they buried you and grieved more piteously than you ever could for them. There was no greater affliction than losing a child. So count yourself and your father lucky.

→>

A thin teenage girl in a tight black trouser suit opened the door of the undertakers and made a formal nod as he entered. She appeared under instruction not to speak, or she was impaired in some way. As she gestured him towards a chair in a little red waiting room, his thanks sounded too cheerful. She made a placatory gesture with both hands and vanished behind a red velour curtain. The room was tastefully without magazines. On the wall was a framed photograph of a river, too narrow and fast flowing to be the Styx. More like the East Dart, where he had once fished illegally in his teens and caught a large trout with hook and worm—a method to outrage a proper trout fisherman, he learned later. He gutted the catch and roasted it over a campfire and ate it with Francesca, the Italian he had met at the bar of the Crimea Inn, Aldershot. They had a fine weekend, he thought, sleeping rough on Dartmoor in a borrowed tent when he might have been at school, studying for university entrance. But when they got back she wrote to say that she never wanted to see him again. A mystery he failed to solve.

He became aware of a drizzle of sound from a hole in the ceiling above his head, a sustained chord on a whispery synthesiser, backed by far-off breaking waves. After a minute the chord shifted minimally. New Age death music. He was in what was once the living room of a modest house, set between a bike shop and a pharmacy in a low-cost Edwardian terrace. The pine coffee table almost touching his knee had tiny bubbles and the black hair of a brush or perhaps a scalp, trapped in its heavy dark stain—a handmade restoration. None of the chairs matched. The waiting room's makeshift air touched him. Bromley & Carter were trying their best with not much money. They faced the same hard problem as the designers of the grandest tomb, like Napoleon's in Les Invalides, where Roland had once queued with Alissa: the departed was here, then not here—and was not coming back. Polished red quartzite or genteel improvisation, what difference could it make?

He felt anxious, as if his father's death had not yet happened. A suspended outcome, as for Schrödinger's cat. Only the son's presence as witness before the corpse could collapse the wave function and kill the father. He recalled sitting in a room like this with his mother, waiting to be called into the doctor's surgery. As a child of eight he had breathing problems, to which the words sinuses and adenoids were intimately attached like additions to his Christian name. Rosalind also did not know what they were and used them interchangeably. A deadly contest developed between them when they sat before the ear, nose and throat surgeon. Nauseous with dread, Roland listened to his mother exaggerate his symptoms. Shy as he was, he forced himself to butt in and convince the specialist there was little wrong. A little breathing difficulty was nothing to him. On low shelves by a deep square sink were sinister white bowls with dark blue rims where soon might lie some ruined organ torn from his body. He had heard them called kidney bowls. He would say anything, deny everything, to dissuade the doctor from reaching into his wall cupboard where needles, scalpels and steel pliers were stored. No one had explained to him that the procedure he might undergo would take place in the future, elsewhere and with an anaesthetic.

Today's procedure would be without such relief. As for his mother, he would come with her the next day. The curtain parted and the girl's father came towards him with his hand extended. Roland stood to shake it and listened to Mr. Bromley's pleasant expressions of condolence. His resemblance to his daughter was comic. They shared a button nose over a strong jaw. But where her pallor had a retropunkish appeal, his looked like a skin complaint. He needed to get outdoors more.

Roland followed him along a narrow corridor to the back of the house into a larger room. Here the tranquil New Age music was louder. The smell was of a department store cosmetics counter. The body was laid out in the coffin that Rosalind had spent much time choosing. Black suit, white shirt, black tie and shoes, with a hint of grey socks. The ruched and frilled satin lining gave a suggestion of cross-dressing. The Major would have loathed it. But there had been an embarrassing mistake. This was not him. It was gone, the little toothbrush moustache he had first grown during the war, when he became a sergeant major, no longer combat-fit after Dunkirk, and was drilling recruits on the parade grounds of Blandford and Aldershot. The mouth was an enormous slit of a smile, a postbox mouth, round which the entire face was formed. Across the forehead it forced a thoughtful frown that had never been his. Roland turned in bewilderment to Mr. Bromley.

The undertaker calmly anticipated him. "This is your father, Major Robert Baines. His mouth was likely wide open at the moment he passed away. The muscles of course would not have retracted."

"I see."

"I'm sorry. Now, you'll probably like some time alone."

"Would you mind turning that sound off?"

With a sympathetic smile Mr. Bromley pulled up a chair and left him. The synthesiser gave way to the hum of traffic. Roland remained standing. He put out a hand to touch his father's chest. Iced mahogany beneath the thin cotton shirt. There was nothing so surprising or horrific about a corpse after all. Merely a banal absence. What else could he have expected? How easy and tempting, to believe in the soul, in an element that had fled. He stared into the coffin at the closed eyes, looking not for some final truth in the Major's unfamiliar face, but for some feeling of his own, some decent sadness. But he felt nothing, no sorrow, no liberation, no angry accusations, not even numbness. His only thought was of leaving. As at an awkward hospital visit when the conversation flags. What restrained him was what Mr. Bromley might think of a man who could not spare a few minutes beside his father's remains. But he was that man. The sort who takes his lead from a score of half-remembered movies and bends across the coffin for a final kiss. Except this would be the first. The forehead was colder than the chest. As he straightened, a taste of perfume clung to his lips. He wiped them on the back of his hand and left.

The funeral four days later was a dull affair rescued by comic error. It was the day after the general election, the reckoning of New Labour's landslide victory. A 179-seat majority—far beyond expectation. The right's long hold on power was broken. The John Major government had become tired, divided, soured by trivial scandal. Blair and his ministers were young, they had a thousand new ideas, their confidence was boundless. They would shake off the old left and be business-friendly. They would pay attention to the concerns of ordinary voters—classroom sizes, hospitals and crime, especially among the young. Supporters and activists wore their "pledge cards"—five policy promises—with pride. The shift was also cultural. It had already been decided that to be a member of Cabinet and openly gay would no longer be a matter of scandal and dishonour. Tony Blair had been to see the Queen and was in Downing Street giving his first speech as prime minister. Copious hair, good teeth, an energetic stride—he was received like a rock star. The flag-waving crowds along Whitehall were vast, the general euphoria was intense.

Caught up in final preparations for the 5 p.m. funeral, Roland followed events in London with some detachment. He was at his mother's house, phoning Mr. Bromley several times, discussing details of dress with a cockney bagpipe player who specialised in what he called family occasions. Susan thought the sandwiches, beer and tea were not enough. The order went out for sausage rolls, cake, chocolate fingers, crisps, lemonade and cider. Roland glimpsed the TV coverage in the living room between errands. Old habits of mind as a Labour Party member made him suspicious of people waving Union Jacks. No good ever came of it. He could have tried for an association between the demise of a Tory administration and his father's death. But it wouldn't fit. The Major was a Glaswegian working-class man at heart. Many times, he had told the story of being a teenager looking for work in the shipyards along the Clyde. Early in the morning a foreman would address the crowd through the gates. Six day-jobs going. The men gathered there would compete among themselves to bid the pay rate downwards. The jobs went to the lowest bidders. That left a mark.

Robert Baines, unlike his fellows in the officers' mess, was always warm to the idea of a trade union. He had been contemptuous of the attempted takeover of the Labour Party by the hard left. Electability was the thing. "Get power first. Then if you need to, go left!"

Working alongside his mother, Roland set out sandwiches on plates and covered them with clean tea towels. Behind them, the TV's inadequate speakers broadcast the tinny roars of the crowds. For Rosalind, keeping busy was a balm. She had entered a heightened state of normality. She issued instructions in the form of timid prompts. But she had aged and shrunk, she couldn't sleep, the skin under her eyes showed deep wrinkles, like a walnut. The funeral guests were all family on her side, with a few neighbours coming out of respect for her. They had rarely spoken to the Major and he never could remember their names. No one had come from Scotland. For the first time in his life, Roland, surveying the spread, little of it to his taste, realised a simple fact. His father had no friends. Colleagues in the army, drinking pals in the sergeants' and officers' mess—force of circumstance. They had not been in his life for many years. Only now was he beginning to come into clear view. The lawnmower story was one small element. An isolated man; too dominant and forceful in his opinions and a little too deaf for friendships, for being in easy company in the local pub; impatient with ideas that differed from his own; high intelligence frustrated of purpose, by a lack of formal education; no interests beyond his daily newspaper; his devotion to military order and time-keeping grew obsessional with age and masked a profound boredom; drink made everything tolerable, at least to himself.

But he warmly greeted Roland whenever he made one of his widely separated visits. Always keen to sit into the night, drink beer, talk politics, tell stories. If he had not repeated them so often, Roland would not remember them now. Those welcomes became warmer still as the Major aged. A robust smoker from the age of fourteen, he tasted frailty and illness for the first time in his late sixties. Soon, he depended on the tall oxygen cylinder by his chair. Even as he knew he was dying, that his lungs were giving out, he wanted to keep going, to be merry and not complain. What was to be done with the memories of adventures with him in the desert to hunt for a scorpion, of firing a .303, learning to swim and dive, climb ropes, to balance on those broad slippery shoulders while he counted slowly. Where was the son to place his pride in the tough captain, service revolver on his belt, pacing across the oily sand of Gurji camp? How was he to place the hours fishing with him on the banks of the Weser? He would patiently untangle the boy's line from the bushes several times in an afternoon. He taught him to play snooker in the officers' mess, in a panelled room of an old German schloss, was always keen to take the boy out for steak and chips, to repair his toys, help him build camps. And who else in the family would sing so readily or take out a mouth organ? To find people singing ordinarily in company, you'd have to leave England and go to Scotland, Wales or Ireland. Robert Baines entranced his grandson with his absurd bagpipes and growling noises. He had got his hands bloody helping the injured motorcyclist.

He had got up in the night, past 3 a.m., to drive forty miles to collect eighteen-year-old Roland from a motorway hitch-hiking drop-off. And was cheerful when he greeted him. Always keen to press a five-pound note into the teenager's hand. Gave him his first driving lesson, reminding him that when he sat behind a steering wheel he was in possession of a three-quarter-ton steel weapon. Perhaps Robert had taught Roland how to be a father. If so, there were things to unlearn. The man whose love for him was so fierce, so possessive, so frightening when he was small, was also the man who hit Rosalind, who swindled a widow and boasted about it, who dominated all domestic occasions, often drunkenly, who mercilessly repeated his thoughts, who had done some untold thing to earn Susan's hatred. In everything his father was, Roland was implicated. So much he would prefer to set aside and forget. The untangling of these lines would never be complete.

The plan devised by Roland and his sister was to have a Scots piper in kilt and sporran approach slowly from among the trees of Aldershot crematorium while playing "Will Ye No Come Back Again," until he arrived in front of the congregation, and while he continued to play, the coffin would begin its slide towards the furnace. The piper said he only did "Amazing Grace."

The simple ceremony, stripped of hymns and eulogies, as

requested by the deceased, proceeded well enough, with a dignified address from the civil celebrant recommended by the undertakers. When she had finished, she looked across at Susan, who gave Roland a nudge. He went outside to signal to the piper to begin his lament. It had been agreed that he should wait by some leylandii trees on the far side of the car park, a hundred yards away. But an unseasonable mist had descended and Roland could not see his man. He began walking in his direction, but just then the pipes started up and Roland went back inside. The congregation listened as "Amazing Grace," distant but clear enough, slowly began to fade. The piper was marching towards the wrong building. The sound receded to nothing. Roland went out again to look but the mist had thickened and there was no sign of his man. He returned and apologised to the assembly. He said it was likely that the piper was now entertaining the bathers at the Aldershot Lido up the road. The Major would surely approve. Everyone, even Rosalind, laughed. Then the official stepped in and, raising her hand for silence, suggested a minute of contemplation. As it ended, the Major began his last journey, feet first towards a green curtain.

➤➤

Two weeks after she lost her husband of fifty years Rosalind came to stay in London. On the nights that Daphne and her children came over Roland was gratified to have his mother see him as part of a noisy cheerful family. Greta and Nancy immediately attached themselves to her. The three were often in a huddle. For the first time in their lives, Roland and his mother talked at length. The Major, even at his most benign, was a jealous presence. The past was his preserve. He set the terms and the limits. He had been angry when Roland asked him once how and when he had met Rosalind. When he asked his mother the same question, she was loyal and evasive. The standard account remained intact. After the war. 1945.

Rosalind did not seem to be in mourning. She had cared for her husband tenderly to the point of exhaustion, she had lived a half-century in his domain as a compliant army wife. Now, after a glass of sherry before dinner, she laughed easily, she was animated, expansive. Roland had never seen her like this before. She had met Sergeant Robert Baines in 1941, she told Roland and Daphne when the children were in bed.

"You mean '45," Roland said.

"No, 1941." She seemed unaware that she was contradicting the usual version. The lorry runs with the driver, old Pop, were not made to an army depot in Aldershot, but to one by Southampton docks. The sergeant at the gate was "a brute," fussy and meticulous with documents and "very gruff." But he asked her to a dance in the sergeants' mess. That was difficult. She was scared of him and she was a married woman with two children. She declined. He asked her again a month later. This time she faltered. Her mother got out an old dress and between them they altered it. The dance was an awkward tongue-tied affair but Rosalind and Robert started "going about" together, "but no more than that. I would never have done a thing like that, with Jack a soldier at the front." Jack's mother, known to Roland as "Granny Tate," came to hear of what she thought was an affair and was furious. She wrote to her son to tell him what his wife was up to. He had been in the North Africa campaign and was now stationed in Malta.

"When he got the letter Jack went absent without leave and came back to England."

"Without papers, from Malta? In 1943? Not possible."

"Or he got compassionate leave. I don't know. When he came home he said to me, I want to meet this man you've been seeing. So they met over a couple of pints in the Prince of Wales, across the road from the gasworks."

Roland remembered the coking station. Mothers used to take their children to stand about in the yard breathing the fumes to cure their colds and coughs.

Rosalind paused, then spoke directly to Daphne. Another woman would understand. "Jack gave me the run-around for years. Now it was his turn."

So it was an affair, but Roland said nothing. The meeting, Rosalind said, "went all right." That was hard to believe. Jack, an infantryman, took part in the D-Day landings—June 1944—and months

later entered a wood near Nijmegen, was surrounded by German soldiers and shot in the stomach. They left him for dead. He was found
by his own platoon and brought back to England and taken to Alder
Hey hospital in Liverpool.

"The first thing he said to me when I went into the ward was, I led
you a terrible life, Rosie."

Rosalind's pass allowed her to stay for two days. Ten days after
she got back, he died. Eight-year-old Henry was already living with
Granny Tate. Susan had been sent to a place in London founded originally for the daughters of able seamen who had died at sea. In the forties, it kept up a tough regime. She was miserable there but was only
allowed back after she developed a cyst in her throat, which required
surgery. The children were away from her, Rosalind said, "While I
tried to sort my life out."

One old mystery solved. No need to ask why Granny Tate hated
Rosalind. "She died of cancer, screaming in pain."

Rosalind hesitated. She was drifting away in her memories. The
walnut skin around her eyes was a deeper brown, closer to black, the
eyes were sunk and stared out with the unknowing look of the old.
What she said next revealed a side of her he had never known. A message from a harsher time. The form of words was unfamiliar too.

"God takes his debts in more than money."

Roland didn't express surprise at this revision of the past or challenge his mother with the old account. He wanted her to keep telling her history. During her stay in Clapham she spoke less of Robert
than of Jack. Before the war it was always the village policeman who
brought him back after he had vanished for weeks or months. While
Jack was away Rosalind would be destitute and "on the parish"—
living off meagre state assistance. It was obvious that Jack did not go
off to sleep under hedges, or not alone. Despite that, he now appeared
to flourish in Rosalind's memory as a romantic figure, reckless and
unfaithful but thoroughly interesting. He was no longer a forbidden
subject. Unlike her second husband it was adventures he craved, not
discipline and order. He had fought in North Africa and Italy, France,
Belgium and Holland and had died for his country. He shone now and
she could claim him.

To have sexual relations with a woman whose husband was on active service during a war would have earned Robert Baines a dishonourable discharge. In a small village like Ash, Rosalind would have been an object of shame and disgust. Perhaps this was why she moved from her parents' cottage to lodgings in Aldershot. When Roland asked her on another evening she was vague and confused and started to fall back on the old story of meeting Robert at the end of the war. He didn't press her too hard. Later he regretted it. He now understood why Jack Tate was a forbidden subject, the secret blemish on the Major's spotless army record, and why he chose overseas postings when he had the option of returning to England, to Aldershot and its environs. There were many in the area who would still remember Rosalind Morley betraying her husband with Sergeant Robert Baines.

In a bout of insomnia during his mother's visit, Roland recast his parents' story, not as one of shame and concealment, but as a grand passion. Two young people, the handsome sergeant, the pretty young mother falling in love despite themselves, against all current notions of decency. In their innocence they thoughtlessly harmed two children. A tale haunted by a soldier's death, such as Thomas Hardy might tell. Later during that sleepless night the story appeared dreary and sad, and there loomed in the darkness of Roland's bedroom a montage of cigarette clouds, beer puddles on concrete floors, never enough money, of lives ruined by war or constrained by army regulations, by class and the narrow hopes of women's lives.

He borrowed Daphne's car and drove his mother home. She was cheerful at first as they made their slow way through south London. At last she was talking of Robert. She was in a mood to forgive and celebrate him. He was very intelligent and loved a good time and they had lots of good laughs, especially when they were young. He worked hard to get where he did and he was devoted to her really, and she "never wanted for anything." Then she recalled again the very first time she saw him as she and Pop stopped their lorry at the barrier by the guard house. Sergeant Baines came out, straight-backed and glowering, and demanded to see their bona fides and their lists. He scared Rosalind to death.

Roland said, "What year was this?"

"Oh, after the war, son. 1947 it would have been."

He nodded and put the old Beetle into gear as the Wandsworth traffic moved forward again. It had gone from her. The usual story was 1945. She and Robert were married on 4 January 1947. The unease he had felt on and off during her stay was growing. He was too hot. He wound his window down an inch and turned the conversation to ordinary things—the traffic, the weather, the children. She joined in and told him how she adored Greta and Nancy. Gerald, she thought, was a little too withdrawn. She had spent as much time with the girls as with Lawrence.

"When are you going to get married, son?"

He made himself sound earnest. "I'm thinking about it very seriously."

"That's what you always say. It would be good for you."

"I think you're right."

He closed the matter down. He knew what good sense it made to others. Daphne was warm, clever, kind, brilliantly organised. Still beautiful, while he was looking ragged. Lawrence was for it. Her children were wonderful. He also knew what held him back. He couldn't talk himself round. It was not a matter for reasoning. It came down to everything he could not think about now.

When he pulled up outside his mother's house she hunched forward and began to cry silently. He put a hand on her shoulder and murmured useless comforting words. She partly recovered and leaned back in her seat, staring straight ahead. The seat belt was still around her. Delicately, he unfastened it. But he was not prompting her to get out.

She said, as if to herself, "Married fifty-one years."

It took him longer than it should have to make the calculation. Not correct, married in '47, so fifty. Either way, even after fifty years, a good marriage or a bad one was a cause for tears. Recovering more, she repeated the number, her number, in a tone of wonder. Divisible by seventeen, Lawrence would have told them. He liked pointing out such things.

"Mine didn't last two. I'd count yours as a triumph."

She didn't respond. They were parked in a close of ten semi-detached houses, twenty years old, in bright red brick and unenclosed front lawns in the American style, but tiny. He did not know how he could leave her here alone. He had in mind his father's armchair by the window monotonously declaring his absence.

"I'll come in with you for a cup of tea."

The suggestion of an immediate plan helped her out of the car. Indoors, she rallied as she asserted herself over her realm. She wanted him to fill the bird feeder with nuts, to mow the back lawn, move the TV nearer the wall. Writing out a shopping list for him made her cheerful again. The empty chair was no threat. When he came back from the village his mother was setting out a cream tea and arranging pink and white delphiniums from her garden in a vase by a lemon cake she had conjured from an instant mix. While he was unpacking her groceries he saw on the top rack of the fridge, next to a piece of cheese, a bar of soap. He put it back on its dish by the kitchen sink. She was animated over tea. It was possible she could be happy here, on her own for a little while. Soon, she would go to live with Susan and her husband Michael. The house would be sold. When he reminded her of that, she said, "I haven't seen Susan in two years. She doesn't speak to me now."

"You saw her last week."

She looked up, startled, and struggled to make the adjustment and her confabulation. "Oh, *that* Susan."

"Which Susan were you thinking of?"

She shrugged. They chatted happily and afterwards she took him round the little square of back garden to show him the beds crowded with flowers in full bloom and the Penelope roses growing above the patio. She was cheerful as she went out to the car with him and took on a maternal role, asking him if he had enough money to get home. He reassured her but she had a one-pound coin ready in her hand and pressed it into his palm and wouldn't take it back.

Ten miles into his journey he was looking for a place to stop. In his distraction he had already taken a wrong turn and was heading along a minor road in exactly the wrong direction. Mile on mile, southern England appeared to be an infinite suburb interspersed with parades of shops. Tyres, coffee, baby clothes, dog parlours, burgers, new exhausts infested a land whose rich soil and decent rainfall had once nurtured woodland of giant oaks, ashes and wild cherry. Now lonesome survivors lurked on housing estates, at roundabouts, among nettles and litter on the borders of garage forecourts. Traffic and provisions for traffic were the dominant feature. Every van was driven by a teenage madman, every truck pumped out a blue stench. Every car was superior to his. He came to the town of Fleet. As he crossed a bridge, he saw a canal. Perfect. There would be a towpath.

The Basingstoke Canal was beautiful, and he took it all back. The modern age was not yet lost. He walked away from the town and considered the string of instances during his mother's visit, not the minor moments of forgetfulness, but vivid failures of cognition, brief delusional episodes. *She doesn't speak to me now.* There had been a previous soap-in-the-fridge moment while she was staying in London. Later, a vegetable knife. His mother had less than a working brain. The wreathed trellis was tilting at an angle to the actual. He doubted that she could live alone, even for a few weeks. He took out his mobile phone. It was still a novelty, to be able to call his sister on this compact device from under a weeping willow along a deserted stretch of canal. After she had heard him out she told him she had reached the same conclusion. She was intending to phone him to talk about a scan.

He said, "If it's neurodegenerative, they can't do anything."

"It will tell us what to expect."

Afterwards, he kept walking. A canal was a set of thin lakes arranged in steps. A brilliant invention. He would never have thought of it. Or anything else in the built world. A month ago he had taken Lawrence for a walk in the country one Sunday afternoon. They were in the Chilterns, a few miles north of Henley, walking along a track near a farm. Lawrence left the path to look at a wreck of abandoned farm machinery. He trod down a thick growth of nettles.

"Dad. Come and look."

He wanted Roland to count the teeth on a rusting cog. There were fourteen. Then Lawrence asked him to count the teeth on a larger cog that meshed with the first. Twenty-five.

"See? The two numbers are relatively prime. They're co-prime!"

"Meaning?"

"The only number that divides them both is one. That way the teeth of the cogs wear out evenly."

"Why would that be?"

But he did not follow the explanation. In the management of his life he was foolish. In mathematics, moronic. His IQ must have halved, for here was another of those moments when he knew he had reached the summit of his understanding. A ceiling, a mountain fog through which he could not pass. His eleven-year-old son was on higher ground, in a clear space his father would never know.

As he walked he thought that, apart from raising a child, all else in his life had been and remained formless and he could not see how to change it. Money could not save him. Nothing achieved. What happened to the tune he had started to write more than thirty years ago and was going to send to the Beatles? Nothing. What had he made since? Nothing, beyond a million tennis strokes, a thousand renditions of "Climb Every Mountain." He blushed now to read his earnest poems. His father was cut down in an instant. His mother was beginning a decline into mindlessness. He knew that a scan would confirm it. Both fates spoke to his own. In theirs he saw the measure of his own existence. He remembered his parents well enough at his age now. From then onwards nothing changed for them apart from physical decline and illness.

How easy it was to drift through an unchosen life, in a succession of reactions to events. He had never made an important decision. Except to leave school. No, that too was a reaction. He supposed he had put together a sort of education for himself, but that was messily done in a spirit of embarrassment or shame. Whereas Alissa—he saw the beauty of it. On a windy sunlit midweek morning she cleanly transformed her existence as she packed a small suitcase and, leaving her keys behind, walked out the front door, consumed by an ambition for which she was ready to suffer and make others suffer too. Her new novel set in Goethe's Weimar was already in proof and on its way to him from Rüdiger. According to the publisher's flier one of the novel's key moments was the meeting between the poet and Napoleon. "Power, reason and the inconstant heart!" was the publicity tagline.

At this point he turned back along the canal towards Fleet. He remembered his mother's question. Marrying Daphne because everyone said it was a good idea would not be a break from his past but a continuation. So would not marrying her. There was no third way.

Two hours later, when he entered his house, he sensed a difference. Lawrence was over at Daphne's, but that wasn't it. He went into the kitchen. Tidier than usual. His suspicion grew as he walked up to the bedroom. Also neat. He understood moments before he had proof. It was not the first time a woman had deserted this bedroom. He opened the wardrobe where Daphne kept her clothes. Empty. As he turned away, he saw her note on his desk. He sat on the bed to read it. It was hardly necessary. He could have written it for her. He too would have made it short: it was clear that they were not going to move forward. With the pressures of work and family and school runs etc. she could no longer manage to live in two houses. She was sorry for the secrecy but she had been talking to Peter. Since Roland was reluctant to commit, she and Peter were going to make another attempt, not only for the children but for their own peace of mind. She hoped that Roland would remain her close friend. Lawrence must continue to come and play or stay whenever he wanted. She was sorry too that he should read this letter so soon after his father's funeral but Peter had turned up yesterday, unexpectedly. She didn't want Roland to hear her news first from Lawrence. She signed off with "Love."

As he went downstairs, he thought it was her reasonableness that cut him. Nothing to say against it, nothing to contest. Even her secret conversations. If she had told him about them he would have suspected that she was trying to frighten him into marriage. No right to feel wronged. But how reasonable was it, to live with a man who had been violent towards her?

Roland had arrived by the kitchen table. A fine old battered surface of pine, clear from end to end. That wouldn't last now. He took a beer from the fridge. He was not going to fall for the cliché of getting drunk. He would sit and consider. The new government wanted the nation to drink like southern Europeans. From Collioure to Monte Carlo, thoughtful sipping. Outside, it was still light, still warm, but he preferred to be in here. So, it was simple. The old life, he and Lawrence together here in the little house as before. Occasional suppers for his friends and their friends. With or without Daphne. He could try to persuade himself that by his inaction it was his decision, not hers. Holding out for something—but he didn't want to think about that.

He stood and began to pace around the table. Soon, he would give Lawrence a call. He would walk round and fetch him, but he was not ready to face Daphne just yet. He arrived by the piano and paused. To one side, on the floor, were four deep piles of sheet music, mostly arrangements of old favourites, standards, that he used for his work at the hotel. Here, on top, assembled in a long-ago moment of organisational zeal, were a few grouped under the heading "Moon": "Fly Me to the Moon," "Moon River," "Moondance" . . . A minute later, he was searching faster, passing "What a Wonderful World," "Yesterday," "Autumn Leaves," and letting a pile topple across the floor. Next, his old jazz books. Jelly Roll Morton, Erroll Garner, Monk, Jarrett. He kept going. An idle wish had become a need. He was three-quarters through the third pile before he pulled out a Schumann collection. Pure chance. Schubert, Brahms, anyone, anything would do. He sat and opened out the dog-eared assortment of Grade 8 pieces on the stand. All over the page were a fifteen-year-old's pencilled fingerings. These days he never bothered. The music fitted around wherever his fingers happened to be. He leaned forward frowning and attempted to take instructions from his teenage self as he picked his way through the first few bars. Perversely difficult. Tuneless. It was said that Schumann was a hundred years ahead of his time. Sure enough, it sounded atonal. Like a short piece he once knew by Pierre Boulez. He started again. It took him fifteen minutes to make some stumbling partial sense of twenty seconds of music. Irritated, he tried once more, and then he suddenly stopped, stood and walked out of the room. He had banished this kind of music from his life the day he left her, the moment he got on the London train at Ipswich station and he was never going back.

# Part Three

# 9

Lawrence's train from Paris was due into Waterloo at midday. Roland went out to the garden gate, hoping to see his son come along the street with his oversized backpack. He wanted to observe him as he himself had been once, in the three weeks he went travelling abroad alone for the first time. To see him as entirely distinct from himself, not as a son but as others saw him, a young adult with a loping stride and a distracted inward look. As he stood under the robinia tree and waited Roland recalled his own various early excursions—to northern Italy and Greece, long-haul hitch-hikes southwards through the autobahn system, selling his blood in Corinth to buy food, washing dishes in an Athens hotel kitchen and sleeping under an awning on the roof. Never exactly carefree. He wrote postcards to Berners friends, defiantly proclaiming happiness. They were stuck at university, while he was the free spirit. But he could never quite believe it. In his off-duty hours in the afternoons, instead of exploring the city he lay on his rooftop camp bed and made himself read *Clarissa* and next, *The Golden Bowl*. He hated them both, so unsuited to the city's heat and din, but he was fearful of falling behind. Soon he would stop caring and would abandon books in favour of travel subsidised by boring jobs—his lost decade. Lawrence had no such diversions and hardships. He had a roaming train ticket and an offer of a place at a sixth-form college.

After a few minutes Roland returned indoors to finish his preparations for lunch. By the time he had finished it was past one thirty. He checked his mobile and made sure the house phone was properly on its cradle. He had bought Lawrence a phone to travel with. If he had lost it, there were public phones at Waterloo station. Upstairs at his desk he saw the email. "Dropped off at Sams. Back late tonight. x L." Lawrence knew that his father rarely looked at text messages. Roland tried not to mind about the absent apostrophe. Or the mild downward sensation of being dumped. This was a parent's rite of passage. There had been no specific arrangement about lunch. He had been caught out, believing himself proud of Lawrence's independence, then thoughtlessly assumed he would hurry home to see his father. At Lawrence's age Roland had never hurried home. He often caused disappointment with a sudden change of plan. His turn now. Staying cool, saving face, he wrote, "Welcome back! See you later." The email address, he saw now, was Sam's. Probably his laptop.

Roland ate alone, with yesterday's folded newspaper propped against a teapot. The Enron scandal. George Bush had deep connections but was presenting himself as the scourge of corporate corruption. And the bringer of war. Lawrence should have phoned. But no complaining. This was the beginning of the transition, of letting go, though Roland had never heard anyone speak of it, this form of parental dismay. You think of your child as your dependant. Then, as he starts to pull away, you discover that you are a dependant too. It had always cut both ways.

Enron insiders sold their shares before the company crashed. Bush sold his shares. Carl Rove was mentioned. So was Donald Rumsfeld.

There would be more moments like this, slights, and Roland would pretend not to notice. It didn't suit him to become an object or source of guilt. Nor could he risk conflict. Lawrence might be in a vulnerable state. He had come back with a story Roland needed to hear. He must keep his sticky feelings to himself.

He woke just after one to the sound of his son coming up the stairs. His tread was heavy and irregular. There was a pause before he reached the landing. Roland lay on his back listening, waiting to choose the right moment to get up. A long piss with the bathroom door open, then prolonged splashing at the basin, silence, and the tap ran again. Drinking perhaps. The ancient lavatory needed to be pumped firmly to prompt the flush. But this was too violent. It was wild. The handle must have snapped off, for something metallic crashed against the tiled floor. Roland waited for Lawrence to get to his room, let a few more minutes pass then took his dressing gown and went to see him. The overhead light was on. He was on the bed, lying on his side, fully dressed. On the floor by the night table was his backpack and a plastic bucket.

"You OK?

"Feel like shit."

"Drunk."

"And stoned."

"Drink some water."

He gasped, possibly in exasperation. "Dad, better leave me. Just want to lie here."

"Fine."

"Till the room stops spinning."

"I'll take your shoes off."

"No."

He did it anyway. Not easy, levering the high-backed trainers off. "Jesus. Your feet stink."

"So would . . ." But the boy didn't have the will to finish. Roland covered him with a blanket, patted his shoulder and left him.

Before falling asleep he read thirty pages of *Sentimental Education*. Young Frédéric Moreau has fallen deeply in love with an older, married woman. She has touched his hand in farewell at the end of a social evening and soon after, walking home across the Pont Neuf, he stops and in his enraptured state is "seized by one of those tremors of the soul in which one seems to be transported into a higher world." Roland read the sentence again. A touch of her hand. No possibility, at this stage, of sex between them. She probably knows nothing of his feelings. According to the introduction in Roland's paperback, Flaubert himself had fallen in love at the age of fourteen with a twenty-six-year-old woman, also married. She remained in his life, with many gaps, for almost half a century. On whether their love was ever consummated, scholarly opinion differed. Roland turned off his light and though sleep was moving in on him, he stared into the darkness, trying to recall his own higher world. No sound from the other bedroom. With Madame Cornell had he once been one step ahead of Flaubert and his Frédéric on Pont Neuf or one step behind? He didn't think a mere touch of a hand could ever have raised him to such an exquisite state. Madame Arnoux had put out her hand to her other guests and when it was Frédéric's turn he had felt "something permeating every particle of his skin." An enviable highly wrought state denied to children of the 1960s in their carnal impatience. He closed his eyes. Strictly formal social norms, extended denial and much unhappiness would be necessary to feel so much after a courteous handshake. As sleep was dissolving his thoughts the answer came clear: he had been many steps behind.

They did not see much of each other the next day. Lawrence slept into the early afternoon and came down for coffee just as Roland was leaving for Mayfair and his Friday afternoon piano session at the hotel. Father and son hugged briefly, then Roland set off. He had a playlist with him which he had to show to one of the managers—usually a formality. Following the New York and Washington attacks last year, it was advisable to arrive early in order to clear the newly installed security scanner at the staff entrance. In his previous job, the pianist was permitted to come through the main doors used by the guests. He now joined a queue of cleaners and waiters coming in for the evening shift. Mohammed Ayub was the cheerful head of security. Roland raised his arms to be frisked.

Mo said, "You playing 'My Way' tonight like I requested?" The West Yorkshire accent was strong.

"Never heard of it. How does it go?"

Mo turned a shoulder, extended his palms and sang a snatch in a beefy baritone. The little crowd behind laughed and applauded. Still smiling, Roland went downstairs to the basement to change into his dinner jacket. The tea room where he was to play was thickly carpeted and panelled. The grand piano was on a dais fringed with ferns and a brass rail. Over the years he had come to like it here. The air was sweet with the perfume of lavender polish. The high-ceilinged room was orderly and tranquil, there were oil paintings on the walls under antique downlights, of racehorses and favoured dogs. In the centre was a tinkly fountain surrounded by sprays of white lilies. It was turned off when he started playing. The sandwiches and cakes—he had first choice afterwards when there were spares—were excellent. He had hated it, all of it, back when he started. It suffocated him. Now, in his mid-fifties, the tea room was a comfort and a refuge suspended in time, where he had no other business, no past, a soothing contrast to his Clapham home and all its accretions.

And it was here he played his pleasant music. He showed his list to Mary Killy, the manager of the day. She was small and neat, acutely aware of her status. At their first meeting she had told him he should address her as ma'am. He said nothing, but he never had. She had a sharp nose, slightly raised, with flared nostrils, that gave her a well-intentioned interrogative look, as though she was hungry to know all she could about everyone she met. It was a couple of years before he discovered that she knew about music. She had been a third desk violinist at the Royal Opera House and gave it up to raise three children. People said she was too controlling but Roland liked her.

He would be starting with "Getting to Know You," he told her, and would follow with a medley of other show tunes, ending with "I'll Know" from *Guys and Dolls*.

"Fine." Mary pointed further down the list. "Chopin? Nothing thunderous please."

"Just a sweet little nocturne."

"Begin in four minutes."

The room was starting to fill, the tea came out with the cake stands and, cushioned on the weak murmur of elderly voices, Roland drifted off through his boundless repertoire. As long as he knew the tune, he could improvise the harmonies—and he knew many tunes. The other managers didn't notice, whereas Mary objected if his chords became too jazzy. His list was useful as a prompt, but usually one number suggested and flowed into the next. He could daydream while he played. He sometimes wondered if he could fall asleep and keep going. But one element of the job troubled him as much now as it had on his first day. He did not want anyone he knew, anyone from his past, to come in and hear him. An element of pride lingered. None of his friends knew about his promise as a classical player, but some had known him once as a jazz pianist. A few might have remembered him on keyboards with the Peter Mount Posse. He kept quiet about his job unless asked, and then he would dismiss it as very occasional and very dull. He never let Alissa or Daphne come, or any of the others. Lawrence especially was forbidden, though he had never expressed any interest in his father's workplace. He would have loathed it. Secrecy also heightened Roland's sense of the tea room as his sanctuary.

He was coming to the end of "I'll Know." Like all these numbers, he had played this one too often to have much feeling for it. But he remembered the reinvention of the show twenty years back. The director, Richard Eyre, went for a brass sound with jazz harmonies— the sort of thing Mary did not want in the tea room. A lot of neon on stage, and Ian Charleson, who died of AIDS. The Falklands year. But who was with Roland when he saw it? Before Lawrence. Before Alissa. It wasn't Diane, the doctor. It wasn't Naomi from the bookshop. He was thirty-four, in his prime. Certainly not Mireille. As he played, he struggled to summon her. Someone he was with, very lovely, and she was gone from him, no name, no face. He may even have been in love but the mental space was empty, a vacant seat. Around that time he had made a list of people he knew who had died of AIDS. It was savage, but no one spoke much about it now. It was the shame of the living, the helplessness of no cure. Nor did people speak about the Falklands. Awkward in a different way. The years slid over old deaths like a heavy lid. Nearly everything that happens to you in life you forget. Should have kept a journal. So keep one now. The past was filling up with blanks and the present, the touch and scent, the sounds of this moment at his fingertips—"The Girl from Ipanema"—would soon be extinct.

That day there was another pianist on the post-dinner shift and Roland was back home by eight. Lawrence was waiting for him, looking scrubbed pink after a long bath and feeling, he said, only slightly fragile. They walked together through the Old Town to the top of the High Street, towards the Standard Indian Restaurant. Lawrence talked about his trip. Paris, Strasbourg, Munich, Florence, Venice. So far, he was avoiding the important part. The roaming ticket worked well, he liked the cities, crossing the Alps was amazing, he had met up with school friends along the way. This afternoon he had phoned a plumber to fix the broken lavatory. Then he called round at Daphne's for tea. She confirmed the offer of a lowly job for him at the housing association. Six months. Gerald had decided he wanted to go to medical school. He had put his name down for the wrong A levels and would have to persuade the science teachers to take him on. Greta was on her way back from Thailand, Nancy was still hating Birmingham, the town as well as her course. Roland knew all this but he listened as if he didn't. He was relaxed and happy for the moment, walking slowly, catching up on his son's news and feeling the last warmth of the city's day rising from the pavement. Soon he would have to hear the Munich story. Last night's drunkenness confirmed his suspicions. He had tried to warn his son off his plan.

The Standard was empty. It was resisting the modernising trend sweeping through London's Indian restaurants. Here they kept to the old ways of flocked wallpaper, failing spider plants and a wide framed print of a lurid sunset. They took their usual table in a corner by a window and ordered lagers and poppadoms. They were silent in acknowledgement of a change of mood. Not all the details would come out at once. They were to return to the story a few times in the week ahead. Roland was serious about keeping a journal and Lawrence's account would be his first entry.

"OK," Roland said at last. "Let's hear it."

Even before he got there, "Munich was shit." His train stopped outside the station and did not move for two hours. There was no announcement, no explanation. When they pulled into the station the passengers were kept on the platform for half an hour, then escorted by police to one end of the station to wait along with a thousand others. Lawrence had enough German from school and his grandparents to understand what was going on. A bomb scare, the third in a month, probably some al-Qaeda affiliate. But that did not explain why the public should be kept in the station. It annoyed him, the way the German passengers appeared so compliant. Suddenly, again without explanation, they were permitted to leave. He found a cheap hotel and in the afternoon, on Roland's recommendation, visited the Lenbachhaus to look at the Blaue Reiter paintings. He thought his father was wrong. Kandinsky was far superior, far more ambitious and interesting than Gabriele Münter.

Late the next morning he visited Rüdiger in his office. His idea was that the publisher would not be able to resist giving him his mother's address when he was confronted in the flesh. Facing each other over his desk, they chatted for a while. Then Rüdiger was called away to deal with something. Lawrence prowled around the office. Sitting by a pile of books on a windowsill was an out-tray filled with mail. On a hunch he went through the envelopes and there it was, a letter to his mother, a typed address. He couldn't risk being found writing it down. So he memorised it, the town, the street and the number. Rüdiger took him out to lunch as promised. During it Lawrence asked him where his mother lived. The publisher shook his head. He said there was a long history. At the end of it, she had told him never to interfere again in her personal affairs or try to intervene or even mention her family to her or give out her address, otherwise she would take her next book elsewhere.

The manager at the hotel was helpful. It was a village, not a town, twenty kilometres south of Munich. There was an occasional bus from a street near the station. He kindly phoned for some times, and so, by lunchtime the next day Lawrence was walking along her road, looking for the house. The village was "a nondescript sort of place" cut in two by a busy road and set in flat farmland. Her street was on the way out of the village, more a kind of suburb. The houses were modern and looked vaguely like ski chalets but "kind of squat and totally ugly." They were set well apart and he was struck by an absence of trees. Not the sort of place a famous writer would choose to live in. Then he was standing right outside her house. It was like the rest, squat, with heavy beams and plate-glass windows. It looked dark inside. Under its thick overhanging roof the house seemed to be "frowning." He wasn't ready to go to the door so he walked back the way he had come. He was feeling shivery and sick. A man getting out of his car was staring at him. Lawrence took out his phone and pretended to be talking on it.

Five minutes later he was back outside the house, still feeling shaky. He thought about walking away. But what then? His bus back into Munich was not due for three hours. He put his hand up to the bell and took it away instantly. If he pressed it, he thought, his life would change forever. Then, like diving into cold water, "I just made myself do it." He heard the ring from deep in the house and hoped she was out. He heard footsteps on the stairs. Too late, he saw a small enamel sign in Gothic script, mounted at waist height. *Bitte benutzen Sie den Seiteneingang.* Please use the side entrance. His mouth went dry as he heard a lock turn and a bolt withdrawn, then another. The door did not open in an ordinary way. With a loud sucking sound of air pressure against rubber draft excluders, the door was wrenched open, and there she was, "angry as hell," his mother.

"Was wollen Sie?" The tone was loutish. Burglar, fan, delivery boy, she didn't care. She was going to see him off.

"Ich bin—"

She pointed down at the enamel plaque screwed to the wall. Irritation caused her forefinger and its glossy vermilion nail to quiver. "Das Schild! Können Sie nicht lesen?" The sign! Can't you read?

"I'm Lawrence. Your son."

Everything went still. He thought, Anything can happen now. She didn't soften and draw him to her in a spontaneous embrace—one of the possibilities he had played with. There was to be no moment of Shakespearean reconciliation—he had been made to read *The Winter's Tale* at school. Or was it *The Tempest?*

Alissa clapped her hand to her forehead and said loudly, "Christ!"

They looked at each other, making their reckoning. But Lawrence's was vague. He was too nervous to notice or remember much. He thought there was a "sort of shawl thing" round her shoulders. She had a cigarette in her hand, half smoked. Also, she had perhaps a cardigan and perhaps a thick corduroy skirt, even though it was a warm day. There were deep lines around her eyes. She had a "kind of crumpled look."

Roland said in the restaurant, "Probably writing. Rüdiger has told me how she gets furious when she's interrupted."

"Yeah, great. But this was *me*. Let's order. I want something gross, like a vindaloo."

For her part—Roland tried to imagine it—she saw a gangly teenager with a strong gaze in a large head which was shaved close, a style which endearingly enlarged his ears.

Finally, Alissa said in a voice at normal volume, "My question remains. What is it you want?"

"To see you."

"How did you get this address? Rüdiger?"

"I dug deep on the Internet."

"Why didn't you write first?"

A quick shot of anger helped Lawrence out. "You never reply."

"That would have been your answer."

His anxiety, the sickness—what he called his jitters—had vanished. He had nothing to lose. He said to her, "What's up with you?"

She started to speak but "I took the liberty of talking over her—and Dad, it felt great." He said to her, "Why are you so hostile?"

But she took his question seriously. "I'm not asking you in. I took a decision many years ago. Too late now to undo it, do you understand? You think I'm rude. No, I'm being firm. Get this straight." She said it slowly. "I am not taking you on."

He was trying and failing to find words for a knot of thoughts. Something like, why can't you be big enough to write books *and* see me? Other writers have children. But he was also beginning to feel that he might not want this hunched and angry woman in *his* life. It wasn't so hard then to turn away from her. She was making things easy for him.

And then she made them even easier. After he had gone a few steps, she called out, "Are you having treatment for cancer?"

Baffled, he stopped and turned. "No."

"Then grow some hair." She went inside and tried to slam the door behind her but it made the same soft airy sound.

End of story. Brutal and consistent. Father and son contemplated it and sipped their drinks. Roland said, "And then?"

Lawrence walked slowly to the bus stop, then past it and into the village to a *Gasthaus* where he drank a beer. Just one. Then he went back to the bus stop, sat on a bench and waited a long time for his bus. His meeting with his mother had lasted barely three minutes.

Two days later, when they revisited the scene, Lawrence told him that after he reached the bench he started to cry. He "really blubbed" and it went on for several minutes. He was relieved no one walked past. Making up for all the time that he'd missed out on having a mother, all the letters he had written, that scrapbook, all of it—and had never cried. Afterwards, he felt calm and told himself that he was better out of it. She was so obviously a terrible person and she would have been a terrible mother.

Early evening the next day they sat in the garden at the rusty metal table Roland always intended to paint. Further down the garden was the long-dead apple tree he still had not cut down. He was used to it being there. Between father and son, two beers and a bowl of salted nuts. Lawrence had just said in a casual tone that he was beginning to think he hated her. For Lawrence's sake Roland wanted to defend her. It would do him no good, he said, to carry a grievance when there had been none before. He had, remember, tried to talk him out of going to see her. But this was not the time to be speaking up for Alissa. Lawrence could have no clear view of his mother until he had read her, and this he refused to do, and always had. Fine. Best not to come at her novels too early. What could her impassioned advocacy of "rich and warm-blooded rationality" have to say to a committed young mathematician? One that knew so little of literature and history, was yet to fall in love, yet to be disappointed in it and had, as far as Roland could tell, no sexual experience. Build on *Cider with Rosie*, *The Old Man and the Sea* and whatever else his school had put his way. He was still better-read than his father had been at sixteen. Books came in their own time.

Instead, Roland said, "From what I've read, she's become a recluse, a famous hermit."

"In a crap house in a crap place. I can't believe she's any good."

"What are your plans for tonight?"

He was suddenly cheerful. "I met someone on the train from Paris."

"Yes?"

"Véronique. From Montpellier. What do you think about this shirt?"

"You wore it yesterday. Take one of mine."

Lawrence stood. "Thanks. What are you up to?"

"Staying around."

After Lawrence left, he went upstairs. In a drawer in his bedroom, among his old self-important poetry notebooks, was a smaller book bound in fake leather, 250 lined pages, a Christmas present from a forgotten donor, every page a blank. He brought it down to the kitchen table. Recently, before Lawrence's return, he had been out most nights—to suppers in the houses of friends, and two late-evening sessions at the hotel. Like a gong struck minutes ago and still resounding, his head was full of voices. Not just Lawrence's, but a chorus of entangled conversations, loud and contentious, a tumult of analysis, fearful predictions, celebration and angry lament. His life was pouring away from him. Events of three weeks ago were already receding or lost completely in a haze. He had to make himself catch some of it, just a little, or it would have been hardly worth living through. What he and people he had seen lately were thinking, feeling, reading, watching and talking about. Private and public life. Nothing of his own failures and gripes and dreams. No weather, nothing about winter becoming spring at last, about fear of ageing and death, or the accelerating flight of time or the lost goods and harms of childhood. Only the people he saw and what they said. He would make himself do it, half an hour a day at least. Spirit of the age. Start a new notebook every year, full or not. He might fill three in a year. Twenty years, thirty if he was extremely lucky. Ninety volumes! So grand and simple a project.

For an hour and a half he wrote down what he could remember of Lawrence's story. Within fifteen minutes he was vindicated. If he had left it a week half the details would have been lost. Like her painted finger trembling as she pointed at the sign. *Das Schild!* Nothing to be done about the past, but the present could be snatched from oblivion. Now to the other voices. This was more difficult, a concatenation of opinion. Same old cast.

He saw a fist gripping a shirt front over a dinner table and shaking it. But that did not actually happen. Wednesday at Daphne and Peter's. Thursday at Hugh and Yvonne's. But now he intended to spread himself across most of this year. He thought he would line up the opinions, who held them, the setting, the amount they drank, the time they left, drunk and hoarse. But once he had started, he wanted only the opinions, and all the voices in one room, talking at once.

*That* Guardian *fellow was right. They had it coming. A second landslide victory. Come on, man! It's an amazing endorsement. A cause for celebration. The Booker? A bunch of timid time-serving mediocrities. Plus punishing fellow Muslims who change or lose their religion? Total crap, one of the worst thought-systems ever devised. What's he got to hide, dragging his feet over a Freedom of Information Act? This is Thatcher mark two. The wealth gap is widening. North of Watford they're beginning to hate him. You're so wrong, in fact you're not even wrong—Frayn, Hensher, Banville, Thubron, Jacobson, Self—these are serious talents. Screw the lot of them. Comfortable white men of a certain age. Their time is up. And where are the women? Have you seen* City of God? *We walked out. Yeah, of lost elections. But it's a work of genius. That opening shot, that chicken running! There's a purity and beauty in Islam. In a globalised world, it gives meaning to the dispossessed. Oh come on! Unemployment is low, so is inflation and so are interest rates. Minimum wage, the Social Chapter. Your leftier-than-thou stuff makes me vomit. I tell you, when the bodies hit the ground the building shook. Student fees—criminal. Dispossessed? Bin Laden is a bloody trust-fund kid! I don't give a shit, as long as healthcare remains free at the point of delivery. With Diana he was doing his duty. It was always Bowles. That bullshit slogan! Blair is stuffing the NHS with managers. I'll tell you what faith is. Groundless belief and those guys in the planes were men of faith. Daphne's Peter's gone over to the other side. He had lunch with Bill Cash. First step to the break-up of the union. We'll lose all our Scottish Labour MPs, then watch out for English nationalism. It will eat us alive. I'm all for Scottish independence. Fascists with a religious veneer. Then you must hate the Scots. Instead of Whitehall they'll get Brussels. He writes a satirical column for the* Telegraph. *We got drunk and talked Shakespeare. It's not satire, it's lies. Brussels is fine by me. Absolutely no way they'll invade. They know Saddam has nuclear weapons. It's all surface, truth-massaging, paranoid media management. Morally bankrupt. The voters you claim to care about don't agree. You must think they're idiots. Remember his Chicago speech? The so-called just war?*

*It's coming. Now he's got his head right up Bush's arse. Come on Baines. Speak for Scotland. The crappy relativism that's sweeping through the left. Perhaps you think Iraqis enjoy being tortured. They're getting ready, those two, to do something truly catastrophic. You wait, when the SWP and non-violent Islamism make common cause . . . Nifty idea, calling the slaughterers of Muslim schoolgirls freedom fighters. I heard it from Goff— Frayn will win it and by God he deserves it. So these little kids said yeah, we boiled a baby for lunch and buried the bones under the lawn. The therapists, social workers, the court believed everything because they wanted to. The police dug up the lawn—nothing. But they still gave her forty-three years. I'm telling you, if they go in, al-Qaeda will rule Iraq. Have you seen the 500-euro note?*

He took a break to make a sandwich, then wrote until midnight. Fifty-one small pages densely covered. He was woken at two thirty by the pressure in his bladder. That never used to happen. He wondered, as he stood draining into the bowl, whether he should be worried that his stream was so weak. He thought of Joyce, of Stephen and Bloom at the end of their day, pissing side by side at night in the garden. Ithaca. Once Roland had possessed Stephen's trajectory, "higher, more sibilant." Now he had Bloom's, "longer, less irruent." Roland didn't much like his doctor. He wouldn't go.

Afterwards, he stood at the window of the bathroom, which was jammed under the flat roof of a tiny back-addition. He looked down into the garden. The July night was cool, the sky had cleared and a waning moon illuminated starkly the table where he and Lawrence had sat hours before. Strangely, it appeared brilliant white and the grass beneath it black. The two chairs were set at the angles at which they had left them when they separately stood. The dogged fidelity of objects, to remain exactly as they had unthinkingly placed them. He shivered. It was as if he was seeing what he was not meant to see— what was there when he was not, how things would look when he was dead. On his way to his bed, out of habit, he peeped into Lawrence's room. Not back. He thought of phoning. But he wouldn't interfere. Lawrence would soon be seventeen and things might be going well with Véronique. He went back to bed and slept deeply, without dreams. The next morning a few minutes after nine he was woken by the phone. At first, he thought the voice was familiar, from someone in his past. He was still half asleep, vulnerable to all dream-like possibilities. It was a policeman asking politely if he was speaking to Roland Baines. *Sentimental Education* hit the floor as he sat up straight, heart thudding, palm already damp against the receiver, and listened carefully.

→→

In his late twenties, when he took his education in hand, Roland sustained only a mild interest in science. He kept at it but he believed it lacked the human touch. The hidden processes of volcanoes, oak leaves or nebulae—all fine on that, but they did not attract him. When science set itself up on that vital ground where people succeeded or failed to thrive alone or together, where they loved or hated or made decisions, its offerings were weak or contested. It proposed dressed-up truisms, physical accounts of what was already known, of events in the brain long understood or investigated in the parallel universe of the mind. Personal conflict, for example. Known and discussed in literature for 2,700 years since a marital spat between Odysseus and Penelope, when he limped home after a twenty-year absence. Ithaca again. Interesting, perhaps, to know that oxytocin among much else ran through Penelope's arteries at the moment of their later reconciliation, but what more did that tell us of their love?

But Roland persisted. He read science books for the layman, driven less by curiosity than by fear of being left out, an ignoramus for life. Over the course of thirty years he had gone through a half-dozen books about quantum mechanics for the general reader. They were written in bright enticing terms, promising to nail finally the related enigmas of time, space, light, gravity and matter. But he knew no more now than he did before he read the first. It helped that a famous physicist, Richard Feynman, said that nobody understood quantum mechanics.

Some half-remembered concepts remained, probably his own distortions. Gravity affects the flow of time. It also bends space. There is no "stuff" in the world, only events. Nothing goes faster than light. None of it meant or helped much. But there was one little story, a celebrated thought experiment, well known even to those who had never heard of quantum mechanics. Schrödinger's cat. A cat concealed in a steel chamber is either killed or not by a randomly activated device. The cat's state is not known until the chamber is opened. In Schrödinger's account it is both alive and dead until that moment. In the good outcome, at the reveal, a wave function collapses, the live cat jumps into the arms of its owner, while its other version continues as dead in a universe inaccessible to the owner or her cat. By extension, the world divides at every conceivable moment into an infinitude of invisible possibilities.

The Multiple Worlds theory seemed to Roland no less improbable than Adam and Eve in the Garden of Eden. Both were powerful stories and he often summoned the cat when an uncertain matter was about to be resolved. A general election count, the gender of a baby, a football score. The cat came to him in his son's form, that morning in bed when the phone rang and a policeman spoke. Lawrence was simultaneously in a police cell waking with a hangover, or on a brushed steel surface under a sheet, in a morgue. Two states, both real, in perfect equilibrium and he could no longer bear the policeman's politeness—he was asking Roland to confirm his address. Whatever a wave function was, it was about to collapse, and he could do it himself. Heave it over the edge.

"Where is he? What are you telling me?"

"And postcode, if you wouldn't mind, sir."

"For God's sake. Just say it."

"I can't proceed without your—"

"I'm in Clapham. The Old Town." He was loud.

"All right sir. That will do. My name is Charles Moffat, detective constable, and I'm calling you from Brixton police station."

"No."

"I work in the office of recently retired Superintendent Browne."

"What?"

"He last came to see you some years ago, let's see, way back. 1989. Concerning your missing wife."

Emerging from his partial dream-state, reconciling himself to the fact that his son still lived, Roland could only grunt. He could hear him now in the bathroom.

"That was resolved satisfactorily."

"Yes."

"I'm phoning in the hope that you might agree to be interviewed about another matter arising from your conversations with Superintendent Browne."

"What about?"

"I'd rather discuss this with you face to face. Would this afternoon be possible?"

At two o'clock they sat facing each other across the kitchen table, just as Roland had years ago when Chief Inspector Browne called round. Moffat was a wiry fellow with a bright look—in fact, he had a light-bulb-shaped head and face—broad forehead, powerful cheekbones, dainty chin. He was wide-eyed and had negligible eyebrows, which gave him a locked appearance of surprise. Far back, perhaps, Chinese blood in the mix. They passed a few minutes in small talk. Browne was their only point of contact. Two of his three sons had followed their father into the Met. They were at different stations near Enfield.

"That's a tough beat," Moffat said. "They'll learn a lot."

The eldest boy had joined the army and passed through Sandhurst with distinction. About to be posted to Kuwait as part of a small detachment.

"Scoping out the Iraq border?" Roland said.

Moffat smiled. "Cause of great pride all round."

When the small talk was done, he said, "My area is historic sexual abuse. This is just a preliminary enquiry and you're not obliged to answer any of my questions. I'll be very brief." He opened a folder containing Browne's typed notes.

"A colleague was going through Doug's files looking for something else and they noticed an item of interest. First, would you mind confirming your date of birth?"

Roland obliged. He was feeling shivery, but he was confident that it didn't show.

Then Moffat read out, *"When I brought it to an end she didn't fight me . . . et cetera . . . murder hung over all the world."*

"Ah yes."

"These words were from a notebook of yours which Doug Browne photographed."

"Correct."

"There was some misunderstanding that they referred to your missing wife."

Roland nodded.

"And in the course of clearing the matter up, you said you'd been referring to a previous affair with another woman. A sexual affair."

"Exactly."

"How old was this lady?"

"Mid-twenties, I suppose."

"Would you mind telling me her name."

A particular image of Miriam Cornell came to him. The rainy night she threw him out, her tears, the shed key in her hand, about to chuck it onto the floor. According to the theory, there actually existed a realm in which he married her in Edinburgh and was still alive. Contentedly or wretchedly married. Bitterly divorced soon after. All of those, and every other possible outcome for them both. Believe that then you should believe in all the religions and cults of the world at once. Somewhere out of sight they were all true. As were all lies. Stephen Hawking had once said, "When I hear of Schrödinger's cat I reach for my gun." But the idea continued to haunt Roland. More than that, it enticed him. All the routes not taken, alive and well. Down through a rent in the veil of the real he was still in his pyjamas, now in his fifties, living the simple life.

He said, "Why should I tell you her name?"

"I'll come to that. And this murder refers to?"

"At the beginning, the beginning of the affair. The Cuban Missile Crisis. Before your time. Everyone thought there was a chance of a nuclear war. Mass murder."

"October 1962. So you'd just turned fourteen when this relationship began."

"Yes." Roland felt a sensation, not pleasurable, rising up through his spine and an urge, which he suppressed, to stretch and yawn. Neither boredom nor tiredness. Moffat was watching him, waiting for more. Roland held his gaze and waited too.

His determination to find Miriam and confront her had ridden waves and troughs of resolve and inaction. Over the last ten years, mostly the latter. One serious effort was in 1989, after the letter came from the school telling him she had gone to Ireland. He went to the Royal College of Music. A receptionist was helpful. She confirmed from a ledger that Miriam left the college in 1959 with high grades. He returned another day and was introduced to an elderly professor of piano and theory. Miriam's name caused him to frown and say that he vaguely remembered her. Very gifted indeed and he'd never heard from her again. But, he said, he might have been confusing her with someone else.

Around 1992 he made another attempt, crossed Greater London on the Tube to visit, near Epping Forest, a national institute of registered piano teachers. She wasn't on the books. As late as the mid-nineties it was difficult to discover facts about anything or anyone, and no one minded at the time. Your neighbour might move four streets away, live an open life and be near impossible to trace. Every idle enquiry entailed a letter or a phone call, or a journey and a search, or all four. He had the Internet by '96 and for all its radical promise it had nothing on her.

Other daily impediments to systematic sleuthing were child rearing, grubbing a living, tiredness. Then came another element. In the late nineties he went through a Charles Dickens phase. He read eight novels in succession. He had a passion for the novels' delight in human variety, for a generosity of spirit he could barely conceive of in himself. Was it too late to become a better and bigger person? Then he read two biographies. One episode in the life had an effect. When he was eighteen, Dickens, an obscure court reporter with literary ambitions, fell deeply in love with the very pretty Maria Beadnell. She was just twenty. At first, she appeared to encourage him but after returning from finishing school in Paris she rejected him. He had no prospects and her parents had never approved of him. Many years later, when he was more famous than any writer had ever been while still alive, Maria wrote to him. In that stretch of his life Charles was tiring of his marriage to Catherine. In three years it would be over. He had been longing for the erotic intensity of his youth. Now Maria Beadnell revived memories of a great and unfulfilled passion. He could not get her out of his mind. He began to write to her what seemed like love letters. Soon it became clear to him that he had never loved anyone else. Failing to win her when he was young was the greatest failure of his life. Perhaps it was not too late.

Maria, now Mrs. Henry Winter, came to tea at Dickens's home by Regent's Park at a time when Charles knew that Catherine would be out. One look at this lady and the dream dissolved. She was "extremely fat." Her conversation was lame, she was garrulous. Where she had once been whimsical, now she was plain stupid. Their tea together was a polite nightmare. Afterwards, he made sure to keep her out of his life. But what could he have expected? Twenty-four years had passed. The story revealed what Roland had never fully thought through. It was almost forty years since he last saw Miriam. He dreaded what she might have become. He wanted her preserved as she had been. He did not want a bloated sixty-five-year-old matron down on her luck taking her place.

At last, the young policeman said, "She was someone you knew already?"

Roland considered. "You want to bring a case."

"That won't be my decision. Was she a friend of the family? Someone you met on holiday?"

Roland was trying to summon his fourteen-year-old self. A craze for winkle-picker shoes had run through the school. He had begged his mother to buy him a pair. She used her new sewing machine to transform his regulation grey flannels into drainpipe trousers. When he came to Miriam's door on a Saturday morning in October, that's what she would have seen—his Hawaiian shirt unbuttoned almost to the waist, farm mud up his drainpipes, the scuffed footwear of a medieval jester. He had that splay-legged swagger of a boy alive to fresh bulk between his legs. At the height of fashion. Turning up on his bike, unannounced, to get his oats before the world ended. For a woman in her mid-twenties he represented a specialised taste.

He said, "I need to think about it."

"Mr. Baines. You're a victim of abuse. This is a criminal matter."

"You must have more pressing cases. Gruesome ones."

"Historic ones too."

"Why put myself through it?"

"Justice. Your own peace of mind."

"It would be hell."

"We provide expert support. You're probably aware, there's a whole new culture around this. What used to be ignored or dismissed no longer is. The good news is we now have targets. So many successful prosecutions in a year."

"Ah, yes. Targets." He would not tell Moffat that he had once been an enthusiast. Instead, he said, "What's the point of that?"

"If we're good, and I believe we are, our funding goes up and we put more abusers in prison."

"Ever tempted to tilt the evidence? To hit the uh . . . ?"

Moffat smiled. His teeth were unnaturally white. He had made a poor choice at the dentist's. Should have gone for the natural off-white, like Roland had two months before. He was still proud of his new look, effected at cut-price by an old girlfriend turned hygienist. Competitively, he smiled back.

The policeman was gathering up the papers. "So say the press. We've more watertight cases than we can deal with." He paused, then added, "Something savage in the male psyche."

"Clearly."

"But female on male. We only get a few cases like yours."

"Targets for those too?"

Moffat stood and handed his card across the table. "You'll see I've written down a case number. If you came forward, it would help others. Men and boys."

Roland saw the detective constable to the door. As Moffat stepped out of the house he said, "Should have asked you this at the start. Were you damaged by it?"

Roland replied quickly. "No, not at all."

Again, Moffat waited for more, and when it didn't come he turned away, raised a hand in casual farewell and went to his car. Roland closed the door, leaned with his back against it and looked down the hall-way past the banister post into the kitchen. Damage. Here it was. The missing, cracked or loosened floor tiles. Under the frayed and stained stair carpet was dry rot. In the hall, skirting boards were rotting too. The plumbing was failing, the heating system was thirty years old, the window woodwork was turning to dust in parts. He had come to accept he would never afford to move out of the house. It needed a new roof. The wiring safety certificate was dated April 1953. Some ceiling insulation contained asbestos. A builder, a good sort, Roland thought, had said the whole place needed "the works." He and Lawrence lived reasonably well on the weekly money his piano playing and occasional journalism brought in. Nothing left over for the works. One day there would be less. A letter from Alissa's lawyer had given notice that her monthly payments would cease when Lawrence turned eighteen. She would send him cheques via Rüdiger from time to time and take care of any tuition fees in Europe or the US. Very reasonable.

The state of the house was the outward show of a set of conse-quences whose origins he didn't care to think about too closely. The lost decade began at the end of his rooftop stay in Athens, when he binned his half-read Henry James. Back in England he played for the Posse, worked mostly on small building sites, but also in a can-ning factory, as a swimming-pool lifeguard, a dog-walker and in an ice-cream warehouse. Hotel lounge pianist, tennis coach and list-ings magazine reviewer came later in the sequence. His travels, with friends, sometimes alone, included road trips across the States, a spell in the caves of Ios, a long road trip with two Vietnam-draft-dodging friends from Mississippi, to Kabul then Peshawar by way of the Khy-ber Pass. They took their ease in the Swat Valley. When his money ran out and he came back, he slept on sofas and floors and spent time in a squat. There were interesting girlfriends, rock and jazz concerts, festivals, movies—and labour, hard or boring or both. In the seven-ties it was easy to find temporary work.

Those were the days when people talked about "the system." He was against it and cast classical music as integral to it. It suited him to tell people that the piano as made to sound by Bach or Debussy was a tainted remnant, a historical ruin. His twenties were slipping by. He assured himself that he had his freedom and he was having fun. He could control his occasional anxieties about the aimlessness of his existence. But they swelled and finally broke through and could no longer be resisted. He was twenty-eight and not living a useful life. He signed up at the City Lit and the Goethe-Institut. At Labour Party meetings he declared himself a "centrist." His higher education took up almost ten years of on-off study. He sat no formal exams. Many people wasted their twenties or their whole lives in offices, on factory floors and in pubs and went nowhere beyond the beaches of southern Europe. So it had been worthwhile to be carefree, live hand to mouth and not be like everyone else. The very point of being young. Whenever he caught himself thinking or saying things like that, he knew it was himself he needed to convince.

He continued to lean back against the front door. A relief, now that Moffat had gone, to stop pretending that he was not rattled. It was not the shock of learning something new. He had charged her many times, in many ways—but only in his thoughts. The shock was to hear it said out loud by an official of the state. *This is a criminal matter.* Not *was,* but *is.* A second jolt was in the form of a challenge. Was he now prepared to do something about it? The affair had remained coiled snugly below the threshold of action, like a snake in deep shade on a hot day. *And me in my pyjamas for the heat.* It was something between himself and his past, never to be spoken out loud. It did not feature in his thoughts as a secret. Those two years were simply—what exactly? What he once heard a writer call her mental furniture. Not to be rearranged or sold. He had spoken about Miriam only once, to Alissa as they walked through the Liebenau snow. Nothing, no shadow of that confession, no artful recasting of it had appeared in any of her novels. He would have liked to take it back from her so it would remain entirely his own. Moffat was asking him to travel in the other direction and make those Erwarton days available to the court, its officials, its frowning judge, its public gallery, the press. Justice? He was being asked to take revenge. On his Maria Beadnell. Forty years on, not twenty-four. He decided he needed Lawrence's help.

His son now worked a forty-hour week at Daphne's housing association near Elephant & Castle. There were a few weeks before he started at a new school. He earned less than the minimum wage to make coffee, run errands, type simple letters and help set up a website. The place had functioned for years without him. Daphne, his surrogate mother, was doing him and Roland a favour. It was his first job ever. He accepted the routine, the 7:30 alarm, the Northern Line commute, without complaint. He had a firmer work ethic than his father had at that age but he had inherited a similar sense of entitlement to pleasure. He usually went straight from work to see friends. Véronique, who had acting ambitions, was waitressing in Covent Garden. She was his girlfriend and Lawrence was no longer a virgin. Their first sexual encounter, in her room, part of a shared flat near Earls Court, was "shambolic." He didn't want to tell his father what went wrong. But the second, in the deserted graveyard of St. Anne's Church, Soho, was "amazing." Roland could not imagine that the grounds around the famous Wren church were ever deserted, especially in the small hours. Nor could he imagine talking to his own father about such things. He felt flattered. To cross this significant line, Roland thought, might help distance Lawrence from the bad moment with his mother. He had listened to his father's homily on the vital matters of consent and contraception with some impatience.

"Don't worry. You won't be a grandfather just yet."

Roland was not able to talk to Lawrence until late Saturday morning. They were at the garden table again, drinking coffee. There was someone from his past, Roland said. He would like to be in touch with her again. Would Lawrence try and track her down on the Internet? Was this an ex-girlfriend? No, this was his old piano teacher. He had always wanted to know what happened to her. She might not even be alive. He gave some details, including her date of birth, 5 May 1938, she grew up near Rye, from '56 to '59 attended the Royal College, then Berners Hall from '59 to '65, after that perhaps lived in Ireland. Lawrence went indoors and was back in minutes with a sheet of paper in his hand.

"Dead easy. You're in luck. Alive and close by. Balham. Still teaching. There's even a phone number."

Lawrence set the page down on the table but Roland did not pick it up in case his hand shook.

All afternoon he was distracted. He found her street in the *A to Z*. Balham. Two stops away. He forced himself to mindless tasks, cut the lawn with the manual mower, cleaned up the kitchen, phoned an electrician. He walked up and down outside for a few minutes, went indoors and made the phone call. Then he took a shower.

After six, as he was drinking a beer in the garden, Lawrence came out to say goodbye before heading into town. He was meeting Véronique when she came off her day shift at the pizza restaurant. But he sat down heavily and gave his father a look, one of cocky challenge that Roland knew well. It sometimes irritated him. It said, I've something to say and don't pretend you don't know what it is.

"I've got a few minutes so, uh . . ."

"Great. Get yourself a beer."

"I won't, thanks. Look, there's something . . ."

Roland waited. His heart made an ectopic beat, just one. Perfectly harmless.

"It's this. I'm sick of maths. Sick of studying. I don't think I want to stay on at school." He watched his father as this sank in.

Lawrence had earned a coveted place at a sixth-form college that specialised in maths. Roland did not speak for half a minute. He understood that Véronique was part of this.

"But you're brilliant at—"

"No, I'm OK at it. Brilliant compared to you, Dad. If I went, the college would show me what brilliant really is."

"You can't know that." Roland was trying to suppress the sense that he was the one, not Lawrence, who was about to lose his sixth-form place—again. The vicarious living that parents must do.

"I wasn't even the best at school. Ah Ting was always ahead. She didn't even try."

"Your teacher said you had more imagination."

China rising. Nothing could prevent it. Trade opened minds and societies. With commercial success, the Chinese Communist Party must wither away—one good outcome Roland was certain of. He said, "Perhaps you need a year out. They can hold open your place."

"The college doesn't do that."

Roland sighed. He had to be careful, he should stop arguing. To oppose Lawrence now would raise his resistance. So he said, "All right. What is it you want?"

This was the question. Lawrence looked away before speaking. "I dunno . . ." He didn't want to say it. It was going to be a terrible plan.

"C'mon. Spit it out."

"I've been thinking about acting."

Roland stared at him. Yes, Véronique.

Lawrence looked down at his lap. "Rada or the Central. Or. I don't know. Perhaps in Montpellier."

He shouldn't argue with him. He should hear him out. But Roland argued. He avoided Montpellier for now. "The kids who get into Rada are driven. Stagestruck. You've never been interested. You weren't in a single school play. You don't read plays. You've never wanted to come with me to any—"

"Yeah. That was a mistake. I'm taking an interest now."

"So what have you been—"

"Nothing yet. Look, Dad. It's not the theatre. It's television."

It was important not to raise his voice. But he raised it, spread his hands in theatrical bafflement. "But you hardly ever watch TV."

"I will."

Roland pressed his palm to his forehead. He was a better actor than his son. "This is summer madness!"

Lawrence took out his phone and checked the time. He stood and came round the table, behind Roland's chair and looped his arms around his neck. He kissed his father's head.

"I'll see you later."

"Promise me one thing. You've got time. Don't go cancelling your place tomorrow. It's a life decision. A big one. We need to talk."

"Uhuh."

Lawrence had taken several steps towards the house when he stopped and turned. "Did you get in touch with her?"

"Sure. And thanks for your help. I booked a lesson."

➤➤

He walked because he was cautious. No, uptight. He did not trust the Tube. Only a minuscule faction, credulous and cruel, believed that the New York hijackers reclined in paradise and should be followed. But here, in a population of 60 million, there must be some. Chosen from among the bearers of "Rushdie Must Die" placards or the burners of his novel, or from among the younger brothers, sons and daughters. That was chapter one, thirteen years ago. Chapter two, the Twin Towers. The next chapter was likely to be a story of punitive revenge, of military invasion, not of Saudi Arabia where the attackers came from, but its murderous neighbour to the north. Two-thirds of the American public were persuaded that Saddam was responsible for the New York slaughter. The prime minister was inflamed by traditional loyalty to the US and successful interventions in Sierra Leone and Kosovo. The country was preparing for war.

Earlier in the year emergency services paralysed central London with a rehearsal for a terrorist bomb on the Tube. The vulnerable obvious place. Tight spaces to amplify the explosion, usefully dense crowds, no easy rescue in dark tunnels blocked by steel wreckage obscured by poisonous fumes. A shortcut to paradise. He thought about it often, too often. Never take the Underground again, was Roland's current thinking, though he failed to persuade Lawrence. The buses too could not be trusted. So he went on foot. From Old Town to the far side of Balham, cutting across the Common, was barely two miles.

He thought he could pass a forty-minute stroll preparing himself, settling himself. What did he want from her? To fulfil the promise he had been making for most of his adult life. Meet her, bring an adult understanding to the episode of his late childhood and never see her again. Simple. But he dreaded meeting her. All morning, dry mouth, however much he drank, loose bowels, constant yawning. He had eaten no lunch. And his thoughts would not remain fixed on what immediately lay ahead. They were entangled with the national obsession—also a matter of dread. There was only one conversation. Hard to banish it, even for half an hour. The drift into war, driven by a government he had supported with some disappointments along the way. Since Berlin, he had lived within a misty sense of political optimism. Last year such hopes were degraded when the towers and their human cargos dissolved into the ground. The response was going to be violently irrational. What he also feared were the consequences. They rose in his thoughts as a black hammerhead cloud of international disorder, its malevolence and direction aggravated by unknowable elements. It could be hell. So too could meeting Miriam Cornell.

He passed the Windmill pub and ten minutes later stopped outside Clapham South Tube. He leaned with his elbows resting against black railings by a tangle of locked bicycles. He needed to concentrate. The dictum from childhood still held: nothing is ever as you imagine it. So he should imagine her now and exclude the worst. An overheated top-floor flat, cramped, unaired, a mantelpiece crowded with mementoes, heavy odours of recent cooking, of her lotions and talcs. Bitterness in the air too. A nuisance of a small dog or many cats. A piano somewhere. She would be hideous, with a clumsy smear of red lipstick, and overweight. There would be shouting, even screaming, hers, his, both.

He made himself walk on. He did not have to go. He could send cash for the cancelled lesson, scrawl apologies over his false name. But he kept going. He wouldn't forgive himself otherwise. A precedent came to mind. Dragging himself round Aldershot, delaying his arrival at the funeral parlour where his father lay. But this corpse would be alive, disinterred from the deepest tomb of memory by an earnest police constable. *Dirt of the grave in her hair.* Soon he would be attending his mother. Her mind, her personality was going but still she hung on in her dreamworld, her no-man's-land, not unhappy, sustained by certainty that her suburban care home was a grand hotel, sometimes a cruise liner. Occasionally she believed she owned the ship. This time he would be better prepared. He would sit by her open coffin, perhaps in black, probably alone in that same room, his hands folded on his lap. These days he often thought of James Joyce. *She, too, would soon be a shade . . . One by one, they were all becoming shades.*

Where he was arriving now was once a joke, the last place in London anyone would want to be, its reputation fixed by Peter Sellers's mock travelogue sketch, "Balham, Gateway to the South." Now, it was on the turn, young professionals and their money were cleaning the place up. But old Balham still commanded the high street. A fading Woolworths, the usual betting and charity shops, a Poundland store. The old energy lingered too. On the pavement, barring his way, a barker was calling out fruit and vegetable prices and tried to press a brown paper bag of tomatoes into Roland's hands.

After he had left the gateway to the south he crossed the road and turned west down a side street. He had memorised the *A to Z*. Three blocks on he went south again then made a right turn. These Victorian villas would have turned into rooming houses in the early thirties. Now they were on their way back to single-occupancy. Scaffolding, builders' vans, men up high ladders repointing the London stock. This was her road. The large detached house was at the far end, on the corner. She had asked him on the phone not to arrive early. Nothing in her voice had sounded familiar. Seven minutes to go. No scaffolding at her address, for the work was already done. A sapling cherry was the centrepiece of a wide rectangle of closely mown grass. It may have been artificial lawn. He walked right past, not wanting to be observed lingering outside and set off around the block.

The student before him, a woman in her early twenties, was just leaving the house as he returned. He slowed his pace to let her go then mounted two granite steps to the entrance. There was only one doorbell. It was the original generous ceramic with grey hairline fractures, set in concentric circles of unpolished brass. He made sure not to hesitate and pressed it, though he felt sudden doubt, a mild bewilderment. The door opened after seconds, and there she was. But she turned away from him instantly, pulled the door wide open as she went back into the house and called out over her shoulder, "Mr. Monk. Marvellous. Do come in." Well used to a daily succession of faceless students. The hallway was broad and long, its floor brightly tiled, a grander version of his own. A staircase of milky limestone rose and curved in shallow ascent. Perhaps the place was Edwardian. He followed her into the sitting room, two rooms knocked together in the conventional manner. But the steel joists were tucked out of sight beyond the ceiling whose mouldings had been refashioned into an oval in the Adam style more than fifty feet in length. Such space and light and order. He saw it all and understood, for it was much that he had idly planned to do in miniature to his own place. And would have if the Epithalamium money had come. Wide dark floorboards, white walls, no paintings, a single armchair in the bergère style, French windows onto a quarter-acre flower garden. The only shelves held sheet music. Dead centre was the piano, a Fazioli concert grand. Someone with money must have entered her life.

She had her back to him, returning music from her last session to the shelves. She was still slim, and taller than he remembered. Her hair was white, tied back in a long ponytail. Without turning she waved him towards the piano stool. "Please sit down, Mr. Monk. Bear with me while I put these away. Play me something. Give me an idea of what you're about."

This time he thought he caught a familiar inflection in her voice. Memory's smoke and mirrors. But he didn't doubt that it was her. He went to the piano, adjusted the stool's height and sat, surprised to find that his heart was steady. In all that he had imagined, her invitation to play was the only element he had accurately foreseen. His name was not chosen at random. Positioning his hands then pausing, he played a major chord. Instantly, he felt it—the action of the keys so silky, the sound so beautiful, rich, enveloping—and amplified in the carpetless room. He felt and heard it in the hollow space below his sternum.

"Do you have a first name, Mr. Monk?"

The facetiousness he remembered.

"Theo."

"Go on then, Theo."

He played " 'Round Midnight" as he remembered the 1947 recording, a little more sweetly perhaps, with a meditative tempo. After the intro and the first line she was suddenly there on his left, standing too close.

"What do you want?"

He broke off and stood to face her. Now that he saw her clearly he recognised the face he once knew and imagined he understood the connection, the line of descent from 1964 to 2002. It was as if he was seeing a mask, one formed from, perhaps, her mother's face with Miriam, the real Miriam, behind it pretending not to be there.

"I want to talk to you."

"I don't want you here."

"Of course you don't." He said it sympathetically. He was not leaving yet. The most striking change, he decided, was not so obviously the coarsening of age as the lengthening of her face, of its youthful roundness. It had drawn her features minimally downwards to give her an imperious look. The high-born Roman matron. The eyes, even their green, even the lashes, looked familiar. The nose still had some trace of the slight insufficiency he had once adored. But round her lips, which were thin, were radiating cobweb lines. It was a severe mouth. A lifetime issuing instruction at the keyboard. She was returning his stare making the same kind of reckoning, he guessed. The lesson of the years. Never good, but she had come through them better than he had. Her mid-sixties against his mid-fifties. She had kept all her hair, he had not. She was still trim around the waist. He was not. Her forehead was smooth while his had three deep parallel lines. His face was a permanent salmon pink from the tennis-court years. When he shaved in the mornings he was irked by the bloated mass of his nose, by its enlarged pores. His teeth at least were respectable. Hers more so. Neither wore wedding rings. She had a gold bracelet. He had a fat plastic Swatch. That was it: she looked—he had to concede the notion—more expensive, obviously richer, better cared for, more at home in her world than he was in his. But he was not intimidated. After all, Balham! If he had been more confident about such things he would have said that her cream blouse was of wild silk, that her skirt bore some high-fashion label, Lanvin, Celine, Mugler, as did her pale blue high heels. He was aware of her perfume. Not rosewater. There was progress.

She had been staring at him in silence for an indecisive half-minute, no doubt wondering how to get him out of her house. She turned suddenly and went to stand by the French windows. Her heels sounded brisk in the long room.

"So. Roland. What is it you'd like to discuss?" Mock patience. She was speaking down to him. He didn't like it when she spoke his name.

"We're going to talk about you."

"Well then?"

"You know well enough."

"Go on."

"I was fourteen."

She turned from him and opened the double doors to the garden. He thought she was about to invite him outside. He would have resisted. But she came back, took a pace towards him and said simply, "Say what you have to say then get out."

Her lack of indifference encouraged him. She was as troubled as he was. He had a few options but without considering them he came to the point, a half-truth. "The police are interested in you."

"You went to them?"

He shook his head and paused. "They know something and they came to me."

"So?"

"They don't yet know your name."

Miriam was not perturbed. "I taught you piano a long time ago. Will that interest them?"

He came away from the piano stool and went to stand by the armchair. To sit would have suited him but this was not the time. He said, "Oh, I see. Your word against mine."

She was staring at him hard. He thought he remembered that this was how she used to be before they had a row. Or he was inventing.

She said it pityingly. "Poor thing. You haven't got over it, have you?"

"Have you?"

She too did not answer. They continued to look at each other. For all her poise he could see in the shifting folds of her blouse her altered breathing. Finally she said, "Actually, I think this would be the moment for you to leave."

He cleared his throat noisily. He felt scared. There was an inconvenient tremor in his right knee. He steadied himself against the chair. "I'll stay a little."

"You're trespassing. Please don't make me call the police."

His voice sounded feeble in his ears. He made himself speak up. "Go ahead. I have your case number with me."

"I don't care. You're an unfortunate man with an unpleasant fixation."

The phone was on the floor by the piano at the end of a long lead. As she went towards it, he said, "I still have my birthday present."

She looked at him blankly. The receiver was in her hand.

"Receipt for reserved seats on the Edinburgh train in our names, a hotel letter in response to yours, looking forward to welcoming us to our suite on the day before my sixteenth. Papers for our registry office wedding the day after."

He had not planned to speak of it so soon. But once he had started he did not know how to stop.

Nothing changed in her expression but she had put the phone down. He wondered about Botox. He was always poor at spotting it. She spoke carefully. "You've come to blackmail me."

"Fuck off." The words were out before he knew it.

She flinched. "Then why are you here?"

"There are things I want to know."

"So you can 'move on.'"

"If you don't want to talk to me now I'll hear it in court."

She was standing by the piano, her left hand resting on it, her forefinger soundlessly stroking or worrying the lowest key. She was scathing. "A confession. An apology. Under threat."

"That sort of thing."

"And record it all on your special little tape recorder."

"I don't need it and it doesn't exist." But he removed his jacket for her to see and dropped it on the chair. He folded his arms and waited. She stepped through the French windows and stood with her back to him. Weighing her options. But there were only two. While she couldn't see him Roland stooped to put his hand on his shaking knee and squeeze hard. It made no difference. The minute vibrations in the muscles were steady, like those of an electric motor. Shifting his weight to the other foot helped a little. He squeezed again harder.

Then he straightened abruptly as she turned and came back into the room. "Very well. Let's talk," she said brightly. "Come down to the kitchen. I'll make us a hot drink."

It was her bid to take control. Show off her fifty-foot kitchen. Turn him into an appreciative guest. Her place, not his.

"We'll stay here," he said quietly.

"Then at least have a seat." She was about to take the piano stool.

"We'll stand." He longed to sit. He thought that at any moment he could lose everything, that only a fine gauze separated him from leaving in despair, from crashing through into another dispensation in which a self-annihilating spirit would obliterate his will to proceed. There was nothing between them, no protection. What they each saw filled them with disappointment and dismay at their own reflected decline. What threatened to overpower him was the past.

"I want you to describe it from the beginning from your point of view, what you felt, what you wanted, what you thought you were doing. I want to hear everything."

She came away from the piano stool and took a couple of steps towards him. Even though he had offered her little choice it surprised him, her sudden compliance. But he was still frightened of her. He didn't want her to come any closer.

"All right. That day in October when you showed up at my—"

"Stop there." He held up a hand. "The beginning. You know that wasn't the beginning. I'm talking about the lessons. Three years before."

She appeared to sag a little as she stared at a point on the floor. He thought he saw her shake her head and he was expecting resistance. Impossible, to talk to a stranger about such intimate things. But now her voice was different, not only lower but more uncertain. He could only wonder at the sudden change in register. It was a transformation.

"All right. I suppose this was always going to happen. And if that's what you want, I'll tell you."

Her gaze was still downwards as she drew breath. He waited. When at last she lifted her head and she spoke again she still did not meet his eye. "It was a terrible terrible time. I was at the Royal College of Music and I'd had a serious affair with a student in my year. More than that. We were in love, or I certainly was. We lived together for two years. But in my final year I got pregnant. Back then a calamity. Somehow we managed to scrape together the money and arrange an abortion in the Easter vacation. My friend, his name was David, had to sell his cello. Our parents knew nothing. It wasn't straightforward, there were all kinds of medical complications, the person I saw wasn't a proper doctor. I was ill, then the relationship fell apart. I got through finals. I went to County Hall for an interview and was offered the job at Berners. I thought that getting away was the best thing. Lick my wounds. But I hated it. The head of music, Merlin Clare, was kind to me, but the rest of the staff . . . those morning coffee breaks in the staffroom in the main hall . . . in those days, an unmarried woman was a sort of threat and at the same time a lure, a challenge. Whatever it was, I felt isolated. Same thing in the village. A young woman living on her own. Unheard of in 1959 in rural Suffolk. I think they thought I was a witch."

"Am I supposed to feel sorry for you?"

She paused then she said, "It might help you to stop seeing it all through the eyes of a child."

A silence fell on them. Roland thought that the eyes of the child he had been were precisely what he needed. He said nothing and finally she went on.

"The abortion upset me badly. I was devastated by the end of the affair. I'd been so close to David. I missed my friends, and I was hopeless at teaching, either one-to-one on the piano, or to thirty kids in the classroom. Then you started your lessons. You were quiet, shy, vulnerable, a long way from home. It set off something in me. I tried to explain it away as frustrated maternal feeling. And my loneliness. Or because little boys can be pretty, these were buried lesbian feelings I was discovering. I wanted to adopt you. You were so quiet and unhappy. But it was more than all of those. I knew that really, but I couldn't admit it to myself. The other thing was that very soon I could tell that you were gifted. There was one time you came in. I thought I knew you well enough by then to be convinced you were lying when you said you'd been practising the first Bach prelude. But I was wrong. You played it so beautifully, expressively, with such a lovely touch. Impossible sounds, coming from a child! I had to turn away because I thought I might cry. Then, I couldn't help myself, I kissed you. On the lips. As my feelings about your coming each week got stronger the only way I could deal with them was to be or pretend to be very strict with you. I mocked you. I even hit you, slapped you hard."

"You used a ruler."

"And there was that other time. Before or after the prelude, I can't remember. I was so ashamed. By then, I was hopelessly obsessed. I touched you. And when I did I almost passed out. I knew this was not going to stop easily. It was not maternal. Or it was all of that, and everything else."

"There was a sadistic element."

"No, it was never that. It was possession. I had to have you. It was madness. A sexually immature little boy. I couldn't make sense of it. A scruffy little boy among scores of other scruffy schoolboys. I thought of giving in my notice but I couldn't. I just wasn't strong enough. I couldn't leave. But I arranged for you to have your lessons with Merlin Clare and even as I did that I invited you to come and have lunch in the cottage. Madness. I was in a bad state when you didn't turn up. But I also knew that it was lucky for me. I can't bear to think what would have happened. I convinced myself that I had to get close to you in order to nurture your talent. It was my professional duty. You were clearly going to be a superb pianist, right out of my league. You certainly were when I last saw you. You were already playing the first Chopin ballade. It was astonishing. There may have been some sense in wanting to be your teacher but I was fooling myself. It was you I wanted.

"After I handed you over to Merlin Clare I stayed clear of you. If I saw you in the distance . . . and how I longed to see you, just *see* you. But if I saw you coming towards me, I'd walk away."

They had crossed a line with these memories and now he felt free. He spoke over her, unable to hide his anger. "You should have left the school. You keep coming across as the victim, the poor unhappy girl swept away by feelings beyond her control. You the victim, not me. Come on! You were the grown-up. You had choices. You chose to stay."

She was silent, nodding slightly, considering, perhaps agreeing. But when she continued he thought there was something clammy and impregnable in her account. As if she had never let the air in, never exposed it to anyone else.

"You said you wanted my point of view, my feelings. That's what I'm talking about. My feelings. Not yours. Not yours. I was living on the edge. I thought I should have therapy of some kind but Ipswich in those days had nothing. And I couldn't imagine ever telling anyone that I was sexually obsessed by a little boy. I didn't dare use the word love. It was too ridiculous. And far more than that. Disgusting. And you're right, cruel. I couldn't tell my closest friend, Anna, even though she knew there was something wrong with me. It was simply too pathetic, laughable. Criminal. But at night, alone in that little house, I returned again and again to those shameful moments when I touched you and kissed you. Those memories thrilled me Roland. But in the morning—"

"Don't use my name. I don't want you to say my first name."

"I'm sorry." She watched him, waiting for more. Then she said, "Slowly, slowly, things began to get better. There were times when I relapsed and became depressed but generally I was improving. Convalescing. There was someone I met in Chelmondiston and we came close to having an affair though it didn't quite work out. The less I saw of you the stronger I became. I knew that soon you'd be an adolescent, a different kind of boy. The child who obsessed me would be gone forever and I would recover. And if I didn't then I could wait longer if I had to, until you were eighteen or twenty—and then see. I was beginning to enjoy the work, I was accepted in the staffroom, I helped Merlin put on *Der Freischütz*, then that terrible opera, *The Emperor's New Clothes*.

"Two years passed, then everything came apart when I saw you out of the window. You came in through the garden gate and threw your bike down and strode up to my door. You looked like you knew what you wanted. Of course, you had changed physically, but one glance was enough for me. My feelings were the same. I felt myself sinking." She paused. "If only you hadn't come that day . . ."

His anger was colder. "My fault, was it, turning up like that? Come on Miss Cornell. Please get the timing right. And the details.

And the responsibility. Three years earlier you put your hand on my cock. You, the teacher."

She flinched again.

He said, "It had an effect, do you understand? An effect!"

She sat down heavily on the piano stool. "Believe me . . . Mr. Baines. I accept that. Every part of it. I harmed you. I understand that. But I can only tell this story as I remember it, as I remember feeling it. I know it was my responsibility, not yours, that I sank to this. You're right. I shouldn't have said if only you hadn't come. What I did *caused* you to come. I understand that."

Now he did not like the desperation in her voice. She was working too hard to keep him from revealing her name to the police. Was that too cynical? He didn't know. Perhaps there was nothing that could ever satisfy him. He said, "Go on then."

"You came in. Even then, I was telling myself it would be good to catch up with your playing. That's how I proceeded, step by step, try-ing to persuade myself of things I didn't *really* believe. As if someone invisible in the room was watching and I had to keep up appearances. So we played a duet, a Mozart four-hander. Your playing amazed me. You had a fantastic touch. I could hardly keep up and all the time I was thinking that afterwards I would show you to the door and at the same time knew that I wouldn't. We went upstairs. No, you're right. Let me say it again. I took you upstairs. And then, well, you know."

From far away came the continuous high-pitched sound of chil-dren playing. Beyond that, the softest murmur of traffic. He took his jacket from the chair and sat down. His knee was no longer giving him trouble. He said, "Carry on."

"That was the beginning, one of many beginnings. Before any-thing else I should just say this. It's the horrible truth. For the rest of my life I never again experienced—"

"I don't want to hear about the rest of your life."

"Let me just say that it was intense. I became very possessive. I knew I was taking you away from schoolwork, friends, sports, every-thing. I didn't care. I wanted to take you away. Early on, just one time, I thought I'd come to my senses and I could break it off. I didn't see you for several days. But I was too weak. Hopeless. Without you, without . . . it, I was physically ill. I ached, my bones hurt." Suddenly, she laughed. "There was a song going round. I couldn't get it out of my head. Peggy Lee singing 'Fever.' And that sonnet, one of his best, 'My love is as a fever longing . . .' "

Roland felt vague disquiet in the face of an unfamiliar cultural reference. It sounded like Shakespeare. He interrupted roughly. "Let's stay with the situation."

"So I got you back and we continued. Amazingly, I still tried to reassure myself with that same lie, or quarter-truth—I was giving you hours of piano tuition a week. In fact, you were making incredible progress. You were leaving me behind. We gave that concert in Norwich. The time went so quickly and as I saw it, there was an intolerable situation ahead of us, ahead of me. Kept back from school, from revision and all that, you might fail your exams, they wouldn't let you back and I wouldn't see you again. Or if you scraped through and started in the sixth you'd be preparing for university or whatever and you'd begin to grow away from me. The more obvious that was, the more inevitable, the more extreme I became. Which was what those two weeks in the summer of sixty-five were all about."

"Sixty-four."

"Are you sure? You failed your exams. Because of me. But that busybody Neil Clayton got involved and they let you back in anyway. I was frightened of your returning to school. I knew it would be the beginning of the end. I wasn't going to let it happen. So another beginning, a terrible one. Locking you in the house. Piano summer school in Aldeburgh. I couldn't keep my mind on the work. These kindly retired people fixated on recovering the lessons they gave up on half a century before. Dead set on their grade exams. I hated them. I could only think of you waiting for me in the cottage.

"Then came the worst. The worst of me. You were thinking of the first day of term, talking about rugby and working harder and seeing your friends again. I had no intention of letting you go. Your set books were locked in your trunk along with your school uniform. It was a bizarre state of mind I was in. If I could be happy, I reasoned, then you would be too. Selfish and cruel by any other standards but my own. I was driven. I had only one thought, one ambition. To keep you with me always. I had fantasies, not completely unreasonable, that I would encourage you to go to the Royal College. And I'd come to London with you. After three years help you with your career, be your manager. The same old self-deceiving lies. All I wanted was you. I wanted you and so I made my plans for Edinburgh. Again, I was able to make it seem rational. You would never find anyone who understood you so deeply or would care for you more devotedly. Neither of us would ever find greater sexual fulfilment. Marriage was the obvious next step. It was always where we were heading and a wedding would be legal in Scotland. I was so caught up in my schemes that I didn't expect resistance from you. I wasn't used to it and I was furious. But even then, in the middle of all that, I was making another plan. Let you start at school then I'd come and get you, reel you in like I did before. I'd have you back and we'd continue as usual. I managed to wait four days. But you hadn't appeared on the first day of term. Then the school office told me you were never coming back. I was distraught. I had your parents' address in Germany, but I didn't write. It was my only successful piece of resistance."

Silence again. She seemed to be waiting for his judgement. His decision. When it didn't come she said, "I've something to add if you can bear it. I don't know if you went to another school or what you did with yourself over the years. But I do know that you didn't become a professional, a concert pianist. I know because for years I kept looking and asking around and hoping that somehow the damage I did might be lessened by your success. But it never was. Perhaps it never could be. And I'm very very sorry for what I prevented you from having, and the world that loves music from having and for the madness I unleashed on you."

He nodded. A great weariness had come over him. Also oppression. Their encounter was corrupt, distorted by a withheld history— his own. He was the cocky little sprat who came looking for instant sexual initiation for fear that the world was about to end. In his tiny boys-only sphere she was the only available one he knew. Attractive, single, erotically inclined. He came itching with purpose and was pleased and proud when he got what he wanted. Now, forty years later, he had come to accuse this dignified lady, demand under threat

a session of self-criticism. Like a young guardian of the Cultural Revolution, one of a self-righteous mob, tormenting an elderly Chinese
professor. He had come to hang a sign round the neck of Miss Cornell. But no, this was all wrong. This was the victim's customary self-
blame and guilt. He was thinking like an adult. Remember, he was
the child, she was the adult. His life had been altered. Some would say
ruined. But was it really? She had given him joy. He was the stooge of
current orthodoxies. No, that wasn't it either!

The tipping falling tumult of these contrary notions sickened him.
He could not listen to any more from her and he could not bear his
own thoughts. He rose from the chair feeling the weight in his limbs.
As he put on his jacket she got up too. It was over. For a moment they
stood uncertainly, avoiding each other's gaze.

Then she led him to the front door and opened it. She said quickly,
"One last thing, Mr. Baines. It's become clear to me while you've been
here, while I've been describing those events. It's a sudden decision
but I know that I won't change my mind. You said that if you brought
charges you'd hear me in court. It won't happen. While you've been
here I've made my decision. If there's a case brought against me, I'll
plead guilty. There won't need to be a trial. Just the sentencing. You
have the evidence anyway and I can't fight it. But it's more than that.
My husband died seven years ago. We met too late for children. I've
no siblings, just various old friends, ex-pupils and my graduates from
the Royal College. And there's my amateur music group. What I'm
trying to say is, I've no dependants. I'll take what's coming to me.
Now I've met you I'm ready."

He said, "I'll remember that," and turned and walked away.

# 10

Roland Baines's progression through his late fifties and beyond took the form of premature decline. He mostly did not want to leave the house. He wanted to read—in the evenings when he was not on duty at the hotel, all weekends, in bed some afternoons, on and off through the night, at breakfast with a book propped against the marmalade jar. He took no exercise. He gained eight kilos over several years, most of it about his waist. He was feebler in his legs, feebler everywhere, including his lungs. Sometimes he paused halfway up the stairs and persuaded himself it was a thought, the recollection of an interesting line of prose that arrested him when it was his breathing and his aching knees. But he was not feebler in his mind. After eight years, his journal was still alive at volume fourteen. He reported on everything he read. Most weeks, he crossed the river to poke around in second-hand bookshops or attend a reading at the Poetry Society in Earls Court or at the Southbank Centre, just as he had—though rarely—in his twenties.

Back then, in the mid-seventies, he had formed a poor impression of British writers. It was a defensive posture and dismissive. He saw them on TV arts programmes as well as on stage. He could not take seriously these chaps in ties and suits or tweeds who wore brogues and cardigans when at home all day, who belonged to the Garrick and the Athenaeum, who lived in solid north London villas or Cotswold mansions, who spoke loftily, as one might after a lifetime pontificating from All Souls, Oxford; who had never risked a peep round the doors of perception by taking a drug other than tobacco or alcohol, which they peevishly refused to accept were psychoactive addictive substances; who had, most of them, been to the same two old universities where they all knew each other; who smoked pipes and dreamed of knighthoods. Too many of the women wore pearls and spoke in the snappy tones of a wartime radio announcer. None, men or women, in their writings, so he thought then, ever paused in wonder at the mystery of existence or fear of what must follow. They busied themselves with social surfaces, with sardonic depictions of class difference. In their lightweight tales, the greatest tragedy was a rumbled affair, or a divorce. None but a very few seemed much bothered by poverty, nuclear weapons, the Holocaust or the future of humankind or even the shrinking beauty of the countryside under the onslaught of modern farming.

When he read at all, he was more at home with the dead. He knew nothing of their biographies. The dead lived suspended above space and time and he did not need to be troubled by what they wore, where they lived or how they spoke. During those years his writers were Kerouac, Hesse and Camus. From among the living, Lowell, Moorcock, Ballard and Burroughs. Ballard had been to King's, Cambridge but Roland forgave him that, as he would have forgiven him anything. He had a romantic view of writers. They should be, if not barefoot bums, light-footed, unrooted, free, living a vagabond life on the edge, gazing into the abyss and telling the world what was down there. Not knighthoods or pearls, for sure.

Decades later he was more generous. Less stupid. A tweed jacket never stopped anyone from writing well. He believed it was extremely difficult to write a very good novel and to get halfway there was also an achievement. He deplored the way literary editors commissioned novelists rather than critics to review each other's work. He thought it was a grisly spectacle, insecure writers condemning the fiction of their colleagues to make elbow room for themselves. His ignorant twenty-seven-year-old self would have sneered at Roland's favourites now. He was reading through a domestic canon that lay just beyond the great encampments of literary modernism. Henry Green, Antonia White, Barbara Pym, Ford Madox Ford, Ivy Compton-Burnett, Patrick Hamilton. Some had been recommended to him long ago by Jane Farmer from her *Horizon* days. His former mother-in-law had died

unhappily, estranged again from her daughter because of a memoir
Alissa had written—a savage account of her Murnau and Liebenau
childhood. In Jane's honour Roland read the lesser-known novels
of Elizabeth Bowen and Olivia Manning to make up for not being
invited to the funeral. Lawrence was also barred. It was better for
everybody that way, Alissa had told Rüdiger, who passed the message
on to Roland.

Now, in 2010, a week before the general election, he abandoned
an afternoon of reading to go leafleting in the Lambeth area. He had
long ago left the Labour Party but he stuffed pamphlets through letter
boxes for old times' sake and because he had promised. He was not
optimistic as he went from house to house and that wearied him. It
wasn't yet May, it was too hot and he was too old for this lowly task.
At the local party HQ there were no familiar faces. New Labour had
run its course. The Project was exhausted. Good things accomplished
and forgotten. Iraq, the deaths, careless American decisions, sectarian
slaughter had caused some of the best local people to return their party
cards. For the past two years the general preoccupation was the financial crash. A deregulated financial sector and greedy bankers were to
blame, voters said, even as they drifted to the right. The disaster had
happened on Labour's watch. The electorate reasonably assumed that
economic competence must lie elsewhere. Gordon Brown had lost his
initial air of compassionate resolve. Down at the Rosendale Road HQ
they were saying that on the campaign his "mojo" had gone missing
in action.

In the evening Roland set off for Somerset House to hear a talk
about Robert Lowell. He had two reasons for going. One was that
around 1972, long before he took his own education in hand, his
friend Naomi took him to hear Lowell read at the Poetry Society. He
should have been at the top of the contempt list. He was posh Boston,
a Yankee Brahmin. But he had been an eminent opponent of the Vietnam War, and his apparent distraction or incipient madness that night
gave him immunity. Between poems he appeared to forget or not care
where he was and he free-associated about *King Lear,* the scientific
classification of clouds, Montaigne's love of life. Lowell was a culture
hero, the last poet writing in English to speak for a nation until Sea-

mus Heaney was established. At the end, as if by popular demand, though no one in the audience had yet spoken, Lowell read "For the Union Dead," in that regretful lilting nasal Bostonian voice that lifted the poem to its finale with lines that were already famous, *Everywhere, / giant finned cars nose forward like fish; / a savage servility / slides by on grease.*

Tonight, the talk was by a professor from Nottingham University. The immediate subject was Lowell's 1973 volume, *The Dolphin,* for which the poet plundered and plagiarised and reshaped the anguished letters and phone calls from the wife, Elizabeth Hardwick, he was leaving for another woman, Caroline Blackwood. She was pregnant by him and he was determined to marry her. The larger subject was the ruthlessness of artists. Do we forgive or ignore their single-mindedness or cruelty in the service of their art? And are we more tolerant the greater the art? That was the other reason Roland was there.

The professor read rather beautifully one of the poems, a sonnet from *The Dolphin.* It was disorienting to acknowledge that the poem was very fine and might not have existed had Lowell been more sensitive to Hardwick's feelings. Then the lecturer read a passage from a sad letter of hers on which the poem was based. Parts of it had been lifted word for word. Then he read letters to Lowell from friends—Elizabeth Bishop: "shocking . . . cruel," or from another, "too intimately cruel," and another, the poems "will tear Hardwick apart." Other friends thought he should go ahead with publication, believing that he would do that anyway. In partial mitigation the lecturer showed how Lowell agonised over his decision and for how long, with various changes of plan, including many rewrites and restructurings and an idea for a limited edition only. In the end perhaps those friends were right, he did what he was always going to do. Elizabeth Hardwick, not consulted, saw her own words in book form for the first time. Her daughter with Lowell, Harriet, was also represented. To one critic she appeared as "one of the most unpleasant child figures in history." The poet Adrienne Rich condemned *The Dolphin* as "one of the most vindictive and mean-spirited acts in the history of poetry." So how did it stand now, thirty-seven years later?

It was the professor's view that *The Dolphin* was one of the poet's finest works. Should it have been published? He thought not and believed that there was no contradiction in saying so. As to whether one's view of Lowell's behaviour should be tempered by the quality of the outcome, he thought it was irrelevant. Whether cruel behaviour enabled great or execrable poetry made no difference. A cruel act remained just that. This judgement ended the lecture. A murmur ran through the audience—of pleasure it seemed. To feel ambivalence in such a civilised context was agreeable.

A woman stood to ask the first question. There was an elephant in the room, she said. Surely what was under discussion was the behaviour of male artists towards their wives and lovers and the children they had helped bring into the world. The men abandoned their responsibilities, had affairs or got drunk and violent and, for just cause, hid behind the demands of their high calling, their art. Historically, there were very few cases of women sacrificing others for their art and they were likely to be condemned harshly for it. Women were more likely to turn on themselves, deny themselves children, in order to become artists. The men were judged more kindly. Where art was concerned, poetry, painting or whatever, this was merely a special case of banal male entitlement. Men wanted everything—children, success, women's selfless devotion to male creativity. There was loud applause. The professor seemed baffled. He had not considered the matter in these terms, which was surprising given that feminism's second wave had established itself in the universities a generation ago.

While he and the woman argued it out Roland was thinking of the intervention he was about to make. It was causing his heart to beat harder. He already had his first line—I am a male Hardwick. It might get a laugh but he did not have a question. He had a statement to make, just the sort of thing the chairman had at the start of the open session asked the audience to resist. I was once married to a writer whose name will be familiar to you. *No manifestos please.* She abandoned me and our baby and I can tell you for a fact that you are wrong. You have to live it to know it—the quality of the work absolutely matters. *Sir, will you please come to your question.* To be left for the cause of mediocre work would be the ultimate insult. *Next question then.* Yes, I forgave her because she was good, even brilliant. To achieve what she did she had to leave us.

But he did not raise his hand quickly enough. Other hands went up for other questions. The moment passed and as he listened Roland began to doubt himself. He had not thought closely about this business in years. Perhaps he no longer believed in his version. Time to reconsider. Such virtue in forgiveness could have been his way of protecting his pride, of arming himself against humiliation. What was true of Robert Lowell in the professor's view had to be true of Alissa Eberhardt. The novels brilliant, the behaviour inexcusable. Leave it at that. But he felt confused.

On the way home in a minicab he acknowledged that what had passed between Alissa and himself was irrelevant. Too much time had passed. It was dead business. What he or anyone thought made no difference. If there was damage, it was done to Lawrence. Their son represented another problem, as he tunnelled, crashed or soared through his late teens and early twenties, much as his father had. Various jobs, various lovers in sequence, an adopted country, Germany. For a while he had wanted to settle somewhere and finally get some A levels and a degree. It was going to be Arabic. Then, he had to make a living, so, computer science. After that he rediscovered his passion for maths, for an ethereal branch of number theory that had no practical application—precisely its allure. But gradually over the last four years the focus had been tightening. It was the climate that troubled him. He understood the graphs, the probability functions, the urgency. He had drifted towards Berlin, to the Potsdam Institute for Climate Impact Research. Miraculously, given German thoroughness in these matters, he had persuaded people there, by way of some interesting mathematics, to accept him as an unpaid coffee-bringer and low-level research assistant until he had a good degree. In the evenings he waited tables in Mitte.

How was success in the young to be judged? He kept himself in shape, was kindly, reticent, trustworthy, often, like his father, short of money. Not everyone needed a degree in maths from somewhere like Cambridge. For Lawrence, much followed from meeting when still sixteen a French girl on a train.

Roland thought his son had poor judgement in his women friends. Lawrence would deny it but he preferred danger, rawness, instability, emotional extremes. Some were single mothers with complicated stories. Like Lawrence, like Roland for that matter, they had no profession (Roland did not think of himself as a musician), no tradeable skills, no money. Lawrence's affairs often terminated in an explosion, each starburst with its own spectacular quality. His ex-lovers did not remain in his life as friends. There, at least, he differed from Roland. Everyone said that Lawrence would make a wonderful father. But each affair as it ended looked like a lucky escape for both. Lucky too that so far no child was left behind.

Roadworks had closed Vauxhall Bridge and an accident was blocking traffic by the Chelsea embankment. It was past eleven thirty by the time Roland's minicab pulled up outside his house. As he entered where his gate used to be—someone had stolen it two years ago— and walked under the robinia that now blocked direct sunlight from the second floor, Roland felt himself to be unusually restless for the time of night. He would have liked to call someone but it was far too late. Besides, Daphne was in Rome for a housing conference. Peter was with her, scouring the city's political scene for Europhobes. Mere sceptics were not enough for him. Too late to call Lawrence. He too was an hour ahead. Carol's days started early and were long. She ran an entire channel for the BBC and was usually asleep by ten. Mireille was in Carcassonne tending her dying father. Joe Coppinger was in South Korea for a conference. Roland's old Vancouver friend, John Weaver, would be deep into his afternoon teaching.

On the kitchen table was the debris of his lunch. As he carried a couple of token dishes to the sink he sensed that he would not sleep easily. The Lowell event had stirred up old stuff, a reminder of his own shapeless existence. Usually around this time Roland made a mint tea and took it to bed and read into the night. Tonight he allowed himself a Scotch. The bottle took some minutes to find. A five-month-old Christmas present, almost full. He took it along with a jug of water and a glass into the sitting room.

A year before her death, after she had fallen out with her daughter, Jane had got in touch with Roland. She assumed they shared a villain.

When he told her how much he admired the novels she pretended not to hear him. Her own process of re-evaluation was complete and final: Alissa's fiction was boring and overpraised. Jane and Roland kept up occasional phone calls until her illness became too serious. She would remember to ask after Lawrence and would want to know just a little about Roland's life but her true interest was Alissa's perfidy. Jane felt profoundly misunderstood, even persecuted. Dark suspicions were troubling her. Certain small objects of sentimental value had gone missing from the house. It was likely, she thought, that Alissa had come in the night.

"All the way from Bavaria?"

"Writers have time on their hands. She knows the house and she knows how to hurt me. I've changed the locks but she still gets in."

Mental decay of some sort. Paraphrenia. He had noticed before this irritable paranoia in the elderly. But Jane was right in the essentials. Alissa had come at her with a knife—she had named and blamed her mother in a bestselling memoir. It would be in print for years, Jane said. Its harshest passages, diffused across the Internet in book-blogs, retweets, reviews and on Facebook, would last as long as civilisation. Nasty letters from anonymous locals had appeared in Jane's post. The lady in the *Bäckerei* smirked whenever she came in. Friends gave their support but were appalled by what they had read and did not know what to believe. She was probably right when she said that she was gossiped about.

*In Murnau* described a rural Bavaria in which small-town Nazis, too low down the pecking order to be of interest to the Nuremberg courts, slipped back during the late forties and early fifties into local government and industry and into the networks of agricultural administration. Alissa named them all, their roles during and after the war. Everyone at every level remained in denial about what had happened. One passage in the book was just as Alissa had described it once to Roland—certain streets, certain empty houses, filled with the ghosts of those who had been taken away to unmentionable destinations. No one talked about them. Everyone remembered the names and faces of their neighbours who were once there, so they knew well the ghosts and the children of the ghosts. There was hatred for the

Americans at the local bases even as their Marshall Plan money was welcome. Somehow donor and donation were separated. As the economy started to recover, so began a scramble for stuff, for consumer goods that buried deeper the collective memories. A new house was being built by murderers on a foundation of corpses. Territory well charted by historians and novelists—Alissa made reverential references to Gert Hofmann's novel, *Veilchenfeld*. What was new was her exceptional prose, its lyrical bitterness. She was contemptuous of the view that in the early years after the war, Germany could only be rebuilt by means of collective amnesia.

Then she went in closer. The chapters narrowed down to the personal. Alissa was torn in two directions. The exaggerated fame of the White Rose angered her. It was a fig leaf for the obscenity of national denial. At the same time, she accused her father of disowning the movement to which he had given brave support, if only from 1943. Heinrich was the solid burgher who grew fat and lazy and feared the bad opinion of the closet Nazis who were his clients or who ran the nearby town halls or law associations. The way she described him, Heinrich was a barely animated drawing by Georg Grosz, far from the man Roland remembered by the fire, pouring schnapps, amiable, tolerant, good-natured, baffled and to a small extent intimidated by his wife and daughter. By her account he was disappointed to have a daughter not a son. He had little to do with Alissa's upbringing, never encouraged her in anything she did, looked bored whenever she spoke. In fact, he never seemed to hear her. He left her to the mercies of her mother.

Here the real damage began. *In Murnau* presented Jane Farmer as an embittered woman hollowed out by a sense of failure. Her literary potential and ambitions were not destroyed by her own decisions. It was her child who ruined everything. Little Alissa was made to suffer in the loveless cold. Maternal punishments were frequent—sharp smacks to the legs, hours confined to her bedroom, rare treats withdrawn on a whim for crimes she could not remember. She struggled for her mother's affection and grew up in the long shadow of her rancour. Her childhood was without outings, holidays, jokes, special meals, bedtime stories. No one ever cuddled her. Her mother lived in a cage of unspoken resentments. Even when Alissa broke away and went to London her mother's dead hand was heavy on her own sense of purpose. It took so long to write those two early novels, so weak in conception, so timid and apologetic.

The day Alissa as a young mother left her London husband and child behind and went to Liebenau to confront Jane was one of the most vivid moments in the book, dramatic, intense, seething with emotions too long held back. It was the scene that critics lingered over. Only Eberhardt, they agreed, could manage so adroitly, with such delicate evocation of pain and anger, the many cross-currents of feeling, of mutual misunderstanding. What interested Roland was that Alissa's account was close to the one Jane had given him so many years ago, on that warm evening in her garden.

Alissa's memoir was a bestseller in Germany and other countries, including Britain. The vile childhoods of others were not only a comfort to many but a means of emotional exploration, and an expression of what everyone knew but needed to keep on hearing: our beginnings shape us and must be faced. Roland was sceptical and not out of loyalty to Jane. In the fifties many fathers were not much involved with their children, especially their daughters. Embraces, expressions of love, were thought too showy, too embarrassing. His own childhood was typical. Smacks to the legs, to the bottom, were common. Children, however loved underneath it all, were to be managed, not listened to. They were not there to be engaged with in serious conversation. They were not beings in their own right, for they were just passing through, transient proto-humans, endlessly, year after year in the graceless act of becoming. That was how it was. That was the culture. At the time it thought itself too soft. A hundred years before, the duty of parents had been to break a child's will with a beating. Roland thought that those in his own country who itched to get back to those times, the eighteen or nineteen fifties, should think harder.

He believed that *In Murnau*, however engrossing, was Alissa's least good book. Untypically self-dramatising. He was aware of Jane's asperity but she was not cruel. Naming her, specifying the village and the house, was a bad mistake. A month after her funeral Roland met up with Rüdiger in the dusty American bar of the Stafford hotel by

Green Park. The success of the memoir had prompted in its author some guilt. It grew stronger at her mother's funeral, where Alissa saw for herself that many of Jane's friends had not turned out for her. At the wake afterwards Rüdiger told her about the abusive letters Jane had received.

"But only because Alissa asked me. Otherwise, I would have said nothing."

"What was her reaction?"

"She's like a lot of brilliant writers. There's something naive, you know? She was burning to write this book. She didn't think about the consequences even when we warned her."

Rüdiger, completely bald, rather stout and grand in manner, was now CEO of Lucretius Books. He could afford a little distance on his famous author. He had others. "She decided after the funeral that she wanted the book withdrawn, the unsold copies pulped. We persuaded her that this would look bad for her. Like a confession of a terrible mistake. We told her. The damage was done. She had to move on. Perhaps write a different book about her mother."

→-

It was 1 a.m. Roland's Scotch, a small measure, heavily diluted, had been intended as a nightcap, a modest shot. But the bottle was at his elbow and he poured a larger one and was cautious with the water. Alissa's unlikely defender was Lawrence. He had been moved by the memoir, he told his father on the phone. He thought Roland's scepticism was "out of order." He was unusually forthright.

"You weren't there. You met Oma and Opa years later when they'd softened, the way people do. And it's irrelevant that this was how it was at the time, that this was how people treated their kids. It was her experience. If you want you could say that she's speaking for a whole generation. If the culture was crap that's not on the mind of an eight-year-old sent to her room without supper. This was her life and she has a right to describe how it felt."

"Her truth."

"Don't put that one on me, Dad. *The* truth. I have friends who've told me all about their shit childhoods with horrible parents. Then I meet them and they're sweet as anything. I don't then go thinking my friends are self-deluding liars. Anyway, I think you've got other reasons not to like this book."

"You may be right."

For this conversation Lawrence was somewhere in the American Midwest for a conference on farming and climate change. Roland had not seen him in six months and did not want a serious argument over the phone. His son had better reasons than he did not to like the memoir. That he was touched by it was admirable, generous. But if Jane had harmed her daughter, what of the harm that daughter had done her son? Where was the novelist's honest reckoning? And as with the mothers, so with the father. Roland's restless marginal life of truncated education and serial monogamy had become Lawrence's. It wasn't exactly a gift.

Whenever he entered a pleasing neutral zone such as a Scotch might bring on at the end of a tiring day, he tended to think that the lifelong mystery of Alissa was at the very least always interesting. There was no one remotely like her in his life. Miriam apart, no one so extreme. To most people, including himself, life just happened. Alissa fought it. He had not seen her since that night in a Berlin alley, when the Wall was falling in fifty places. Almost twenty-one years. He doubted that he would ever see her again. That in itself had a fairy-tale element. She was big. In forty-five languages she took up space in the minds of several million people.

She re-emerged in his life with the English translation of each new book, roughly every three years, and with the occasional news-cutting forwarded by one of Rüdiger's assistants. Roland had asked long ago not to be sent the full press folder. In between, she rarely crossed his mind. Whatever he read about her always disturbed his peace and sent him off in some new direction. Last year was a good example. There arrived a cutting from the *FAZ*, a long essay about the Nobel Prize in Literature which ended with speculation on who would be announced in October. Every year there were rumours, not always unfounded. There followed a list of usual suspects. Roth, Munro, Modiano. But surely, the piece concluded, it was time for the German language to be honoured again. There had been nothing since Elfriede Jelinek. Who else this year but Alissa Eberhardt? Of course! That morning Roland walked to a bookmaker in Clapham High Street and asked at the counter for the odds. The lady there had to go away and consult on the phone. This writer was not on their list. The answer came back from head office. Fifty to one. He put down an extravagant £500. An eighth of his life savings. £25,000 to be extracted like ambrosial juice from the fruits of his ex-wife's success—there would be some justice in that. When October came around and the announcement was made the German language was indeed honoured but not in Alissa's name. In her place, Herta Müller. Too bad. Not the kind of justice he'd hoped for. He had to accept the lost bet as a fair verdict on their failed union.

Thirty years ago he would have poured himself a third then a large fourth and the night would gape open, the way it did in the months after Alissa took off. But now, when at last he stood, somewhat dizzy at the sudden exertion, three-quarters of his whisky remained in the glass. Better there than in his gut, primed to wreck his sleep. He took from a shelf his copy of *The Dolphin* and headed upstairs, yawning and turning off lights as he went. He had once heard a close friend of Lowell recall on the radio that when she visited him one morning in hospital she had found him sitting up in bed rubbing marmalade into his hair. Completely mad and yet the poetry was magnificent. Hearing that long ago and recalling his own abandoned poems, Roland had sometimes thought there was hope for himself.

➤➤

When he looked back on the first several years of the new century he often remembered the two-minute silence in Russell Square in honour of the victims of the Tube and bus bombings. If he summoned the scene he always pictured the cordoned-off wrecked bus nearby, in everyone's sight, a crime scene still under forensic examination. Media pictures overlaid on false memory. The bus exploded elsewhere, in Tavistock Square, and was taken away for examination.

That morning in July 2005, intrusive thoughts had crossed and converged where Roland stood in the gardens with several hundred others. During the silence he tried to keep his thoughts on the dead and the unknowable minds of their "clean-skin" murderers, but his mother's illness kept breaking in. Illness and death were much on his mind. Jane had died the month before the attacks. For years Rosalind's decline had been slow, now it was accelerating. For a long while her speech had been a tangle of upended grammar and sense. Her conversation could be lyrical, like an opaque poem by E. E. Cummings. Lately she barely spoke at all. Now there was concern about her breathing.

He was standing at the back by the gates of Russell Square Gardens in order to get away quickly. He needed to travel out to west London to meet his brother and sister. Susan had told him she had momentous news about the past. Talking about it on the phone was not possible. They would visit Rosalind first then go to a café. Susan had to pick up a grandchild later from school and had asked him not to be late.

Henry and Susan met him at Northolt Tube station. They went in Henry's car from there to the care home, three terraced houses knocked into one in a residential street. On the way, some desultory small talk then silence. A helper led them to their mother's tiny room and they crowded in. She was sitting on a straight-backed armchair with her back to a hand basin. Her head was slumped forwards so that her chin touched her chest. Her eyes were open but she did not seem to be aware of her visitors as they arranged themselves around her, Susan and Roland on the bed, Henry on a chair the helper brought in. The room smelled of disinfectant. Susan was sitting closest to her. She put her hand on her mother's and tried some cheery greetings. Roland and Henry joined in. No response. She made a humming sound and then a word they could not make out, then less than a word, a vowel sound, ah, ah, ah. Then only the sound of her breathing, rapid and shallow with a grating sound as it passed over mucus snagged in her airway. Her head hung lower. They sat and watched her as if waiting for her to revive. There was nothing to say. It did not feel right to be speaking among themselves. Roland supposed he would not see her alive again but after ten minutes that did not stop him wanting to leave. On the contrary.

As he saw it she was already dead and he was already grieving but could not do it in her presence. He was determined not to be the first to get up. A sense, not of significant leave-taking, but of politeness held them there. He had spent many hours in this overheated room. For years her life had been one long receding tide. As it withdrew it left behind random pools of stranded memory. The large one that should have contained the half-century marriage to Robert Baines was missing. It vanished early on when she could still recognise her children, though not her grandchildren, and could recall other isolated stretches of her life. When Roland experimented with references to his father she spoke only of Jack Tate. Susan had hung her father's picture on the wall. Rosalind's stories of her first husband were lucid. She had told them to Roland long before she was ill. Not all the memory pools were from the distant past. She remembered a visit to Kew Gardens with Roland five years before. The memory of her mother, who died in 1966, was also strong and the focus of her anxieties. She hadn't seen her in so long and she must get to the village and visit her, for she must be so old and frail by now. Sometimes Rosalind packed a carrier bag of gifts and essentials to take with her. An apple, biscuits, fresh underwear, a pencil, her alarm clock. Tucked beside it were folded scraps of paper she said were bus tickets.

The helper came in to relieve them. It was second-sitting lunch, she said, and they would have to leave. Then this would be the last time he ever saw his mother, slumped at a table with a dozen old people who were chatting loudly. It seemed impossible that she could eat. Her head still protruded forwards, her eyes were open and so was her mouth. She was staring into a bowl of mashed food and did not hear her children as they said goodbye. Roland kissed her head, so frail and cool, and noticed again a wide bald patch just below the crown. It was good to step outside into the shaded street crowded with parked cars. As long as he was with his brother and sister he felt nothing much. He would need to be alone. He assumed it was the same for them, for as they walked to the café, Susan and Henry discussed other care homes they had heard of that were less well-run and more expensive than this one.

The café was on the premises of a failed charity shop. Two friends of Susan were "making a go of it" for a low rent. It was a sad place trying hard to be cheerful, with red gingham tablecloths and pots of geraniums and framed jokey signs on the wall in melting graphics that a local pub must have donated. *You don't have to be mad to work here but it help's*. Roland's gaze was fixed on the apostrophe, surprised that it moved him. They were all doing their best to get by with what they had.

He was not in the mood for momentous news. They had squeezed round an undersized table and ordered tea. No one was hungry. The sight of his mother's puréed lunch in a plastic bowl had made Roland feel nauseous. It was assumed that Susan's news could not be delivered until the tea was brought. She and Henry were approaching their seventies. All the usual signs in their faces and posture and speech declared his own future ten or twelve years ahead. But they were doing fine, he wanted to reassure himself. Unhappy first marriages, calamitous break-ups now never mentioned, contentment second time around while he pushed on alone with dwindling energy and purpose. He had at least a party of friends, including ex-lovers on hand for the occasional supper. But over the years some of them had also been settling to tranquil second and third marriages and he was seeing less of them.

When the tea was before them in thick white mugs too hot to touch, Susan took from her shoulder bag a brown envelope. She had received a letter from a Lieutenant Colonel Andrew Brudenell-Bruce of the Salvation Army. His work was to help people trace lost family members. For a while he had been dealing with a case that may concern her. He had found Susan through her first husband's unusual name, Charne. If her mother's maiden name was Rosalind Morley of Ash in Hampshire then she might be interested to know that she had a brother. He had been adopted soon after his birth in November 1942. His name was Robert William Cove and he would like to get in touch with his biological family. Colonel Brudenell-Bruce assured her that if she did not wish to be contacted by this person the matter would be closed and she would hear nothing more. If she wished to proceed, he would be happy to put her and her brother in touch.

Henry and Susan exchanged a look. 1942, when they were already away from home and their childhoods began to unravel. Away from their mother, away from each other. In the early forties, their father was fighting in the Western Desert Campaign. So it was obvious. The Christian names alone. Robert—of course, and William was the name of the Major's father and of an older brother. Susan and Henry looked at Roland and he nodded. This was *his* full brother.

Into the silence he said weakly, "Well . . ."

Well what? In the first instance stupidity. It was so obvious that it seemed to him now that he had heard the news before and failed to pay attention. Or was too well defended against the old family story to understand what he was being told. Or didn't want to know. The news was not a shock, not yet. More like an accusation. When Rosalind came to stay in Clapham after the funeral—he was trying to think this through as the three of them sat in silence—she didn't misremember the date, 1941, on which she first met Robert Baines. Their mother had simply forgotten to lie. She remembered to exclude the baby boy but she came close to telling him the truth. Her children were packed off "while I sorted myself out." What else could that have meant? If he'd been attentive, one intelligent follow-up question would have unlocked the history. She was wanting to tell it. There must have been other occasions when she was ready to free herself of the secret. With the Major dead and the events so far behind her there was nothing to lose. But his mind was partly elsewhere whenever he dealt with his parents. A little more focus—or was it love that he lacked?—and he could have got it out of her and she would have been relieved of the sixty-two-year-old burden she had carried alone. He and his sister and brother could have helped her. They could have learned the real history of the family. She was round the corner, staring at her lunch and could tell them nothing of her hidden son because she was, in effect, dead.

Roland sat back and felt the weight of the near future. The questions, the stories to be rewritten, a stranger to be greeted as a brother, Rosalind's sadness and preoccupation explained at last. He saw it unrolling before him, vanishing and reappearing distantly, like a track over hilly terrain. And here was the past, even more obscure than before, with its blurred figures in a mist. Robert Baines fathering a child with the wife of a serving soldier. Rosalind pregnant by another man while her husband was abroad fighting for his country. The shame and secrecy, the fury in the family, the gossip in the village. Jack dying in 1944 in the liberation of Europe, freeing Robert and Rosalind to marry. Did Sergeant Baines command and arrange for Rosalind's children to be dispatched to clear space for his affair? Did he insist on the baby's adoption to save his army career? He faced the prospect of a court martial. If Roland included himself and his boarding school, then all four of Rosalind's children were expelled, banished to their new postings. At each parting Rosalind must have wept. He had seen her shaking shoulders as she walked away that time his parents put him on the coach to go to his new school. She must have thought then of the other three children and wondered how she could have let it happen again.

Susan and Henry never referred to their wartime childhoods. It was gone, buried. Now it was back. In old age the three of them would go on trying to make sense of it—of meek Rosalind, domineering Robert and all they had made between them. Exile, loneliness, sorrow, guilt. The children must go on trying to understand, Roland thought, and it would never end. But he had to stop now and deal with what he knew for certain. He had a brother, another brother, a full brother. That needed to be separated out from the deception and the questions. Was it a cause for celebration? He could not feel it yet. Only his own stupidity.

He asked Susan's friend for three glasses of water.

Henry cleared his throat and said, "I think I sort of knew it at the time, when I was eight. Not about the baby, of course. The affair. Then I forgot all about it. I blocked it out. When I was allowed to go and see Mum he was always there. That man. That's what I called your dad, Roland, in my mind, that man. He gave me a present, a toy tractor I think it was. Painted yellow. But I remember I refused to take it. I must have had my reasons. Loyalty to my dad, I suppose."

Susan: "I can't remember much. Or anything. My memory's a blank. And thank God for that." She passed the envelope to Roland. "This is yours to deal with. I can't be the one to meet him first. It's too much."

"When you've seen him," Henry said, "you can tell us about it. Then we'll see him."

That evening Roland wrote to introduce himself to Lieutenant Colonel Andrew Brudenell-Bruce. The reply by return of post was affable. He had written to Mr. Cove, who would be in touch directly with Roland. The colonel lived in Waterloo and was happy to drop by. He came two days later and sat in the chair at the kitchen table that Roland immediately associated with the policemen, Douglas Browne and Charles Moffat. Perhaps it was because, like them, Brudenell-Bruce was in uniform. Whenever Roland met religious figures he felt obliged to protect them from his disbelief, which was so complete that even atheism bored him. He was always friendly in an exaggerated way with the local vicar when he met him in the street. But no protection was needed for the colonel, a decent and unshakeable man, Roland decided, a big fellow with muscular shoulders and arms and a loud generous laugh. He said that in his youth he had been an amateur weightlifter. Much appeared to amuse him, even his own remarks. This was his last case, Andrew explained, because he was due to retire. He had therefore given it his special attention. He laughed.

"You'll like your new brother. He's a good sort."

"As a family we're pretty strange."

"In thirty years I've yet to meet one that isn't."

Roland laughed along with the colonel.

A letter arrived from Robert Cove. It was friendly and to the point. He was sixty-two, married to Shirley, with one son and two granddaughters. He lived in Reading, not far from where he grew up in Pangbourne. He had been a carpenter-fitter most of his working life and was determined not to retire before he had to. He understood that Roland lived in London, so how about meeting in the middle? There was a place just outside Datchet, used to be a pub, now a conference centre and still called the Three Tuns. He named a day the following week and suggested 7 p.m. "It will be tremendous to meet you."

In the days before, Roland pitched between a foreboding he could not explain and pleased anticipation, curiosity, impatience. Then back again to a sense that coming his way was a set of obligations towards a stranger. He did not need his life to become more interesting. He wanted to read books and see the same handful of old friends.

He arrived late. The train timetabling was awkward and the Three Tuns was nearer Windsor and further from the station than its website promised. He walked a dusty main road out of Datchet and turned towards the conference centre up a driveway lined with saplings in plastic tubes. He approached a cluster of new buildings designed in the redbrick pastoral style of eighties supermarkets. Automatic sliding doors brought him into a large high-ceilinged bar, almost empty. He paused by the entrance wanting to see before he was seen.

Sitting alone at a table with the remains of a glass of red wine was a version of himself, not quite a mirror image, but Roland as he would have been after a different life, another set of choices. It was the Multiple Worlds theory made real, a privileged glimpse into one of the infinite possibilities of himself that were fancifully supposed to exist in parallel and inaccessible domains. Here, for example, was Roland as he would have been without glasses, with the straighter back he always intended to have and the weight shed from round his waist. This man appeared to Roland to have a more settled expression. Robert Cove seemed to sense that he was being stared at, for he turned and stood and waited. In the three or four seconds it took to reach him Roland felt he had passed out of the ordinary into a form of hyperspace and was floating across a dreamscape, hardly aware of who he was. Outside of dramas and fictions such an encounter was impossibly rare. But as soon as he arrived in front of his brother the altered reality collapsed into the banal, or the comic, for no conventions existed to smooth such a meeting. One extended his hand, the other made to embrace. Later Roland could not remember which impulse had been his. The brothers stumbled against each other, stepped back and settled on the handshake as they announced their Christian names in unison. Roland pointed at the wine glass and Robert nodded.

When he was back from the bar they touched glasses and began again. They passed a few minutes agreeing that the Salvation Army did fine work bringing people together, and that the colonel was a wonderful man. Then an awkward pause. Somehow they had to begin. Roland proposed they each give a short account of their lives and circumstances.

"Good idea. You go first, Roland. Show me how it's done."

There was in the accent a hint of the softly rolled "r" which Roland associated with his mother. Hampshire, which sounded to his ear halfway to the West Country. Roland's story was one of automatic redactions. He left boarding school early because he was impatient to start earning. His marriage to a writer ended after a year. For the first time in his life he described himself as a "lounge-bar pianist." He promoted Lawrence to a "climate-change scientist," but about "our mother and father, our half-brother and half-sister" and the unhappy past he provided a more detailed picture. His life as he spoke it hardly added up to much. He ended by saying, "You're joining, if that's the word, a very fractured family. We didn't grow up together and you're the extreme case of that."

Robert went to the bar and came back with a full bottle and fresh glasses. The first thing he wanted to say was that he had been well cared for and loved by his adopted parents, Charlie and Ann, and he felt no bitterness and needed no sympathy.

"That's good to hear."

He did not know he was adopted until his father told him, against his mother's wishes when he was fourteen. But he'd already had hints which he had managed to forget—he had been teased at school for not having "real parents." Somehow, the rumour had got around. As a teenager, little by little, he learned how it happened. In December 1942 Ann had seen an advertisement in the classified section of the local paper. Robert unfolded a photocopy of the page and passed it across. The entry was brief. Above was *Violin, Saxophone, Clarinet and Trumpet required urgently for newly formed band. Immediate cash,* and below, *We purchase for cash saleable second-hand furniture.* In between was *Wanted, Home for baby boy, age 1 month; complete surrender— Write Box 173, Mercury, Reading.* Complete surrender—the Major, surely. He could have written "unconditional." Elsewhere—Roland could not help glancing across the page—in 1942 the war had drained the labour market. There was a need for "boys of seventeen" and "experienced gentlemen" to fill in for the absent men.

He gave the page back. Rosalind and her baby and her younger sister, Joy, he now learned, took the train from Aldershot to Reading. That train arrived late as they often did during the war. By arrangement, the sisters waited until all the other passengers had dispersed. They had with them, Ann Cove remembered, a brown carrier bag stuffed with baby clothes. Robert was handed over to the Cove couple by the ticket barrier. Ann was troubled for years by the memory of Joy turning her back because she could not bear to witness the moment the baby left her sister's hands. Rosalind looked numb and said little.

A month after their first meeting, Roland and Robert would go to see their Aunt Joy in the village of Tongham, not so far from Ash. It was, of course, an extraordinary reunion and Roland mostly kept out of the way and listened. Joy had lost her husband the year before and she was frail but her memory was good. When all the exclamations and embraces were done they settled down over tea and walnut cake and she told her story. She had spent much time looking after baby Robert while her sister went out to work and had become closely attached to him.

"You were a beautiful little thing," she said as she patted Robert's knee.

On the train to Reading she had tried to get her sister to change her mind. It wasn't too late. They could avoid this couple at the station, catch the first train back and go home with the baby.

"She wasn't having it. All Rosalind kept saying in a quiet voice over and again was, 'I have to do it. I have to do it.' I've never forgotten, when she spoke she wouldn't look at me."

Even on the way home to Aldershot, when both sisters were in a state of great distress, Joy told Rosalind that they could still go back, tell the Coves she had changed her mind, bring little Robert away. Rosalind wept and shook her head and would say nothing. When they were back on the platform at Aldershot station she made her sister swear never to speak of what they had done. Joy kept her silence. She did not even tell her husband in forty-eight years of marriage. She talked about that terrible morning for the first time with Robert sitting next to her on the sofa. He touched her shoulder as she started to cry.

In the Three Tuns bar Robert continued his history. He had a normal and boisterous childhood. There was never much money but his parents were kind and he was happy. He became head boy at school but was glad to leave several months ahead of his sixteenth birthday. He hated the classroom, he said, even more than Roland. He got a factory job where he was the youngest on the assembly line. By some traditional and violent rite the women workers wanted to lay hands on him, strip him naked and dress him in an outsized baby's romper suit. He was having none of that and fled. They chased him down a flight of steel stairs, across the factory floor and out into the street. It was a close thing. He never went back. Eventually, he entered a tough five-year apprenticeship as a carpenter-fitter. Over a lifetime he had worked on many building sites in his area, and these days often drove past houses whose floor joists or roof trusses he had installed. He made a speciality out of constructing bespoke staircases. He married in the mid-sixties and remained happy with Shirley. Their son, daughter-in-law and the granddaughters were the centre of their lives. Robert's other passion was his football team, Reading. He went to all their games, home and away.

As Robert spoke Roland was studying his face and remembering his own time on building sites in the late sixties and seventies. With time pressures, unreliable supplies of labour and materials, and overlapping trades creating confusion, they could be difficult contentious places. No unions, terrible safety records, no facilities for the men, occasional fights. The days of "the lump." The older men, he remembered, after years of weathering disputes, developed a certain tough-minded detachment. He thought he saw it in his brother. Not easily drawn into arguments, he guessed, and implacable when they happened. It was a broader face than his own, he now saw, more open and generous. The hands that held their glasses gave the story of their different fates. Robert would have no use for the soft white fingers of a lounge-lizard pianist. His had visible calluses and scars. His life sounded more intact, more integrated—a lifelong marriage, a neighbourhood dotted with the dwellings he had helped construct, the local team he urged on in all weathers, and especially the pretty granddaughters whose photograph Roland was now inspecting. No acid trip by the Big Sur River to disconnect Robert from ordinary ambitions, no single-parenting, improvised careers, sequential lovers, political disappointment and pessimism. But Robert's life had been tough. His mother's early death, the void of knowing nothing of his origins, the whipping-boy apprentice years and hard work. Most of Roland's problems had been self-inflicted, mere luxuries. But would he swap places with Robert? No. Would Robert swap? No.

"After my mother died and I turned twenty-one I decided to trace my biological parents. I got a fair way along with it, got my birth details then I gave up. Busy with other things. And I thought, well, if my blood parents haven't come to find out how I am, they probably don't want to hear from me. So I left it—for almost fifty years."

Roland thought he caught the tone, the inflection, perhaps the methodical attitude of the Major, the ghost of the other Robert in this one. He had brought his birth certificate and showed it now. Born 14 November 1942. Where? At a private address in Farnham. Away from the big military hospital in Aldershot. That made sense. A few inches to the right was the truth, the mother named as Rosalind Tate formerly Morley, of 2 Smith's Cottages, Ash, and there beside it was the lie, the father written in as Jack Tate of the same address. A few days before, Henry had sent Roland some documents—Jack Tate's service record, his army Pay Book. He had served with the 1st Battalion of the Royal Hampshire Regiment. It fought in the Western Desert in 1940 then moved to Malta in February 1941. It remained there during the long siege, then took part in the invasion of Sicily in July 1943 and afterwards of Italy. No way home for a humble infantryman. No chance of conceiving a child in England to be born in November 1942. Jack's battalion was not back until November 1943, when it began training for D-Day. It landed on Gold Beach on 6 June. Jack got his bullet in the stomach in October near Nijmegen and died in England on 6 November.

Roland stared at his brother Robert's birth certificate, at the square that contained the lie, as if the paper could dissolve to reveal a long-ago passion then regret, of Rosalind giving birth to a child and six weeks later, on a wintry railway platform, delivering him into the care of two people she didn't know and would never see again, of her desolate return by train, perhaps her sister's arm round her shoulder, but empty-handed and alone, of how that morning defined her life. *I had to do it.* See it her way and through the prism of war. Keep the baby and she would have confronted the fury of her husband returning from the front, the contempt of the village, and attached to her child the stigma of illegitimacy—a vehement social disgust that would quietly fade away in Roland and Robert's lifetime. She would have set herself against the will of the man she loved and feared. Unless the child was erased from their lives, Sergeant Baines faced ruin.

At last, Roland said, "You should go and see our mother. She might not have long."

Could he and Robert love or hate each other in the way of brothers? Too late. But the connection with this stranger—he felt it now—was complete, inescapable. Together they kept saying the words self-consciously and making it true. Our mother, our father.

Roland took from his pocket the one photograph he had brought to show Robert. He put it on the table between them and they looked at it together. It was a studio portrait of their mother with Susan on her right, Henry on her left. All three were in best clothes. Susan looked about fifteen months old, Henry around four years. That would date the photograph to 1940. Almost certainly taken for Jack to keep with him through the war. Henry had an arm across his mother's shoulder. Susan was standing on some form of support, out of shot, that brought her face level with her mother's. But it was Rosalind the brothers were looking at. She wore an open-necked blouse that revealed a glimpse of a pendant chain. Thick black hair tumbling to her shoulders, no need of make-up, a steady confident gaze, a slight smile and an air of tranquillity. This was a young woman of great beauty and poise.

Robert said, "And I never knew her."

Roland nodded. He thought but did not say that he too never knew her. The mother he knew was fretful, bowed, meek, apologetic. Now he understood that distant sorrow that hung about her and what she grieved for. The young woman in the photograph vanished on Reading station in 1942.

➤➤

Rosalind's vascular dementia did not run a straight course to its terminal point. Her body would not give up and it dragged her mind back into the world for several more months. His mother staring into a plastic bowl of mashed food was not the last Roland saw of her. She was not already dead. A week later, she was sitting on the edge of her bed and though she did not recognise him, though she called him "aunty," as she had every visitor for the past year, she spoke whole sentences, meaningless in context but with a touch of poetry about them. On this occasion, after accepting Roland's embrace, she said, "Daylight delights you."

"It really does," he said as he took out a notebook and wrote the three words down. There were other lines on that visit. She spoke them unprompted over the course of an hour's disjointed conversation. They seemed to belong together. He had finished telling her, for what it was worth, of Lawrence's work in Germany when she suddenly said, "Love just follows you."

As he was leaving, she gave what sounded like a blessing. The words amazed him. He turned back and asked her to repeat them. But she was staring out the window and had already forgotten what she had said. She had also forgotten his presence in the room and greeted him afresh. He knew she had quiet religious feelings but he had never heard her invoke God before. Or love. He typed the lines up that evening, without alteration, except for a final line break. When the time came he added her poem to the back of the order of service pamphlet for her funeral in St. Peter's Church, Ash. *Daylight delights you, / Love just follows you. / Our hearts rejoice. / God in all His glory / Take care of you.*

He arrived with Lawrence. They passed the hearse containing Rosalind's coffin parked in a lane beside the graveyard. As he entered the church, Roland saw various relatives, some in their nineties, some not yet a year old. His siblings and their spouses, including Robert and Shirley, were already in the front pews. The undertakers brought their mother in and settled her coffin on the trestles. The vicar began her welcome. Impossible not to stare at the coffin where Rosalind lay in the dark. But she wasn't there, or anywhere, and here it was again, the simplest feature of death, always startling—absence. The organ played a familiar introduction. Ever since his truculent fourth form at Berners Hall, he could not bring himself to sing a hymn. However sweet the melodies or the rhythm of the lines he could not get past the embarrassment of their blatant or childish untruths. But the point was not to believe but to join in, to be part of the community. They were starting with "All Things Bright and Beautiful," Rosalind's favourite. Lovely for small children but how could an adult mouth this creationist nonsense? Not wishing to offend others he stood as usual, holding the hymnal open at the right page. Same again for "Pilgrim." Hobgoblin! Foul fiend! During this one he glanced across at his brother, his new brother. Robert was standing erect, not holding a hymn book and not moving his lips.

When the subdued ragged singing tailed away Roland went to the pulpit to deliver the eulogy. Henry, the eldest, had not wanted to do it and nor did Susan. Facing Roland were many who'd had only the briefest education. He did not know how much history they knew. Speaking without notes he reminded the congregation of the year of Rosalind's birth, 1915. He said it was hard to think of another historical period when a single lifetime of ninety years could have encompassed as much change as hers did. When she was born, the Russian Revolution was two years away, the First World War was only just beginning its terrible slaughter. The inventions that would transform the twentieth century—the wireless, the car, the telephone, the aeroplane—had not yet touched the lives of the villagers of Ash. Television, computers, the Internet were years away and unimaginable. So too was the Second War, with its even greater slaughter. It would shape Rosalind's life and the lives of everyone she knew. Ash was still a horse-drawn world in 1915, hierarchical, agricultural, tightly knit. A visit to the doctor could be a serious financial setback to a working family. Rosalind wore callipers on her legs at the age of three to correct for malnutrition. By the end of her life a spacecraft had entered the orbit of Mars, we contemplated the unknowns of global warming and were beginning to wonder if artificial intelligence might one day replace human life.

He was about to add that several thousand nuclear weapons stood in constant readiness. But the vicar, who was standing close behind him, meaningfully cleared her throat. His pessimism was out of place. He moved on to the correct form of celebration, and spoke of her devotion to family, of her cooking and gardening and knitting, of how tenderly she nursed her husband Robert through emphysema. He missed out the baby she gave away and the new addition to the family. Henry and Susan were still raw about it. Nothing against Robert, they had insisted, but they did not want their mother's secrecy and shame to be part of her "send-off"—Susan's phrase. Roland ended by saying that their mother had once told Henry's wife Melissa "with all the authority of a mother-in-law," that the journey to heaven took three days.

"That means she will have got in around 5:30 p.m. on the 29th of December. I'm sure we all hope that she's comfortably installed."

He returned to his pew feeling false. He could say this at the end, however lightly, but he could not sing the harmless hymns.

➤

Daphne had told him on a few occasions during his thirties and forties that he was sexually "restless" or "troubled" or "unhappy." This was said from the outside. She said it from the inside more pointedly when they lived together across two households, back in the mid-nineties. She repeated herself in their last weeks together, not long before Peter limped home from Bournemouth and her and Roland's complicated arrangements came to an end. But on all occasions, it was never a charge. That was not Daphne's way. It was more of an observation, grey-washed with regret—for him rather than for herself. She was a busy woman, capable of keeping him and his problems at arm's length. Now, five years later, in the autumn of 2010, with Labour gone and when the country was being readied to pay for the greed and folly of the financial sector, Daphne's husband left her for the second time. Peter surprised everybody with a consuming devotion to a wealthy older woman. She had something to do with his laughable single-issue political passion. He had sold his stake in the electricity company to a Dutch equity group. The *Financial Times* disclosed a sum of £35 million. Together, he and Hermione would help fund the dream of taking Britain out of the European Union.

Roland was two years into his sixties. Time had dissipated his restlessness. Daphne's children and his child had left home. She knew him well, better than anyone. It seemed worth the risk, after much reflection, to ask her—at last—to marry him. To his surprise she said yes—in a casual instant. They were at her place in Lloyd Square one evening, shoeless by the fire, the first of the season. Daphne's immediate assent made the nicely proportioned rooms seem larger. The walls, the doors and architraves glowed. Everything glowed. A full kiss, then she went to the kitchen to fetch a bottle of champagne. This was how to steer a life successfully, Roland thought. Make a choice, act! That's the lesson. A shame not to have known the trick long ago. Good decisions came less through rational calculation, more from sudden good moods. But so too did some of his worst decisions. But that was not for now. She filled their glasses and they toasted their future. Daphne was sixty-one. In the long business of modern old age they were neonates. They stoked the fire and made their plans like excited children. Peter would be giving her his half of the house as part of their clean break. Once the house was purged of Peter's possessions, Roland would move in and transfer ownership of the Clapham place to Lawrence. But not before the overdue renovation. Daphne knew the right people to do the work. She would continue at her housing association for another five years. Then they would travel. He had in mind Bhutan, she was for Patagonia. A perfect contrast. Roland would walk to the Angel Tube most afternoons and continue his sessions at the Mayfair hotel. He would allow her to meet him there for a drink, and even to make requests. She said she'd like him to play "Doctor Jazz." He knew it well. The ex-violinist manager, Mary Killy, wouldn't like it. But he'd play it. In Daphne's sitting room his old upright would go along the wall behind them, under her Duncan Grant portrait of Paul Roche, the artist's lover.

So it went on happily until a thoughtful silence fell between them. Roland got up too quickly from the cat-scoured Chesterfield and stood still, waiting for a dizzy spell to pass. Then he rebuilt the fire, sat down and exchanged a look with his wife-to-be. She had kept her hair long and it was still blonde, artificially so, he imagined. She remained tall and strong and he easily conjured the face of the mother of three young children, the woman who helped him through the months and years after Alissa left. Inevitably, into their silence the past pressed in. There was so much of it now. Without forethought—another good decision—Roland said, "There's a part of my life I've never told you about." As he said it, he was wondering if Alissa had told her long ago.

But Daphne looked up with interest. He was certain she would tell him if she knew. And so he began the whole story, from the early piano lessons when he was eleven, Miriam Cornell's cottage, the sudden end on a rainy night, the policeman's visits when Lawrence was a baby, another policeman eight years ago, the visit to Balham, why he played " 'Round Midnight," the parting on the doorstep, how she had said she would plead guilty.

When at last he finished she was silent, taking it in. After a while she said softly, "So what did you do?"

"I'd never had such power over another person and I wouldn't want it again. I did nothing for a month. I had to be sure that whenever I thought about it, I arrived at the same place. And I did. Nothing changed. My feelings about it were no different from when I walked away from her house. Seeing her settled everything. I couldn't send her to prison. She may have deserved it, technically or fully, humanly or whatever. But the impulse for revenge or justice died in me once we'd met."

"You still felt something for her?"

"No. The whole thing ceased to matter. Complete indifference. And I couldn't get myself past the thought of my own role in it. My complicity."

"At *fourteen?*"

"To bring a case against her from a position of detachment . . . too cold-blooded. This wasn't the same woman. I wasn't that boy." He paused. "I'm not being very convincing. Even to myself."

"She had a lot to answer for."

"I think she knew that."

"What would you feel if it had happened to Lawrence?"

Roland considered. "Fury, I suppose. You're right."

"Well . . ." Daphne stretched out and studied the ceiling. "Then call it forgiveness."

"Yes . . . virtue. But it wasn't what I felt, or feel now. It was beyond forgiveness. It wasn't even about moving on or whatever they say. Closure. I no longer cared—about her, about what I might have been. All gone and I don't give a damn. How could I send her to prison, even for a week?"

"So you wrote to her."

"The police didn't know her name and I wasn't going to leave a trail. I phoned and told her what I'd decided. She started to say something. I think she wanted to thank me but I rang off."

The log basket was empty. Together they carried it to a walk-in cupboard off the kitchen where the wood was stored. When the fire was going again and they were settled Daphne said, "You've kept this to yourself all this time?"

"I told Alissa once."

"And?"

"I remember it well. Her parents' place. Deep snow. She said, 'That woman rewired your brain.'"

"And was she right! But rewired means forever. How can you say it's all gone and it doesn't matter and you don't care?"

To this he had no reply but they would surely return to the subject. Their marriage had begun.

An event at work the next day seemed at one with that late night. It was as if asking an old friend to marry him had stirred up disparate floating elements of his past and caused them to cluster and reappear. He was on pre- and post-dinner sessions. It was accepted that there was no London tourist season. In a fully fashionable world city it was always the tourist season. Each year, more Russians, Chinese and Indians came, as well as the usual Gulf Arabs and Americans. Even tens of thousands of French thought London had something over Paris. The hotel was usually full, though the clientele remained unyouthful. It was a place valued not so much for tradition and Old England as for being dully tranquil. One could depend on nothing happening. Many guests were regulars. The concierge desk had good ticket connections to the mainstream popular shows. The reliable restaurant served residents only—no need to go scrambling after hot-ticket chefs across town. The hotel was expensive but unregarded by noisy pop and film stars and bond traders or any other section of London's beau monde. After dinner the lounge bar was crowded and over the years, among the regulars, there developed a muted following—secured by Mary Killy's judgement—for Roland and the kind of approachable music he played. Sometimes he arrived on the dais to timid applause. Mary asked him to acknowledge it with a gesture, a faint bow would do. He obliged. The management now treated him as an asset, one cut above the waiting staff. He was allowed to arrive for work through the front doors. He was permitted, even encouraged, to be seen ordering drinks in the lounge before or after his session. If he would mingle with the guests, all the better. This he did his best to avoid.

In the evening he arrived mildly hungover from the night before. They had gone to bed at four and made love before they slept. They did not see each other at breakfast. Daphne had an early routine hospital appointment and he tried to sleep in. After half an hour, he gave up, made coffee and with it wandered around her orderly house and imagined himself living there. There was a tiny room off a landing she said he could have as a study. He peeped in. Piled with suitcases and childhood furniture, two high chairs, cot, tiny desks, waiting for the next generation. Daphne's eldest, Greta, was pregnant. During the morning he had felt immune to his customary reflections on time and life spinning away from him. He was making a new start. He would be reborn. A neonate! He had phoned Lawrence to tell him his news, though he could not help thinking that he was asking for his son's approval. The answer was simple—"yes, a thousand times yes!"

Now, at work, as he went to the piano for his first set and nodded in three directions to the scattered clapping, he noticed four people at a table close by on his left. A couple of about his age and two young women. They were drinking beers and looked a little out of place. All four possessed that look, the focussed gaze that an extended formal education was supposed to bestow. For his own good reasons he did not believe in any of that. His face-recognition had grown poor over the years but within seconds he knew who they were and there came to him, as well as delight, a long-forgotten stab of guilt. His hands were already on the keyboard and he had to get to work. There were more guests from the States than usual, according to Mary. That meant starting with "A Nightingale Sang in Berkeley Square," a secondary national anthem for a certain kind of American in London.

He was playing through his usual show-tune medley when he looked across at the group. They were watching him intently and as he met their gaze they smiled nervously. He lifted a hand in greeting. He had arrived at a staid Scott Joplin ragtime and imagined Daphne as his wife, sitting alone at a table while he played Jelly Roll Morton's "Doctor Jazz" in a thumping stride style. That would certainly happen and thinking of it filled him with delighted anticipation. Now he played something sentimental. "Always." He took another quick look at the four. A waitress was setting down four fresh beers. The idea came of sending them a message, a memory. His break was a few minutes away. The last number of the set would be one he had never played before, here or anywhere. He knew it well enough, the chords were simple and as he started to play, he managed to replicate its gently swaying rhythm, and found that his right hand, all by itself, knew the introduction and how to copy the tender guitar notes that lifted the chorus. *Linger on your pale blue eyes . . .*

When he finished and looked up the woman was crying. The man was on his feet coming towards him and the two young women were smiling. One had an arm round her mother's shoulders. The general buzz of conversation dipped and the lounge guests looked on with interest as Roland stepped off the dais and went into a long embrace with Florian and then with Ruth. Hanna and Charlotte joined in and they made an affectionate scrum of an embrace. Well, he had been asked to mingle with the guests.

As they straightened Ruth laughed. "Jetzt weinst du auch!" Now you're crying too!

"I'm just being polite."

They walked the few steps towards their table. He had Hanna on one arm, Charlotte on the other, the girls with the astounding whispered secrets, his German-language instructors on the black plastic sofa. One of the waiters was setting down a fifth beer.

They had twenty minutes before the second set. The stories tumbled out, the four Germans sometimes talking at once.

"How did you find me here?"

When Florian and Ruth were arrested and the flat was searched, their address books were confiscated. Finally, when they knew they were coming to London, Hanna tracked down Mireille on a French *"amis d'avant"* site and she told her about Roland's piano bar. Hanna was an Erasmus student in biology in Manchester, Charlotte was working in a bookshop in Bristol to improve her English. Ruth was teaching in high school, Florian was a doctor and they had moved to Duisburg in 1990. Both parents looked older than their years, many lines around the eyes, and Roland noticed something subdued in their manner. They had both put on weight. He told the family that as of last night he was to be married to his best friend. On an impulse he phoned Daphne. She sounded far away. She was just finishing up at work, she said, and would join them in an hour. Champagne then, afterwards!

The Heises had never met Lawrence but they knew of him and asked for his news. As a part-time mature student, he was studying for his maths degree from the Free University in Berlin. Until then he was a waiter in the evenings and making himself useful unofficially at a climate institute in Potsdam. That morning he had told his father that he thought he "might be in love" with an oceanographer called Ingrid.

Roland ended an exuberant second set with some Kurt Weill tunes, "Mack the Knife," then "Ballad of the Easy Life." He stood from his last number to scattered applause, slightly more emphatic than usual. More than his playing, the drama of the reunion had touched a few. News of his marriage plans had spread to the bar. On the table there was a bottle in an ice bucket and five glasses with a note of congratulations from the night manager.

After the toasts the Heises' story came out. In answer to Roland's question, no, the records and books he had brought to the house had not caused problems. But Schwedt was a grim place and it was a grim time. Ruth worked as a cleaner in a hospital, Florian was in a paper mill and then, slightly better, a shoe factory. The system pressed down on them and worse, the neighbours were hostile. None of it was so bad as being without the children. Suddenly, after two months, they had them back. They had not been separated after all but they were not in a good state. The sisters nodded as Ruth was saying this. But the last eighteen months had been lightened by growing hope. News trickled through about people, whole families, crossing into Austria from Hungary and the Russians were doing nothing about it. Then of course, the Wall. The journey west from Schwedt in March 1990 was complicated. They met up at last with Ruth's mother, Maria, in Berlin. The authorities had never allowed her to visit. Ruth and Florian finally got her to a hospital in the West, in Duisburg, where she died in '92.

It had been a wonderful break when Florian, at the age of forty-one, was given a grant to go to medical school. But it was hard sustaining the family on Ruth's wages as a lowly assistant in a school for difficult children. Things got worse, Florian said, when the girls turned themselves into teenagers from hell. Hanna and Charlotte squealed in protest.

"All right. How about one teenage pregnancy scare, police complaints about graffiti crimes, alcohol, drugs, dyeing your hair green, bad school reports, loud music in the street, coming home at 2 a.m., urinating in a public . . ."

The longer his list, the harder the sisters laughed. They clutched at each other. "It was behind a bush!"

"Wir wollten einfach nur Spass haben!"

"Just trying to have fun? What about the petition of the neighbours?"

Ruth turned to Roland. "They wanted these two sent back east!"

The girls dissolved completely. It was hard to imagine graffiti and green hair now that they were cool and educated Westerners. It was the parents who bore the marks and drank most of the champagne. Their children barely touched theirs. Some minutes passed, then Hanna and Charlotte glanced at each other, nodded and stood. An Italian friend whose English boyfriend had a flat in Holland Park was having a party and they needed to get going. They would see their parents in the hotel at breakfast. Their elders stood to be embraced and they watched the sisters hurry across the lounge. Roland had mixed feelings. He did not envy them a party starting this late. But he missed in himself what he remembered so well, that impatience, that hunger to be there at the crucial event. The thought dissipated as he saw Hanna and Charlotte step aside at the entrance to let through his future wife. Even before she had reached their table Florian and Ruth had knocked back their children's drinks. They ordered another bottle and fresh glasses.

After the introductions and a fresh round of toasts, Daphne was given a brief history. She remembered the family from Roland's accounts. He recalled how she had introduced him to a contact in the record industry who located a rare bootleg Dylan that Florian had been pining for.

He said, "I was happier when I was longing for things." He stood and, muttering about the stupidity of the local smoking laws, went out for a cigarette.

While he was gone Roland gave a running translation for Daphne as Ruth told them that Florian had not been as happy as herself and the girls. The clinic where he worked was in a tough part of Duisburg, near Oberbilk. He saw the worst—the drugs, the poverty, violence, squalor, racism, the way women were treated in the white as well as immigrant communities. Ruth called it the worst; every country had its worst. But he said it was the reality and no one was confronting it. He could never defend the old East but he wasn't happy in a united Germany. He loathed the traffic jams, the graffiti everywhere, the litter around the clinic, the stupidity of the politics, the commercialism. When an ad came on the TV he left the room. He thought the neighbours looked down on him but really, Ruth said, they were nice people. When the girls were at school he was always complaining about poor discipline in the classroom. It was embarrassing. In fact they got a good education. On the roads, he said that most drivers were criminally insane. German pop music drove him mad.

"He has all the music he likes, his own music but he never plays it. When you played the Velvet Underground song he was very sad. We both were, for the old times that we never want to see again. Anywhere!"

Roland felt uneasy listening to her talk about Florian in his absence. There was more complaint than sympathy in her tone and he suspected that she was trying to enlist him in a marital grievance. He hoped none of this had come across in his translation. He glanced at Daphne, who was sitting beside him. Since joining them she had seemed withdrawn. He took her hand and was surprised to find her palm hot and damp, in fact wet.

"Are you OK?" he asked quietly.

"Yes, fine." She squeezed his hand.

Ruth leaned forward suddenly. "He's seeing a woman. He denies it. So we can't talk about it."

But Roland did not translate for Daphne. He could see Florian approaching, followed by a waitress with another bottle. When he sat down, he insisted on opening the champagne himself.

Daphne gave another squeeze. Roland took her to mean that she wanted to leave soon. He looked at her and nodded. She looked worn out. She'd had a long day. But Florian had returned in an expansive mood and was filling the glasses and wanting to reminisce about the late eighties and the forbidden books, which he hadn't touched since. Then he got on to the subject of NATO. Its expansion east was madness, a ridiculous provocation to the Russians with their national inferiority complex. Roland started to disagree. Surely Florian did not need to be reminded. The old Warsaw Pact countries had suffered years of Russian occupation, violently enforced. They had good cause and every right to make their own choices. But entering the debate was a mistake and it took almost half an hour to disengage, swap phone numbers and emails. Then they stood for farewell embraces which, for Roland, had lost their innocent exuberance. The moment was tainted. He wished Ruth had not told him what he did not need to know. He felt sad for them both, and some misplaced guilt about his own happiness.

There was more delay as they were leaving. Some of the staff wanted to shake his hand and be introduced to Daphne and offer congratulations. She was friendly in response but he could see that it cost her an effort. He suspected that Peter was causing problems. Perhaps he was wanting to come back. Not a chance. At last, arm in arm, they walked along the groomed backstreets of Mayfair towards Park Lane to pick up a taxi. She asked him what Ruth had said and he told her. She made no response and as they went along he felt her clinging to his arm as if she feared falling. Once they were in the taxi heading east he moved closer to her.

"What's the matter Daphne? Tell me."

She stiffened suddenly and a shudder went through her. Though she took a deep breath before speaking her voice was very small. "I've had some bad news." She was about to tell him, but she couldn't. She turned from him and began to cry. Roland was shocked. If it was one of the children she would have told him already. He put his arm round her and waited. Her shoulders and neck were hot. The cabbie slowed and asked over the intercom if there was anything he could do. Roland told him to keep going and then he switched off the microphone. He had never seen Daphne cry. She was always so capable, strong, concerned for others. He felt the mute amazement of a child before a weeping parent. He found some tissues in her bag and pressed them into her hand. Slowly she recovered.

"I'm sorry," she said. And again, "I'm sorry."

He hugged her closer. Finally she told him. "I had some test results back this morning." As she said it, he guessed the rest.

She said, "I should have told you. But I thought it would be nothing. It's cancer, grade four."

Though he tried, for a few seconds he could not speak.

"Where?"

"Everywhere. It's everywhere! I don't stand a chance. In their own complicated way they said as much. Both doctors. Oh Roland, I'm so scared!"

# I I

He lifted it from the drawer where he kept his sweaters and placed it on his desk. It was a weighty ceramic jar with a screw-top inlaid with cork and it was wrapped in a single sheet of two-year-old newspaper. Before that it had stood for five years in the window of his bedroom until he had grown weary of being reminded of the reason for his delay. Now, just before midnight in early September, everything was packed and piled in the hall. His rented car, the cheapest machine he could find, was parked round the corner. He gently laid the jar on its side and unrolled it free of its covering. Two years sat lightly in memory, like two months. Time's gathering compression was a commonplace among his old friends. They routinely shared their impressions of an unfair acceleration. He had forgotten that in a spirit of glum irony he had chosen this page. He put the pot to one side and spread the paper out. 15 June 2016. A half-page photograph showed Nigel Farage, leader of the UK Independence Party, and Kate Hoey, a Labour MP, in the prow of a boat, leaning back against the railing in buoyant mood. Behind them was Parliament. Alongside was a packed pleasure boat decked out in Union Jacks. There were other boats, partly out of shot. It was a celebration and a promise that soon Britain would vote to leave the European Union and take back control of its extensive fishing waters.

But Roland was not interested in Farage and Hoey. An elbow, upper arm and part of a shoulder in the foreground of the picture were the reason he had chosen the page. A perverse choice. They belonged to Peter Mount, one of the major donors to the cause. For a year he had been pestering Roland to dispose of Daphne's ashes and involve him in the rite. Lately, Peter's calls had increased. Roland had explained many times that her wishes had been specific and that he, Roland, was not in contradiction of them. His delay was in order. A couple of times he had hung up on Peter. It was not only personal. He had come to loathe everything the man stood for.

He wrapped the jar in a fleece, stuffed it into a spare backpack and took it downstairs to put with the rest of his stuff. Hiking boots under a broad-brimmed hat, another backpack, a small suitcase, a cardboard box of groceries. He went into the kitchen and wrote a note to Lawrence and Ingrid. They were coming from Potsdam with six-year-old Stefanie to house-sit and enjoy London. His instructions were mostly about his cat, which he had not seen in two days. On his return, they would celebrate his birthday with a dinner. What a pleasure, not to return to an empty house.

On a separate sheet he wrote a zany welcoming letter to Stefanie, with drawings and jokes. Over the past two years they had been building on a special friendship. Here was a surprise, a love affair, an affair of love, as he entered his seventies. He was touched by the way she sought him out to present her solemn reflections or considered questions, or to insist that he sit by her at mealtimes. She wanted to know about his past. He was awed by the clear evidence of a six-year-old's thriving inner life. He was swept back more than thirty years to Lawrence's childhood. She listened with a fixed concentrated stare to her grandfather's stories. She had her mother's blueish-black eyes, an oceanographer's submarine gaze. He thought she regarded him as her ancient and extremely precious possession, whose frail existence she was tasked to preserve. He was flattered whenever she put her hand in his.

Half an hour later he was in bed and, as he expected, unable to sleep. Too many things to remember, like a sharp knife, his blood-pressure pills, the best route out of London. He should take a different bank card to replace one that was out of date. Cars no longer had CD players, so he should look one out if he was to play her favourite disc. He took a zopiclone and as he waited his thoughts settled on Peter Mount again. It seemed that once the Referendum had gone his way he was spending his time falling out with the woman he lived with and

rediscovering his love for Daphne. He and Hermione had fought the
campaign together, given it money, triumphed, and now they were
fighting in court over properties they jointly owned. Mount's posthu-
mous love for his ex-partner had narrowed to an obsession with her
ashes. He knew where she wanted them thrown. Thirty-five years
ago, she had marked the place for him on a map. He had recently
offered to go and do it himself. That was not going to happen. Her
remarks to Roland as well as her letter were specific. That letter was
in his luggage. Peter had left her twice and done it messily, and there
were the episodes of violence, which he owned up to without contri-
tion. At the time, apparently, he claimed she had driven him to it. In
her last weeks, Daphne had decided not to forgive him.

The pill was slow to come on and caused him to oversleep. He
should have taken a half. All through the night Peter Mount was in the
tangled lines of his dreams. His mother was there too, needing something, calling for help but in mumbled words he could not understand.
He woke in a blurred state at eight thirty. His plan had been to get on
the road by six and beat the rush hour out of town. Now, with slow
movements, he was losing more time straightening out the kitchen for
Lawrence and Ingrid, then needing an extra cup of coffee for the road.
It was almost ten before he brought the car to the front of the house. It
was that time of day when traffic wardens were fresh and hungry on
the job. He loaded the car at speed and was turning back to the house
to lock up when he confronted the figure from his dreams. In his state
it seemed unsurprising. Mount was standing by the railings outside
the house holding a canvas bag. He was wearing a tweed jacket with a
country look, a baseball cap and heavy brogues.

"Thank God. I thought you might have left by now."

"What do you want, Peter?"

"The children told me. I'm coming too."

Roland shook his head and pushed past him. As he entered the
house he glanced back to see Peter trying to get into the car. Then
he tried the boot. He came towards the front door and called out,
"Enjoying my house, are you?"

Roland slammed the door and sat at the bottom of the stairs to
think things through. This was indeed Peter's house once, bought

with the electricity money. Then donated to Daphne to pay off his debt of guilt. That was an ancient argument and a while back Roland had changed the locks. After ten minutes he went out again. Peter was still there, waiting.

Roland chose a tone of tranquil reasonableness. "I don't know why but I'm sure you do, Peter. She didn't want you involved."

"You're lying, old fruit. I loved her far longer than you did. I have a right."

Roland went back into the house and in determined mood spent the rest of the morning paying bills and writing emails—good to get this done. Where he was headed had no Internet connection. At twelve thirty he looked out the bedroom window. Peter had gone and there was still no parking ticket on the windscreen. An hour later he was heading west on the M40 towards Birmingham and beyond.

Long drives usually settled him into sustained reflection, somewhat grim and plodding like the traffic itself, but usefully detached. His little car, nimbler and more spacious than he expected, was a thought-bubble pushing north through a country he no longer quite knew or understood. Approaching Birmingham he slipped into a mode of magical thinking. The cooling towers, outsized pylons, the fenced blank-walled warehousing round the industrial fringes suggested a toughness and resolve about leaving the Union he could almost admire. The trucks and trailers he passed were larger, noisier, more assertive and numerous—they had the vote.

In fact, the Birmingham vote was finely balanced. It was a cosmopolitan city. In 1971 he played a gig there with Peter's band. A discerning small crowd appreciated that the Peter Mount Posse modelled itself on American southern rock, on the Allman Brothers, on Marshall Tucker. Peter insisted that the Posse wore grey fedoras, t-shirts and black jeans. They didn't play covers. Peter and the bass guitarist wrote all the band's material. They were in an obscure venue in the basement of a guitar shop near the New Street station. One of their best nights ever, before marriages, children and the onset of punk broke the band up. It was the night that Peter brought along his new girlfriend, Daphne. She and Roland talked for hours while Peter was off somewhere getting drunk. From then on, there was unspoken jeal-

ousy and rivalry. But Mount was a cool lead guitarist with an assertive personality, a knack of getting his way and, just occasionally,
into fights, proper ones with clenched fists. A self-doubting part-time
keyboard player could not compete. And here was the same Peter,
a wealthy man of convictions, a defector from UKIP, a conspicuous
donor to the party of government, within a tongue's length of a peerage, according to *Private Eye*. It had turned out there was nothing
inevitable about the egalitarian spirit of rock music. The confrontation on the pavement that morning was less to do with a few pounds
of ashes than a continuation of an old struggle. Seven years on, everything led back to Daphne. Which of them would own her memory?

The months that separated diagnosis and death were the most
intense of Roland's life, at a few points the happiest and during the
rest, the most miserable. He had never felt so much. After the immediate shock and terror she had arranged a second opinion. He went with
her and took notes while she asked the questions they had worked on
together. It seemed so abstract, she kept telling him. She was feeling
nothing unusual apart from an occasional pain in her side which she
rated for the consultant at three, on a scale of zero to ten. They were
married in a registry office with no family or friends present, only
a couple of witnesses plucked from the street. For days they talked
over the consultation and the results of a further set of tests. Then
she made her decision. She summoned her children, including Lawrence, to Lloyd Square and broke the news. That rated high among
the worst events. Ten on the pain spectrum. Gerald, recently qualified
from medical school, went quiet and left the room. Greta wept, Nancy
got angry—with her mother's news and with her mother. Lawrence
put his arms round Daphne and both cried.

When things were calmer and Gerald was back in the room she
told the family what she had decided to do. Apart from serious pain
relief, not yet necessary, she would refuse treatment. The side effects
were vile, the success rates at this stage negligible. The children went
back to their lives and Daphne and Roland worked on a plan. It came
down to three parts. First, while she was still strong enough to travel,
there were places she wanted to see again. Among them the spot where
she would like Roland to dispose of her ashes. Second, she would be at

home to organise her affairs and keep doing that until it was the third stage and time to concentrate on being ill.

Roland made the hotel and travel arrangements. In summary, the entire process was practical and businesslike. But along the way there was more crying and many angry outbursts. She didn't stoop to "why me?" but, like Nancy, raged against the indecency of fate. She turned on Roland for his apparent detachment, his "bloody clipboard"—in fact, sheets of paper resting against an art book—his pen at the ready "like some prison bureaucrat." Prison? Because he was free and she was trapped. But their reconciliations were immediate and tender.

First, a family holiday in an unpretentious hotel on a small island off the south coast of France. Daphne wanted Lawrence to come. In response to their pleading the Potsdam Institute set him free at short notice. Greta, Nancy and Gerald knew the hotel from childhood. The proprietor remembered Daphne and embraced her. He was not to be told. The week gave them a first taste of many violent reversals of feeling, from dank anticipation of the tragedy drawing closer, to ordinary holiday merriment improbably obliterating everything. They turned out to be irrepressible, the family jokes, memories, teases, delight in the surroundings. During a two-hour meal they could move more than once between these poles. At dinner they sat outdoors overlooking a modest bay and the sunset. To take a picture that included Daphne was to see already the photograph which would posthumously survive her. She wanted no *omertà* about her condition. That was no easier than tactful silence. On the first evening, when it was time to say goodnight, the embraces felt like rehearsals for a final farewell, everyone was aware of that and there were tears. They were in the garden under a eucalyptus tree, in a circle-embrace. Nearby was the chef's illuminated tank in which lobsters pressed their armour against the glass with a muted clicking sound. How different this was from the communal embrace with the Heise family in the Mayfair hotel, a few weeks before.

Daphne said, "In the face of this crap, being here, doing this is the very best, the most joyous thing I can imagine." At which, Lawrence became overwhelmed and everyone had to comfort him. When he recovered they teased him about stealing Daphne's limelight and she joined in. So it went on for six nights, up and down. Her trick was to persuade them that, high or low, there should be no restraint or guilt about merriment and sadness. She gave the impression of being happy and though the family did not believe it or her, the illusion lifted the mood.

There were no cars on the island. There was one paved forestry track and many footpaths through the holm oak woods. They hiked, swam and picnicked on the cliffs together. One afternoon Daphne and Roland walked alone to the far end of the island to a sandy beach by a bamboo thicket. They were oblivious to the beauty of the day as she set out ideas that would evolve over the coming weeks. She dreaded the helplessness, the humiliation at the end almost as much as the pain. She was experiencing the first stirrings of a sharp rending sensation in her side. The pain, she thought, was going to be big, "like a tower." It frightened her. So did the thought of losing her mind if the secondaries reached her brain. As for the sorrow—not seeing the four children further into adult life, never knowing the grandchildren to come, not being with him into old age, not discovering the marriage they should have started long ago.

"My fault," Roland said.

She did not contradict him, merely squeezed his hand. Later, on the walk back to the hotel, on that same subject, she murmured, "You were a restless fool."

Back on the mainland at the end of the stay they said their good-byes on the quayside in a normal affectionate manner. For now they were purged of high emotion. The young adults were sharing a taxi to Marseilles to catch their planes to London, and to Berlin via Paris. Roland and Daphne were driving north-east in a rented convertible to stay in a rural *pensione* some way out of Aosta. She had cleaned rooms there for two months after leaving school. Four hundred miles in a leisurely four days, and Daphne would drive. They were to go by minor roads wherever possible, with Roland navigating by the large-scale maps he had bought in advance. No GPS. He had also booked three stopovers in remote country locations.

The island apart, this was the most successful of Daphne's dream itinerary. The demands of driving on narrow mountain roads, choosing the ideal picnic lunch spots, the pleasures of arrival at the end of each day, the occasional backtrack when Roland made a navigational error kept her mind on the present. The *pensione,* the Maison Lozon, was much as she remembered it. The owner let them peep into her old room. In this hotel she had lost her heart to a Bulgarian waiter and in this tiny room, a day short of her eighteenth birthday, she made love for the first time.

At supper they talked about their teenage years, about the children as teenagers and of the condition in general and when it had acquired its special status. Roland put it down to a symbolic moment, when Elvis released his first hit, "Heartbreak Hotel," in 1956. Daphne put it five years earlier, during the delayed post-war boom of the early fifties and the extension of the school-leaving age. It may have been that talking about that time in their own lives added depth to a sense of a shared past; it may have been that they yearned for each other as teenagers; it could have been their elation at the end of a successful road trip and the brilliance of their island week or her delight in the Fats Waller song he played for her on the *pensione*'s ancient piano; above all, it was the certainty that it was all to be taken from them. They had been friends a long time and they loved each other the way old friends do, but later that evening in their second-floor room under a heavily timbered roof, they fell in love—like teenagers.

That feeling remained but the trip became less delightful. Things went downhill literally as they became bound to a timetable and descended from the mountains to join a torrent of traffic towards Milan's Malpensa airport to deliver their rental car and catch a flight to Paris. Turin would have been better. Roland's mistake. Daphne grimly committed herself to the vernacular driving style, flashing her lights and tailgating at high speed in the packed fast lane. Roland sat tensely and kept quiet.

They had grown used to beauty and peace and found they were not suited to Paris. The apartment was on the rue de Seine. The streets around it were crowded with tourists like themselves. The morning coffee in the local bars tasted vile, both muddy and weak. They decided to make their own in their apartment. In the Michelin two-star restaurant she wanted to show him, wines he had bought for around £15 in London started at 200 euros. These were banal tourist gripes. But in the Petit Palais, which Daphne had not visited in thirty years, Roland had what she liked to call "a moment." He retired early from the paintings and waited in the main hall. After she had joined him and they were walking away he let rip. He said that if he ever had to look at one more Madonna and Child, Crucifixion, Assumption, Annunciation and all the rest he would "throw up." Historically, he announced, Christianity had been the cold dead hand on the European imagination. What a gift, that its tyranny had expired. What looked like piety was enforced conformity within a totalitarian mind-state. To question or defy it in the sixteenth century would have been to take your life in your hands. Like protesting against Socialist Realism in Stalin's Soviet Union. It was not only science that Christianity had obstructed for fifty generations, it was nearly all of culture, nearly all of free expression and enquiry. It buried the open-minded philosophies of classical antiquity for an age, it sent thousands of brilliant minds down irrelevant rabbit holes of pettifogging theology. It had spread its so-called Word by horrific violence and it maintained itself by torture, persecution and death. Gentle Jesus, ha! Within the totality of human experience of the world there was an infinity of subject matter and yet all over Europe the big museums were stuffed with the same lurid trash. Worse than pop music. It was the Eurovision Song Contest in oils and gilt frames. Even as he spoke he was amazed by the strength of his feelings and the pleasure of release. He was talking—exploding—about something else. What a relief it was, he said as he began to cool down, to see a representation of a bourgeois interior, of a loaf of bread on a board beside a knife, of a couple skating on a frozen canal hand in hand, trying to seize a moment of fun "while the fucking priest wasn't looking. Thank God for the Dutch!"

Daphne, who at that point had eight weeks to live, put her hand on his arm. Her smile, indulgent and sweet, melted him away. She was giving him a lesson in dying. She said, "It's lunchtime. I think you need a drink."

The travel and tourist routines in a lively city began to weary her and she longed for home. They cut their visit short by three days and took the train to London. There was still one more journey ahead and it was better for her to rest up in Lloyd Square before they set off. Five days later she was in good shape as they loaded up her car with provisions and hiking gear. Again she insisted on driving. Her last chance, she kept saying. On her instructions he had rented a cottage in the Lake District, by the River Esk. She had stayed there at the age of nine with her father, a country doctor and an expert amateur naturalist. She remembered how pleased she was to have him to herself. Together father and daughter were going to climb Scafell Pike, the highest mountain in England, if not in the world. The cottage, Bird How, in the upper reaches of the valley, had no electricity and it was part of the excitement, to be allowed to light the candles and carry them into the bedroom among the creepy shifting shadows.

As Daphne drove them over the Wrynose and Hardknott passes, Roland recalled a time when Lawrence, then fourteen, announced that he wanted to climb a mountain. Two days later, they were staying in a pub in the Langstrath valley, setting out early for the climb up the same mountain.

"I was amazed by how fit he was, the speed he made me take that ascent."

Daphne laughed. "You sound a little sad."

"I miss him."

There was low cloud and fine rain when they arrived at Bird How two hours before dark. The cottage was reached by a rough track and the low-slung car scraped loudly over protruding rocks. Roland carried their stuff in across a garden of uncut grasses, while Daphne prepared the cottage. Even in the flat light he could see how beautiful the surrounds were. The fells rose on both sides. The Esk, invisible under a line of trees, was down a sloping meadow framed by drystone walls. The cottage was simple. No bathroom—one washed at the kitchen sink. Down below was a cobbled cellar and a chemical lavatory.

Next morning the rain had stopped and the clouds had partly cleared. The forecast was for periods of sunshine. They loaded their packs and set off along the farm track, following the river upstream. They crossed to the east bank by the footbridge at Taw House Farm. Daphne had in mind a certain place she wanted to show him. The going was easy underfoot but they went slowly, resting every twenty minutes or so. While she was sitting on a high ladder over a drystone wall she took a painkiller and soon after she walked with more confidence. It took them three hours to cover a few kilometres. They arrived at the spot, the crossing at Lingcove Bridge. She was excited. It amazed her that the simple arched stone structure was exactly as it was over fifty years before when she sat by it with her father and he told her about the war. He had been in the Medical Corps, tending troops as they fought their way across the north German plain towards Berlin. He was not, she told Roland, a demonstrative man but he held her hand as he told her about his work and explained as best he could to a nine-year-old the system of triage. As their unit pushed further east, further from home he had written letters to Daphne's mother.

"I asked him what he wrote about. He said he described everything, even the wounds he had tended and told her that he loved her very much and that when he got back, they'd get married and one day have a little girl like me. I can't tell you, Roland, what a joy it was to hear him say that. He was an extremely reserved man. I'd never heard him use the word love. People didn't in those days, not to children. To hear him say that he loved my mother gave me a great glow of love for him. He told me he had watched engineers build a pontoon bridge at speed across the River Elbe. When he crossed it in a lorry two wheels slipped over the edge and they were close to tipping into deep water. The soldiers had to climb out carefully, one by one.

"As he told that story, and he told it really well, he turned it into a kind of thriller. I was gripping his hand and the water was rushing down the river and down the waterfall behind us. The lorry was tipping but the soldiers were going to be safe. As I listened I thought that I was the happiest I had ever been."

Daphne and Roland went onto the little bridge and looked downstream. After a silence she said, "I'm so happy here with you, and the two happy moments are almost the entire span of my existence. I'd like you to come here alone with my ashes. Getting all the children here at the same time would be hopeless. Don't come with a friend, don't bring any of your lovely ex-lovers. Especially don't let Peter barge in. He's made me miserable too often. Anyway, he hates walking and the big outdoors. Come alone and think about our happiness here. And tip me in the river." Then she added, "If the wind's blowing you can go down and do it from the bank."

This last, its bathos, was too much for them. They fell silent and hugged. Such talk of happiness, Roland thought, was absurd. The approach of a team of hikers, scarring the landscape with their electric blue anoraks, made them self-conscious and they let each other go. There was not enough room on the bridge for them all to pass, so while the friendly group waited, Roland and Daphne returned to the east bank and went a few yards up Lingcove Beck, in front of the first waterfall and ate their picnic.

By the time they had finished Daphne was too tired to go on, so they began a slow descent to Bird How. For the rest of the day she dozed on the bed and Roland, who had brought a biography of Wordsworth to read, couldn't face it, or him, and instead flipped through country magazines left by other guests. In the early evening he stepped outside and looked across the valley towards Birker Fell. The faint breeze against his face carried and amplified the sound of the river. He thought he heard footsteps behind the house at his back. He went to look, but there was no one. The steady tread resolved itself into his heartbeat. As he returned to his view of the river he saw a barn owl fifty yards away, flying low directly towards him, coming up the meadow, its pale face full on to his view. For an instant, he had the impression, more of a hallucination, of a human face, ancient, utterly indifferent, gazing at him. Then the image passed, the owl banked to its right to fly upstream, parallel to the river, then it turned left, crossed the river and disappeared behind a stand of trees. When he went back indoors he heard Daphne stirring and took her a mug of tea. He didn't mention the owl. He told himself that she would have been sad to have missed it.

Two days later he did the driving back to London. Daphne slept part of the way. When she woke they were level with Manchester. She took a disc out of her bag, highlights of *The Magic Flute*.

"OK?"

"Sure. Turn it up."

At the first fat chord of the overture Roland felt himself thrown back to 1959, to the smell of fresh paint on the flats that depicted a spooky wood and on the heavy cotton apron he was made to wear; bewilderment at where he was supposed to be and what he was supposed to do; the unacknowledged numbness at being so far from his mother. Two thousand miles. He saw in the road surface rushing towards him the patterns of the lino in the Berners Hall music block. That the overture began its familiar merry scurrying did not release him. He had been holding himself together in the situation and now the Mozart and the memories were softening him. The hopelessness of Daphne's courage threatened to undo him. He was in the middle lane doing seventy-five miles an hour, passing a long line of trucks and his vision was beginning to blur. How warm she was, how pathetic, how hard she was trying when she was bound to fail.

"Need to pull over," he murmured. "Something in my eye."

She turned in her seat to watch out of the rear window as he accelerated along the line of the endless convoy.

"Go in now," she said.

With her help he tucked himself into a gap between two lorries and pulled onto the hard shoulder, hazard lights flashing. She already had a tissue in her hand. He took it and got out. The uncaring industrial roar of the M6 restored him as he stood in a dust storm, wiping his eyes. As he was starting the car she put her hand on his wrist. She knew.

Now he was fine, inured to the opera. They had gone ten miles or so when she said, "Poor Queen of the Night. She hits those top notes, but she knows she's going to lose."

He glanced across at her and was reassured. She meant it. She was not referring to herself.

At home the next evening, when he came in from his session at the hotel, he found her on her knees in the sitting room surrounded by photo albums and hundreds of loose photographs, some of them black and white. She was annotating as many as she could so that the children would know the names of their remoter relations and her friends. Also, her children would be reminded of precise locations and dates of their childhood holidays. She wrote long letters to each of them, to be read six months after her death. On and off, sorting the photographs took her more than two weeks. She arranged through her GP for a Health Service visitor to help look after her when she became incapable. She began emptying her wardrobes and drawers of clothes, some to be chucked out, others to be washed, ironed and folded by her and taken by Roland to a Red Cross shop. She gave away all her overcoats. She would never see another winter. It was ruthless, Roland thought, and what if she did not die? He was holding on to that hope. Stranger things had happened in illnesses.

Daphne had no doubts. "I don't want you or the kids to be doing this. Too grim."

She formally withdrew from her housing association and with the help of a lawyer friend formed it into a collective. She went to the office and made a farewell speech to her stricken staff and came back in high spirits with flowers and boxes of chocolates. Roland was suspicious, suspecting she would crash at any moment. But the next morning she was in the garden, in her hiking boots, turning over the soil in the raised beds. In the afternoon, the same lawyer came round to help her make arrangements for the house. Peter had provided generously for the three children to buy places to live. Daphne wanted to make over her house to Roland. When he protested she explained her conditions. It was not to be sold while he was alive. It would remain the family house. Lawrence too could have a bedroom. Useful for the kids if they lived out of London, useful for Christmases.

"Keep the place going," she said. "I'd feel so settled if you would."

After consultations by phone with the children it was agreed. Roland's Clapham house would be sold. Plans for doing it up were abandoned. Lawrence could use the money on a place for himself in Berlin where prices were lower.

The paradox was, Roland thought, that all this preparation—phase two—was a way of not thinking about what lay immediately ahead. She had already been to her doctor for what she called an "upgrade" of her pain medication. Late mornings and late afternoons she slept. She ate less and most evenings she was in bed before ten. Alcohol of any sort repelled her because it tasted of decay, she said, and that was just as well. Not drinking preserved her energy.

Neither the beginning of phase three nor its nature was in Daphne's gift. Her talent for organisation partly concealed its arrival, which was piecemeal. A second upgrade of the pain medication, even earlier nights, even less food, moments of disorientation, moments of irritability, visible weight loss, a vivid pallor, all advancing so slowly as she busied herself. These were the trickling pebbles that preceded the avalanche. It came in the dead of night with a scream. The pain in her side and stomach had soared beyond the reach of the latest pills. Roland was at the foot of the bed in a daze, pulling on his jeans while she writhed on the twisted sheets. She was trying to tell him something between bouts. Not to call an ambulance. But that was precisely what he intended to do. She was no longer in charge. The paramedics came within ten minutes. It was impossible to get her dressed. In the back of the ambulance one of the medics gave her morphine as they raced towards the Royal Free. She dozed on a trolley through the fifty-minute wait in A&E. Roland and a porter took her up to her ward, where they seemed to know about her and had her notes. Her GP must have anticipated this. Roland waited by the nurses' station while they "made her comfortable." When he went back in she was on a drip, in a hospital gown, sitting up. The oxygen supply hissing into her nostrils had restored some colour to her face.

"I'm sorry," were her first words.

He took her hand and squeezed it and sat down. He apologised. "I had to get you in here."

"I know."

After a while she said, "Nothing's going to happen tonight."

"No, of course not."

"You should go home, get some sleep. See me in the morning."

As she gave him a list of things to bring, which he typed into his phone, he sensed the old Daphne back in command and he left the hospital at 4 a.m. filled with irrational hope.

⤞

Just after six, in rich late summer sunlight he turned onto the track that led to the cottage. The surface no longer seemed so rutted or the car was slung higher. Before unloading he went to look inside. Everything just as it was, even the smell of polished wood, even copies of *Country Life* magazine on a table in the corner and the resounding stillness. But this evening there was honeyed sunlight on the meadow down to the river and right across the valley. And he was no longer sixty-two. It took him four trips to bring in his stuff. As he had expected, her absence in the deep silence was oppressive. He kept himself busy with his unpacking. He even put his spare clothes into drawers when he was staying only two nights.

Finally, he poured a beer and took it outside and sat near the front door on an improvised bench set into the drystone wall. It was peaceful to sit and look out over the valley and wait for them to recede—the lingering vibrations in his body from the small car's overworked engine. Seven years. What took him so long? Her letter was clear. He could take as long as he wanted. It was not enough that for all this time he had lived in, even owned, her house, made her study his own, nightly used her well-worn pots and pans, slept in the bed they once shared. Nor were they enough, the several Christmases in the house with Lawrence, Ingrid, Stefanie, Gerald, Nancy and Greta and their boyfriends, girlfriends, later husbands, wives, then children. Daphne's memory was strong in all of that, but he still needed the actual last vestiges of her physical presence and he would not let them go, the carbonised essence of his wife and her coffin. He had to keep her by him. Only after five years, when the jar became above all else a reminder of his delay, did he roll it into the sheet of newspaper and tuck it into the bottom of a drawer.

Later, as he prepared his supper, he felt the sadness coming down again. It had been a while since she was so much in his thoughts. It hurt. That was another reason for delay, his reluctance to re-engage with the loss. Better if she had been buried whole in a London cemetery where he could have sat by her regularly. Being an active gloomy celebrant in the final disposal of all that was left of her—it was stirring up too much. He should have done it straight away, within two weeks of her death, stayed at the inn in Boot, walked upriver without coming near the cottage. He had booked Bird How without thought. It was morbid to come back here. He wondered if he should pack up and leave. But he knew that a change of location would improve nothing.

Until her ashes were in the Esk, heading towards Ravenglass and the Irish Sea, there could be no relief. He must get on and do it. To suffer was appropriate. His plan had been to hike onwards from the bridge up to Esk Hause and return by the waterfalls of Lingcove Beck. But he had studied the map more closely and seen that it was far too demanding a hike for a man of his age and condition. Now it was clear, he would do his duty at the bridge, come straight back, pack up the car and leave. He could not spend another night in Bird How.

He was on the track before nine, following the valley upstream, crossing to the east bank by the footbridge at Taw House Farm as before. Except he was trying not to think in these terms. He had to keep her, her walking with him, from his thoughts. He was not hiking into the past but out of it. He was soon by Bursting Gill looking across the river to Heron Crag, less than ten minutes from the bridge. After recent rain, the river to his left dashed magnificently against granite boulders, the ferns on the fells rising around him were still green and in the air was the sweet scent of water on stone. But water and stone had no smell. He took off his backpack. The ceramic pot wrapped in a fleece and his two litres of water were heavy. He knelt by the river to splash his face with cupped hands.

He had not realised how short the journey was or how fast he had covered the ground. That day, Daphne had needed to rest several times. He took his pack and climbed up to his right in the direction of Great Gill Head Crag, onto a knoll among the ferns and rested. He was a hundred feet above the path with a long view downstream. Wednesday morning, the school summer holidays over and no one about but for one lone hiker, perhaps a mile and a half away, perhaps two. He or she appeared to be standing still. He sat down and took out the letter. Instantly her voice was close in his ear.

My dearest one, you can drop me in it whenever you want.
It doesn't matter if it takes you twenty years. As long as you
can make it all the way unaided to the bridge, stand where we
stood and think about us and how happy we were. I fell in love
as a teenager with a Bulgarian. He told me that he would one
day be a famous poet. I wonder if he made it. Lives are so hard

to predict. I came back to the same place more than forty years
later to fall in love with you or discover that I had long ago.
How wonderful it was driving us there through the mountains.
Thank you for your map-reading and for playing at my
request a sentimental song on the *pensione*'s out-of-tune piano.
Thank you for it all. I know this will be a painful trip for you.
Another reason to thank you. I'm so sorry you'll have to make
it alone along the beautiful river. My darling, how I love you.
Don't forget! Daphne.

The proximity and clarity of her voice sharpened his memory of
her courage, of the pain she was in when she wrote her note in the
overheated ward with the green curtains drawn around her narrow
bed and the morphine pump's tube fixed into the base of her thumb.
Her brave words in loopy copperplate enhanced his awareness of the
valley, its generous light and space, its sonorous river tumbling south-
west, of the feel of the coarse grass under one hand and now, as he
drank deeply, the cold water-bottle in the other. He was lucky to be
alive.

Her letter was an essential part of the rite. After he had read it
again he stood—too resolutely, perhaps, and had to wait for his sudden dizziness to pass. Then he descended towards the river. He used
to have the knack of getting down steep slopes at a half-run, leaping
onto rocks and ledges below him like a mountain goat. Now, mindful
of his knee joints, he descended sideways with care onto the path. He
approached Lingcove Bridge in a contemplative state of mind. He had
forgotten that on this side there was a drystone wall sheep pen. He
went past it and stopped in front of the bridge. It was a popular place
for picnicking or stopping to take pictures and have a swig of water.
This morning he had the place to himself. The bridge was just wide
enough for a couple of sheep side by side. He went onto it and stood,
as instructed, in the place at the top of the tiny stone arc where they
had stood together. He took the backpack off and put it between his
feet, but he was not yet ready to take out the jar. Here was the occasion and he wanted to give it time. He gazed downstream. The breeze
was slight and he could pour the ashes from here. He thought that if he

could magically transpose himself into anyone's skin at that moment, he would choose to be Daphne's quiet medical father, feeling the tight grip of the little girl's hand in his as he told her stories of the war and of his love letters home to her mother. That was benign, but summoning a doctor was a mistake. It led him not to recollections of shared happiness but to what happened afterwards during Daphne's last weeks. He couldn't help his disobedient thoughts. They tended towards her agony and the agony of the children when they came to see her. She shrank in the bed, her face grew tight around her skull, her teeth protruded so that they all struggled to see the face they knew behind a new mask. Her skin burned. She hated sleeping so much, the morphine dozes, the dreams—frightening, she said, because they were as vivid as life and she fought to escape them. Her tongue was covered in white sores, her bones, she said, were on fire. The rending pain in her side was as she had dreaded and worse. The choice was between the pain or the morphine and the suffocating dreams that disguised themselves as reality, though the consultant insisted that patients on morphine had dreamless sleep. When Roland asked Daphne if she wanted to come home, she looked frightened. She said she felt safer where she was. For the same reason she wouldn't be moved to a hospice. Soon the drugs did nothing for her pain and she longed to die. Here was the humiliation she had always feared, but pain rendered her insensible to it. He heard her beg a doctor in a small voice to release her. She tried it with the nurses, who were now her friends, to allow her an overdose that no one would know about. But the staff, kindly as always, were bound by law to their medical duty to keep her alive in pain until she dropped. They were prepared to kill her by omission, by denying her food and drink. Intense and unremitting thirst was added to her ordeal. Roland moistened her lips with a wet sponge. Her lips were cracked as though she had crawled across a desert. Her eyes were yellow. Her breath smelled of something rotting. He took the "nil by mouth" sign off the foot of her bed and went to the nurse's station to insist that she be given water whenever she asked for it. They shrugged OK, that was fine by them.

Not long before, legislation had come before Parliament yet again that would have allowed Daphne to choose the moment of her death.

The Church worthies in the Lords, the archbishops, fought it. They hid their theological objections behind lurid tales of greedy relatives wanting to get their hands on the money. The divines were beneath contempt. In hospital, though never in her presence, his scorn—his "moment"—was reserved for the worthies of the medical establishment, the grave principals of the royal colleges and societies who would not relinquish their control over life and death.

Roland said all this to Lawrence in a hospital corridor. One of his careless rants—doctors were probably walking by and heard him. Two centuries passed before the establishment thought it worthwhile to look down a microscope to examine the micro-organisms Antonie van Leeuwenhoek had described in 1673. They set themselves against hygiene because it was an insult to the profession, against anaesthesia because pain was a God given element of illness, against the germ theory of disease because Aristotle and Galen thought otherwise, against evidence-based medicine because that was not how things were done. They clung to their leeches and cupping for as long as possible. Into the mid-twentieth century, they defended mass tonsillectomy of children, despite the evidence. In the end, the profession always came round. One day they would come round to the right of a rational person to choose death rather than unbearable unrelievable pain. Too late for Daphne.

Lawrence heard him out then put a hand on his father's arm "Dad, they must have fought off loads of bad ideas too. When the law changes, they will."

They were walking back towards Daphne's ward. "They will, but they'll fight it to the last."

Sitting with her day after day, tending to her, watching her grotesque decline, he had to have someone, something to blame. Blasphemously, he longed for her to die. He wanted it almost as much as she did.

Later they let him stay with her through the nights. When she died, at 5 a.m., he was asleep in his chair and couldn't forgive himself. He had woken to see someone pull the sheet over her face and he became agitated. A Filipina nurse was firm with him. "She didn't wake, darling. We made sure of that."

So that, he thought on the bridge, was also what they shared during four weeks and, in the final moment, failed to share. The kind nurse could not have been aware of everything. He had dozed off for more than an hour. He would never know if Daphne had woken and called his name as she felt herself going down, lifted a hand in hope of reaching his. He could not bear to think about it and had never spoken of it to the children. He didn't doubt that Lawrence would have something rational and comforting to say. That would have made it worse.

He still had the bridge to himself. He turned round to look upstream and then up Lingcove Beck, towards the waterfall where they had eaten their lunch. There was their happiness to consider yet, the rite demanded it, but he was in no hurry. He could still remember what they ate. They never held with fussy sandwiches. Instead, they took a sharp knife to a hunk of bread and a slab of Cheddar. With tomatoes, black olives, spring onions, apples, nuts and chocolate. Exactly what he had in his bag today.

When he turned back to the downstream view he saw a hiker appearing round a slight bend in the river. Probably the person he had seen from the knoll, now a couple of hundred yards away. He watched, frowning, and then, on an impulse, bent down to take his binoculars from a side pocket of the backpack. He raised them, turned the focus wheel, and sure enough, there he was, Peter Mount, moving across the uneven ground with hesitancy and distaste. His natural surface was the pavement. Or the pile carpet. Yes, here he was, Lord Posse Mount, formerly of Clapham Old Town, coming to reclaim Daphne from him by some tainted logic: I met her before you did. He was minutes away. Roland knew that he could end all argument by consigning her ashes to the river now. But he was not going to be pressured or bullied. He was under instruction and his meditation on their happiness had hardly begun. He put the binoculars away and crossed his arms. His dead wife's ex-partner—not husband— the father of his stepchildren, was picking his way along the path. It looked like brogues had not been suitable for crossing the various becks that poured off the fells into the Esk. For someone who lived in reasonable hopes of a peerage, assuming he'd handed across enough cash to the party, the baseball cap did not look right either. It may have been intended to convey a youthful look. It failed, for the face, as worn as Roland's, was that of an old buffer in the grip of irritation and distress.

Roland was now eager, looking forward to the confrontation. The ceramic pot was safely wrapped in his pack, which sat between his feet, between his heavy three-season boots. He adopted a bright welcoming smile as Peter stopped by the bridge and gazed up at him.

"Well now, Peter," Roland called down, raising his voice above the sound of rushing water, "this is a surprise."

"Feet are bloody soaked and I think I've pulled a muscle." He sat wearily on a boulder. He was carrying no luggage.

"Poor you." Roland was seized with great joy. He slung the pack onto one shoulder and went down onto the bank.

Peter took off his cap and mopped his brow with it. "Have you done the deed?"

"No."

"Good. Is this the right bridge?"

"Absolutely."

"OK then. Just give me a minute."

It was impressive, the way Peter spoke as though the conversation yesterday morning had not happened. He had always had that knack of getting his way. He just kept going, ignoring all obstacles until he got what he wanted. Useful, way back, when they turned up at venues, always as the support band, and the sound system or the lighting was not right and the management was unmoving—at first.

Roland said lightly, "So, where are you headed?"

"Right here."

In imitation of Peter, in tribute to his methods, Roland said, "If you cross over and head up to the left you'll get to Esk Hause. Turn east at the top and you'll have some fine views down into Langdale."

His adversary got to his feet. He was smiling as he nodded at Roland's pack. "You've got it in there."

"I think I'll wait until you're on your way, Peter. You know, you could stay on this bank, go up Lingcove Beck there and see some rather lovely waterfalls. If you like that sort of thing. Then you could shin up Bow Fell."

"Come on, Roland. Let's get it over with. I've booked a table for lunch at Askham Hall."

"It's quite a drive. Don't let me keep you."

"I tell you what," Peter said reasonably. "I'll do it and you can watch." He took a step towards Roland with an arm outstretched as if to take the backpack from him.

He stepped aside. "She didn't want you involved. She was quite clear about it, I'm afraid."

Peter folded his baseball cap and pushed it into the inside pocket of his tweed jacket. He looked away, seeming thoughtful as he massaged his earlobe between forefinger and thumb. "I think it must have been in Stockholm. Thirty-five years ago. She was pregnant with Greta. She told me what she wanted if she happened to go first. I told her what I'd like if it turned out to be me. We made solemn promises. Later, when we got back, she drew a circle for me on a map. Which I've kept ever since."

He pulled it partly clear of his jacket pocket, Ordnance Survey, an old sixth edition, one inch to the mile.

"Long time ago," Roland said. "Before Angela, was it? Before Hermione? Before you hit her?"

To Roland's surprise, Peter took a decisive step towards him. This time he did not step back. Again, rather brilliantly, Peter continued as if Roland had not spoken. "And I always keep my promises."

They were standing close enough, face to face, for Roland to catch the scent of Peter's cologne.

"Me too," Roland said.

"So the sensible thing is, we do it together."

"Sorry, old friend. I've told you why."

Peter took hold of Roland's open-neck shirt, just below the top button. He held the cotton material loosely, almost fondly. "You know Roland, I've always liked you."

"I can see that." As he spoke, Roland brought up his right hand and encircled Peter's wrist. It was somewhat thicker than he expected, but Roland's forefinger just met his thumb as he tightened his grip. It was only now, too late, that he understood that they were going to fight. Incredible. But there was no way out of it. They were of equal height and the same age, given a month or two. He knew that Peter never exercised, whereas he had behind him thousands of hours on the tennis courts. They were well behind him but he was sure he had retained residual fitness and strength. There was certainly power in his racket hand, for Peter gasped as he let go of Roland's shirt. At the same time Peter brought up his free hand and gripped Roland's throat. So it was serious. As Roland knocked Peter's hand away, the backpack slid off his shoulder onto the ground. That was just as well, for now the two men scrabbled to get an arm round the other's neck and use their legs to try to pivot the other to the ground. Countering each other's moves they went into a clinch. For a full minute they stood there, two old men swaying and grunting on the bank of the Esk. No other sounds but the rush of water. No birdsong. No hikers came by to be baffled by the sight. They had the Lake District to themselves to settle their affair.

Even as he struggled, Roland thought he had one disadvantage. He had time to think that what they were doing was absurd. To know it was disabling. Was he fighting or pretending to fight? Whereas Peter was driven by the blessing of absolute rectitude and a single purpose, which was to win. To win the ashes.

Roland freed his right arm and drove the heel of his hand under Peter's nose and pushed hard, forcing his head back. At last he had to let go and step away. His nose was bleeding. Roland had his back to the river. He checked on his pack. Safe to one side, against the wall of the sheep pen. Breathing heavily, they stood facing each other, about twelve feet apart. To his surprise Peter made a grunting sound and suddenly bent low or crumpled up, as if his heart or some other internal organ was failing. Roland was about to go forward and help, but Peter was upright again, and in his hand was a rock about the size of a tennis ball. Only now did Roland understand that in this fight, as in all fights, there were unspoken rules, or there had been. They were about to be discarded.

Peter wiped the blood from his upper lip. "Right," he whispered as he drew his arm back.

"If you throw it," Roland promised, "I'll break your neck."

He threw it clumsily and Roland clumsily ducked right into its path. It struck him, not quite full on, high on his forehead, well above his right eye. He didn't go down. Instead he stood swaying, conscious but immobilised, aware of a continuous high-pitched sound. Peter saw his chance and ran at him and shoved him hard with both hands in the chest, sending him backwards over the steep rocky slope to the river. In a bad situation, he fell well, or not disastrously. Just before he lost his footing, he managed to twist round and hit the ground and the shallows along the whole length of one side of his body. His left arm broke some of the fall, and the water cushioned his head. He was under for only a few seconds and lucky to be away from the surging main current. Still, the impact was colossal, like an explosion, and he was winded, fighting for air. As he dragged himself up he already guessed that he had fractured some ribs. He got the upper part of his body out of the water and lay on his side half on the bank, getting his breath back, listening to the sound in his ears diminish. It was only then that he remembered Peter. He twisted his head to look. He was on the bridge emptying the last of Daphne's ashes into the midstream tumult. He saw Roland, lifted the jar above his head football-trophy style and gave him a cheery smile. Roland closed his eyes. None of it mattered. Whoever put them there, her remains were in the river, heading towards the Irish Sea, just as she wanted. He could let himself go, float alongside her all the way.

He got his legs out of the river and pulled himself into a sitting position. A few seconds later he heard Peter's voice above him, at the top of the slope.

"Got to rush. Late for lunch. Sorry we couldn't do the business together. Looks like you'll survive."

Roland sat for half an hour recuperating and checking his arms and legs for breakages. He was fortunate, if that was the word, to be out here on a warm day. Finally he stood and made his way a few yards downstream where it was easier to gain the bank. The empty jar was resting against his pack, which he searched for painkillers, paracetamol and ibuprofen. He took a gram of each with a long pull of water. It hurt, raising his arms to put on his fleece. He opened out a collapsible hiking pole and, with difficulty and loud groans, got the pack onto his shoulders. After twenty minutes he was making good progress. The path was easy and the descent along the valley imperceptible. His boots made a homely squelching sound, the painkillers were doing their business. What weighed on him was the fact of his defeat. He tried to fight it off. It was death that had stolen Daphne, not Peter. Various daydreams of revenge helped him along the path but he knew he would do nothing. Back at the cottage, where there was no bathroom, no hot shower, he changed his clothes, lit a fire and sat before it, eating his provisions—nuts, cheese, an apple—then he fell asleep.

It took a long while to load the car the next morning. His aches had magnified overnight. Before setting off he raided the pharmacopeia in his backpack for more painkillers, along with some modafinil to keep him alert and focussed on the road. It made the journey almost pleasurable. In tribute to Daphne, he played her *Magic Flute* selection on the machine he had brought and listened without being thrown back to the past. He was sustained by the prospect of dinner with Lawrence, Ingrid and Stefanie.

After three stops along the way he was parking outside the Lloyd Square house in the late afternoon. He walked into a surprise. The hall was filled with balloons and cheering children. Lawrence and Ingrid had arranged for Nancy, Greta and Gerald to be there with their families. In the kitchen, over a mug of tea, with Stefanie on his lap, he described how he had slipped from the path and tumbled into a river. The children gasped at the notion of an old man being allowed out on his own to risk himself on such a mad adventure. Before Roland took a shower, Gerald, now a registrar paediatrician, examined the injuries. He was recently married to David, a curator in the Department of Greece and Rome at the British Museum. The young doctor was not troubled by the lurid bruises and grazes down Roland's left arm and upper legs, or the heroic wound on his forehead. It didn't need stitches. He was, however, interested in the bruise on Roland's chest. The freckly little boy who used to come after school for a sleepover with Lawrence now possessed the bland authority of a seasoned medic. He recommended an X-ray. A fractured rib could puncture his pleura.

Before joining the party Roland bit off another fragment of

modafinil to get him through the evening. They were fifteen squashed around the dining table, as well as two babies in high chairs. Stefanie had asked to sit at his side. Now and then she took his hand and squeezed it to reassure him. She tugged his head down level with her lips and whispered, "Opa, ich mach mir Sorgen um dich." Grandad, I'm worried about you.

Later, Roland gazed at the company, at the boisterous good-willed family: a climate-change mathematician, an oceanographer, a doctor, a full-time mother, a housing specialist, a social worker, a community lawyer, a primary-school teacher, a curator. Perhaps they were all, in the spirit of the times, the newly irrelevant. For now, in this small corner of the world, it was Peter Mount and his kind who ruled. In an instant of dissociation, he saw the family members as figures in an old photograph and everyone in it, including the babies, Charlotte and Daphne, had long grown old and died. There they were, those people from 2018, expert and tolerant, whose opinions were lost to time, whose voices had faded away until they had left hardly a trace.

Lawrence stood to propose a toast, not only to his father on his seventieth but to the memory of his stepmother and to all the children at the table. Feeling sharp twinges in many places, Roland stood to thank everyone and lifted his glass to his wife and the grandchildren. He tasted the plummy richness of southern Europe and there came to mind the hike he and Daphne had taken across the Mediterranean island, down to the beach with the bamboo grove and the still water in the dark blue bay and on the return the scent of wild herbs crushed beneath their dusty boots. When she was still strong enough to take the day's warmth and distance in an easy stride. His hand went involuntarily to his chest, to the sore constricted part below his heart and he thanked them all again.

# 12

The fall, the second in three years, occurred in June 2020, not long before the end of the first lockdown, as Roland descended the stairs. He had finished a first draft of a piece, "The Thatcher Legacy," for an American online magazine. $125 for 1,000 words. Why her, why now? He did not ask. As a part-timer at the hotel he was not in line for furlough money, so his hip Japanese employers, keen for bebop and edgy blues, had told him. He had a state pension and less than £3,000 in savings. Relaunching as a journalist at any price was all he could think of.

He descended with care, keeping one hand on the banister, as constantly reminded by Gerald. Falling, in showers, out of bathtubs, on pavements, over carpet edges, off buses, down slopes was how many among the old started to die. Roland's destination was the kitchen and a late lunch, a can of sardines in olive oil on a toasted slice of pumpernickel bread with a cup of strong tea. Tastier than it sounded. On his way down the stairs he was wondering how he might improve his article. It was plodding, earnest, lifeless. On the website men and women one-third his age turned in copy with a joke and a jab in every line and still managed a stern face of bookish or political know-how. Nearly thirty years after leaving office, her legacy, her mark on the country's psyche ran deep, so he had written. Her fingerprints were all over the present and she would not be forgotten: a housing crisis due to the collapse of social provision, a deregulated and crazed City whose greed the country paid for with austerity, a disabling notion of national grandeur, a general distrust of Germans, of the French and the rest, medium-sized towns across the north Midlands, Wales and the Scottish central belt still comatose from her free-market rigour, national assets sold off, shareholder frenzy, fabulous disparities of wealth, reduced fealty to the common good, workers without protection, rivers bubbling with privatised sewage.

He was just an old Labour hack. He was trying too hard with "fingerprints all over the present." For all he knew, it was a cliché or a steal. He needed some jokes. On the positive side? Brought down the fascist dictatorship in Argentina, rescued the ozone layer and briefly, before she turned her back on the subject, spoke to the world about climate change. Also, opened shops on Sunday, reformed the Labour Party, lowered inflation and taxes, helped Reagan face down the Soviet Empire, busted some corrupt unions, granted homeownership to the many, showed women how to cow overbearing men in their pomp and entitlement. Equally unfunny.

Such striving for even-handedness must have disturbed his sense of balance. He was two steps from the bottom and in that he was lucky. The transition was instant. He felt the pitiless steel lasso tighten around his chest then a meteorite flare of pain streaked to the left of his sternum. His unlucky shooting star. He clutched at himself and tipped forwards. The wondrous automatic routine kicked in and his hands flew out from his body to protect his head as he landed with a thump and sprawled unhurt across the hallway tiles. When he sat up pinpricks of starry light floated across the view but the pain had gone. Not even an after-touch. Not a thing. He got to his feet slowly, stood with his back against the wall, leaning forwards, knees slightly bent, and waited to see what would happen next. Nothing. It was nothing.

He brushed the dustballs off his trousers and continued into the kitchen. As usual he had left the radio on. A man was shouting in fury at a weeping woman. *The Archers.* Unbearable. He snapped it off and set about his preparations. It was serious work, not for the weak, pulling on the ring that would peel back the tin lid and let the light into his neat array of three sardines topped and tailed as if for a kids' sleepover. He could have broken his neck. But only a fool would show up in hospital at the emergency department, complaining about his heart. And go down with the plague inhaled from some unmasked moron wandering about the waiting room. Then days later taste the ventilator's cold nozzle on his tongue before the induced coma, and accept a one-in-two chance of return. Besides, it was not his heart. He was sure it was his ribs, a piece of bone somewhere poking into muscle tissue like a cocktail stick though an anchovy. The X-ray had shown only hairline fractures, which were supposed to repair themselves. But he was the patient and he knew his theory was sound. A microscopic splinter of bone was skewering a nerve end. When he moved in a certain way, pain and a sensation of tightness radiated across his chest, though never as severely as just then. Gerald, backed up by Lawrence, wanted to send him to a heart specialist. But Gerald was in paediatrics. Children's hearts were different.

Roland took his tea into the front sitting room, unchanged since Daphne's day but for the dust and a few thousand photographs spread across the carpet and three cardboard boxes with more pictures stacked inside. Inspired by her, one of his lockdown projects was to annotate and arrange the random heaps by date. Not easy. His progress was slow. Too many photos set off memories and sessions of wondering about dead or long-lost friends or prolonged struggles to remember names and places. He wasted much time envying his youth. Too many shots from the time of his lost decade showed him with a backpack looking strong and cheerful against gorgeous backgrounds of mountains or desert, wildflowers or lakes. Where was that, who pressed the button, what year? He was a stranger to himself, a stranger he envied. Now it looked precious, perhaps the best thing he ever did. After childhood and boarding school, before tennis coaching, munch music and greeting cards, when had he ever been so free, so intent on celebrating life itself? Relax, he wanted to tell the young man staring up at him. Wandering among Indian paintbrush flowers across meadows, along streams, 2,000 metres up in the Cascade mountains, high and dreamily joyous on mescaline in the company of good friends, the base camp five miles behind—it had to be accounted as success.

From 2004 for ten years his photography came by way of digital cameras. After that it had come by digital phones. Cameras for non-specialists were now defunct, like typewriters and alarm clocks, and soon to be extinct, like valve radios and bathing machines. He had emailed large selections of his JPEG files to a company in Swansea to be printed up at some expense, ready for his annotations. Then he realised that he should have worked the other way round and digitalised a selection of his pre-2004 prints. Then he could have handed or emailed to his family the entire production, easily replicated.

He was plausible within the digital age, like a man in cunning disguise, but he remained a citizen of the analogue world. That single starting error was undermining his sense of purpose and slowing him down. Too late, too expensive to go back, boring to continue. He lacked Daphne's discipline. But she had worked to the ultimate deadline. His was softer. Therefore he would never come near to finishing. Occasionally he went into the front room, picked up a photograph off the floor, gazed into it and faded into a reverie. When he came out of it he jotted down a few lines on the reverse. Since the beginning of the first lockdown he had written on the backs of fifty-eight photographs. A ridiculous way to proceed.

These days he ate less, drank more and thought a lot. He had a chair, a view, a certain glass he favoured. Among his subjects were other single starting errors that multiplied through time into a fan-shaped array. On close examination the errors dissolved into questions, hypotheticals, even into solid gains. On this last he may have been deluding himself. But in surveying a life it was inadvisable to acknowledge too much defeat. Marrying Alissa? Without Lawrence there would have been no joy, no Stefanie, Roland's new best friend. If Alissa had stayed? He had reread *The Journey* in February and early March when he and most of the people he knew locked themselves down three weeks ahead of the government. Her novel remained exquisite. Leaving school early? If he had stayed, Miriam, by her own admission, would have hauled him from the classroom and he would have been sunk. Even now that thought, as if in prospect, stirred him just a little. Abandoning classical piano and the chance of becoming a concert pianist? Then he would never have discovered jazz, would never have run free in his twenties or learned to respect manual labour or developed a snappy backhand. He would have been bound to five hours a day practice for the rest of his life. Not sending Miriam to prison? For as long as she was inside, the connection between them would have remained bleak and strong. That was one reason. There were others.

Marrying Daphne just as she started to die he understood as inevitable, necessary, perhaps the best thing he ever did. Should he have stayed in the Labour Party to argue for its liberal and centrist traditions? He would have been driven miserable and mad after four consecutive defeats. So his life was an unbroken succession of correct decisions? Clearly not. Finally he came to the true turning point, the moment from which all else fanned out and upwards with the extravagance of a peacock's tail: the boy mounting his bike, mid–Cuban Missile Crisis, to present himself to Miriam for a two-year erotic and sentimental education with its ludicrous finale, the pyjama week, that terminated his schooling and distorted his relations with women. This was difficult. When he asked himself if he wished none of it had happened he did not have a ready answer. That was the nature of the harm. Almost seventy-two and not quite cured. The experience remained with him and he could not part with it.

Confined to quarters by a pandemic, grounded by fear of dying on a ventilator while fighting for air, sitting through the winter's late afternoons in the rocking chair—he had brought it from the Clapham house, a chair for old folk and nursing mothers—wondering how soon he could honourably pour himself the first drink of the day, he thought back often to his confrontation with Miriam Cornell in her Balham house, in her bare music room. Just as he had in the Old Town, he took up a position in front of French windows that faced onto a garden. Five years ago, he had planted an apple tree on Daphne's lawn to make up for the one he chopped down in Clapham. It had not grown much but it was alive.

Miriam Cornell's place had grander French windows looking onto a lush designer planting. He remembered how weary he was by the end, desperate to leave. There was a hollowness, a void, a lie in which they were complicit. By silent agreement there were two subjects they would not touch. The easier one first. They could not refer to the delight they shared in music, in playing the Mozart four-handers in her cottage or the thrill of performing on concert grands the Schubert Fantasia in the Norwich assembly rooms, or the rowdy applause at the school concert when the mouse-child brought onstage a flower and chocolate.

Then the hard one. During that confrontation they dared not speak of what bound them, the obsessive engulfing limitless repeated joy that was also illegal, immoral, destructive. They had been naked long ago, face to face in bed in the little sunlit room that looked towards the River Stour. She wouldn't let him go and he did not want her to. A lifetime later, a stout gent turned up at her splendid house to accuse her. She was a different person too. Fully clothed in all that they had become they denied the real story even as they discussed it. They didn't touch, didn't shake hands, as far as he could remember. He played the cool interrogator. She stood on her cold dignity at first and wanted to throw him out, then she confessed. Oh yes, he was a child and it was a crime, but it was something else besides and this was the problem. She couldn't have said it, and he wouldn't have listened. They lied by omission. She had loved him and made him love her. The hostage fell in love with his captor—the Stockholm Syndrome. On the rainy evening he made his escape with his trench-digging wages in his back pocket, he dragged the trunk containing all his possessions across her lawn, but he never got far. That was the damage, the forbidden matter—the attraction. The memory of the love remained inseparable from the crime. He could not go to the police.

He stood and gazed at the photographs that covered three-quarters of Daphne's broad green Iranian carpet. Sorting them into chronological order, once a vital tidying project appropriate to a lockdown, now seemed pointless. Everyone knew memory was not like that, it was not in order. Here by his left foot was an old Polaroid, probably from 1976. He picked it up. It was a smudged unexceptional picture of a round muddy pond. It was laughable how remote it was from what he and his old friend John Weaver had seen at the time, a natural pond set in a clifftop and beyond it the Pacific Ocean. Seen from thirty feet away, from its boggy fringes and right across its few inches of water, the pond appeared to be boiling, seething and writhing with motion. As they went closer they saw thousands of tiny frogs. All seemed to have emerged from their tadpole existence at the same moment. More frog than water. They slithered and wound themselves across each other, a great feast for the right kind of predatory bird. Behind the pond the sun was beginning to lower itself towards an immense plain of reddening cloud, lower than the cliffs and stretching to the horizon. They were still three miles from their camp on the Big Sur River and they set off towards it at an easy run. At the age of twenty-eight it was possible to lope for miles that way without effort. Their path through the Californian chaparral was hard and smooth and gently downhill. What a glorious half-hour that was, gliding through the warm scented air, bare-chested in the weak sun.

There his recollection blanked and picked up again when it was dark and they were at an outside bar where people sat at tables near a heated swimming pool. After such a day they were in celebratory mood. Five years before, John had escaped the oppression of low-level jobs in England and found liberation in Vancouver. This was a reunion. Since freedom was their subject and they were in a high state of exhilaration they slipped out of their clothes and took their drinks into the pool and drifted up and down, talking all the while, until they were interrupted by the bar's owner standing on the pool's edge, hands on hips, ordering them out with a pronouncement they liked to quote long afterwards: "It ain't right, and I know it ain't right."

They obeyed and laughed about it once they were dressed. But it was a public place, a family bar, after all, and it was only eight o'clock. They had no business or need to be seen naked. The owner was right. His phrase, the way he had crisply deployed it at that moment, haunted Roland for many years. The categorical imperative? Hardly, for this was a matter of context and social convention. But when he thought of his own various errors through life it seemed in long retrospect that he lacked that immediate hands-on-hips automatic and grounded sense of the right course. Who else but Roland had entered his seventies semi-impoverished, living in an expensive house that he owned by accident and could never sell—a house paid for by a man he despised, recently ennobled and a junior minister in the Johnson government? It wasn't right, and he knew it wasn't right, but there was nothing he could do about it. It was too late.

He let the photograph drop from his hands. He didn't feel like writing on the back of it. Too much to say. He went upstairs to his study. The lockdown was coming to an end and all his other unfulfilled projects were in here. The usual thing—read all of Proust, learn another language, another musical instrument. In his case, Arabic and the mandolin. He had resolved to read all of Musil's *The Man Without Qualities* in German. So far seventy-nine pages in three months. Another ambition had been to improve his understanding of science, starting with the four laws of thermodynamics. His assumption was that basic principles elaborated during the age of steam should be easy enough to grasp. But simple starting positions blossomed into such complexity and abstraction that he was soon left behind and bored. Still, in the Second Law, which was the third because they started at zero, he was reminded of a truth obvious to all householders. Just as heat bled out into cold and not the reverse, so order bled out into chaos and never in reverse. A complex entity like a person eventually died and became a disordered pile of disparate bits which must begin to move apart. The dead never sprang into ordered life, never became the living, whatever the bishops might say or pretend to believe. Entropy was a troubling and beautiful concept that lay at the heart of much human toil and sorrow. Everything, especially life, fell apart. Order was a boulder to be rolled uphill. The kitchen would not tidy itself.

The house was disordered though not quite squalid. He did not mind but soon restrictions would be lifted and the children would come to visit. Lawrence and family first, then Greta, her husband and children, along with Gerald and his partner David and after them, Nancy and her family. Roland could not be seen to dishonour Daphne's memory by despoiling her spacious welcoming home. He couldn't afford to keep the cleaning lady on. The children had offered to cover her wages and he was too proud to accept. One person can clean up after himself. Now the price of pride must be rendered. He was obliged to wrench himself from his habitual dream-state and get to work. Today, the day of his fall, he had marked down to begin.

He was to approach the top-floor bedrooms first, the easiest. The vacuum cleaner and materials were already up there thanks to a false start the week before. He opened the windows in both rooms, wiped surfaces, stripped the beds and remade them, vacuumed the floor.

Ninety minutes passed before he started on the bathroom. He was on his knees, scrubbing the sides of the bath when he paused at a sudden thought—he was oddly content, thinking of nothing but the next task, lost in the present, delivered from intro- and retrospection. He couldn't do it for a living like some had to, but as a form of escapism it ranked high. He should have been doing it all the while, every day. Good exercise. If there ever had to be another lockdown . . . He was at the point of resuming when the phone rang. Reluctantly he put aside his brush and went next door to pick up.

It was Rüdiger. They had Zoomed a couple of times since March. At that point Germany was ordering its plague more efficiently. Roland did not like to hear about it. He was glad that Germany was doing well but he was a patriot at heart and liked to think his country could face down a challenge. In late February he had watched video clips of exhausted medical staff in northern Italy overwhelmed by Covid cases, working only on patients likely to survive. They were running out of ventilators, oxygen, medical-grade masks. Undertakers could not cope with their backlog of corpses. There was a coffin shortage. Austria closed its border. How could the disease not spread here when there were dozens of daily flights from Italy? The UK government dithered. Two weeks later, in mid-March, thousands gathered in Cheltenham for the Festival horse races. Tens of thousands were at football matches. The government held out for another week.

"It's in the national unconscious," he had tried to explain to his German friend. "We feel we've already left you. We no longer catch your European diseases."

Now Rüdiger, who lacked small talk, said without preamble, "I have three things to tell you."

"Go ahead."

"One good, one bad, one could be anything."

"Start with bad."

"Yesterday Alissa had her left foot amputated."

Roland was silent. There was a story about Sartre he was trying to remember. Probably untrue, whatever it was. He said, "Smoking?"

"Genau. Distale Neuropathie. Then the gangrene. It went OK, they said."

"You saw her?"

"Very drugged. She said she was relieved it was off. When I told her that she had smoked for her art, she laughed. So. Now the good news. On my chair here I have a bound proof in English of the new novel."

"Wonderful. What's your view?"

"A copy will go to you today."

"And the other thing?"

"She wants to see you. In a month or so if you can. Clearly you must come to her. She'll pay for your flight."

"OK." He said it automatically. He was being summoned, commanded to board a plane, inhale recycled coronaviruses. To dispel these thoughts he said, "Yes, I'll come."

"I hoped so much you would say that. I'll tell her right away."

"I'll pay my own flight."

"Fine."

"Does she want to see Lawrence?"

"Just you."

He carried the housework material down to the floor below, ready for the next day's work, took a shower then sat in the garden to eat a sandwich. Alissa without a foot was no more alien to him than Alissa the chain-smoker of thirty years. If she was dying Rüdiger would have told him. But there was nothing in the prospect of visiting her that appealed to him. Not even curiosity. His savings would shrink a little. Thanks to lockdown he had come to prefer going nowhere. Alissa Eberhardt was accepted as Germany's greatest writer. Bigger than Grass had been, with no fall from grace likely. Almost as big as Mann. The strongest personal feeling he had about her was anger, long outworn, for her rejection of her son. It rarely crossed his mind. In his mental landscape she was fine as she was, a grand mountain seen from afar, someone famous he used to know when she was obscure, a superb writer, possibly a great one. There was nothing between them, nothing he wanted to tell her, nothing he wanted to hear. She did not need to know from him how much he admired her work. So why go? Because she had lost a foot? Yes, by way of her chosen addiction to a ridiculous substance. No real high. A deadbeat's drug that people smoked to ward off their craving for it. Like an ugly Cleopatra making hungry where most it satisfied. If Alissa needed to speak to him before they were both simplified and dispersed by entropy, let her grow accustomed to a prosthetic foot then visit him in London, here at his old garden table. So phone Rüdiger now and inform him of a change of mind. No. She would already know that he had said he would go. So he would go. He would answer her summons because it would be more effort not to.

Her book took ten days to arrive. By then, though Daphne's house did not gleam as it once had, the rooms were in order. It was July, the lockdown was over and the nation was at play. But nothing changed for Roland. He took the novel, *Her Slow Reduction*, from its package and began to read. It was longer than anything she had written. Here it was at last, here *he* was at last, in chapter one, pulled through the looking glass of her art to become the oppressive bullying and sometimes violent husband that the protagonist, Monique, walks out on one morning, leaving her seven-month-old baby daughter behind. That husband, Guy, is English. The house that Monique quits is in Clapham, south London, in a neighbourhood rendered "detestable" by its congested squalor. She is of Franco-German parentage, fired by political ideals that motherhood had been threatening to obliterate. Back in her native Munich, recovering from the pain of separation from her daughter, she embeds herself in local politics by working for the Social Democratic Party. She becomes a specialist in low-cost social housing. Here, Alissa seemed to draw on Daphne's experience of various tenants, from the reliable rent-paying hard-workers to the chaotic drunken defaulters. All must be housed.

Monique changes her name to Monika. Then for honest reasons, but a brilliant move nevertheless, she becomes an environmentalist and changes party. Her rise through the Greens is rapid. Within five years she is victorious in the local elections and wins a seat in the Land Parliament. She falls in love with a fashionable chef, Dieter, who is heading a revolution in German cuisine, from its sodden base to lighter Mediterranean flavours. The novel's title refers in part to a cooking term. Ten years later she is a well-known figure in Berlin, tactically adroit, heading to the top. But in a surprise move, she shifts her allegiance from stronger to weaker figures within the Greens.

By now it is 2002 and at this point the novel becomes a counterfactual history of German politics. Through a series of mishaps among colleagues as well as political opponents, and ruthless manoeuvring, Monika becomes chancellor. She will hold office for more than a decade but she does not resemble Angela Merkel. From the moment Monika holds the highest office the erosion of her political ideals, the slow reduction, begins. Perhaps, the narrative suggests, her descent began long ago. To enable the "slow reduction" in the country's carbon emissions and to tame its powerful coal interests she becomes the champion of nuclear energy. Her party hates her for it but cannot dislodge her. To encourage inward investment from powerful American tech industries she enters a clandestine agreement with the US government to provide military intelligence and other assistance during the invasion of Iraq. To keep the Alternative für Deutschland party at bay, she closes Germany's borders to immigrants. In order not to offend the important Turkish-Muslim vote she is ambivalent on certain freedom-of-expression issues.

In Brussels she always gets her way. The French are reduced to the status of junior partner as they do her bidding. Monika ensures that Berlin will host the Olympic Games. She determines that Germany must become a full member of the Security Council at the UN. To that end, within a mere eight years of holding office, she has made Germany a nuclear power, with five submarines miraculously extracted from the French. Whatever the odds she never seems to lose a fight. The various political elites of the Greens, the SPD and even a large minority of the right-of-centre CDU come to loathe her. There are massive student demonstrations against her. But in the country at large, among the voters, she is adored. She is beautiful, witty, she has the common touch and she wins elections. The country is thriving economically, with full employment, low inflation, rising wages. National pride soars after a successful Olympic Games.

But in private she is tormented. The cruelty inflicted on her by her ex-husband still haunts her. So does guilt about her daughter, whom Guy prevents her from seeing. Monika is sexually enslaved to Dieter, who refuses to marry her and makes her wretched with his many affairs. She knows, but can never admit, that to achieve success she has had to play one lobby, one interest group against another and reject everything she once believed in.

The reader understands that this is an Icarus story. When Dieter finally abandons her it precipitates a dramatic nervous collapse. She makes a series of spectacular political errors. They culminate in a scandal about kickbacks from the auto industry, which she badly mishandles. She is seen to be protecting the wrong people. She suffers debilitating depression, made worse when a former close aide writes an exposé of a masochistic sex scene he had stumbled across, which involved manacles and whips. Dieter gives a press conference and confirms the article and adds some spice of his own, including the much-quoted "she is vulnerable and deranged." Her opponents in Berlin know that their moment has arrived. Icarus is plunging earthwards. A motion passed in the Bundestag and then the Bundesrat invokes a clause in the 1949 constitution and declares the chancellor mentally unstable and unfit for office. And she is.

Monika's rise and fall is expertly narrated. The novel was quite clearly brilliant. But Roland was bound to take exception to the finale. A year has passed. Driven from office, scorned by the media, rejected by allies, the ex-chancellor travels to London as a private citizen. Guy is still living in the same Clapham house, a decrepit figure, stooped and crippled by gout. He is amazed when he opens the door to Monika. He invites her in. A lifetime in politics has taught her not to waste time in meetings with small talk. Their conversation in the kitchen is brief. She has come to murder him. She takes a knife from Guy's magnetic rack and stabs him in the neck. She washes the blade, checks there is no blood on her clothes and leaves. She is back in her Berlin apartment that evening and Guy's murder is never solved. By the end of the novel, Monika is living in obscurity, further reduced, in a cottage near the Saxon Switzerland National Park, still tormented by her demons, her guilt, her lost love, her discarded ideals.

Roland lay along the length of the sofa where he had been reading. The last of the summer evening's sunlight, filtered through a plane tree, rippled on the wall above him. He should feel honoured that she cared enough about him to need to kill him. She had taken her time. Better to have done with him in her first novel. In the so-called echo chamber of the quarter-century-old Internet, in scores of author profiles, it was routinely noted that Alissa Eberhardt had once lived in Clapham, London and had abandoned her husband and baby to begin a literary career. Scores of female journalists had wondered in print if this was the only way a woman could dedicate herself completely to her art. The profiles to accompany the new novel—there would be dozens in many languages—would assume that Alissa had identified him as violent, that it was not only for her writing that she had left him. It would have cost her story nothing to have made Guy a Frenchman, turned London into Lyons, given the family three children, none of them seven months old. Her novel was a lying accusation, an act of aggression—a fiction, and that was where he knew she would hide, behind the conventions of make-believe.

That evening he called Rüdiger. Over the years running Lucretius Books the retired publisher had learned calm in the face of all kinds of anger.

"I told her you might be upset."

"What did she say?"

"She told me that's his right."

Roland took a deep breath. "It's an outrage."

To this Rüdiger remained silent, waiting for more.

"I was never violent towards her."

"I'm sure of it."

"I was the injured party. I've never criticised her in public. When Lawrence was little I encouraged her to see him. She did everything her own way."

"Yes."

He struggled to suppress his exasperation. "You tell me, Rüdiger. What's going on?"

"I don't know."

"It's still in proof. You could persuade her to change it."

"I'm no longer her editor. When I was, she didn't accept what she called my interference."

"You can tell her how upset I am."

"If you want."

Both men were silent for several seconds, both wondering, Roland thought, how to end the call. Finally he said, "Why would I bother to go and see her?"

"Only you can decide."

When he put down the phone, Roland remembered that he had failed to ask about Alissa's foot. He spent the rest of the evening moodily improvising at the piano in his Keith Jarrett style.

Lawrence and family arrived the next day in the late afternoon. It was an exuberant reunion of the kind being repeated around the country. He had not seen the family since Christmas. Paul regarded him with suspicion and hid behind his mother's legs. Stefanie, almost eight, seemed to have grown two inches. She was circumspect at first, then grew warmer through the evening. When they sat at table for tea, juice and cake and she rested her chin on her hand and appeared to slip into a daydream, he imagined he could see the young teenager in her. The children's supper, then their protracted and separate bedtimes, took up most of the evening. Roland had half an hour on the sofa with Stefanie. She was a shy girl who came to life in a one-to-one. Until she was seven and a half she was averse to reading books on her own. She preferred talking, listening, fantasising. Then the miracle occurred, as Lawrence described in a lockdown call. At bedtime he recited to her from memory "The Owl and the Pussycat." He had forgotten the effect it once had on him. "It was like a sort of pole-vault of the imagination. She wanted it again. And again the next couple of nights. Then she read it for herself, memorised it, recited it at breakfast. Now she's reading. A transformation."

As soon as she had Roland to herself she spoke to him in German and corrected his, just as he had asked her to.

She started, as she usually did with, "Opa, tell me something."

He described how long ago two German girls in Berlin used to give him language lessons.

"Tell me about the olden days."

He obliged with stories of Libya, of going into the desert with his father to find a scorpion and finding one straight away, under a stone.

She had heard that one before but she liked hearing it again. "Would it kill you?"

"I think it would have made me ill for a while."

In return, she told him the names of some new friends and described their characters. She had decided on a career as an organic farmer. Her method for swimming the backstroke was one she had devised herself. He told her about the photographs he was trying to organise. Before she went to bed he took her into the sitting room to show her the spread. He put in her hands pictures of Lawrence on holiday in Greece. She thought it amusing and paradoxical that her father could ever have been four years old.

It was not until ten that the three adults sat down to the supper Roland had cooked. They talked about the children first, then, inevitably, about the pandemic, whether there would be a second lockdown, the race to get vaccines tested and manufactured. The new age of social-media unreason was promoting fake cures, encouraged by the American president. Angry and phobic conspiracy theories were everywhere.

When Roland broke the news of Alissa's amputation Lawrence said, "I'm sorry to hear that."

But it was clear that it meant little to him. Roland had remembered the famous story about Sartre, told by Simone de Beauvoir. He smoked sixty a day and philosophised at length about the pleasures of tobacco. His habit was ruining his health. When his legs gave way and he had a heavy fall he was told frankly by a doctor in the hospital that if he continued smoking, first his toes would be amputated, then his feet and ultimately his legs. If he gave up the habit, his health could be restored. It was his choice. Sartre said that he would need to think it over.

The joke, if it was a joke, was lost on Ingrid. Lawrence was amused. Next, their work. Both were helping with papers for the 2021 IPCC report, due in ten months. The indices were bleak. Carbon dioxide in the atmosphere was up to 415 parts per million, the highest level in 2 million years. The forecasts of seven years before had proved too conservative. They thought that some processes were irreversible. To hold warming to 1.5 degrees was now impossible. They had recently gone with a team and overflown, with Russian permission, vast areas of Siberian forests in flames. Local scientists had shown them shocking data on methane release from antiquated oil wells and had said that passing the news upwards through the bureaucracy could threaten their science funding. The ice-melt data from Greenland, the Arctic and Antarctic were depressing. Governments and industry, for all their rhetoric, were still in denial. Nationalist leaders were living in a fantasy. Forest fires, floods, drought, famine, superstorms—this year would be even worse than last but better than next. It was already here—a catastrophe.

Lawrence was pouring the wine they had brought with them from Germany. He said, "I think it might be too late. We're stuffed."

The windows were open to the warm night air. The three spoke and listened easily, intimately. It often happened like this, Roland thought, the world was wobbling badly on its axis, ruled in too many places by shameless ignorant men, while freedom of expression was in retreat and digital public spaces resounded with the shouts of delirious masses. Truth had no consensus. New nuclear weapons multiplied, commanded by hair-trigger artificial intelligence, while vital natural systems, including jet streams, ocean currents as well as pollinating insects, submarine cliffs of coral and the biological churn of rich natural soils and all manner of diverse flora and fauna—wilting or becoming extinct. Parts of the world were burning or drowning. Simultaneously, in the old-fashioned glow of close family, made more radiant by recent deprivation, he experienced happiness that could not be dispelled, even by rehearsing every looming disaster in the world. It made no sense.

→⊱

Later in July 2020 there was a funeral for a family member, and then in August came another death. First, his sister's husband, Michael, a gentle giant, gifted amateur magician, former medical orderly in the army, then an industrial chemist. A man in command of all kinds of strange and useful knowledge. Only two weeks later, Roland's brother Henry died. Of Rosalind's four children, he had lost the most in childhood. He had been clever at school and head boy, like their "new" brother, Robert. There was not enough money to let Henry stay on and move to a grammar school for the sixth form. Robert and Rosalind should have intervened. But Henry never complained about the course of his life. National Service, then many years in a men's tailoring shop, an unhappy first marriage, retraining as an accountant, and then, his major piece of luck, marrying Melissa.

The funerals were secular and at both Roland read a poem by James Fenton, "For Andrew Wood." It asked what the dead would want from the living and answered the question by proposing a bond.

*And so the dead might cease to grieve*
*And we might make amends*
*And there might be a pact between*
*Dead friends and living friends.*

Melissa heard it at Michael's funeral and asked to have it at Henry's. After the second funeral, when the immediate family had retreated to a corner of a dark pub near the crematorium, Susan said that the poem made it possible for Michael and Henry to remain in their lives as living presences. Melissa started to agree but was overcome by weeping.

Just so. The difficulty lay in reading the poem without cracking up, especially, Roland found, when the poet says of the dead, after they had become "less self-engrossed,"

*And time would find them generous*
*As they used to be.*

Even thinking of the lines caused his throat to tighten. It was Daphne, generous Daphne. Still raw, nine years on. As much as the poem's sentiments, it was the tone of calm and playful reassurance that did for him, and the knowledge that none of it was true. The dead could want nothing, and not all of them were once generous. The poet was being kindly and consoling. It was the artful kindness that moved Roland. The trick, when the occasions to recite came round, was to put his left hand deep into his pocket and pinch his thigh. The bruise from the second funeral overlay the first.

Over half-pints of ale, Roland, Robert and Shirley, Susan and Melissa went through the family story. The baby on Reading station, the lifelong secrecy, the fractured family. Robert, not long out of hospital after a heart operation, was thinking of writing a memoir. He had already done more than anyone in the family to recover what could be known of its past. He was thinking of using a ghostwriter. There was nothing new in the story now but they needed to talk about it together as they had a few times before. The mood, influenced by Fenton's poem, was of forgiveness. That two of the family had gone to join Rosalind and Robert in oblivion softened their judgement. As they were turning over the past Susan said of her mother and stepfather, "They got themselves in a terrible mess and in those times and in their situation, we might have done the same and covered it up forever after."

A sympathetic silence followed. Finally, Robert said, "They gave me away to two wonderful people. I don't hold any grudges."

Was it possible to make friends with the memory of their dead parents, as Fenton proposed? Perhaps not, for just before they broke up Susan said angrily, "But there was something he did and I'll never forgive him for it. Never."

They pushed her to say more.

"I'm sorry, I shouldn't have mentioned it. I'm never going to talk about it." Then she repeated, "I'll never forgive him."

When he phoned her that evening and asked again, she changed the subject.

➤➤

The two deaths and visits from Daphne's children and their families occupied him through August. He had not told Rüdiger that he had changed his mind about the visit. He learned from him that Alissa was in a wheelchair. As the summer weeks passed he was not sure what he wanted to do. Perhaps it was cowardice not to meet her. Perhaps his curiosity about her was greater than he thought. But he dithered. In the middle of the month, Lawrence phoned from Potsdam. Over several years he had read all his mother's novels and he had just finished Roland's copy of *Her Slow Reduction*. While they were discussing it Lawrence asked abruptly, "Did you ever hit her?"

"Absolutely not."

"Did you ever stop her from seeing me?"

"Never."

"She all but names you."

"It's upsetting."

Lawrence must have thought it over and discussed it with Ingrid. On a second call he said, "Dad, you can't let this stand. Write to her."

"I was thinking of going to see her."

"Even better."

In that way the decision was made. By then he thought he might be too late. The best scientific advice was indicating a September lockdown to head off a serious second wave of infection. Cases were rising in the familiar way. But he was playing at the hotel again and could not find a substitute acceptable to the management until the last day of August. He need not have worried. An acquaintance, Nigel, an old friend of Daphne's who worked at the *Financial Times*, came by the hotel one evening and they had a drink after Roland's set. The libertarian right of the Conservative Party, many of them diehard Europhobes, privately referred to the health minister and his advisers as "the Gestapo" for their faith in enforced lockdowns. Temperamentally, the prime minister was inclined to the libertarian tendency. According to Nigel, the word was that he would hold out against a September lockdown.

"Then of course, the cases will keep on rising and he'll have to do it anyway. He hasn't learned his lesson from March."

For the flight to Munich Roland wore a medical-grade mask donated by Gerald and sat tensely through the journey, refusing food and drink, aware that everyone around him was half his age and likely to survive a dose of Covid without even knowing about it. He had a window seat with a view of a trembling wing. Risking his life in order to deliver a self-serving rebuke to a long-ago love, now crippled. Madness.

He spent that night at Rüdiger's. For many years he had lived alone in a large apartment in the Bogenhausen quarter. In all that time Roland had never heard him refer to a partner or a lover, man or woman. It had never seemed right to ask and now it was too late. He was rich from his publishing empire, supported the opera and the Lenbachhaus gallery and various local charities and in retirement had made himself an amateur lepidopterist. He was also a fly fisherman and tied his own flies. What a life. Rüdiger's cook served dinner. Aware of the remote sound of dishes being washed in the kitchen Roland had a rare moment of regret that he was not rich. It might have suited him well. He would have needed a different attitude, different politics. But Rüdiger had always been a man of the left, gave generously to Amnesty and other charities. *Generous*. The word prompted Roland to describe the two funerals. Death led them next to the pandemic. Germany's figures were still relatively low. Chancellor Merkel had shown on TV how well she understood virology as well as the mathematics of risk and was riding precariously high in the polls. The chancellor was a conduit to Alissa's novel. It was due in the shops in four weeks. There had been some advance reviews. Some declared *Her Slow Reduction* another masterpiece. Others grumbled.

"She's our greatest novelist. Teenage school kids are made to read her. But she's white, hetero, old and she's said things that alienate younger readers. Also, when a writer has been around long enough people begin to get tired. Even if she does something different every time. They say, She's doing something different—again!"

But so far no mention in the press of Roland as wife-beater.

"You might get away with it," Rüdiger teased him.

Later he left Roland in the library trying to resume his struggle with Musil's masterpiece and went away to write emails. He came back an hour later and said, "I've been thinking. I should go with you tomorrow. It could be difficult."

"I wouldn't want that."

"At least let me drive you there."

"Very kind of you, Rüdi. But I'd prefer to make this journey without you."

"Then let my driver take you. Phone him when you want to come back."

In the morning, when they reached the village, Roland asked to be set down on the main road by the bus stop. He assumed that this was where sixteen-year-old Lawrence had got out. Roland waited for the car to draw away. He could see Alissa's road a hundred yards ahead, on the other side of the road. He had seen it before through his son's eyes. It was as if he was in the location of a half-remembered dream. Memory and present perception tricked each other to create an illusion of return. Her road rose steeply to where the first of a dozen houses began, a set of minor variations on an architect's forceful idea. A low brooding protected look of glass and shuttered cement. As if a giant had vengefully flattened a Frank Lloyd Wright creation. There may have been an architectural proscription of trees and shrubs to lay bare the purity of horizontal lines. Thirty feet down a very steep slope, virtually a cliff, traffic on the main road rushed in and out of the village. He knew from Rüdiger that she had bought the place in 1988 on the proceeds from *The Journey*. Perhaps on an impulse, before the house was built and without visiting the site. Whatever she thought about it when she settled in, her routines would have kept her here. All those books, papers, research materials. A move would have been disruptive. It did not look like a neighbourly place and she may have liked the anonymity.

He slowed after the second house as he thought his son had. Like him, Roland now felt that he needed more time, when he'd had weeks to reflect. He could remember the insult she had delivered in her book but he could not at that moment summon his anger. What came instead was a mess of anachronistic memories, a bolus of undigested feeling and recollection that he had not touched or tasted in years. Their late-night champagne on a boulder in a burn near Mount Suilven, typing up her novel, her appearance at his Brixton place with a bag of food, the candlewick bedspread on which they decided to get married, Alissa on her knees in paint-streaked jeans, spray-stencilling a junk-shop chest of drawers in their bedroom in the Clapham house, their angry row about East Germany, and sex—on the Danube delta, in French hotels, on a hard bed in Lady Margaret Road, in an orchard by a Spanish farmhouse, just once, quietly, in Liebenau, and the frightening magnificent birth that followed. There was more and they came as if tightly rolled or hammered and compressed by engines of time into a single object. What was it—a shapeless stone, a golden egg? More like a wisp, a fiction, exclusive to him. It would not be shared with her and that was one measure of loss that couldn't touch him now.

But there was that essence everyone forgets when a love recedes into the past—how it was, how it felt and tasted to be together through seconds, minutes and days, before everything that was taken for granted was discarded then overwritten by the tale of how it all ended, and then by the shaming inadequacies of memory. Paradise or the inferno, no one remembers anything much. Affairs and marriages ended long ago come to resemble postcards from the past. Brief note about the weather, a quick story, funny or sad, a bright picture on the other side. First to go, Roland thought as he walked towards her house, was the elusive self, precisely how you were yourself, how you appeared to others.

There was a small white car parked outside her place and he paused by it. It was pitiful that he had to remind himself of the obvious—that he was not the agile creature of his thoughts. He was an old man visiting an old woman. Alissa and Roland lying naked in the undergrowth, in a copse of holm oaks near where the Danube divided to meet the Black Sea, existed nowhere on the planet but in his mind. Perhaps in hers. Perhaps those oaks were pines. He approached the squat front door. Ignoring the sign in Gothic script that told him to use the side entrance he rang the bell.

A small Filipina woman in a brown housecoat opened the door and stepped aside for him. For such a large house the hall was cramped. He waited while the woman shoved the pneumatically assisted door closed. She turned to him with a shrug and a disarming smile. It was not her kind of door and they didn't share a language to talk about it. In those few seconds he recalled his visit to Balham to see Miriam Cornell and he imagined someone like himself, a self-righteous fool, journeying around Europe to make accusations against the women of his past. He forgave himself. This was only his second reckoning in eighteen years.

He was shown into the sitting room that stretched the entire depth of the house and the door closed behind him. The room was as dark as it looked from outside. The air was rich with the scent of strong tobacco. Gauloises perhaps. He didn't know they still existed. She was at the far end of the room in a wheelchair, seated at a large table in front of a flat-screen computer surrounded by several high piles of books. All he saw at first was the gleam of her white hair as she wheeled out from behind the table and called, almost at a shout. "My God! Look at the paunch on you. And where's your hair?"

He approached her, determined to smile. "I've kept both feet."

She laughed gaily. "Einer reicht!" One is enough.

They were off to a crazy start. It was as if he had come to the wrong house. Jocular insult was never her style. A life of public pronouncements, of being a national treasure, had set her free.

Expertly, she steered her chair right up to him and said, "For Christ's sake you can give me a kiss after thirty years!"

He did not know how to refuse her and he was intent on seeming composed. He leaned down to press his lips against her cheek. The skin was dry, warm and, like his own, deeply creased.

She seized his hand and gripped it tightly. "The state of us! We'll drink to it. Maria's bringing a bottle."

It was just past eleven. Roland usually held back until seven. He wondered if Alissa was under the influence of disinhibiting painkillers. Some opioids had that effect. He said, "Sure. We've nothing to lose."

She waved him towards an armchair. While he moved aside copies of the *Paris Review* she lit a cigarette.

"Chuck them on the floor. It doesn't matter."

They were old copies from George Plimpton's time as editor. Someone had told Roland that since then a younger generation had taken over. They might not be sympathetic to Alissa's mix of acerbic rationalism and seventies feminism. She had made unnecessary enemies in the trans debates when she said on an American TV chat show that a surgeon might sculpt a "kind of a man" out of a woman but there was never enough good stuff to carve a woman out of a man. It was said provocatively in the Dorothy Parker mode and got a quick bark of laughter from the studio audience. But these were not Parker's times. "Kind of a man" brought the usual trouble. An Ivy League university withdrew Alissa's honorary degree and a few others cancelled her lecture engagements. More institutions followed and her speaking tour collapsed. Stonewall, also under new management, said she had encouraged violence against trans people. On the Internet her remarks pursued her. A younger generation knew her to be on the wrong side of history. Rüdiger had told Roland that her American and UK sales had suffered.

Maria came in with the wine and two glasses on a tray and left. Alissa poured to the brim.

When they raised their glasses she said, "I know from Rüdiger that you've liked my work. Generous of you but don't talk to me about it. I've had enough. Anyway, here we are. Cheers. How was your life?"

"Good and bad. I have stepchildren, step-grandchildren. And two grandchildren, as do you. And I lost Daphne."

"Poor old Daphne."

It was said lightly but he did not speak. Instead, to conceal his irritation he drank deeply, more than he had intended. She was watching him closely and nodded at the glass in his hand.

"What are you on?"

"Down to a third of a bottle a day. Then a Scotch last thing. You?"

"I start around now and keep going till late. But no spirits."

"And those?" He gestured towards the cloud over her head.

"Down to forty." Then she added, "Or fifty. And I don't give a fuck."

He nodded. He'd had different versions of this conversation with friends his age or in their eighties. Nearly everyone drank. Some had taken up cannabis again. Others, cocaine that delivered in a twenty-minute package a vague reminder of how it was to be young. Others, even acid in micro-doses. But as mind-altering drugs went, alcohol in the form of wine was hard to beat, especially for taste.

Whenever their eyes met, he added to a proper impression of her face. The features he remembered were in there, locked within a puffy enlargement. He had to imagine that the beautiful look of the woman he had loved had been painted onto the surface of an uninflated balloon. If he blew as hard as he dared he would have it, the familiar eyes, nose, mouth and chin fleeing apart, like galaxies in the expanding universe. She was in there somewhere, staring out, trying to find *him* among his own wreckage, the bald and porcine nonentity with the disappointed air. He had claimed to drink less than she did, then emptied his glass when she had hardly touched hers. What had bloated them both was not food so much as carelessness or surrender. They were letting go. She at least had another book or two to write. While he . . . but he was drifting and she was speaking.

"I've told them. I'm not stirring." She said it loudly in protest, as if he too had insisted that she must.

The stump at the end of her left leg was encased within a mannish sock and rested on a white cushion balanced on the footrest of her wheelchair. She had no need to stir. He had sometimes heard successful writers complaining in public about their lot, the distractions, the pressures. It always made him uncomfortable.

She continued, "I said, one interview. One! Syndicated, translated, print, broadcast, Internet, whatever, all at once."

The subject was *Her Slow Reduction*, how it should be publicised. He thought he would get started and try to stay calm. "It's a fine novel. You don't need to do a thing. But Alissa. It seems you're calling me out as a wife-beater."

"What?"

He said it again.

She stared at him, amazed, or pretending to be. "It's a novel. Not a memoir."

"You've told the world many times. You left your husband and seven-month-old baby in Clapham in 1986. So it is in your novel. She runs from domestic violence. Why not from Streatham or Heidelberg? Why not a two-year-old? To the press the implication will be clear. You know I never hit you. Let me hear it from you."

"Of course you didn't. Jesus!" Her head lolled back and she stared at the ceiling. Both hands lay fidgeting on the larger wheels she used to propel herself. Then she said, "Yes, I used our house and I had every right. I remember that shithole well. I hated it."

"You could have used some invention."

"Roland! Really! Did a future German chancellor live in our house? Have I been secretly running the country for the past ten years? Has your throat been cut? Will I be arrested for murdering you with a kitchen knife?"

"The analogies don't hold. You've been laying the ground in interviews for years. The abandoned husband and baby were—"

"Oh come on!"

She said it at a shout but her anger did not prevent her from splashing wine into their glasses. "Have I really got to give you a lesson in how to read a book? I borrow. I invent. I raid my own life. I take from all over the place, I change it, bend it to what I need. Didn't you notice? The abandoned husband is two metres tall with a ponytail you wouldn't have been seen dead with. And blond, from the Swedish guy I knew before you, Karl. Sure, he hit me a couple of times. But he didn't have a scar and nor do you. That was from a farmer near Liebenau, an old Nazi, friend of my father. And Monika, the chancellor, is drawn a little from me thirty years ago. Also from your sister, Susan, who I loved. Everything that ever happened to me and everything that didn't. Everything I know, everyone I ever met—all mine to mash up with whatever I invent."

She may not have been angry at all, Roland thought, just talking at an insane volume. He said, "Then listen to my humble request. One tiny extra step of invention. Move that shithole house out of Clapham."

"Didn't you notice how you were missing from my memoir? I'll tell you what I've been doing for thirty-five years. *Not* writing about you! Godamnit, Roland, I protected you!"

"From what?"

"From the truth . . . Jesus!" She fumbled as she tried to extract another cigarette from a small hole in the top of its soft packet. When it was lit she drew heavily and was calmer. She had thought about this. She had a list.

"From the memoir I could have written. How you stuffed me, eyes, ears, mouth, with your needs. Not only your God-given right to some ecstatic union of minds and bodies in the clouds. But your oh-so-cultivated version of what you might have been. That refined sense of failure and self-pity for what life had stolen from you. The concert pianist, the poet, the Wimbledon champ. Those three heroes out of your reach took up a lot of room in a small house. How was I to breathe? Then you invented fatherhood, parenthood and couldn't stop talking about it. Meanwhile, all around you, junk, squalor, piles of your unwanted crap everywhere. I couldn't move. I couldn't think. To get free I paid the highest price and that was Lawrence. You were a great subject, Roland. Something about men I could have told the world. But I didn't! I never forgot that you were the only man I ever loved."

This startled him. While she was laying out her charges, he had fixed his gaze on the spill that had formed on the glass-topped table. His patient tone was a fake. "Your sexual needs were also pressing. Those rejection slips made you howl—"

"Roland, stop, stop, stop!" At each shouted word, she thumped the armrest of her wheelchair. What remained of her cigarette flew out of her hand and landed on a rug several feet away. But she had not lost control. She waited while he got up, gave the cigarette to her and sat down.

"We're not here for this. Let me say it for you. Around the house I was a slob too. I wanted you to help lots looking after the baby, then I accused you of stealing him from me. I wanted lots of sex and got it and pretended I was only meeting your needs. Having my novels rejected drove me nuts and sometimes I turned on you, even after all your editing and typing. I turned my son away when he came looking for me. So. My novels are filled with stupid, demanding, contradictory women who run away. I used to get it in the neck from feminist critics. But I have stupid men too. Life is messy, everybody makes mistakes because we're all fucking stupid and I've made lots of enemies among these young Puritans for saying so. They're as stupid as we were. The point is, Roland, for you and me, it no longer matters and that's why I hoped you'd come. We're still here and we haven't got long. Me especially. I thought we could eat and get drunk together and remember everything that was good. Soon they'll start printing finished copies.

If it makes you happy, I'll change Clapham and the baby's age and anything else. It's nothing. None of it matters."

As he gazed at her amazed, he at last lifted his glass but did not drink from it straight away. In all her outpouring what still held him was the news that he was the only man she had loved. True or not, it was extraordinary that she should say it. He could not say the same to her, not quite. Instead, he proposed a toast. "Thank you. To eating and drinking together all day."

He had to stand and lean across the table to touch her glass. As he did so she murmured, "Excellent."

At that moment, Maria came in with another bottle. Alissa may have summoned her with a buzzer.

Roland said, "OK. How about this? When I was coming along your road I was remembering various places we had sex."

She clapped her hands together. "Now that's the spirit!"

He ran through the locations for her in roughly the order they had come to him. So—sharing after all.

With each summoned place, her mirth grew. "You remember a bedspread? Men!" And then, "In that wood in the Delta you trod on a thorn and convinced yourself it was a scorpion."

"Only at first."

"You went ten feet in the air."

It surprised him that she had only a faint recall of the day she came to Brixton with her shopping.

"You said the food was for 'afterwards.' That word. I almost passed out."

He too had forgotten certain events that still glowed for her.

She said, "We had stayed the night at your parents'. We went upstairs in the late morning, I think to strip the bed. Before we knew it we were having a quick one, very quietly. I was tense because I thought they could hear us downstairs. The bed squeaked. They always squeak when there's someone around."

"They squeak the truth."

"Don't you remember? When we were done, you couldn't get out?"

"Out of the room?"

"Out of me! I had some kind of spasm. Vaginismus, it's called. Never had it before or since. We were both in pain and your mother was calling up the stairs that lunch was ready."

"I've torn this one from the record. How did I get out?"

"We sang silly songs. Almost in a whisper, to distract me. The one I remember was 'I'm Gonna Wash That Man Right Outa My Hair.' "

"And a year later you did."

Suddenly she was serious. The second bottle was already half-empty. "Come here, Roland, right beside me. Now listen. I never got you out of my hair. Ever. If I had you wouldn't be here. Please believe me."

"OK. Got it." He leaned over and they held hands.

And so the day went on. They had lunch in the garden. They were too old or too experienced to get helplessly drunk. Later he could recall most of what they said and wrote it in his journal. In the afternoon they talked about their health.

"You first," she said.

He missed nothing out. Open-angle glaucoma, cataracts, sun damage, high blood pressure, a fractured rib causing chest pains, the potential, given his girth, for diabetes two, arthritis in both knees, prostatic dysplasia—benign, malign, not yet known. He was too scared to find out.

They were indoors by then. The lowering sun did not bring more light into the sitting room. She told him she had lung cancer and that it had already spread extensively. The doctors thought she was right to refuse treatment. Her other foot would probably have to go. She would not put herself through the stress of giving up smoking.

"I'm done," she said. "I have a novella to write, then I'll sit here and wait."

Next, she insisted, there was to be no more talk of illness. They talked of their parents, as they had many years ago. It was a form of elaborate summing-up in which there was nothing new to tell each other beyond the stories of their decline and death. They did not talk about Alissa's memoir and the rift with Jane. They played some old songs on the hi-fi but weren't touched by them. It was not possible to regain their pre-lunch exuberance. The retreating effects of alcohol dragged on their spirits. Her defiant claim that nothing mattered now seemed puny. Roland had a plane to catch that evening. Everything mattered. He phoned Rüdiger's driver to arrange his ride to the airport.

When he was sitting near her again, he said, "I almost didn't come and I'm glad I did. But there's still a shadow and only you can do something about it. We've avoided the subject. You have to see Lawrence. You have to talk to him. You can't avoid it, Alissa. Given everything you've said, for both of you it has to happen."

She closed her eyes while he spoke and kept them closed for her first words. "I'm scared and I'm ashamed . . . of what I did, and of how I kept it up for so long. I was a fanatic, Roland. I ignored that kid's beautiful letter. D'you know, I actually binned it! I was cruel when he came looking for me. He can never forgive me. It's too late to make a, whatever, a relationship of any sort."

"It could surprise you, just as today surprised me."

She was shaking her head. "I've thought about it. I've left it too late."

"It would change how he thinks about you, long after you've gone. For the rest of his life." She continued to shake her head.

He laid a hand over hers. "All right. Then just promise me this. That you'll think about it again."

She didn't reply. He thought he saw one last shake of the head, but so very faint that it might have been a nod. She was asleep.

He sat watching her while he waited for his car. Her lips were parted, her head tilted to one side and she breathed heavily. He did not doubt that she was dying. The pale and slender large-eyed young woman had become a loud grotesque, some might think. But the more time he had spent with her today, the clearer it became, the face of the woman he had married in 1985. It touched him or touched his vanity that he was the only man she had loved. If it wasn't true he was pleased that she should say it. If it was true, then she paid for her dozen books with two loves, a son and a husband. Now, she had no one, no family. No close friends, according to Rüdiger. She lived in a dark cement bunker of a house, waiting to die alone. Time had degraded him too but by all conventional measures, he was the happier. No books though, no songs, no paintings, nothing invented that would survive him. Would he swap his family for her yard of books? He gazed at her now familiar face and shook his head for an answer. He would not have had the courage to break out as she did, even though men paid a lower price—the literary biographies teemed with wives and children abandoned for the higher calling. Too quick to take offence, he had forgotten that the man in her novel that he mistook for himself was two metres tall, blond, with a scar and a ponytail. She had delivered at full volume her tutorial in how to read.

He heard the bell and the sound of Maria's quick steps as she went to the door. He got to his feet slowly, careful to avoid another of his dizzy moments. As he was leaving the room he turned towards her for one last long look.

➤➤

In the new year, 2021, in a post-solstice eclipse, the third lockdown began, the US president was replaced amid turmoil and at midnight on 31 January Europe was left behind. Roland, alone again in the big Lloyd Square house, was liberated from two obsessions and could devote himself to fretting exclusively over the science and fractious politics of epidemiology. The new lockdown had been delayed, as had the first and second. In deaths per million the country ranked high in the world and the prime minister was popular. More so when vaccinations began with good-natured efficiency while Europe, Germany especially, fumbled. Nothing was simple. The national confinement stretched into a long winter and an icy spring. The harm done by it was beyond measurement. Estimates were conditioned by local experience and political opinion. But all agreed the damage was severe to minds and bodies, childhoods, education, livelihoods and the economy. Suicides were up, as were marital breakdowns, as was domestic violence—generally, code for men hitting women and children. But dying of suffocation without family or friends, tended by overworked strangers in masks, was worse, most thought—and most, including Roland, knuckled down.

By mid-February he had annotated the hundredth photograph—

himself and Daphne on the banks of the Esk, taken, he remembered, by a lone and obliging Japanese hiker. With that the project ended. The selection was across a lifetime—in his mother's arms at six months, short-trousered and jug-eared in the Libyan desert, then most of the rest of his cast, his parents and siblings, two wives, son and family, stepchildren, their families, lovers, his close friends, the separate universe of bare-skinned holidays, backpacks, the frog pond, his London hotel people, the Khyber Pass, the Himalayas, the Causse de Larzac, arm in arm with Joe Coppinger on a glacier in the Upper Engadin, Lawrence at two months in his mother's arms, Rüdiger when he still had an earring, and more. He excluded his one photograph of Miriam Cornell, blurred, standing by the shed where, presumably, his trunk was locked at the time. Then he changed his mind and added her to the hundred, writing on the back, "my piano teacher '59 to '64." Otherwise everyone was named and full contexts were given. The rest, obvious enough or a mystery forever, even to himself, he piled back into three large cardboard boxes, taped the lids down and carried them up an unstable ladder to the attic.

Through February and March he began and concluded the reading of all his journals, usually one a day, forty in all. He heaped them on a bench in the kitchen. That evening he glumly watched a tennis tournament whose contestants were elderly stars of thirty, forty, even fifty years ago. From a distance these men and women looked lean and strong. The eldest was eighty-one. They played doubles, from the baseline mostly and a few steps in, but their strokes, smoothly tooled over a lifetime, were fast and low. They loved life and therefore still minded about losing. There were tantrums around the umpire's chair. By modern standards, as Roland knew, he was old before his time. There was nothing he could do about it.

This time round he felt part of the locked-down communality. He did what everybody did: noted that the days were passing too fast, went online to book a holiday he thought he would never take, made resolutions he did not keep, was in touch with family by phone or Internet video. Alone in the house he led a crowded social life. Daphne's side of the family, regular exchanges with Lawrence and Ingrid in Potsdam then separately with Stefanie. He bubbled-up with Nancy, who drove over from Stoke Newington, usually without her three boisterous sons, at which he expressed routine disappointment but felt relief. In voice, mannerisms, looks, Nancy closely resembled Daphne youthfully risen from the dead. The virus had brought his past to life. He was in touch at last with Diana, who ran a maternity clinic on Grenada, in St. George's, and refused to be pensioned off. Carol had been head of a vast fiefdom within the BBC until she retired. Mireille had followed her father into the French diplomatic service and she also was retired. They mostly talked about children, grandchildren and the pandemic.

He suffered a hot-knife pain in his knees when he took his daily walk. The knock-on effect of arthritis in his knees was weight-gain through lack of exercise. Alissa was right—his paunch was ludicrous. There was one minor recurrence of the chest pain but nothing like the attack that had thrown him down the stairs. He thought about replacing the cat that had wandered off and was still wondering about it when restrictions were lifted in mid-May. He chatted once a week from behind his mask with the merry Sikh lad who delivered the Internet groceries. But Roland occasionally entered a state of catatonia, a black and white world of emotional neutrality that could last an hour or even two. Then, if he had been told he would never see or speak to another human again, he would have been neither sad nor happy. In this state—it was after several weeks—he managed what he'd always considered impossible, except for yogis in a state of grace: to sit in a chair for half an hour and think about nothing.

Those were the hardest times, returning to his shrunken state. Silence, solitude, pointlessness, perpetual dusk. The names of the days of the week meant nothing. Nor did modern medicine, even after his first shot. We are all one with history now, subject to its whims. His London was of the plague year, 1665, of the diseased wooden town of 1349. He felt old, dependent on his family. To stay alive he had to shun them all. And they him. To resume his small existence he would force himself to some trivial act, like standing to return to the fridge a bottle of milk before the central heating soured it.

Somehow he had carelessly let slip, probably to Lawrence, a reference to the pain in his chest. In late February the entire family was on to him, Lawrence constantly, Ingrid gently and from time to time. On one visit Nancy gripped his hand while they were standing in the garden. She was urging him, like the others, to see a doctor. It was as if Daphne was speaking to him. On another occasion Nancy brought Greta along, illegally, and the sisters made their case together. He reminded them of the tumble he had suffered in the Lake District and how he had never been the same since. It was his ribs. One lunchtime Gerald phoned from Great Ormond Street Children's Hospital. He had a ten-minute break. As he spoke Roland could hear the rustle of his plastic protection suit. His voice was flat with exhaustion. "Look, I don't have much time. A man in his seventies with chest pains who doesn't get it checked out is an idiot."

"Thanks Gerald. Awfully kind. But I know exactly what it is. I took that fall walking in the Lakes and—"

"I'm not going to say any more. We've just lost another kid on the ward to Covid. Twelve-year-old boy from Bolton. In a minute I have to go down and break the news to the parents. If you can't look after your own health, well, that's too bad." He hung up.

Chastened, Roland stood in the kitchen by his half-eaten lunch, the receiver in his hand, the embodiment of an old fool. Upstairs in his study he wrote Gerald an email apologising for his frivolous attitude in dire times and praised the young man's courage and dedication. Yes, he promised, he would see a heart specialist as soon as lockdown ended.

He followed the pandemic news and daily consulted the Johns Hopkins dashboard and the gov.uk sites to watch the rising numbers of the third wave. Among those tested for Covid in the previous twenty-eight days, deaths peaked at 1,400 a day. Then there were those who died without a test. Everyone said, even the right-leaning tabloids, that Johnson should have gone for the September lockdown. Roland believed the figures. How common was that around the world, to trust official data? Then it could not be so bad, he told himself in better moments. The instruments of state, its institutions were greater than the government of the day.

He and everyone else who was interested had already learned the pandemic lexicon, "R," the fomites, viral loads, the furin cleavage site, heterologous prime-boost trials, vaccine escape variants, case rate/hospitalisation uncoupling and, most resonant and sinister of all, original antigenic sin. There was nothing novel in another lockdown, nothing to hope for but the lowering of the figures and the lengthening of the days when the clocks leaped forward the week after the spring equinox. What sustained him was his discovery during the first lockdown that he did not mind a little housework. Physical movement was good for him and keeping his cage in order made it seem larger. Holding entropy at bay pleasantly emptied the mind, though there was often little in his. By extension, he began to find pleasure in throwing things out. He started with clothes, armfuls of sweaters, many with moth holes, jeans that chafed and chided him for his change of shape, shirts of bilious colour. He did not need more than ten pairs of socks and did not think he would ever wear a suit or a tie again. He lingered over his hiking gear then left it intact. Books he would never read or read again, old tax papers, old invoices, irrelevant charging cables . . . It was hard to stop. He filled a spare room with bin liners and boxes. He felt lighter, even younger. People with eating disorders, he thought, must be aiming for this giddy feeling as they cast off weight to lift from the ground of their existence, float away, freed from themselves, from the burdens of past and future, reduced or elevated to pure being, happily unencumbered like small children.

The process of purification brought him to the forty journals. His most recent entry was the previous September, a 1,000-word account of his hours with Alissa. There, he had decided, it must end. They had exchanged a few emails but both his and hers lacked—what exactly?—energy, invention, purpose. A future. Their business with each other was concluded. She did not mention her health but Rüdiger let him know that her decline was steady.

Reading back since 1986 did not bring him any fresh understanding of his life. There were no obvious themes, no undercurrents he had not noticed at the time, nothing learned. A grand mass of detail was what he found and events, conversations, even people that he could not remember. In those sections it was as if he was reading of someone else's past. He disliked himself for complaining onto the page—about living hand to mouth, not having the right kind of work, not mak-

ing a long and successful marriage. Boring, no insight, passive. He
had read many books. His summaries were hasty, without interest.
How weak compared to Jane Farmer's journal. She had something
to write about: European civilisation in ruins, heroic young idealists
beheaded, while he was a child of a long peace. He remembered the
lift and twist in her prose. Hers, like his, was unrevised last-thing-at-
night stuff. Her way of setting or unfolding a scene was far superior,
so were the logic and tension that lay between one sentence and the
next. Her knack of knowing how one good detail could illuminate
the whole had the gleam of vital intelligence. This was also the way
of Alissa's prose. Where he simply listed experiences, mother and
daughter gave them life.

That was one good reason to act. When he thought of Lawrence
or a remote descendant reading his journals he knew what he must
do. Nancy and her family had given him a fire bowl at Christmas. On
a dull mid-afternoon in late March, he filled it with kindling, slender
logs and barbecue charcoal. When it was burning he sat close in long
overcoat and woolly hat and, with a mug of tea in one hand, fed the
poorly rendered second half of his life to the flames, one volume at a
time. It came back to him then how he had thrown school copies of
Camus, Goethe and the rest onto a bonfire in Susan's garden. Fifty-
seven years ago. Bookends, the end of books, to frame a life. Had
John Dryden's *All for Love* really burned quicker, brighter than the
rest? On that his memory was poor. He hoped it had.

When the fire bowl held only dying embers the cold drove him
indoors to his usual chair. He held more in memory and reflection
than he could have found in his journals. There were currents, plot
lines, developments that no one could have predicted but in those
vanished pages he had not even posed the questions. By what logic
or motivation or helpless surrender did we all, hour by hour, transport ourselves within a generation from the thrill of optimism at Berlin's falling Wall to the storming of the American Capitol? He had
thought 1989 was a portal, a wide opening to the future, with everyone streaming through. It was merely a peak. Now, from Jerusalem to
New Mexico, walls were going up. So many lessons unlearned. The
January assault on the Capitol could be merely a trough, a singular

moment of shame to be discussed in wonder for years. Or a portal to a new kind of America, the present administration just an interregnum, a variant of Weimar. Meet me on the Avenue of the Heroes of January Sixth. From peak to midden in thirty years. Only the backward look, the well-researched history could tell peaks and troughs from portals.

One great inconvenience of death, according to Roland, lay in being removed from the story. Having followed it this far he needed to know how things would turn out. The book he required had a hundred chapters, one for each year—a history of the twenty-first century. As things stood he might not get a quarter of the way through. A glimpse of the contents page would be enough. Would a catastrophic global overheating be headed off? Was a Sino-American war woven into the pattern of history? Would the global rash of racist nationalism yield to something more generous, more constructive? Might we reverse the current great extinction of species? Could the open society find new and fairer ways to flourish? Would artificial intelligence make us wise or mad or irrelevant? Could we manage the century without an exchange of nuclear missiles? As he saw it, simply getting through intact to the last day of the twenty-first century, to the end of the book, would be a triumph.

The temptation of the old, born into the middle of things, was to see in their deaths the end of everything, the end of times. That way their deaths made more sense. He accepted that pessimism was the good companion of thought and study, that optimism was the business of politicians, and no one believed them. He knew about the reasons to be cheerful and had sometimes cited the indices, the literacy rates and so on. But they were relative to a wretched past. He couldn't help himself, there was a novel ugliness about. There were nations run by well-dressed criminal gangs intent on self-enrichment, kept in place by security services, by the rewriting of history and passionate nationalism. Russia was just one. The USA, in a delirium of anger, delusional conspiracies and white supremacy, could yet become another. China had refuted the claim that trade with outsiders opened minds and societies. Now the technology was on hand, it might perfect the totalitarian state and offer a new model of social organisation to compete with or replace liberal democracies—a dictatorship sustained by a reliable flow of consumer goods and a degree of targeted genocide. Roland's bad dream was of freedom of expression, a shrinking privilege, vanishing for a thousand years. Christian medieval Europe did without it that long. Islam had never much cared for it.

But each of these problems was parochial, local to a mere human timescale. They shrank and tightened into a bitter kernel contained within the shell of the greater matter, the earth's heating, the disappearing animals and plants, the disrupted interwoven systems of oceans, land, air and life, beautiful and sustaining entanglements barely understood as we forced change upon them.

From Daphne's living room—the house would always be hers—he watched the dusk descend on London. If, by some stroke of epiphenomenal luck, he could get his hands on the phantom book he might or might not be reassured. At the least, his curiosity could be satisfied. How soothing it would be, to read that his pessimism was out of control. There was one emollient nostrum he liked: things will never be as good as we hoped or as bad as we feared. But imagine showing a well-meaning Edwardian gent a history of the twentieth century's first sixty years. The combined mega-deaths of Europe, Russia and China would cause him to buckle and weep.

Enough! Those angry or disappointed gods in modern form, Hitler, Nasser, Khrushchev, Kennedy and Gorbachev may have shaped his life but that gave Roland no insight into international affairs. Who cared what an obscure Mr. Baines of Lloyd Square thought about the future of the open society or the planet's fate? He was powerless. On a table at his side was a postcard from Lawrence and Ingrid. The picture showed a luminous yellow beach backed by sand dunes and sparta grass. The family was taking "a cold and windy break" on the Baltic coast. The handwriting was Ingrid's. Just before the joint sign-off, she told him they would come to visit him as soon as restrictions were lifted, which they hoped would be May. This was good news. Roland closed his eyes. Between himself and his son there was an unresolved matter. No unfriendliness, but they needed to talk.

It began last year in September when Roland had been back a

week from Alissa's. He phoned Potsdam and Lawrence picked up. Roland gave an account, entirely benign, of his time with her. He said, "I think you should go and see her. I know she'd like you to."

There was silence. Then Lawrence said, "Rüdiger gave her my email. She wrote to invite me."

"What did you say?"

"Nothing yet. I might not reply."

Roland realised how much he wanted his son to visit. He needed to proceed carefully. "You know she's ill."

"Yes."

Roland could hear in the background Paul and his mother chanting, "Es war einmal ein Mann, der hatte einen Schwamm." Alissa used to sing it to baby Lawrence. Once there was a man who had a sponge.

"Could be important for you. Otherwise, you might always regret it."

"She wants us to make everything OK. It never was and it can't be now."

"You sound bitter. Going could be a way of dealing with that."

"Honestly, Dad. I'm not. She never crosses my mind. I'm sorry she's ill or whatever. So are lots of people I don't know. Why should I care about her?"

Roland said the obvious stupid thing. "Because she's your mother."

Rightly, Lawrence did not reply and nor did he when his father added, "She's Europe's greatest novelist."

They talked of other things. In a later conversation Roland said, "At least reply to her."

"I might."

When the family came in May three days after the general lockdown ended, his impression was that Lawrence still had not written. In her hesitant lilting tone Ingrid had told her father-in-law on the phone that she thought he should let the matter drop. He said he would. But later he considered it his duty to try one last time. Pushed, he would have found it difficult to explain why this business mattered to him. His own visit had settled something. His son thought he had nothing to settle.

The family arrived and quarantined in the house while Roland kept apart in the basement flat. When the ten days were up Lawrence borrowed a car from Gerald and drove Roland to his appointment at a dedicated heart clinic south of St. Albans. A semi-retired consultant there was a former mentor of Gerald returning a favour. Roland disapproved of private medicine but was assured, as if it made any difference, that no money had changed hands.

On the journey, assuming it was his last chance, Roland raised the subject of Alissa.

"I guessed you'd bring it up so I wrote to her. Told her to get lost."

"You didn't!"

"No. I was very polite. I said I saw no purpose in our meeting now and wished her better health. I attached a picture of her grandchildren."

"Ah well."

"I also asked her not to write again."

"OK."

"But Dad, a few days later, a big package arrived. Inside was a wooden case and on it was a note saying, I understand but please have these. Inside, was this *Blaue Reiter Almanac*. 1912."

"Wonderful!"

"We had it authenticated. Amazing. And it's beautiful. Kandinsky, Münter, Matisse, Picasso. We'll keep it for Stefanie and Paul. But also in that box were these seven journals written by Oma. 1946! Did you know about them?"

"Yes."

"Beautifully written."

"I agree."

"It took me a week of free evenings to scan them all. Then I beamed the whole lot to Rüdiger. He didn't even know they existed and he's excited. Lucretius Books are going to bring them out in German in two volumes. A London publisher is interested too."

Roland closed his eyes. "Brilliant," he murmured.

"Rüdiger thinks it will be important to scholars as a source for *The Journey*."

"He's right," Roland said. "But it's a lot more than that."

The clinic, in a Queen Anne country house, with a disused hockey pitch and two neglected tennis courts, resembled a boarding school.

Lawrence stopped in the car park but did not get out. He was visiting a friend in Harpenden and would come back as soon as he received the call. Father and son hugged clumsily in the constricted space. As he approached the building through a stand of trees that concealed the cars, Roland's mood dipped. Sad for Alissa facing death, getting Lawrence's email whatever she deserved, then packing up the treasures she had hoped to put into his hands. And publication at last for Jane. Redemption, but too late. As he pushed through the glass double doors of the clinic's reception, he was no longer so sure that his heart was sound. An entire institution was dedicated to discovering that it was not. How could he face them all down? Even the grey-bearded receptionist at the desk had the grave manner of a specialist.

As he waited to be called he wondered if his son had delivered him, by agreement with the rest of the family, to make sure he kept his appointment. Here was a taste of old age, the possibly paranoid awareness that matters were being settled behind his back. The terminus being, We'll have to get him into a home.

At the start of the morning's ordeal, he spent a brisk fifteen minutes with Gerald's mentor, Michael Todd. The consultant was a huge pink fellow, with a head so bald and polished it showed a faint tinge of green reflected from the shrubbery outside his window. Mr. Todd ran through the schedule. They would meet again when it was complete. The results of blood tests had already arrived. When Roland was asked to describe his chest pain he did not mention his rib theory. Two minutes with the stethoscope then he was led away. Though he was the object of friendly expert attention and nothing hurt, these were two disagreeable hours. An X-ray, a thunderous MRI scan, treadmill, ECG. On an ultrasound screen, he saw in real time his heart busy in the dark on his behalf these past seventy-plus years, precariously squelching. The machines and their skilled minders could not be for nothing. He was ill at heart.

He was shown back into the presence of Mr. Todd. A pile of printouts was on his desk. He was reading through them as Roland sat down across the desk to wait. Hard not to feel that the judgement about to be delivered was moral, not medical. Was he a good or bad person? The heart in question picked up pace. This was a school moment. His future was in the balance.

At last Michael Todd looked up, removed his glasses and said in a neutral tone, "Well Roland—may I call you that?—as far as I can see there's nothing wrong with your heart. I'm looking at the culprit here, an osteophyte, a tiny spur of bone on a rib pressing on a nerve. Hence the referred pain. You might have had a fracture there."

"I had a bad fall two or three years ago."

"Tell me."

"The current junior minister of health pushed me into a river."

"Not Peter Mount! *Lord* Mount. How about that. We were at school together. And he went for you? I'm not surprised. Always a frightful bully. Anyway, my colleague will deal with your osteophyte."

He passed the scan across. Roland could see nothing but handed it back with a nod.

"You should live well into your eighties. But first you must do something about your weight and lack of exercise. Stop drinking every day. Get yourself some new knees. The rest will follow."

He did not immediately phone Lawrence. Instead he went for a slow shuffle round the perimeter of the hockey pitch. The fantasy was irresistible. Here was his school. The headmaster himself had just given him his results. He had passed, just as he knew he would. Eleven straight A's! He stood a chance of reading chapter thirty-five.

At home that evening he phoned Gerald to thank him.

"It's a weight off our minds, Roland. I know a brilliant surgeon for you. She works out of UCH. One knee at a time of course but you could be on court by next Easter."

Greta then Nancy phoned. Ingrid and Lawrence came into the sitting room to clink their wine glasses against his lime cordial. He felt fraudulent. Beyond not being ill he had achieved nothing. But he graciously behaved as if he had.

While Lawrence put Paul to bed and Ingrid cooked he had Stefanie to himself. Now she was reading, there was even more to talk about. They spoke only German. Outside, it was a bright evening but the French windows were shut against a temperature of four degrees and a sharp wind. Roland was in place in the rocking chair and she stood at his side. She had lost another tooth lately and had put it under her pillow. In the morning there was a two-euro coin.

"Ich weiß, dass Mama sie dort hingelegt hat!" I know that Mummy put it there.

That afternoon she had read Tomi Ungerer's *Flix,* about a dog born to parents who are cats. Roland, without her knowing, had read it too. A moral tale, but funny and clever.

Stefanie leaned against his shoulder as she explained the plot. "Opa, er muss gebratene Maus essen und lernen, auf Bäume zu klettern!" He has to eat fried mice and learn how to climb trees. Flix is an ugly little fellow, adored by his parents, and grows up in a cat's world. He learns that his feline great-grandmother had been secretly married to a pug. The canine genes have resurfaced. Luckily he has a dog for a godfather who teaches him canine ways, including dog-talk. But it can be tough, torn between two cultures. Eventually he becomes a politician and campaigns for mutual respect, equal rights and an end to cat–dog segregation.

When she had finished her account, he said, "Do you think the story is trying to tell us something about people?"

She looked at him blankly. "Don't be silly, Opa. It's about cats and dogs."

He saw her point. A shame to ruin a good tale by turning it into a lesson. That could be for later. It was a short step from cats to the poem that had brought her to reading. Together they chanted in English "The Owl and the Pussy-Cat." He told her how her Papa, when he was little, wanted to hear it night after night and always shouted out, You are, you are! His nose, his nose! The moon, the moon!

She said, "Und was liest *du*, Opa?" And what are *you* reading?

"Well, there's a pretend book I want to read. It's very interesting and so enormous that I don't think I'll ever get to read it all."

"Who's in it?"

"Absolutely everybody, including you. And it's a hundred years long."

"Und was passiert da drin?" What happens?

"That's what I'd love to find out."

She looped her arm around his neck, keen to join the game. As usual, she wanted to make everything all right for him. "I'll get to the end, Opa." She thought, then she added, "Ich werde es lesen, wenn ich erwachsen bin und es dir sagen." I'll read it when I'm a grown-up and tell you.

"By the last chapter you'll be as old as me."

The outlandish idea made her smile and he saw again that she had on each side innocent gaps where permanent teeth soon would come. It was a mistake to have mentioned his imaginary history of the twenty-first century. It was not a children's book. He loved her and in the liberated moment he thought that he hadn't learned a thing in life and he never would. He turned and lightly kissed her cheek. "My darling, one day you can tell me all about it. But now your mama's calling us to supper. Will you sit next to me please?"

He rose from the chair, but far too quickly and there came upon him one of his reeling vertiginous episodes when he seemed to float through a dense black medium that rippled faintly. His hand found the chair for support.

"Opa?"

Yes, a mistake to mention such a book when he was passing on to her a damaged world.

Then his head cleared but he still gripped the back of the chair, determined not to fall and alarm the girl.

"I'm OK, mein Liebling."

She spoke softly in the coaxing sing-song voice she sometimes heard her mother use on her little brother. "Komm, Opa. Hier lang." Come on, Grandpapa. It's this way. Frowning with concern, she took his free hand in hers and began to lead him across the room.

# Acknowledgements

I am indebted to the following books and authors: *The White Rose* by Inge Scholl, *A Noble Treason* by Richard Hanser, *Complete Surrender* by David Sharp, *Robert Lowell* by Ian Hamilton. My most sincere thanks to Reagan Arthur, Georges Borchardt, Suzanne Dean, Louise Dennys, Martha Kanya Forstner, Mick Gold, Daniel Kehlmann, Bernhard Robben, Michal Shavit, Peter Straus and LuAnn Walter. My special thanks to Tim Garton Ash and Craig Raine for their close readings and helpful notes, to James Fenton for permission to quote from his poem "For Andrew Wood," to David Milner for his brilliant editing and, as always, to Annalena McAfee, who expertly read many successive drafts. Finally, my thanks to my English teacher, the late Neil Clayton, who insisted I used his name unchanged, and a warm salute across the decades to all the boys and teachers who passed through the strange and wonderful Woolverstone Hall School. No such piano teacher as Miriam Cornell was ever there.

Ian McEwan
London, 2022

## Permissions Acknowledgments

Excerpt from "For Andrew Wood" from *Yellow Tulips* (Faber & Faber, 2012) and *Selected Poems* (Penguin, 2006) by James Fenton, reproduced by kind permission of the author. Excerpt from "Raketa" ("Rocket") from *Zbrane pesmi* ("Collected Poems," Cankarjeva zalozba, 1977) by Edvard Kocbek, translator unknown. Excerpt from "For the Union Dead" from *Collected Poems* by Robert Lowell, © 2003 by Harriet Lowell and Sheridan Lowell, reproduced by permission of Farrar, Straus & Giroux, all rights reserved. Lyrics from "Pale Blue Eyes," words and music by Lou Reed © 1968, reproduced by permission of Oakfield Avenue Music Ltd. / EMI Music Publishing, London W1T 3LP.

## A Note About the Author

Ian McEwan is the critically acclaimed author of seventeen novels and two short story collections. His first published work, a collection of short stories, *First Love, Last Rites*, won the Somerset Maugham Award. His novels include *The Child in Time*, which won the 1987 Whitbread Novel of the Year Award; *The Cement Garden*; *Enduring Love*; *Amsterdam*, which won the 1998 Booker Prize; *Atonement*; *Saturday*; *On Chesil Reach*; *Solar*; *Sweet Tooth*; *The Children Act*; *Nutshell*; and *Machines Like Me*, which was a number one best seller. *Atonement, Enduring Love, The Children Act*, and *On Chesil Beach* have all been adapted for the big screen.

## A Note on the Type

The type used in this book was designed by Pierre Simon Fournier le jeune. In 1764 and 1766 he published his *Manuel typographique*, a treatise on the history of French types and printing, and on what many consider his most important contribution to typography—the measurement of type by the point system.

Composed by North Market Street Graphics, Lancaster, Pennsylvania
Printed and bound by Berryville Graphics, Berryville, Virginia
Designed by Maria Carella